DIVINITY: IMMOLATION: BOOK THREE

SUSAN REID

Divinity: Immolation: Book Three is Copyrighted © 2014 by Susan Reid. All rights reserved.

DEDICATION

This book is dedicated to both of my children who are my life. To the Almighty magnificent presence that surrounds us all and who has been guiding me in both my literary endeavors and life adventures. It is also for all of my readers and each reviewer for their love of the supernatural, paranormal, and fantasy. I appreciate you all!

CONTENTS

DEDICATION	2
ACKNOWLEDGEMENTS	5
I STARLING	6
II CAM`AEL	10
III STARLING	18
IV CAM`AEL	30
V STARLING	40
VI CAM`AEL	46
VII STARLING	53
VIII CAM`AEL	57
IX STARLING	62
X CAM`AEL	76
XI STARLING	83
XII INTERLUDE	89
XIII CAM`AEL	94
XIV STARLING	100
XV CAM`AEL	105
XVI STARLING	110
XVII CAM`AEL	115
XVIII STARLING	123
XIX CAM`AEL	134
XX STARLING	142
XXI CAM`AEL	155
XXII STARLING	162
XXIII CAM`AEL	168
XXIV STARLING	176
XXV CAM`AEL	185
XXVI STARLING	194
XXVII CAM`AEL	201
XXVIII STARLING	208
XXIX CAM`AEL	218
XXX STARLING	226
XXXI CAM`AEL	232
XXXII STARLING	242
XXXIII CAM`AEL	248
XXXIV STARLING	252
XXXV CAM`AEL	256
XXXVI STARLING	263
XXXVII CAM`AEL	271
XXXVIII STARLING	277
XXXIX CAM`AEL	286
XL STARLING	293
ABOUT THE AUTHOR	310

"Love bears all things, believes all things, hopes all things; endures all things. . . Greater love has no one than this; that someone lay down his life for his friends. . ." (1Cor 13:7; John 15:13).

ACKNOWLEDGMENTS

Plot, places, characters, biblical names, and references, are all meant for fictional entertainment and storytelling purposes only. Likenesses to persons living or dead, events, places, and ideas are purely coincidental. Comparisons or ideas about specific, known, and popular Angels or Demons —lies deep in the imaginations and beliefs of each individual reader.

I. STARLING

I had no idea how to turn off the flames that were still burning along my arms and down my legs. I guess I had no choice but to wait for them to die out on their own.

Lovely.

The previous stern, reprimanding, and hard to decipher expressions on each of the elders' faces, instantly morphed into curious elation and joyous surprise. They were all actually—smiling now...with the exception of Spencer and the other two Seraphim girls. Though they were definitely impressed with my essence, my demonstration didn't wipe the glare of suspicion from their eyes.

"Well, there is no question on how you managed to stay safe then. Congratulations on the discovery of your essence, Starling." The woman elder smiled broadly and nodded approval. Then she quickly exchanged glances with the other three elders. They instantly appeared intrigued, all huddling in towards each other and uttering soft spoken words as if I weren't standing here in front of them.

Spencer was busy observing me through narrowed eyes. The brown-skinned seraphim girl suddenly rose up on her tip-toes to pull him down by his shoulder, and then she whispered something close to his ear, too.

Though gradually dissipating, my flames continued to caress my entire body with a wispy, tickling sensation, slowly beginning to wink out completely—one body part at a time. I noted soon thereafter, that I had mostly calmed down inside, too. However, my anxiety remained.

"This is quite remarkable, to finally be able to witness hallowed fire with my own eyes and in person. You are very unique indeed, Starling." The male elder beamed at me. In fact, all four of them were beaming now.

"Tell us, how are you able to bring forth your hallowed fire?" The elder woman sitting next to him asked with genuine curiosity and interest.

"Um, I'm not really sure. It's definitely linked to my emotions though, I think. I can't quite control it." I answered truthfully.

"Hmm, that's a new one. Well, if that is the case, control will come in time with practice."

Spencer suddenly leaned down to whisper something in the ear of the male elder on her right, though his ice-colored, twinkling eyes remained glued on me.

That was such a pet peeve of mine.

What was he whispering about? Hadn't my display been satisfying enough?

No, of course not.

Aon and Aliks told me to avoid the Seraphim. They didn't tell me how that would be possible though. Maybe this was one of the *situations* that they said would be up to me to figure out.

I wasn't sure what to do or say now. I was still the mysterious new girl here and I haven't even started my educational and physical training. I did, however, manage to escape a fallen on my own and that was what they all found suspect.

It was evident that Spencer and the other two female seraphim were homing in on something about me that the elders weren't detecting—yet. I feared that he was already sensing exactly what that something was already and it didn't take long.

Cam's scent.

I felt a nervous knot begin to cramp and twist deep in my gut once again. My face flushed, tingling as beads of perspiration began to dampen my forehead. That instantly quirked Spencers brow, having immediately reacted to the abrupt change in my body heat and chemistry.

Shit.

The elder male suddenly cleared his throat, regarding me once Spencer finished whispering to him.

"Starling, how are you feeling?" he then asked.

Icy apprehension gripped my chest. "I'm fine. Why?" I smiled casually.

"Well," He began, "Your aura appears…somewhat afflicted. Meaning that it no longer appears genuinely yours."

His face appeared contemplative and the other three women seemed to follow suit.

I swear my legs were about to go out from under me. The blood drained from my face and I know that it was evident to the seraphim as they continued to watch me attentively.

"I don't know what you mean." I asked, not meaning for it to come out as anything less than affirmative.

Spencer replied before the elder could even open his mouth. "What he means, is that you definitely don't smell like you should, which is understandable considering what you've just been through. It's one thing to get physically dirty but it's quite another to have that darkness and filth cling to and become a part of your aura like that."

I shrugged, forcing a naive and innocent expression. "I don't know. There was a period of time where I was knocked unconscious and I don't know how long I was out." Much to my relief, the elders nodded in understanding realizing that my answer made sense to them.

"What happened when you awoke?" A female elder suddenly asked.

Her question was more of wonder than accusation.

If I cut out a huge chunk of what happened, would that still be considered…lying?

I didn't have a choice. If this symbol beneath my feet suddenly lit up or something after my response, I was screwed.

"I had a few hall portal gems. Lorelei gave me some when we went into the human realm, to have just in case." I answered while keeping my eyes on Spencer, who didn't seem convinced.

If anything, that answered his earlier question on how I had managed to return untrained and without a map.

"Oh, I see. Well, thank goodness for that then." She smiled.

Spencer spoke up again, "Without disrespect Elder Woods, I've seen that discoloration in auras many times before. Tainting is a high possibility and we shouldn't leave her at risk."

I glared at him.

"I agree but quite frankly, if there was any darkness existing within her, it could not survive or remain, especially after that momentary display of her essence." He countered.

I smirked slightly this time.

Spencer pursed his lips tightly and nodded at me, "Then her aura should have returned back to normal by now. Look at it, it's still tainted." He motioned with his head in my direction.

I felt naked.

The way that they were all studying me made me feel like a slutty anomaly.

Or maybe that was just my own guilt and paranoia.

Damn you, Spencer!

"In my expert assessment, I think it would be wise for her to see a succor for a thorough examination, just to be on the safe side." Spencer added quickly with a respectful nod at the elder.

He had thrown out and played his final card.

I was irritated now.

"Yes, I agree that it would be beneficial. That will be all Starling. Thank you again, for your quick thinking and heroic act of bravery. And of course, welcome back. Spencer, Kaia, and Brynn will escort you to the medical quarters. Your own safety and well-being is top priority now." The elder woman then said.

"I'm fine, really. I don't need to be examined. In fact, I'm just really tired." I rushed to my own defense.

"Don't argue with protocol, Starling. It's for your own benefit. Since I'm in charge of helping you with your training, I'm sure Sean will want me to also assist you with honing your essence too. As a being who can sense physical maladies and changes in biorhythms, I can honestly say that something about yours really needs to be checked out." He affirmed assiduously.

I went rigid with irritation at his insistence despite what I was saying about being fine. Heat began to rise under my skin once again.

He smirked with satisfaction.

I began to panic internally. This is not going to go well.

II. CAMAEL

Content and happy.
Those two words described the euphoria of having Starling once again, being able to communicate with her anytime that I wanted to now, and not hearing from Morning Star since his threat. However, no moment of sweet bliss could ever go on uninterrupted here in the spirit realm.

Starling was in safe hands. She hadn't called out to me since earlier, which made me assume that all so far was going well, but I was still on edge given the current situation. Aon and Aliks were looking after her right now. It was what they were both sent to intercept us for and of course— it was all that they told me.

I appreciated them for that, especially in Starling's current condition. A condition that she was not aware of —yet.

It was still worried somewhat though. She was a warrior, which meant that she would be in battle, fighting, continuing to be targeted for kidnapping, if not more now, and susceptible to injuries regardless of her quick healing ability. I would rather have her here with me permanently in order to avoid all of that.

Morning Star was really going to pull out all stops to hunt down and claim both her and my child—our child. That thought made me furious with anger at myself and the possibility of not being able to do anything about it as long as she was behind the walls of the Divine hall. At least she's able to maintain her status, which was the most important thing that I wanted to ensure.

I went for a swim, later settling in with a cup of spiked passion flower tea, and a book that I had come across a while ago but never got a chance to read. It was written by an unknown San'lioch author from one of the galaxies beyond the many moons of Jupiter.

The cover was an illustration of one of their women looking into a mirror and seeing a reflection of a human woman looking back at her. Some likenesses were similar, like her lips and the number of eyes she had. The distinct differences were obvious though; from her bluish, lilac-colored skin, her large, wide-spaced, slanted opaque-colored eyes, her conical forehead, and her gracefully long, swan-like neck.

The cover intrigued me. The language in itself was complicated and would be difficult to decipher with its abstract form of lines and dots, but that's what drew me to it first among some of the others that I managed to take back with me.

Rahab and Edanai were in the kitchen cooking up something sweet and delicious when I returned. Unfortunately, the sweet mix of vanilla and honey wasn't the only potent thing strong in the air here. I could instantly sense Edanai's anxiety, frustration, and — anger.

I groaned inwardly, quietly padding into the kitchen to make another cup of tea. They both sat in soft conversation over anise and cinnamon coffee to accompany the delicious muffins they made.

There was only one left and I appreciated that they were saving it for me. I figured that I'd enjoy a delicious snack and a moment of peace before heading out to check on Berith. There was no news from Atiro, so I suppose that's a good sign.

I joined them at the table, stirring fresh mint leaves into my tea, and about to grab for the last muffin...before realizing that it was gone.

"Did you have a relaxing swim, my friend?" Rahab struck up the conversation first.

"Yes, I did. How goes the site for your restaurant?" I asked while covertly looking for any tell-tale signs of the vanishing muffin, like crumbs on the table, the tray, or either of their lips.

Rahab shook his head. "I have someplace in mind but we're all undecided on the location. I'd rather we all stayed close in one area, like where we were the last time since we've already been there. I don't know if combining ventures will work out if that's the case. Ryziel wants to be where the celebrities are, and Macai is already tattooing his flesh all over for advertising purposes." Rahab explained with a snicker.

I chuckled, "Well, maybe you two could come to a compromise

and meet in the middle somewhere if you still want to partner up."

Rahab nodded in thought. Edanai remained passively quiet.

"Are there anymore muffins left?" I finally decided to ask anyway.

"Nope." Edanai answered just as Rahab's mouth opened.

His eyes went from hers to mine, and then he began to rise out of his chair. "I can make more. It won't take long." He offered.

"That's okay, Rahab." I waved off, glancing askance at Edanai. She casually thumbed through some kind of gossip newspaper but with an evident attitude.

I eyed her, debating on even asking what I had done this time.

I returned my attention back to my book but considered returning back to the solitude and peace of my den instead. I opened the book to the page where I left off and attempted to read again.

Rahab remained standing. "It's really no problem, Cam."

"Oh? Why look, there is one left after all." Edanai said more to Rahab as she held it up like a prize, turning the scrumptious muffin in her hand for effect on purpose.

It hadn't been there a minute ago. Really childish, Edanai. I scolded her mentally.

"Would you like it, Rahab?" Edanai held the muffin out to him.

Rahab cut his eyes to me innocently and pursed his thick, onyx-colored lips, "Um...no. But Cam would like it." He nodded towards me. His large, bright orange eyes began to glow, traveling between me and Edanai with uncertainty once again.

I lowered my book. She didn't even look at me when she smirked and then— she proceeded to eat it.

I gaped at her silently. If that wasn't an underhanded yet blatant, 'Fuck you, Cam', I don't know of any other gesture that would have been.

Rahab quickly wriggled his sharp-taloned fingers and whispered a brief recipe incantation. Instantly, another identical muffin materialized on the platter in the middle of the table. He slid the platter closer to me. I highly preferred freshly prepared foods and beverages with natural ingredients but I appreciated his thought.

I ignored it, closing and setting my book down on the table, and then slowly leaned forward on my elbows.

"Something bothering you, Edanai?" I asked.

Rahab shifted from foot to foot. "Well, I'd better go. I've got to look at...some...things..." he quickly mumbled. With that, he immediately ghosted out.

"What would be bothering me, Cam?" She replied in short, clipped words, while pretending to be interested in an article about a well-known celebrity who was really the lovechild of an alien being. He probably was, in my opinion.

"Psychic ability isn't one of my strongest magicks but I'm not clueless. You may think that your hostility is subtle but I can tell you that it's about as subtle as a flatulent chasm troll. So, what's wrong with you?" I more demanded than asked.

She remained silent, continuing to purposefully ignore me.

"Fine. If I'm going to be alone, I may as well find a place with less chill in the air." I said, rising from my chair with my book.

"I can't believe you!" She finally blurted.

I looked at her in confusion.

"Don't play dumb. I was really worried about you, Cam."

"What are you talking about?" I began but then I stopped myself. I think I finally got what she was so upset about, I just didn't understand why. I've been with many, many other females before. Even though she was disapproving of it, she was no stranger to my past habits and history.

She cut her amethyst eyes up at me. There was evident jealousy and hurt behind them. Why was she doing this now?

"I came back to check on you," She chuckled sarcastically, "I guess I should have known better." She said flatly.

I sighed and slowly sat back down, rubbing a hand across my cheek and chin.

"Beings getting tortured don't scream that damned much or that damned loud." She then said.

I smiled to myself. I knew it. She evidently heard my and Starling's lovemaking, as if I had any control over or fault in that. Some women remain silent, some moan, some simply pant, and some curse and talk dirty. Then there are those that scream and squeal.

That was Starling.

Edanai shoved the newspaper across the table and then folded her arms beneath her breasts. "I know you can be smooth Cam, but smooth enough to get a divine warrior to lay down her weapons and spread her legs that quickly? I've got to hand it to you, you've definitely got crazy mad skills." Her words dripped with sardonic contempt.

"I know that you aren't jealous." I stated flatly.

She narrowed her eyes at me. "Jealousy has nothing to do with it. Were you making love to her…physically?" She wanted to know.

I pursed my lips and leaned back in my chair with a slow exhale. Obviously.

"You did didn't you? Of course you did. No woman screams like that unless she's getting…"

"What's your point Edanai? Is that why you're upset with me? You already know how I feel about Starling. She remembered me, thankfully, and that's the only reason that I'm still alive right now. For all I know, it could have been the only moment that I'll ever get to have with her." I cut her off. Saying the words, even though I knew that there was no way I'd ever allow that, cut me deeply to hear.

What if that had truly been the only time that we would ever have together?

No. It wouldn't be. Not as long as I existed. Even Elohim wouldn't be able to keep me away from her, let alone the divine warriors. She was carrying my child and I would kill any being to protect the both of them.

I was growing annoyed with this conversation already. She had completely doused my good mood since returning from my swim.

Her brows knitted together in confusion and chagrin.

"She remembered you?" Her tone had simmered down considerably. "How?" She shook her head in disbelief.

"I don't know. It was way more than I could ever hope or wish for though, so I'm not going to dare wonder how or why."

"Does she remember us too?" She wanted to know.

"Given time, I'm sure she will. She remembers Rahab."

I shut her up for the moment. Her mind was working and I think I know what she was thinking.

"Cam'ael—did you impregnate her?" her jeweled eyes pierced me with the question.

I hesitated, biting my bottom lip as my eyes flicked away from hers briefly.

"Oh shit." She exaggerated each word. Her eyes widened and then she exhaled in exasperation.

It hadn't really dawned on me why Edanai was this upset over my encounter with Starling but now I was finally getting it.

She already knew that was inevitable. I've wanted Starling for so long. We had been granted the opportunity and I took it. She was mine now— in more ways than one.

Demons and fallen were incredibly virile and potent. Pregnancy was nearly one hundred percent, which was why I steered clear of actual vaginal contact with women, until Starling. Edanai was both hurt and upset because it was the one thing that she had always wanted and tried to have. It was part of the sin that had gotten her cast out. I would not allow her to have it with me either, which both hurt and infuriated her but I had my reasons. It took her a long time to accept it though and I know that this news definitely doesn't help.

She slowly stood up, a hand covering her mouth in thought as she paced the length of the table, her other hand fisted against her hip.

I let the silence remain in between us while wondering how Starling was faring right now. I had no choice but to trust the angels. They couldn't lie and I knew that they wouldn't let anything happen to her.

"No pun intended but you've really screwed her now, Cam." Edanai suddenly spoke. She turned her head and her eyes narrowed in accusation, "You did it on purpose, didn't you?" She finally whispered.

Did I? Maybe I did. Was it wrong? Very. Would it end up badly? More than likely. I averted my gaze from hers.

A sharp breath of annoyance seeped out of her lips as she turned her back to me once again and shook her head.

I could tell that she didn't want to face me on purpose. I had nothing else to say in regard to her question. I didn't have to say anything.

"Where is she now?" She asked. Her back still facing me.

"The hall."

Her head shifted and cocked slightly, "How was she able to return?" She inquired with surprise.

"I'm not entirely sure."

"Sadly, she's going to be the last to know. She'll be kicked out of the divine hall and shunned eventually. And you've finally given Morning Star every reason to pursue her now that you've given him exactly what he's been wanting from you. He will find out eventually." Edanai warned.

I took a tentative pause. "She's being guarded and protected."

Edanai raised a brow. "Oh? By who?"

"Aon and Aliks. They met up with us as I was showing her around the neutral area. They were sent by Elohim."

That silenced and shocked Edanai.

She was gauging my expression. I had no reason to lie to her about that. I was just as shocked as she was when they relayed that message to me in Angelic.

"Sent by Elohim? So…this is already known and allowed?" She asked softly. An incredulous and confused expression masked her face.

I nodded.

Bewilderment now contrasted her initial confusion.

"That…isn't the only thing." I slowly said.

Her eyes snapped up to mine waiting for me to unleash another bomb.

I shifted and sighed, unsure at first if I should even tell her.

"Since we were together," I started carefully, "We've developed the ability to communicate telepathically too."

I expected the look on Edanai's face to shift into further disbelief but her expression remained cool.

"What else did you expect?" She mocked.

I looked at her irreverently. "What's that supposed to mean?"

She shook her head as she strode alongside the table, ending up behind me.

She leaned in over my shoulder and spoke softly, "The conduit that established the link between you two is the child growing in her right now. At this rate, it won't be long before she gives birth. I'm a little curious as to how all of this will play out but I suppose if the angels are aware of it and you're still alive…" She trailed off.

It was quiet.

Of course. That made sense.

I didn't know how this was all going to work out either because it wouldn't be long before someone there would pick up on it, like that damned seraphim.

"Would you please keep this to yourself? I don't want anyone else to know right now, not even Rahab." I told her.

She gave a soft snort of disbelief. "I don't know how long you think it will go unnoticed but sure, I won't breathe a word of it. I'm going to go. I've got plans with friends." She added abruptly.

Edanai didn't need to leave like this not when other dangerous threats still loomed.

I stood up. "Edanai, please be careful. I'd much rather you keep Rahab with you."

She pressed her lips in annoyance, "I think Rahab has better things to do than to shadow me around as a bodyguard. I'll be fine. I can take care of myself, no need to worry." "Rahab cares deeply for you, like I do. That means that I'm not going to let you get away with worrying about me if I can't worry about you. I would feel better if you had others with you, and that you at least make sure that you keep in touch with me often.

" I wasn't going to breathe a word of Morning Star's threat to Edanai. I know her. It would just make her that more militant in daring him to do something or make a move She lifted her chin and pierced me with a hard stare, "No. Your plate is beyond full right now. I can promise the first part but the second is a no go."

"That's not fair, Edanai."

"Fair, is a not a term that we as Fallen are familiar with anymore. It's a good thing that you waited, I suppose. If she were still a simple human rather than super, she wouldn't survive giving birth— let alone physical sex with you. You're an absolute demon in bed." She winked and then she began to ghost away.

I stared at the blank space where she stood a moment ago, cringing at her words and the thought. My child would possess half of what I am. Darkness by virtue of being a Fallen. I've already doomed this child to a lifetime of having to fight and resist the permanent cursed wickedness that he or she would inherit.

I was suddenly overcome with a feeling that this would be the last time that I ever saw Edanai. I had been helpless to make her stay.

"*Rahab.*" I called out telepathically.

"*You don't even have to ask, my friend. I will never be too far behind her. I promise that I will not let her out of my sight.*" Rahab answered back right away.

"*Thanks. Your safety is just as important to me too*"

Rahab laughed heartily. "*I appreciate that, my lord.*"

I mumbled my annoyance verbally with a shake of my head. I know that Rahab would undoubtedly protect her, but his assurance failed to make me feel any better about Edanai being away from me right now.

III. STARLING

I'm not sure how long I simply just stood there, staring at the panel of elders, speechless. What else could I say or do that wouldn't appear…questionable?

Spencer, Brynn, and Kaia headed over to the double doors once the elders all stood to signal the end of this inquisition. My pulse raced with chilling dread.

It wasn't so much over what they might discover, I just didn't want to have to think about skirting and reassembling the truth to keep my actions and Cam's name out of any explanation.

I wanted to be a warrior.

I meant every word of the oath that I took but I'd be a fool to think they wouldn't know or eventually find out.

What did Aon and Aliks want or expect for me to do now? Why had I been the only one to see them, and where were they now?

"How is everything going?" Cam's voice suddenly entered my head.

"Not good." I replied.

There was brief pause on his end. I shouldn't have said that. I should've told him that everything was fine.

"Why?" He asked. I could hear the anger building in his tone.
"They want me to get examined by the succor here."
"Did they explain why?" he wanted to know.
"They don't have to. I already know what they're looking for and it wasn't their suggestion, it was Spencer's."
"Who the hell is Spencer, so I'll know who to hurt when I see him?"

I wanted to laugh at Cam's humor but somehow I don't think he was joking about that. "He's one of the earthbound Seraphim."

There was another long pause on his end.

"I've seen him." Those three words sounded so powerful, I swear I could already feel the heat of his mounting anger swirling around inside my brain.

"Something wrong, Starling?" Spencer's voice cut into our personal mental conversation just then.

I snapped my head up and turned to look at the three of them standing at the double-doors, waiting for me.

The elders had already cleared the room and only two warrior guards remained. I bit my lip, suppressing an urge to say something smart.

I joined them at the door, not venturing to meet either one of their eyes as I walked past them and out into the corridor.

"Cam, don't do anything, please."
"I didn't promise you that. This is different." He replied.
"I've got this. I'll keep you posted, don't worry."
"Can you get away afterwards? Even if you have to meet me at the very edge of the Divine Hall grounds where it meets neutral land?"
"I'll try but I don't know how long this may take."
"I don't mind waiting. I'll be watching in the meantime."

Brynn, the seraphim with light, faintly glittering, gold-colored skin asked softly, "Why do you seem so distraught?"

Kaia, the sienna colored seraphim flanked my other side, and Spencer remained behind us.

The sound of her voice was soothing, kind of reminding me of a relaxing lullaby, and she actually sounded genuinely concerned.

I cast a sideways glance at her with just my eyes. "I'm not distraught. I'm tired and I'm not really enthused about being poked and prodded." I answered.

Remaining just a step or two behind them, I let the both of them lead the way down the corridor, up a small flight of steps, and then hooking another right into a wide, arched breezeway.

I wasn't sure what kind of examination this was going to be but I'll be damned if I was asked to put my feet up into any stirrups.

"Poked and prodded?" Kaia intruded.

"She's new. She doesn't know how the succors work." Spencer added in his two cents from behind us.

I didn't even turn around to address or acknowledge him. I would have cursed him out if I did.

"Ah, I almost forgot. Don't worry Starling, you'll be fine. This is standard practice for any warrior who's been either badly wounded or…"

"Tainted?" I cut her off brashly. I didn't mean to snap and sound bitchy but it couldn't be helped.

She didn't seem surprised or affronted by my outburst or choice of a word but it did silence her for the moment.

"What's happening?" Cam's voice was insistent.

"Nothing yet." I replied.

Two warriors were emerging out of a set of wooden doors that loomed ahead on the left. The placard set in the stone wall above the doors read:

Medical Aid and Examination. All Weapons Prohibited. Please Retract Before Entering.

The female wore a bandage around her neck and the male with her held her steady for support as they walked together past us.

"Why is she wearing a bandage? Don't we heal on our own—and fast?" I asked all of them as Spencer moved ahead to open the doors for us.

Kaia answered, "She was probably poisoned by a hell thorn."

"What's a hell thorn?" I followed behind her and Brynn into the medical quarters.

"They're a poisonous and dangerous annoyance because the thorns are small but they contain a large dose of both paralytic and hallucinogenic properties. Once its venom enters your system, it's almost impossible to dispel." She explained.

"I'll see if Ilka or Rubie are available." Spencer spoke as I continued to follow behind Brynn and Kaia into an octagon shaped sitting area. Nothing but several wooden chairs, a few books, and three potted plants adorned the room. The light sources came from bowl shaped sconces lining the walls, and they were filled with bright yellow and orange illuminated rocks, which I found unique and interesting.

I sighed and remained standing, fidgeting with anxious impatience as they both took a seat.

"So, where do hell thorns grow? The Darklands?" I asked.

"A hell thorn is a vine-like creature not a plant, and they thrive in sludge pools and underground caves over there. They're very hard to see until it's too late, especially in the dark. That's why you should never venture anywhere near the Darklands on your own. Many of the demons and the fallen like to use hell thorns to coat their weapons." Kaia answered.

I raised my brows in alarm. "Like they need anything else to use against us. Most of them have magic and that's an unfair advantage as it is." I commented.

"Their magic isn't always fully effective against you guys, depending on what it is and where it hits you first. But you'll be learning all about that in your classes." Brynn answered.

"I admire you, Starling. You're a lot tougher than you look." Kaia then said.

I glanced at her in surprise. "Why do you say that?" I asked her. She simply smiled.

I wasn't sure how to take her words or her smile but before I could say anything else, Spencer peered around the corner and beckoned me forward with his index finger.

I sighed internally and trudged over towards him.

"Last room on the right down that way." He pointed.

Without a word, I followed his direction not bothering to wait for him if he decided to follow me.

The heavy wooden door was propped open. I stopped just inside of it to take in the examination room. I was surprised to see a simple long slab of stone covered in a soft pallet of blankets sitting in the middle of the room. It was much like the one I had been placed on when I first awoke here. There was a wall of small, square shelves that were full of all sorts of liquids, powders, and bandages.

A petite, young woman sat at a long, wooden table. She was clearing away some items that she had been using before turning her attention to me with a warm, friendly smile.

"Hello Starling, come on in." She waved me forward as she stood up and walked over to greet me. I wasn't sure what I was expecting her to look like, and I wondered if she were of the human species at all or if she was like Spencer.

She wore a long, white kimono-style top. Though her face was smooth and young, her hair was completely white and cropped with short- peaked spikes all over. She didn't have any brandings either, like Lira and Diana.

"You needn't stay, Spencer. Thanks." She smiled pleasantly, meeting and blocking Spencer from entering into the room.

He grinned sheepishly. "Right. I think I'll wait though. I want to make sure she's alright."

"You can leave now." I snapped with agitation.

He seemed injured by my sharp words.

"I'm the succor here. She'll be fine. Bye." Ilka further insisted as she gently closed the door in his face.

I felt relief once she did but now I was really both nervous and wary.

She chuckled, shaking her head, "He's something else isn't he? Anyhow, I'm Ilka. Why don't you go ahead and lie down up there and just relax," She pointed to the slab examination table, "This shouldn't take long. You look fine to me."

She crossed back over to a water basin at the other end of the wooden work table.

I sighed softly as I slowly walked up the small set of steps onto the platform surrounding the slab, and then slowly turned with my back to it.

I reluctantly sat down already feeling uncomfortable.

"Oh and go ahead and remove your jacket for me too, please." She added.

She was gingerly washing her hands in a basin and I took my time slipping out of the jacket

"Sorry, I may be a little offensive. They didn't give me a chance to bathe or change let alone breathe since I've been back." I told her.

She laughed, "So I've heard. No need to apologize for that. Congratulations on making it back safely. You have my undying gratitude and respect for what you did to save a fellow warrior. Returning on your own, especially as a brand new warrior, is not something that we're used to seeing, which is why we're all even more adamant in making sure that you're okay— both physically and metaphysically. That's mainly what we succors do, by the way. We affirm that your energies, both spiritual and mental, are aligned and still positive. We also use touch to search and heal all sorts of internal damage that may not be visible to the eye or healing well on their own." She quickly dried her hands on a towel and then walked back over to me.

"Succors possess stronger healing energies than that of regular warriors and we transmit that extra power unto the injured, that's all." She assured me with a pleasant smile to ease my obvious apprehension.

"I'm not injured." I said flatly.

She looked me over in a brief flash. Her level of intelligence didn't match what she looked like to me. She reminded me of the girl in my photo album, China. I instantly felt a connection to that aspect of her.

"I believe you. However, some things can manifest later and begin to cause ailments, so this is more of a precaution." She smiled again.

"Are you going to use magic?" I asked.

She shook her head, "No, no magic. It's a healing talent. So tell me, how are you feeling right now?"

Her teal colored eyes observed me closely. Though she appeared to be simply glancing over me, I could literally feel that she was doing much more than that. There was a definite warmth that gently caressed my skin. Was she literally x-raying me with her eyes?

"I'm fine. Never better."

She gave me a customary nod. "I'm sure you are but your aura speaks differently. Why don't you lie back and just relax. I want to check a few things." She urged.

"Spencer didn't fill you in?" I finally gave in, swinging my legs up and over onto the slab to recline flat on my back.

The sooner I cooperated, the sooner I could get out of here and plot Spencer's severe ass kicking from the privacy of my room.

"I'd rather hear it from you. Just keep looking straight up." She instructed.

She held a golf ball-sized, clear crystal or quartz in front of my eye. A milky white substance swirled slowly around inside of it and then it began to glow softly. Ilka studied my eye carefully.

"What's that for?" I asked.

"It can detect signs of change within your body. The eyes are the windows into the mind and soul after all." She smiled.

The crystal maintained its soft, milky white glow, shifting into a slight bluish hue in its center by the time she was finished. I found it mesmerizing. Apparently not seeing anything unusual in the first one, she did the same to my other eye.

"All clear?" I finally asked after a few minutes.

She nodded. "All clear." She affirmed and then slipped the crystal into the pocket of her kimono shirt.

That was a relief, though part of me wondered that if Cam's essence was still lingering in me, how would it show itself other than tainting my aura?

Ilka began softly stroking her fingers through the curls in my tangled hair. Her fingertips softly began to graze my scalp and I instantly fell into a state of relaxation that left me feeling weightless. My lids began to flutter, feeling heavier with each passing second.

Was she trying to put me to sleep? Or was I finally succumbing to everything that's happened up to this point and my intense love-making with Cam? Speaking of, he's been silent since we last spoke. I hoped that meant that he would stay away from the vicinity of the hall until I filled him in on what was happening.

I reverted back to her original question of wanting to know what happened to me in my own words, assuming she was politely still waiting for my response.

"When I tried to save Jamie, the fallen dropped her and held onto me instead. Then...she eventually dropped me. Next thing I know, I blacked out. I was able to return because I still had some portal gems on me." I continued on, reconstructing the events carefully.

"Dropped you? And you survived the fall?" She was impressed.

"She didn't get that high up." I quickly added, already feeling guilty for telling that lie.

"Ah, I see. Well, thank goodness for that. I hear hallowed fire saved your life too. I'm honored to provide aid to one who is gifted with such an incredible power." She said softly.

Her hands were gentle and soft as she examined my neck. She gingerly pressed on several pressure points that immediately took away all of the knots and kinks. Wow, the touch of a succor was like the hands of a magical masseur.

Her hand then went to gently rest over my heart.

"So far, so good." She said. I guessed that she was either listening or counting heartbeats. She was right though, I felt remarkably soothed and much better than when I first arrived.

"Did you run into trouble at all? With any dark being?" She then asked.

My pulse began to beat rapidly. She was still holding a hand over my heart. I think she was trying to gauge my reaction to her questions while she worked.

I shifted slightly and sighed to play off the sudden acceleration of my erratically thumping heartbeat.

"None that I wasn't able to defend myself against." I answered simply.

"Hmm. Spencer said he was told that you arrived through the portal pretty banged up, with a dislocated shoulder and broken arm."

I sighed and nodded.

Her hands went to examine and stroke my shoulders, elbows, forearms, and then my brandings. She took a moment to admire them.

"Well, you're right. You seem absolutely fine to me so far," She then chewed her lip as her hand traveled to my torso, pressing gently to spread the healing warmth emanating from her hands and fingers deep into my tissues and muscles.

Her hands continued to slide further, taking care to barely touch and apply a small amount of pressure to specific areas that made me flinch a bit. I was very aware of the powerful yet soothing energy coming from her palms and fingertips.

A sudden vibrating shock made us both gasp simultaneously and I automatically jack-knifed upwards into a sitting position. A faint, tickling spasm flitted inside of my abdomen as I recovered from the strange reaction. The look on Ilka's face worried me.

She gaped, transfixed on my abdomen and unable to meet my eyes.

"What happened? What was that?" I asked first.

Her eyes were as wide as saucers and she rubbed her fingertips together slowly.

Had I hurt her? What the hell had I felt inside of me?

She slowly shook her head, finally snapping out of her momentary stunned lapse and looked at me. "I'm...I'm not sure."

She said as she swallowed hard. "Lay back. I'm going to try again." She said.

"Try what again? What did you do?"

"Nothing that I haven't been doing. I need to be sure though so please, lie back down."

There was a knock at the door.

"Is everything okay in there?"

It was Spencer. No doubt, he had picked up on the sudden change in both of our bio-rhythms just now.

Ilka shook her head and sighed, frustrated that Spencer was even still around.

"Everything is fine, Spencer. If I need you I'll get you, okay?" She called out.

Though he didn't reply, she was sure that he was still lingering.

"That means that I don't need you hanging out by the door either. Go bother Rubie!" She called out to him.

After another moment, we finally heard Spencer retreat. He was really getting on my nerves now.

Ilka turned her eyes back to me. There was a serious edge in them this time.

"Starling," She was whispering now and I wondered why.

"When you came to, did you feel different in any way?" She then asked me.

My heartbeat began to pick up speed again and I didn't care if Spencer could sense it or not.

"Different in what way? Of course I felt different. I was knocked unconscious." I told her.

She knew something. Something that she wasn't telling me but she didn't have to. I already knew what that something was.

Cam's essence clung to me like another layer of flesh that wasn't my own.

She shook her head, "That's not what I meant. I need to check again just to be certain." She said as she forced me to lie back once again.

I wanted to resist because she was making me even more nervous but I knew that if I continued to act suspicious, she'd probably figure it out.

I acquiesced as she rubbed her slender, soft hands together first and then closed her eyes as if concentrating. Her hands hovered over my abdomen briefly and then she slowly lowered them.

There! The tickling zap responded immediately at her touch and we both gasped once again. I was more surprised because it confirmed the first strange spasm that I felt, and that meant that there was truly something going on inside of me.

Was it the source of darkness that was tainting my aura?

I began to worry.

Ilka's expression conveyed deep concern. Then her eyes went from mine, to my lower belly, and then to the door.

Great. She found my affliction and now she was either going to announce it to Spencer and the other two seraphim, or she was debating it and thinking of going straight to the elders.

She briskly walked to the door, opened it and peered out to scan each end of the small corridor, then she closed…and locked it this time.

Now she was freaking me out.

"What's going on, Ilka?" I sat up and asked her.

No more examinations.

She put a hand to her mouth, pinching her lips together with her index finger and thumb and her other was hand fisted at her hip. Finally, she took in a brief inhalation of breath, "Starling, I'm going to say something that I want you to remain calm about because it can be fixed, understand?" She then said softly.

Calm? Fixed? So something was wrong after all! What would I flip out about? Maybe an accusation? An accusation that was true. My heart was in my throat now.

I nodded once. I couldn't lie about anything else. I didn't want to.

I wanted to call out to Cam but that would only make him angrier about what was happening to me, and then he'd do something that could end up getting himself hurt or killed as well as many other divine warriors in defense against him.

I swallowed, remaining silent in my anxious dread to await her question.

She paced for a moment, looking down at the floor as if thinking hard about how to phrase her words, which worried me even more.

Finally, she looked up at me and spoke, "I think that…I mean, I know that—you've been sexually assaulted."

My eyes nearly popped out of my skull. I felt nauseous and light-headed. There was no way that she could miss the burning red hue that was giving away my obvious reaction to her diagnosis.

Assaulted though? I supposed that would be the natural

assumption.

She nodded. A fearful and sympathetic look was present in her eyes.

"How...w...would you..." I couldn't form any words even though I knew what I wanted to say. How was she able to tell?

I expected her to tell me that she was sensing Cam's essence in me. I expected her to tell me that she knew my story wasn't adding up to an extent. I expected her to confirm that what Spencer sensed about the black that had become fused with my aura had been accurate. I even expected her to have to report it to Sean, Diana, and all of the elders.

It wasn't as if I'd have no place to go. I would be with Cam or back in the city of Indianapolis, like what it had said on my drivers' license. Or I could settle in any place that I wanted to. Either way, it would have to be someplace isolated. However, I would no longer be considered a divine warrior, maybe just a warrior, if that. Would I become an enemy to everyone here then? I didn't know what to expect.

"Because there's definitely another life force emanating from inside of you. You aren't open to possession as a divine warrior, which leads me to conclude that—you're pregnant." She finally whispered as if it were a deadly taboo statement.

Her words echoed in my ears, not really making sense to me right away. I could feel myself growing tingly and numb all over as my body swayed, threatening to topple over.

I did not expect her to tell me that.

Words were forming in my head and my mouth was moving but nothing coherently vocal came out.

"We've never had to deal with something like this before but we might just be able to." Ilka said, briskly walking over to the large wall of cubby shelves and perusing what was contained in the glass jars.

I slowly brought my hand to my abdomen, resting it there to further take in the revelation.

I'm pregnant? How could it be detected already anyway? My thoughts repeated themselves over and over. I'm pregnant with Cam's child.

There's a life in me right now.

What kind of a child would it be? Cam was a supernatural being. Who was it going to look like? What was it going to be? More importantly, how was I going to both hide it and continue my physical training as a warrior?

Maybe that would no longer be an option that I'd have to worry about.

Ilka spoke to me over her shoulder, "I'm not sure how this will work. This is a first for me so I may need to seek additional counsel…"

"No." I suddenly blurted out, almost mechanically.

Ilka was silent and still for a brief moment. Then the sound of her soft footsteps slowly began to approach me. When she stood in front of me, her eyes appeared confused as she searched my face for understanding.

"What do you mean?" She breathed.

"I mean, I don't want to get rid of it." I then said softly.

My mind was still struggling to accept the possibility. Does Cam know? Of course he doesn't. How would he take the news? Would he be just as dazed and stunned as I am?

Ilka's expression turned into surprise and then softened with understanding. She sighed.

"Starling, I understand why you feel apprehensive, believe me. It is a life and it's a part of you too but it was brought about by something that should have never happened. A dark being took advantage of your defenseless state. It wasn't your fault." She said with a consoling hand on my shoulder.

I closed my eyes at her words and bit my lip to choke back the tears that began to blur my eyes. "I won't speak of this once it's done if you wish. I understand your fear of what it would mean to the others if they knew." She then said.

I sniffed, swallowing the dry lump in my throat and turning my eyes down to look at the floor, so I wouldn't have to look at her when I clarified my response. "It didn't happen…while I was unconscious."

Ilka was speechless at first.

"You were beguiled when it happened then, right?" She then assumed. When I slowly shook my head no, it looked as if she were going to faint this time.

IV: CAM`AEL

Dusk was approaching, spreading like spilled dark violet and royal blue ink across a cloudless sky that was now littered with millions of stars and galaxies above. The moon was a pale pink, casting a rosy hue over the tops of the now dark trees; filtering through the cloudbank below the mountain, and spreading sparkles of pink light across the soft rippling surface of the Eternal waters in the far distance.

Even Morning Star's domain seemed obscenely quiet and peaceful for a change, though that didn't mean that nothing sinister was going on over there either. A line of black crows shot upwards from the stone forest, instantly making me wield my sword and ready to infuse it with light. The flock arced upwards, forming a 'V' that hovered for a few seconds, before flying back into the direction of the desert lands.

It was hard to tell if they were truly just birds or if they were a part of the whole demon named Xyn. I had forgotten about him for a moment and seeing the crows reminded me that Edanai was out there somewhere on her own. Even with Rahab not far behind her, I was still worried about them.

I hadn't heard a word from Starling since her non-reassuring reply of, "Nothing yet."

It took every bit of my self-control to remain silent and maintain patience, knowing that I had no other choice as long as she was behind the walls of the hall. Yes, I was glad that Aliks and Aon assured me that she would be able to return to the hall but at what cost? I was going stir crazy inside of my own maddening rage. It threatened to boil over into destructive and out of control, and dark, wild lust began to weave and work its way through me on top of everything else.

I needed Starling again but not just to satiate my lust. Dark lust needed to be released in a dark manner, through use of power, fighting, or doing something malicious. I hated it. I felt the need to cut myself again in order to get some relief but I didn't want to go back to that habit and place again.

I needed her because she calmed me and made me forget about what I am. I feel genuine love with her, one that I've spent thousands of years wishing and wanting to have with a female since being cast down. With Edanai, it was comfort, which only stopped at a close friendship for me.

Starling had my interest even before I knew her and the longer I watched her, the more I fell in love with her. It didn't matter to me that she was still a child at the time I first took notice of her either. I'd never touched or did anything of a sexual nature to her, which was why it was so devastating to me when I thought that she had died in that torrential storm and flood. Knowing that she was chosen, meant that she would be here and off limits. Never in my whole existence did I imagine that she'd be here now and that I'd have a chance to be with her at all. Now, she was pregnant with my child.

Elohim has allowed all of this to happen.

Starling, as a human being and a divine warrior, gives me hope and a reason to exist; believing that I'm more than just a condemned, evil, untrustworthy fallen, incapable of receiving or giving love.

She wouldn't possibly be able to conceal her growing belly for long. Have they discovered that she was pregnant yet? She would have said something to me by now. Maybe after the discovery, she was both angry and in shock. She could be upset with me for getting her pregnant, maybe even disgusted and horrified at the thought of what was growing inside of her. No, I didn't want to believe that about her, not Starling. After all, the child is a part of her too. It was still half human— half superhuman, actually.

The very thought of anyone harming her let alone our child brought my anger to a whole other level. My teeth began to gnash together the longer I fixated upon the structure of the Divine Hall in the far distance. All the while, I calculated all of the possible fractures along the circumference of the impermeable, indestructible, invisible wall. It was made up of runic symbols and it surrounded the entire acreage of sanctified land, in order to keep the dark ones out. I began to estimate just how close I could get to either break through or cause some serious damage without being detected or hurt in the process.

I'd keep my promise to her. I wouldn't kill any divine warriors outside of self-defense but I sure as hell would seriously maim a few in a heartbeat to get to her.

"Starling, what's going on? Talk to me." I called out, not meaning to sound gruff. It was the darkness rising in me.

Silence.

I didn't like this. Something wasn't right.

"Starling!" I called out with more intensity once again.

"I'm pregnant, Cam." She finally answered softly. The shock was evident in her tone.

Words left me. They had indeed discovered it. My anger and lust was instantly suppressed into chagrin and consolation.

"I know." That was all that came to mind as my reply.

"You…know?"

I couldn't tell if she was upset or what and that bothered me.

"Yes."

Silence.

"I'm sorry." I whispered, as heart-breaking as it was for me to say because I really wasn't.

I was beyond happy to finally have what I've always wanted. If I had to exist forever on Earth in imperfect flesh form, this made it all worth the mistake of my original sin.

"For what?"

Her reply surprised me.

For putting you in a position that would ultimately result in your banishment from the hall, and leaving you an open vessel. For knowing that I'd impregnate you when we made love and not bothering to tell you that it was a high possibility. Those were all of the things that I wanted to confess.

It couldn't have been avoided anyway. Fallen don't have or use any form of birth control. No material exists that would serve as a strong enough barrier against our seed.

"For selfishly getting you shunned before you've even begun as a warrior."

"You didn't force me, Cam. I wanted you as much as you wanted me. All things do happen for a reason, right?"

She was right. It happened because it was allowed to happen. Her words made me happy and consoled my pain but I didn't want her to have to suffer for it. I wasn't bound to anything but she was.

"Many instances, yes. Who discovered it?"

"The succor. She seems trustworthy but I don't know for sure. Either way, I'll let you know when I see you."

"Blame me. Tell them that I took advantage of your unconscious state." I then urged her.

"That's what she automatically assumed but I'm not going to tell her that and give her a reason to think that I want it taken care of."

I sighed helplessly.

"If you don't then they'll know…"

"I know. I'll see you as soon as I can get away."

"Alright. I'll be waiting."

I waited a bit longer, my heart aching for what Starling would have to face alone. I had to be ready to go in and get her if worse came to worst. After a while, I reluctantly created a personal portal for entry into the familiar abode that I had chosen once before, and wisped through.

~~~****~~~

I immediately heard voices and laughter once I ghosted into the living area of the farmhouse. It was daylight and cold. Winter had begun to settle in judging by the bare trees and large piles of dead, dull-colored leaves scattered about the ground outside.

The television was on but set to a low volume. One of the voices definitely belonged to Berith and the other was a fallen male. The aroma of many different dishes filled the interior, all coming from the kitchen.

The clatter and scraping of metal utensils floated out from the kitchen. I silently peered around the edge of the arched wall and saw…to my surprise—a smiling Atiro, stirring a bowl of something thick and chocolate scented. Berith was barefoot and wearing comfortable looking yoga pants, tank top, and a food-stained apron with chocolate smeared on her nose and chin.

They both stopped and looked at me as if caught in an embarrassing pose.

"Hey Cam`ael, I…we ah —didn't know that you were coming." She then said as her eyes shifted to Atiro.

I've never seen him smile let alone heard him laugh, which I found interesting and refreshing if this was what I was thinking.

"Just checking in. I see you've grown accustomed to your new habitat." I joked with Berith.

She pursed her lips and lifted her chin as if she didn't want to admit my observation, given her rampant complaints and whining when I initially offered the place to her.

"It'll do. If anything, being in this body has made me more creatively resourceful in many ways."

I looked her over. She had actually managed to thin out a bit. The original body she had taken was a cadaver of a young girl who was a little on the pudgy side. Berith has been working it out but maybe a little too hard.

"Good to hear but remember, you can only handle so much physical exertion before you'll have to change again and Edanai won't assist this time."

"Yeah, yeah I know and I'm actually fine with that. She'd probably give me a hunched back and a clubbed-cloven foot anyway."

I chuckled a bit at her remark and catching sight of the slight rise in Atiro's yellow-tinted cheek. I never would have thought that any being, other than Morning Star and his moronic mob, would have found Berith…interesting or desirable past her looks—of which she didn't have anymore. From what I could ascertain so far, Berith was actually tolerable to be around. Amazing what two people of polar opposites and pasts can sometimes bring out of each other. It instantly made me think of Starling.

Berith was hiding out, having been on the run since Morning Star stripped her of her flesh and power in his childish rage against her meeting and sharing information with me.

She came to me for help and if it hadn't been for her saving me when Xyn nearly killed me, I wouldn't have bothered.

"How are you, my friend?" I nodded with a smirk.

"I'm well Cam`ael, and yourself?" He returned the curt nod.

"No need to complain and no worries."

That was a lie.

"Atiro is an amazing cook and an even better teacher. I had no idea." Berith complimented him with a wide grin.

An array of dishes and brand new cookware was spread out on a few of the counters. There was a whole roast, a whole baked chicken, quail, duck, several different cakes, pasta dishes, cookies, breads, and potatoes prepared in several different ways.

"I can see that. I didn't know either. Expecting guests?" I pointed to the buffet of food.

Berith chuckled. "I guess we got a little carried away."

"Well, Berith did most of the cooking actually. I simply offered to assist." Atiro said.

"Oh don't be modest, Atiro." Berith smiled with a playful nudge.

Was Atiro blushing?

"Well, just mention the word 'food' and put it out there. I'm sure Mac, Ry, Nay, and several others would promptly respond and be more than happy to oblige in helping to sample this spread." I commented.

Atiro laughed and nodded in agreement.

Hearing Atiro laugh at all was a strange sound to my ears. I've never seen him so engaging, let alone speaking since our meeting at my place.

Was he becoming smitten with Berith of all beings? Apparently so.

"Is there any news? Something happening?" Atiro then inquired seriously.

I shook my head. "Not really, no."

Berith looked at me. "Nothing here either, so far."

"That worries me too. Don't let your guards down." I told them.

"Well, I don't have much in the place of defense but I do know a few spells," Berith pointed a wooden spatula at me, "Did you know that there are several underground organic spice stores here in this city?" She then said, making air quotes when she mentioned 'spice stores'.

I raised a brow with low interest. "Really?" I said, perusing the tableau of culinary arts and picking up an herbed baby potato to sample. That didn't surprise me at all.

She nodded. "They're all over the place, if you're of the supernatural plane and you know where to look. Which means, there have been a lot of special shoppers in and out of there. Females gossip and I happened to pick up on several conversations." She grinned as if she held a juicy secret.

I looked up at her as she joined me, standing across from me on the other side of the kitchen island.

"There's a haven of dark divines right here in this city, in the shadier district of downtown."

My gaze fixated on her with interest now. "Gossip or you know this for sure?"

"Both. I haven't ventured over there to verify it for obvious reasons but it's a tip. In fact, there are more and more dark ones coming through from a rift somewhere nearby. I don't know where it is but I've heard that these dark divine's are being protected by a legion of fallen aligned with that schizo-bastard. There's also a group of succubus', para- demons, and high level voids that seem to be focused on both you and the girl too." Berith warned.

Focused? More like the elimination of me and the capture of Starling. Many others have tried to go against me throughout the Millennia, mainly out of spite and jealously but they've all failed.

I wondered if they were remnants of Drakael's liege, perhaps to seek vengeance over his destruction or maybe even Baal's death since I was tied to both.

Though I wish I had been the one to destroy Drakael, I didn't do it. His righteous vanquishing came direct and swift for the spilling of Starlings blood.

Drawing the blood of a chosen while they were still mortal, either intentional or accidental, was vehemently prohibited for both sides per universal laws. It's one law that if broken, provokes instant and direct death straight from Elohim.

"Her name is Starling." I flatly corrected Berith.

She rolled her eyes. "Sorry. Starling. Have you seen her yet?"

My eyes flicked to Atiro, who remained silent and engrossed in carefully ladling equal amounts of the chocolate batter into each cup of a metal baking pan.

"How are you liking college?" I skated over her question.

She eyed me inquisitively and crossed her arms over her chest, "These humans that teach know nothing about the real world around them. They're only breeding a new generation of completely clueless, vulnerable humans. I find listening to them both humorous and boring. I would have stopped attending a while ago but there are a lot of nice vessels there." She grinned.

I gave her a warning glance and then turned to Atiro, still dodging her question on purpose.

"Keep a low profile. I'll check in again soon. Be very careful, Berith. You too my friend." I nodded at Atiro.

Atiro nodded assurance and Berith took my blatant avoidance of answering her as an insult, though I was sure that she knew what my non answer meant.

"Wait. I ah, have something else that might be of some interest to you. I was going to give it to Atiro to bring to you but since you're already here…" Berith began as she turned and padded back into the living area. Her footsteps soon began to thump up the hollow wood stairs.

At first, I wondered why she didn't simply just conjure whatever she had for me into her hands but I forgot, she couldn't.

She was powerless now. Something else I knew was getting difficult for her to get used to.

"She's right. I saw some activity when I accompanied her to the food store. It's mounting. When you're out there among the humans, you can sense it right away. The time must be growing near." Atiro offered as he put the cupcake pan into the oven.

I found the scene humorous. Formerly silent Atiro, as huge as his bulk was, and an expert fighter; was now in an apron baking cupcakes.

"What do you make of it?"

Atiro began removing the apron, "They're gearing up for something else, something really big. That much is certain. Ry, Mac, and Nay are on the western coast of the North American Continent, some place he called Hollywood California, I believe. He's been looking for a crowd to better blend in with and I think he's found it," he laughed softly. "He says there's so much dark activity out there, that none of them pay much attention to each other. They're having way too much fun."

Berith returned, carefully holding a small, extremely old, yet spectacularly preserved, yellow-gold and authentic mother's pearl decorated box.

I furrowed my brow as she delicately handed it to me.

"What's this?" I questioned, carefully taking it from her. I examined the design and details in admiration, recognizing the age of the precious metal. Curiously, I turned it over in my hands gingerly and then gently opened the cover to reveal its hidden contents.

I was stunned.

The title on the cover of the nearly petrified, brown leather was written in gold leaf script, and in an ancient language. It was some form of angelic to be precise. I ran my hand over the impressive jewels and then carefully opened the cover. The inside of it contained just a few yellowing, superfine pages, all frayed with brittle, browned edges.

"It's part of a tome or texts." Berith whispered.

I looked at her wryly. "Thank you for clarifying that. I meant where did it come from?"

I wasn't familiar with this form of angelic but I could figure it out if I studied it for a while.

"It's something that I took from Morning Star right before everything happened. I hid it where only I could find it, here in the mortal realm." Berith admitted.

"She had me take her to the barren arctic lands near the Northern pole. She sealed and buried it deep. It was a good hiding spot that's for sure." Atiro affirmed.

"I don't know what it is necessarily but if Morning Star had it, then there's something of deep importance in it. If I were you, I'd keep it locked up at your place, or better yet bury it at the bottom of the Eternal Lake."

The text appeared scattered, not forming any uniform continuous lines that would normally link paragraphs together.

"He can't even read angelic anymore." I commented in bewilderment as I glanced over each page in wonder.

There were many pages missing, that much was apparent not even knowing what was written on them. Where or who had he gotten this from? This should have been something that was in the keeping of angels.

In fact, I'm sure that at one time it had been.

So how the hell had he gotten it? Another interesting mystery perhaps. I was fascinated. A feeling of both nostalgia and excited curiosity began to kindle in my mind.

The parchment was crafted from ancient fibrous plants and papyrus trees that were indigenous to the Earth around what is now the Tigris and Euphrates River in the Middle East, after the Great Flood.

I wondered how Berith managed to keep it all in one piece so easily and maintain it so well.

The symbols stoked a distant memory of the speech that I shared with my former angelic brethren once upon a time. Enochian? No, this was different and it was evident it was not written by man.

How many angels or fallen had he killed in order to obtain possession of this?

"I know but some of the newly fallen can and they were helping him to decode some of it in exchange for favors, dominions, and vessels. Either way, I know it was extremely important to him. Maybe it can become a bargaining tool at some point." She then said with raised brows.

"I don't play bargain games with the wickedly insane. Not ones I have any intentions of following through with anyway." I immediately clarified.

She shrugged a shoulder. "You never know."

There was silence between the three of us for a brief moment. Atiro was attuned to something else; taking in scents and noises around the vicinity to ensure that we weren't being tracked, watched, stalked, or surrounded.

"This is the real reason he nearly killed you and is now hunting you down, isn't it?" I finally asked Berith.

She shifted from foot to foot with hesitation. "It's the main one, yes. He was already suspicious and I think he thought that I was trying giving it to you then," She sighed, looking down at her bare toes for a brief moment and then back up at me, "I did plan to. I knew you were the one fallen that he'd have a hard time getting it back from if at all. I didn't want to leave it where it could get damaged or eventually retrieved by one of his minions. He tortured me for days, tearing a piece of me apart each time I refused to tell him where I took it, until there was finally no trace of physical flesh left. When I saw my chance, I fled." She admitted. I had no idea just how fucked Berith was but if it was something that Morning Star desperately wanted back. He was going to have to try and take it from me.

V. STARLING

The last conversation between me and Ilka, after I finally had no choice but to confess, weighed heavily on my mind as I made my way back to my room.

Her reaction and words were not what I expected but I couldn't make her keep this a secret either. She wouldn't.

She told me I had to tell the elders in my assembly soon or she would be forced to do it. I understood her dilemma but at least she was sort of sympathetic, at least that's what she appeared to be to me. I know she was right and I trusted her but I was frightened.

The few people that I bothered to notice or glance at from the corner of my eye were looking at me reverently now, but I felt as if everyone already knew or could see that I was pregnant, even though my stomach was still flat.

I didn't say a word to Spencer, Kaia, or Brynn, leaving them all to wonder about the diagnosis in my silence. I left Ilka to give the report of my clean bill of both physical and mental health, which was essentially the truth anyway. I mumbled about heading to my room to get a change of clothes, bathe, and then nap for a long time. Even though they all three followed me out of the medical quarters, they left me to find my way back to my room alone, which surprised me and I appreciated it.

I was still dazed. I hadn't even called out to Cam since earlier and I know he was probably going crazy with worry. I didn't even know what else to say or do at this point.

"Starling! Oh my God!" I heard a high-pitched squeal from behind me.

Footsteps were quickly tapping towards me.

I managed to turn around just in time for Lira to slam into me, wrapping her thin arms around me in a firm hug. It was a touching greeting and it made me instantly smile as I hugged her back.

"I'm so glad you're back and you're okay! We thought you were gone forever!" She gasped, half laughing and half sobbing, which turned into spasmodic, hitching breaths.

Tears glistened in her big, brown eyes.

"Nope, I'm back." I smiled while forcing back my own waterworks.

She paused to wipe her face, sniffing and hiccupping with a

broad smile.

"Lira, I'm really sorry about what happened." I then began.

"Sorry? What are you apologizing to me for? That was the most fun that I've had since I've been here." She laughed and sniffed again.

"Really?"

She nodded enthusiastically. "Most definitely!"

I sighed. "Still..."

She waved off the start of my self-deprecating speech. "Forget about me. You're back and that's what matters. I thought you were..." Her bottom lip and chin began to quiver and she began to cry all over again.

"Come on, no more tears. I made it back and I'm not gonna allow that happen to me or anyone else again if I can help it, okay?" I smiled.

She nodded with a weak smile.

Though I really could care less, I asked anyway. "Is Jamie alright?"

Lira beamed through her tears and wiped her face. "Of course she's alright. It's you we were all worried sick over. Thank you for saving her."

I pressed my lips in a tight smile, feeling guilty. I hadn't set out to save her entirely. I was careless and not thinking when I did it but I was glad that she was safe.

"What about Durien? Have you seen him today?" I asked her then.

She shook her head no. "I haven't seen him since he and Spencer made it back." She said softly.

"He didn't get in trouble, did he?"

I would be righteously ticked if he did.

"No, but he blames himself for you getting taken. He left and he hasn't been back here since then. I'm guessing that he's at his place in the human realm." She told me.

"He shouldn't blame himself. No one should. Does anyone have a portal gem to his house?" I asked her.

"I don't know. If you set a guest list with the alchemists and give permission, then those who are on it have access to portal gems to your home. I think Anthony and Gabe might be on his list. Do you want me to find one of them?"

I sighed.

"No, I'll ask them myself but thanks. In the meantime, I'll be in my room for a while. If you do happen to see him before I do, will you tell him that I'm back?" I told her.

"Of course." She smiled, "Can you meet us in the dining hall before you retire to your room though? Everyone has been asking about you since you came through the portal."

I really didn't want to see or talk to anyone else right now. I just wanted to be alone to think about what I was going to do but the glimmer in her eyes held hope and excitement that I couldn't rain on. She seemed to be among the few who were genuinely happy about my safe return so far.

I nodded. "Okay."

~~~****~~~

I don't know what the foul crap was that Cam had smeared into my hair but it took forever to wash out. I grumbled about it to myself as I combed through my still damp curls and fought with multiple tangles. Obviously there was no conditioner or blow drying mechanism here and these combs didn't really do the job well. I couldn't wait until I was able to venture back out into the human realm and establish my own home.

If I made it that long.

My hair has been a hot mess since the Eternal Lake skinny dip and then bathing at Cam's place. Maybe I should take Spencer and Sean's advice and just cut it. They said it would be like a handle to the fallen if it wasn't tightly wound into a bun of some sort anyway.

It was so surreal knowing that a baby was growing inside of me right now. This was yet another experience that I never got the chance to have while I was still mortal.

What was I going to do though? What would I end up giving birth to? A supernatural or a human being? Or both? All of those questions scared and confused me. Regardless, I'm going to be a mother and that realization began to stir up an automatic protective instinct within.

Once I finished fixing my hair, I lingered in front of the mirror and stared at my reflection. I narrowed my eyes to fixate on my aura out of sheer curiosity. The bright, white light began to form a soft halo around me but there was something different now.

There were dark smudges in random spots that broke the solid continuity of the light surrounding me. The darkness smeared into my aura was definitely noticeable, and it was nothing that I could even attempt to hide. With another deep sigh, I closed my eyes.

"*Starling.*" Cam's voice returned to me in a soothing, somewhat seductive tone.

The sound of his voice in my head when he said my name automatically created a frenzy of erotic sensations throughout my entire body. I could still feel him inside of me, and the phantom aftershocks of the multiple orgasms that left my legs feeling both rubbery and too weak to even kneel.

My breath caught. I was already literally craving him again.

I bit my bottom lip, keeping my eyes closed and answered him softly. "*I'm here.*"

"*I couldn't wait anymore. Are you alright?*"

"*Yeah.*"

"*What did the succor say?*"

"*She's leaving it up to me to confess. If I don't then she will, which is fine. I plan to. I don't have any other choice.*"

I heard him sigh softly. "*I'm sorry. I didn't mean to put you in this predicament and make you compromise what you were destined to be and have chosen. I don't regret any of it though. I'd do it all again. Everything.*"

"*I don't regret anything either and stop saying sorry. I'm not.*"

Then I paused. "*Do...*" I hesitated to ask the question because for me there was none, but given the fact that he kept apologizing about it made me wonder.

"*Do you want me to get rid of it?*" I asked softly.

"*You can't be seriously asking me that.*" He sounded hurt.

"*I just want to be sure, that's all.*"

It was silent on his end for a moment. "*Are you sure? Though I'd do everything in my power to convince you otherwise, I'd understand if you...*"

I would have been offended if it wasn't apparent that Cam really wanted this child. I could hear it in his voice.

"*I won't lie to you, I'm am afraid but that thought never came to mind as an option. This baby...no matter what he or she is, will be a combination of the both of us and will have the same free will that all beings have.*"

"*You're not alone. You'll never be alone. In fact, I'd rather you* be here with me anyway."

I paused. I believed him though I still felt an emotional tug at my heart.

"I know. I just didn't think as an immortal...that I could even get pregnant or that you as...a supernatural spirit being could...you know." I don't know why after all we did together both in the spring behind the waterfall and in his bed, that I couldn't even say the words. I felt silly.

"Though we fallen can still switch back and forth between our original spirit forms and physical flesh at will, ultimately we've been condemned to endure for eternity in flesh form, which means that I'm no longer perfect. Everything that comes with being of the male species applies. You're female... and still human." He explained.

It was then that I finally understood why he was so apologetic. Because he was keenly aware of all of that and I was clueless. I had to wonder if Cam had planned this. Fallen wanted female warriors to breed with and I assume that's why they were all after me, especially Morning Star. But why just me when they could create whatever dual race of beings they wanted with other female warriors? Have they been able to? What made them think that they'd be able impregnate me? Well—Cam had been able to.

I didn't want to follow where my mind was going to next. I didn't want to believe anything bad or negative about Cam but he was a Fallen, and I was told never to trust anything that a Fallen did or said. But what if... no, I wasn't gonna even go there and think that at all. I swallowed thickly, my heart pounding slow and hard. Warm tears began to pool in my eyes.

There was an air of silence and sudden curiosity gnawed at me again. *"Will you tell me why you fell now?"* I asked.

"No."

Was he serious? Why was he keeping it such a guarded secret? This was going to drive me crazy. His evasiveness about it was making me suspicious, which wasn't helping given my current thoughts.

"Why not?"

"I don't want to continue to talk about this like this. I need to be able to see and hold you."

"I won't see you at all until you tell me."

This time, he was silent for a long time. I thought he had abruptly ended the conversation for the sake of maintaining his secrecy and it was slowly breaking my heart.

"Ok, you win, but afterwards you'll owe me something."

His response surprised me but it made me smile. Maybe I was overreacting and jumping to conclusions. I'd almost forgotten that Cam is an incubus. Whatever that something was, I was certain that it involved physical contact—not that I wouldn't have given in to him anyway.

"I suppose." I agreed softly.

"You don't even know what I want."

"Um, yeah, I think I do."

He laughed. *"I'll see you soon."*

"Okay." I smiled to myself.

Returning to my room to put my things away before heading to the dining room to meet the others, I stopped short in the doorway. Sitting on the writing desk, next the notebook for my journal, was a simple crystal vase filled with small white, bell-shaped flowers, surrounded by long, slender, vibrantly green leaves. The bouquet was beautifully arranged and a hint of fresh floral dew clung to the air. It struck a memory of springtime, filling my room with a relaxing, soft scent.

I raised a brow of curious surprise as I walked over to examine and smell them up close. Was this a welcome back gift or something from Lira and the others?

"Those are lily-of-the-valleys." I heard from behind me.

I turned around to see Jamie, leaning against the doorjamb with her arms around her middle. She appeared softer, more toned down. Her long, dark brown braid hung loosely over her shoulder.

"They're beautiful."

She nodded. "Those should last a long time too."

It was almost as if she were having a hard time maintaining eye contact with me, like a sheepish avoidance.

"Did you leave these here?" I asked her.

She shifted and inhaled. "I thought you'd like them. They're...sort of a...welcome back thing...and," She glanced at the floor, shifting her stance again, and then to my surprise— she began to cry.

VI. CAM`AEL

She had me in the palm of her hand, already wielding the power that women had over men...that she had over me. It didn't take long. I'd do anything for her.

I smirked to myself.

I was going to have to be seductive and clever to get out of telling her my history. She wanted to know what I did to fall. It wasn't that it was horrible, I was both embarrassed and ashamed of it. Even more so, by the existence and activities that I took part in thereafter. I was already wearing my shame, seeing the permanent black marks whenever I revealed and spread my wings. Wasn't that enough?

The dark symbols that ruined my once great wings, and my formerly gold brandings, now cursed to blood red, were more than visual proof and constant reminders.

Edanai, Ry, and Rahab were the only ones who knew the basic truth, but no one knew the whole truth in its entirety except for Elohim. Of course, Morning Star knew much of it too but he was the last fallen that could judge or measure any of our sins or disobedience against his own. I didn't want Starling to see me as desperate and foolish, and in my opinion it was pointless anyway.

I sealed and hid the book that Berith gave me behind the largest bookshelf in my bed chamber. I would need a good amount of time to attempt to read it and I may not even do it here or the human realm.

I decided that I would head into another dimension later, a place that would offer quiet and privacy. A place that Morning Star and his clan knew nothing about—so that it would remain safe from his eyes and repossession.

I was cloaked and only a few feet away from the border of the sanctified grounds of the Divine hall while we were engaged in our mental conversation. I had to see what was happening up close. Though I had already been detected by the all-white, strange animals that roamed freely on the grounds, and a few of the warriors, none of them made any move or attempts to confront me.

I began to retreat, slowly backing further into the trees of the neutral zone, still listening and watching. A sudden streak of white luminescence whizzed past me, embedding itself deep into the trunk of a tree right next to me with a solid thump. Wood creatures and implings chittered and scampered away to hide in the leaves and bushes.

I tensed and abruptly whirled around, wielding my sword but remaining cloaked, just as another projectile zipped right over my head. Thrusting a palm forward, I conjured a shield of dark energy in front of me, which stopped the next five shots dead in their tracks. It allowed me to see what they were more clearly too.

Glowing silver bolts.

It was obvious that the attacks were meant to get my attention. Whoever it was would have had a clear shot the first time. Though I had an idea of who these belonged to, I wasn't taking chances.

The trapped bolts, leaving them suspended in the field of dark energy that formed my shield, until they finally began to dissipate into wisps of bluish white smoke. Durien stepped out from behind a wide-girthed tree several yards away.

He cracked something in his fist and made a motion of throwing it down. A portal shot upwards, glimmering in a kaleidoscope of muted colors. With one last glance over his shoulder at me, he ventured through and I followed him.

~~~****~~~

There was already a fracture in the protective wards surrounding his place, so I simply ghosted in. He was standing at the panoramic window, looking at the evening sunset over the water in the distance. His feet were planted shoulder width apart, fists at his waist, and I could feel unstable anger wafting off of him.

"I guess you must have forgotten that you guys still cast shadows when the sun is high." He spoke first, not turning to face me yet.

I smirked. That fact was the main reason we cloak at night. In the darkness, it was near impossible for the warriors to see or detect us by sight. So, the hall did manage to offer these future warriors something of value.

"Ah, that explains your extremely bad aiming then but I could have been any one of the others." I reminded him.

He grunted sarcastically. "Your scent is distinct. You don't smell like all the others. No one in your circle does." He stated flatly.

I nodded, approaching him slowly and stopping halfway just as he turned around to face me.

"You just don't quit do you, man? Now you're hanging out that close to the vicinity of the hall? For what? If you're looking for Starling…she's gone! She got taken and she ain't coming back, okay?!" His teeth were clenched and he was fuming.

Durien looked like…shit.

His eyes were bloodshot and there were worry lines between his eyebrows that made him look a lot older than his young age.

He was upset with me, that much was clear and I knew why. He slowly relaxed his arms but his fists were still clenched so tightly, prominent veins protruded from the tops of his hands.

I kept my eyes on his and debated joining him at the window.

"Why didn't you tell me that her essence was hallowed fire?" I asked, keeping my accusing tone even.

Durien appeared confused but still angry. "What the hell are you talking about?"

"She possesses deadly fire. Deadly enough to kill darkness on contact. You didn't know?" I asked him with a raised brow.

I finally joined him at the window. He continued to look up at me inquisitively with a hint of surprise though he still scowled.

"How do you know? You saw her use it? You're still alive so it couldn't have been too deadly, unless..." the fiery heat of anger and a challenge began to burn in his eyes once again.

Was he really going to try and fight me?

"Don't be ridiculous!" I spat back through clenched teeth.

I meant that in more ways than one.

It took him a minute to simmer down but he was still agitated.

"I didn't know what her essence was, none of us did but that's beside the point now!" He was getting angry again.

"She's fine." I said, looking down at him indignantly.

His face instantly morphed into dumbfounded confusion.

"Say what?" he asked, brows furrowed.

"I said she's fine. She's safe at the hall right now as you stand here yelling and dancing on the minefield." I repeated slowly, my eyes glowing malevolently on purpose to remind him of exactly who he was threatening.

His anger began to subside and he recoiled, taking a slight step away from me, and pausing to think.

"Seriously?" His entire demeanor had suddenly shifted from rabid attack dog to foolish chagrin.

"Why would I lie to you about that?"

After a moment, he pursed his lips and sighed deeply through his nose. "Oh."

The tension began to slowly unravel from his body as he wiped a hand down his face and then moved into the kitchen, opening the refrigerator.

"I kind of knew something like that was gonna happen and it just about ended badly but I take full responsibility and blame. I won't be doing anything like that again so you can forget about asking," Durien said as he pulled out a bottled water out and pointed it at me. "You're on your own with her. If she doesn't remember you, you should just leave her alone altogether. It's gonna cause major problems."

He unscrewed the cap of the water bottle, leaned back against the arm of the couch, and took a long drink.

"I understand and I take responsibility as well. I hadn't expected you to invite the whole gang and I certainly didn't anticipate Baal showing up, though it didn't surprise me." I said.

He looked pointedly at me. "Like I said, that wasn't my fault. No such thing as a private conversation around the hall. Everyone pretty much invited themselves. In the end though, I'm kind of glad they did. I have some idea why they all want her as a female divine warrior, and I know why you want her, but do you know the real reason why they all seem so drawn to Starling in particular?" Durien then asked.

I hadn't expected that question from him but it was a good one. Yes and no, I wanted to reply but instead I shook my head no.

He sighed. "It's gonna be really hard for her, especially there more so than in the human realm. The training we get may not be enough." He shook his head.

"It isn't." I frankly agreed.

His eyes flicked up to connect with mine. We were both thinking the same thing.

I offered to train Starling but I don't know if I'd extend it to Durien. He'd have to make a choice. I wasn't about to train him so that he could share anything with a group of warriors dead set on killing me and my friends.

"So, what ended up happening? How did you get her back? And what happened after that? Did she remember you? What did she say to you?" He eagerly wanted to know and asked in one breath.

I shot him an irritated grimace with a hint of unbelieving sarcasm at his sudden barrage of probing questions. Yes, I liked Durien and I trusted him to an extent—as much as he trusted me. He did me a huge favor and risked a lot so that I could see Starling again. For that, he had my undying gratitude but any information past that was none of his business…at least most of it would remain unknown until Starling began to show.

"If she wants you to know anything then I'm sure she'll share it with you." I simply said.

He pressed his lips and narrowed his eyes.

"What did you have to do? Cast some sort of a spell on her? I'm sure she was terrified being that she was untrained and all. Is that when she used her fire?"

More questions.

This time I simply nodded.

A slow smile began to spread across Duriens brown face. "Sweet. Good for her." He said more to himself.

"Is that all you wanted to know?" I then asked him, getting ready to ghost out of his home.

He hesitated, taking a quick inhalation of air as if he did want to say something else but instead chewed his bottom lip. "Yeah.

Thanks again." He gave a nod.

"I didn't do it for you or any of the others at the hall." I reminded him.

"I know." He replied.

VII. STARLING

I could only stare silently while Jamie broke down in front of me. She was trying to fight it and I knew I should be doing something to comfort her, but I just stood there.

"Anyway, welcome back." She quickly hiccupped, sniffed, and began to walk away, still unable to meet my eyes.

"Jamie, wait." I called out.

She stopped but didn't turn around to face me.

I walked towards her slowly. "You don't have to thank me. It was a given and I don't regret it." I told her.

Her shoulders shook as her breath hitched. She only nodded.

"If…if you ever want to talk about anything…"

"I'm fine." She cut me off and began to walk away once again but then she stopped again briefly, looking back at me over her shoulder.

"He saved you, didn't he?" She then whispered.

I furrowed my brows.

Her words caught me off guard and my pulse began to race at the thought of who she might be referring to.

I felt the burn of guilt begin to warm my face.

"He who? What are you talking about?"

She turned to fully face me again, the hint of a sad and crooked smile on her face, "The only way you managed to make it back." Then her smile slowly turned into a frown, "Don't ever give them his name." She warned in a hushed whisper with her index finger to her lips, before finally walking away.

Confounded and thrown, I watched her until she turned the corner at the end of the corridor.

She knows.

I didn't expect those last words from her. What did she mean by that? I remember Durien telling me that she had a thing for supernatural beings. She was either messing around with Spencer now or had been in the past.

Damn, Jamie was the last one that I wanted holding that piece of information. She was a hard one to figure out and I couldn't trust her. All I could do was continue to play stupid once that information got back to the elders— and it would. I remembered her expression after she practically kicked my ass out on the training field the other day, and Spencer was trying to hold her back and calm her down. She looked like she was trying to keep herself from crying then, too.

I didn't spend too much time pondering what her issues were. I made my way back to the now thinned out crowd in the dining hall, catching the others in the midst of setting up an impromptu welcome back celebration.
Was that cake?
My stomach growled jubilantly and I began to salivate. After I entered the dining hall, all heads turned to look at me. It was like I was re-entering once again on my first day here.
It took me a moment to realize that they weren't just looking at me, they were all looking behind me.
I turned around— and my mouth fell.
I had a trail of divine elementals following and crowding around after me. They all stopped when I did. Their freakishly human eyes and faces studied me curiously without a sound.
Oh God. They were sensing that something wasn't right with me, and if they were sensing it, then the others would definitely be alerted to the change too.
"Well don't just stand there, come on. We're all waiting…" Lorelei's voice was in front of me.
I turned back around to look at her when she stopped in mid-sentence.
Her grin slowly staggered, "Wow, you're like the pied piper of elementals. Aren't you special today? That's weird." She commented.
Scarlet and Crystal joined us to see what everyone else was gawking at as well.
"What's going on?" Scarlet asked before seeing the posse of white animals spread out behind me just outside of the doorway to the dining hall. They sat silently with their attentive eyes focused on me.
"What, they don't follow people around?" I joked, growing edgy.
"Not in a pack like that." Crystal pointed.
"Well, there's a first for everything I guess." Lorelei shrugged, "Come on. We hope you like chocolate cake." She smiled.
With one last glance at the elementals, I let Lorelei pull and guide

me over to the table that they had decorated. The cloth napkins were creatively shaped in Origami-like flowers and the medium-sized, chocolate frosted cake sat in the center of a paper cut doily in the middle of the table.

Anthony and Gabe were already seated and waiting to dig in, and Lira was busy setting out plates and silverware. No sign of Durien or Spencer.

I hoped Durien wasn't beating himself up over this. I tentatively pressed my palm against my lower belly, an automatic new reaction for me since finding out that I was pregnant.

"Well, well, well...looking and smelling much better." Gabe quipped.

I smiled. "Thanks. I'm definitely feeling much better."

"That's good to hear." Anthony said as he stood up to pull a chair out for me.

That was nice. I slowly sat down.

"This wasn't necessary but thanks." I said to everyone.

"No need to thank us. You're safe and that calls for a celebration, so I hope you have a sweet tooth. This is a rare indulgence here." Scarlet smiled as she began to cut the first slice.

A rare indulgence? Given the daily food choices, I could see that.

"Even if I didn't, I'm starving so don't be shy on my slice." I told her.

I tried hard to separate all that's happened and the present company of my friends, especially all the elementals that were still sitting over there in the open doorway, still watching me. It was making me really uncomfortable and nervous now.

"What's with all the elementals?" Anthony thumbed over in their direction with a questioning quirk of his brow.

Everyone stopped to look, further making me want to sink through the floor and disappear completely, more so because everyone else in the dining hall began to make the connection too.

Crystal dismissed it with a shrug and a wave of her hand, "I wouldn't worry about it. They're real sensitive to auras and since yours is a little off right now, they're probably just worried about you. That's all."

My heart began to race.

"Mine is— off?" I asked, searching all of their faces and eyes for more explanation.

I already knew what they meant. No doubt it will probably get worse and more noticeable as the baby begins to grow. I assumed that was the reason why.

Lorelei shook her head. "Not in a bad way. It's probably stress. You just got back. It may take a few days." She assured me with a smile.

I suddenly didn't feel like eating anything anymore.

VIII. CAMAEL

I called out to Edanai upon returning home. She was stubborn if anything and it drove me insane—that's where we tended to bump heads at times. Instead, Rahab assured me that she was fine and so far, no incidences. Ry, Nay, and Mac were having a ball in Hollywood, so I doubted that I'd see them anytime soon unless something dire transpired.

All I could do was wait until I saw Starling tonight. I had plans, and after ducking out into the human realm once again to retrieve a few items for our date, I noted that it was nearing the holiday feasting of turkeys and soon to be gift giving time. The traditions and events of other beings all over the world fascinated me. I didn't care anything about their significances, I simply enjoyed the festivities and the décor.

Starling didn't pay much attention to the birthdate on her drivers' license. Of course, she wouldn't have made the connection anyway given that she had no concept of human realm time as opposed to time in the spirit realm.

Her birthday, via human realm time, was coming up and I wanted to both do something and get something exceptionally unique and special for her. Realizing that I should have given Starling her phone, or at least had her make a few calls before taking her back, didn't dawn on me until I saw it going off again. Glimpsing at the display, I saw that she had numerous text messages and her voicemail notification light was flashing once again.

It was of course, China.

I never asked what Edanai told her last but apparently it wasn't enough to keep her from calling again. I'd have to think of something else for now and have Starling call her back herself. I texted back an, 'I'll call you tonight,' and left it at that. I'm sure she would wonder why she was avoiding her again and didn't bother to answer just now but oh well. I hoped that what I was doing didn't end up distancing their friendship in the end.

I retrieved the book that Berith had given me, handling it delicately as I placed it gently on the square cocktail table, and then proceeded to fix myself a cup of tea. This was going to take a while to decipher but I was determined to make some sense of it, even if this wasn't the whole text.

With a pad of paper and a pencil, I started with the first line, taking each repetitive symbol and notating how many times it appeared. I did the same with the next one and so on, until I essentially created a key of some sort. Trying to focus on each symbol and match it to that of my distant memory of the language was proving to be more difficult than I thought.

After five cups of tea, four glasses of burgundy wine, and half a dozen bread buns stuffed with lamb and spices that Rahab made the other day, I had only managed to decode two words that I was certain of: 'Arrogance and weapon.'

I was even more puzzled now than I had been since starting this. Who wrote this? Why had it been written, and why does Morning Star have it much less want it? Those two words burned into my mind, allowing me some form of an idea and picture. Was this key to the final days of humans? Did it have something to do with Morning Star's coming invasion?

"Cam'ael, I must speak with you. A new task has been requested by Elohim and it must be done with haste."

It was Aliks' voice, or what sounded like him.

I paused, scowling at the mere disturbance let alone what he was saying.

Another request? Again? Since the last one, when Drakael had apparently manipulated my loyalties to Elohim and tricked me into becoming a pawn for his own plans for Starling, I was less enthused and wary.

"I'm done with requests, especially if it involves releasing anyone." I flatly replied.

There was silence on his end.

"You refuse even though Elohim has granted you all that you have most desired, and has allowed everything that has come to pass?"

I clenched my teeth in frustration. So he was playing that card now? As much as having another request irritated me because it might take me away from Starling, I had no choice.

To Elohim, I have always been loyal and obedient and I still am. Anything he asked of me, I would risk myself to do or complete and I have up until the incident with Drakael.

"I'm outside." Aliks then said, reading my silence accurately.

I ghosted outside of my home, seeing Aliks' slight, glittering form and silver and pink flowing hair, standing at the peak of the mountaintop. It was adjacent to the spot where I had spoken to Drakael.

My wings were out when I manifested back into flesh form, meeting a smug Aliks.

"I'm impressed by your loyalty to Elohim. I understand why it is that he has not lost faith or favor in you." Aliks complimented.

"Just get on with it." I snapped.

He began to pace.

"This is a nice view. One can see…everything from here." He mused as he gazed out onto the landscape, more so, the side facing the Dark Lands.

I already didn't like where this was going.

Against the purple horizon, a carriage of faded blue ghostly forms, all corralled into a lasso made of glowing green vines, was being pulled by a pair of aural bandits, accompanied by a Psyren. They rode on the backs of poisonous, scorpion-tailed, winged, black Pegasus'. Her shriek of elation pierced the air with such a sharp, nearly deafening pitch, it nearly made my nose and ears bleed.

Judging from the cluster of pale, ecto-plasmic forms bundled behind them, and the howls and catcalls ululating from the bandits, I'd say that they had just rounded up a large bundle of souls.

I haven't seen very many of them at all lately, so this was interesting to me. I wondered from where they had acquired so many.

Aliks turned to me, a furtive side grin affixed to his pale face. "They all know who you are, don't they?"

"What are you getting at? What is the request?" I was short of any patience.

"Your name and presence strikes both fear and veneration among many of the dark ones, including many other fallen." he began.

"Don't forget loathing. Those aren't necessarily good things either." I quipped.

Aliks shrugged a single shoulder and nodded in agreement. "Nonetheless, it's a level of respect. Gain and maintain an alliance with the aural bandits and the Psyrens. That is the request."

I wasn't sure if I'd understood him right.

"What? An alliance? Is this a joke?"

Aliks pursed his lips. "Elohim would not request anything without a reason. You know that."

Yes, I did know that but after my last experience, I wasn't really motivated.

"Does he realize what he's asking and how difficult that will be if it is possible at all?" I asked, incredulous.

"Obviously he does." Aliks smirked.

I was already having doubts. Why? Why did Elohim want me to even try to associate with those scavenging lowlifes, let alone create an alliance? It was pure and extreme madness.

"For what purpose?" I asked anyway.

"That will come to pass. Will you do it?" Aliks then asked.

I wanted to say no, absolutely not, that it was a complete waste of time and energy but I couldn't. Not to Elohim.

"He refuses to speak to or hear me anymore. I want some proof that this has come directly from Elohim before I even consider it." I finally replied.

Aliks' expression turned to surprise and then he paused. "It has been done." He simply said. "Will you do it?" He repeated again.

"What has been done?" I asked suspiciously, scanning the sky and the vicinity around us, searching for something telling or a uniquely visual sign from Elohim.

"Will you or won't you accept this request?" Aliks patiently repeated yet again.

I bit my lip, hesitation furrowing my brows at his nerve.

What proof did he give?

I finally gave in. "I'll try."

"No trying. You must do it!" Aliks snapped.

"I said I'll try! There are no guarantees with them!"

"Where there is a will, there is always a way. It is imperatively important. Go about it however you need to." Aliks added and he began to ghost away before I could even ask or protest anything else.

Was he serious? What was Elohim thinking? I didn't have time for this. I already had everything I ever wanted and needed. I had Starling...thanks to Elohim.

I sighed heavily, gazing above into the vast heavens.

"I get it. I don't understand it but I get it." I whispered out loud.

With one last glance in the direction of the distant Darklands, I finally ghosted back inside.

I had no idea how I would go about approaching any kind of an alliance with those asinine rejects who cared more about riches, bullying, and stealing than they did about any kind of life. Does Elohim really think I can trust them to work with me in establishing and maintaining an alliance? They were more prone to worship and serve Morning Star before me, being that they associated and dealt with him often.

   I returned to the texts that I had been trying to decode, only to be halted by the revelation in front of me once I picked up the pencil. I had been reverently humbled once again.

   The texts…had been deciphered completely. All of the words were translated for me by Elohim himself—along with something else that hadn't been there before.

   The location of the rest of the book.

IX. STARLING

I was thankful to Lira for loaning me a map of the Spirit realm. Otherwise, I wasn't sure that I'd be able to find my way to the Eternal waters by myself. I knew Cam wouldn't leave me to find my way on my own but I didn't want him to come anywhere close to the hall, just in case. Even though it's only been since early this morning that I was last with Cam, I couldn't wait to see and be with him again.

It was hard to ignore and avoid the elementals that were still watching and following me around. I had no choice but to make direct beelines from each destination and then to my room, and to pretend that I didn't see or notice them. For the time being, I'd rather everyone thought I was weird and loopy than being suspected of something that was forbidden on so many levels.

Once behind the closed door of my room, I took some time to study the map. My journal still lay blank and untouched. There'd be no way I could write about anything that's happened in the last day and a half. Since I couldn't reveal the complete truth, it would be better if I simply didn't write anything at all.

I thought back to the photos and all the people that were in my photo album. My family…my parents, and my grandmother. What were they like? How had they died? When had they died? Were their souls really protected from the dark ones and Morning Star? Cam said they were and I don't think he'd lie to me about that, fallen or not.

Then, I thought about my friends. A large part of me wanted to see them again but how would that go? I had no clue how spirit realm time corresponded to human realm time. How long have I been gone and how much time has passed there anyway? Would they sense something different or wrong with me? I guess that's why Durien said that it wasn't a good idea to venture back to our past lives and associations. I sighed.

Exhaustion finally won out and I was ready for a nap.

~~~****~~~

When I awoke, I had no idea what time it was but it was dark and really dim in my room, save for a soft beam of bright moonlight spilling in from the window. I hadn't been disturbed, thank goodness but I had the indistinguishable feeling that I was being watched. I sat up in my bed and turned to look up at the small square window above the desk.

A large, all white owl sat in the sill on the outside of the glass, calmly and peacefully cocking its head at me. Its large, round, turquoise blue eyes remained unblinking as it studied me with curiosity. I didn't feel threatened but I certainly felt unnerved. Was it spying on me?

"Hello." I spoke, feeling a tad silly until it responded with a soft warbling hoot in reply. That was a pleasant surprise.

Diana said that they don't speak…most of the time and that they could understand human speech. They were messengers and protectors of the hall.

It flapped its great white wings, making a slight hooting noise again, and then suddenly took off in flight.

That was random.

I went to freshen up and change, hoping that there was no curfew and that no one would question why I felt the need to go for a walk at night alone in the neutral areas. Those areas were still prone to the infiltration of darkness from what I've heard. Maybe after all of the recent events regarding my return and all of the strange events surrounding me, people would steer clear of even wondering let alone approaching me to ask.

With my cloak secured around me and dressed in my field gear, I ventured casually towards the North end of the hall and made my way outside.

I stood out in the front field and paused to look up into the dark sky, searching the stars.

It didn't take long for Cam to take notice of me. He must have been watching already. The stars to the east, where the lake was located, suddenly began to slowly shift. The end result were two interlinking hearts.

I pulled the hood of my cloak up and over my head with a smile. Taking one last glimpse behind me, I made off to the East, in the direction of the hearts.

The woods were super dark at night, even with the dappling of moonlight spilling between the canopy of the limbs and leaves on all the massive trees. The hood of my cloak was pulled down over my head and part way down my face. Despite the concealment, my aura made me a literal walking flashlight.

I suppose it was to my advantage in some ways, especially when I began hearing strange noises and things moving among the dead leaves and the bushes in the darkness beyond. It was almost as if the woods were alive with another energy force. I could sense it but it wasn't a negative energy. It must be the guardians of the forest. I remember Cam telling me about them.

Shadows moved. The darkness beyond my range of light was a bit unsettling but I was ready to wield my blades or even flash some fire if I needed it. I suddenly felt as if I were being watched by both the trees and...someone else.

The crunch of leaves sounded behind me and I froze. Immediately, I thought of Cam.

"Cam, I'm on my way. Please tell me that's you behind me?" I called out to him just to be sure.

"I'm not far but it's not me. You've been followed. It's two of your own."

Crap! Two? Who could they be?

"Stay out of sight." I told him.

"Not if I think you're in trouble." He warned.

I drew my blades.

"Hey, you shouldn't be walking out here in the dark, especially by yourself."

I deftly spun around, ready to both attack and defend. I can't stand when people sneak up on me. I don't care who it is.

Crouching low, my arm automatically lashed outward, slashing at...Spencer?

"Whoa! It's me, Spencer!" He dodged away from me skillfully with his hand splayed protectively over his groin.

What the hell? Was he following me around now? What was his deal? So, who was the other one that Cam mentioned?

"Yeah, I know and you were about to become an earthbound seraphim eunuch. I don't like being followed." I replied flatly.

He looked at me in surprise and then frowned. "Ouch, really? You'd better be glad it was me. That was a nice brutal attack move by the way. Going straight for the main source of happiness and joy first is guaranteed to bring down or weaken any male enemy instantly. Where'd you learn that so fast?"

I sighed and rolled my eyes, straightening from my low crouch.

"I thought this area was neutral. I wanted to go to the water." I motioned in the direction of the Eternal waters while pulling in my blades.

He stepped closer, into better view and then looked down at me speculatively.

"This late? There's a safer route through the back field behind the hall so you'll never have to leave sanctified land. Why would you come this way?" he asked me.

In the darkness, the shadows on his face along with the light of my aura, made him look ghastly and intimidating. The extra eerie effect of his nearly glowing, sparkling and swirling eyes didn't help much either.

"I have no problem finishing what you attempted. The eunuch reference was hilarious. I've been waiting for him." Cam's suddenly spoke. There was definite malice in his tone.

"Please don't, Cam. He's arrogant and by the book but he's no threat to me." I replied.

Other than being a possible snitch, I then thought to myself.

"He certainly won't be when I'm done with him."

I tensed, hoping that Cam was simply talking.

"Because I told her to meet me out here. We were going for a walk. She wanted to see the lake and I told her that I'd show her where it was." Came another familiar voice from out of the darkness.

When she pulled back the hood of her cloak, the yellow gold aura around Jamie highlighted her face.

This took me by complete and total surprise.

Spencer appeared confused when he glanced at her and then back at me in question.

"Now? This route? Do you two have any idea how late and dangerous that could be?" he then said.

"Relax, she's with me. I wanted to talk to her. Nothing of darkness will survive when she gets angry anyway. We'll be fine so you can go now." Jamie said calmly.

How did Jamie know about my fire? I was just as speechless as Spencer was but given recent events and the fact that I saved her life, I think that explanation was good enough for Spencer to allow it and back off.

"Do you have any hall portal gems?" he asked Jamie.

"Take the night off, Spencer. I'll catch up with you later." She smirked.

He pursed his lips and glanced at me once again. Then he reluctantly turned to leave but if I knew him, he wouldn't be completely far away.

"Come on, the water is this way." Jamie nodded, walking onward past me.

I hesitated. This was not good.

"We may not be able to meet tonight after all. I'm sure Spencer is lingering back there somewhere, and I have no clue what Jamie's intent is but I don't want her to see you." I told Cam.

"Then let me handle it." He replied matter-of-factly.

"No! Don't do anything that will even remotely give them the idea that you're out here." I warned him.

I kept a few steps behind Jamie. She seemed to know exactly where she was going and the smell of crisp, fresh water soon began to ride in with the gentle breeze.

Fragrant blossoms permeated the night air and tiny, high-pitched chittering sounded all around us.

They were the impling creatures that I remember seeing when Cam showed me around this area.

A few fluttered by, resembling huge moths with glowing, human-like bodies. They left sparkling trails of geometric designs in blue, red, and yellow dust in their wakes.

"Did you really want to talk to me?" I suddenly asked her. I strained to listen, attempting to catch Spencer following us again.

"I can create a distraction." Cam suddenly said.

"No, that won't work. I'll handle this. Don't do anything." I replied.

Cam was silent but knowing that he was somewhere nearby watching over us made me feel safer.

"Were you really trying to take a walk in the dark to the lake by yourself?" Jamie asked over her shoulder.

I swallowed, feeling an icy lump form in the back of my throat, nearly restricting my breath. She knows. Somehow she knows and she wasn't going to buy my story.

The only thing left to do at this point was turn around and head back. But how would that look?

When we reached the shore of the Eternal waters, it was a breath-taking, artistically designed scene

The illuminated, ice-blue water rolled, rippled, and lapped calmly against the glittering white sand of the shore. It looked so much more different at night, at least this side of it anyway. I had no idea which part me and Cam were skinny dipping in earlier.

Small streaks of light darted playfully just beneath the surface. The living waterlings of the Eternal waters were apparently wide awake and playful tonight.

"It's always this beautiful especially at night when the moon is high." Jamie commented as she gazed out onto the vast sparkling surface of the immense lake.

"Yeah, it is." I agreed.

Silence fell for a few moments.

I felt awkward, wondering if Spencer were out there still creeping around.

"You never answered me." She suddenly said.

"Answered you about what?"

She smirked. Even in the darkness I could see it.

Her voice was low and hoarse, a bare whisper when she spoke again, "About why you really came out here tonight."

I eyed her. She was waiting for me to respond. I didn't.

She sat down in the soft, warm sand, bringing her knees up and wrapping her arms around them.

I wasn't sure what to make of her intentions.

"Why is she getting comfortable?" Cam was irritated.

"I don't know. She's weird. But I think she knows…about you—about us."

"How do you know?"

"Something she said earlier."

"Can she be trusted?"

"We didn't exactly hit it off."

"I see. You saved her life though. She's been humbled."

"Maybe but I doubt it."

"Great, then I'll have to knock her out."

"Stop." I gently scolded Cam.

I slowly knelt down onto the sand across from her, leaving about three foot gap in between us.

She softly chuckled, "You're gonna have to learn to be a lot more discreet and less obvious than this."

I didn't want to say anything. If she already knew, I didn't want to confirm or deny it.

"How do I know, you ask?" She simpered at me.

I remained quiet. She didn't continue right away.

I heard her sigh softly and then she chewed her lip.

"I saw him at the club. He definitely commands attention by virtue of his looks alone. I studied the way he was watching you. It wasn't lust or something sinister, it was...adoration and longing. He loves you." She looked at me with a hint of envy and sadness in her pause, "Devlin would still be here...if he had been around." She then whispered.

My eyes widened when I looked at Jamie. He who? Cam? The silhouette of her face was as still as a statue in the moonlight. She was looking out at the water.

"If who had been around?"

She turned to me. "Do you remember those texts in the library? The ones that they have locked and sealed away?"

"Yeah."

I had wondered why they were locked away the first time I was in there, when I met and talked to both Sean and Diana during a brief orientation.

"They have the ability to summon, bind, and banish them...if they know their true God-given names. If they think you've become soul-tied to one...to him, which I can already tell that you are, then that's what they'll try to do first. That's what they did to him. But he wasn't like the others. He was different. He was good."

Her words were hushed, her voice cracked in her attempt to be loud enough for me to hear but low enough not to carry. Okay, she obviously wasn't talking about Cam. One of the good ones though? A fallen like Cam and his friends?

She then peered at me curiously, "I know you had no memory of him. So how did he get you to remember him? Was it a spell or were you just beyond captivated by his looks? How come you weren't afraid of him?" She wondered.

I truly didn't have the answer to all of that and I wasn't going to tell her anything even if I did.

She harrumphed. "That's fine, I don't blame you. If Devlin had kept her mouth shut about him too...they'd both still be here now." She then whispered softly.

My heart began to pound and I stared at her in disbelief. Was she telling me what I think she was telling me? Was this the whole reason why Jamie came at me the way she had in the dining hall my first day? She had been referring to Cam then, even though I had no idea what or who she was talking about at the time. It had been hypocritical of her evidently, so why was she being so open and candid about it now? I didn't know what to say or think.

"He would have been able to save her too. Just like yours saved you. It's ironic in a way when you think about it," She paused again, licking her lips and thinking of her words.

"They were angels, guardians in the beginning. Some never lost that aspect of themselves and they've remained protective even after having fallen. When they love, they love deeply and loyally; and when they're angry or wronged…it's terrifying and deadly." She barely whispered.

"Cam, do you hear what she's saying?"

What was I thinking, of course he could hear her.

"Yes."

I wondered what he thought about all of that.

"Who was that fallen? One of your friends?"

"I would have no way of knowing for sure unless she tells you his name."

"Don't you have any friends that went missing all of a sudden not long ago?"

"I only keep a small circle of close friends that I maintain contact with all the time. Fallen aren't like humans when it comes to relationships."

Oh. I guess I can understand that.

"Did you know that the elders have the ability and power to do that though?" I was fearful.

"Yes."

"Why didn't you tell me?"

"Because it's a non-issue. Cam'ael isn't my true Elohim given name and it takes a lot more than a name to summon a fallen anyway. However, a demon created or born of darkness, that's a different story. Whoever she's talking about, couldn't have been a fallen—if he was, then he was really stupid to have revealed his true name to anyone, especially a warrior."

I was about to go off on Cam, about how that wasn't stupid at all. It meant that he trusted her —like I trusted him, and I certainly hoped that he trusted me. In a way, I did understand Cam's point but I for one still wanted to know his.

"Or maybe he just really loved and trusted her. He probably even told her why he fell, too." I said on purpose, wondering what his reply to that would be.

I could hear him chuckle a bit but he remained silent.

"They'll do everything they can to get it out of you. Believe me, they know something already. They're leaving the guilt and faith in your own oath to come clean up to you."

Or in my case, one of them already knows. Ilka. For all I know, she could have told them already but she swore to allow me time to do it myself.

She turned to look at me, awaiting either a reply or a reaction to her words but I remained fascinated and quiet, letting her speak. Even Cam was silent.

She chuckled softly. "They practically hounded Devlin for a confession and a name until guilt made her give in. That was her biggest mistake." Jamie sighed sadly.

"She might still be alive." I finally spoke up but the sound of my voice was timid, and I was uncertain that even I believed my own words.

Jamie gave a sarcastic snort and shook her head. "It doesn't matter. She's been gone too long. She's an enemy now."

I stared at her incredulously.

"You would be too if you had been gone any longer than you were. You wouldn't have been able to return." She then said.

"So let me get this straight. No one has any faith that she could still be alive; and after all this time, with all the scouts and elementals that we have at the hall, no one has ever tried to find or rescue her either? That right there is bullshit. No one counts on her coming back in one piece but heaven forbid that she does manage to escape and return, only to be shunned from the only support and family that she has and knows now. Where's the loyalty? She's one of us, a divine warrior and we're chosen for a reason. I was told that darkness can't touch us easily because we're not open vessels. And no being of darkness or light can ever take away her free will. As long as she has that it's never too late for her." I stated with fierce passion in my tone.

My convictions and how strongly I felt about them took her by total surprise. This time Jamie was speechless, staring at me for several minutes, blinking. Her expression turned to chagrin and a single tear began to roll down her cheek. She quickly wiped it away and turned away from me again.

"Very well said. I'm speechless and even more in love with you than I was only moments ago. I didn't think that was possible. I can't wait any longer, either get her to leave or I will cast a spell to put her out and kidnap you right this second." Cam's voice insistently cut silence in my head shortly thereafter. The urgency dripping in his tone was filled with both love and lust. My physical reaction from the obvious desire in his words began to warm my blood.

Jamie cocked her head, listening. I heard her inhale deeply and I wondered what she was doing, until the scent reached my nose too. Earthy cinnamon and fresh rain.

"He's here. I'd recognize that scent anywhere. He doesn't smell like a Fallen to me," She inhaled deeply again, *"He smells...incredibly desirable."* She said through a slow exhale.

Then she smirked with deviance and her voice was purposefully low this time, "He's an Incubus, and a powerful one at that. Sweet and taboo on so many levels. No wonder you're rendezvousing so soon after having just been with him. You can practically feel his magical energy and aura stroking and caressing your skin. But you'd better be careful, that combination among their kind makes him extremely dangerous too. Shit!" Jamie then hissed.

"She may be weird but she nailed my presence. She's good." Cam commented, apparently impressed.

Damn. How the hell had she managed to assess all of that so quickly and accurately? Just how fascinated and into these supernatural beings was she and for how long?

Jamie suddenly wielded her weapon and was on her feet in a split second. I instantly stiffened once the thick, silver, retractable chain linking her double, hand-held, scythe blades together, took form in each of her hands. Her brandings had a hint of a glow to them, just like mine began to do in automatic reflex to the looming, impending conflict and fight. I jumped to my feet and wielded my blades too, just in case she tried to attack Cam.

"What are you doing? I said to wait, I've got this! Don't make me have to attack her over you!" I urged.

"She's not attacking me. That damned seraphim is quickly making his way back towards you two right now, and there's two fallen and several imps who have spotted you both. I'm getting you

out of here!"

"Me? What about them?" Adrenaline began to surge from the anticipation and the current gravity of the dangerous situation.

"I don't care about them."

"That isn't right, Cam!"

Before I could even register or comprehend what just happened, Jamie disappeared in a blur, running stealthily into the dense trees. After a grunt and what sounded like a body slamming hard onto the ground, I ran over swiftly to see if she needed help.

To my astonishment, Spencer was lying on the ground —out cold with his illuminated lightning Bo still in his grip.

"You two had better get out of here now. He won't be out long." She urged and then her head snapped over to the left.

I smelled them now. The wind was picking up and the odor was foul, like old sulphur, rotten flesh, and wet feathers.

"Damn, too late! You're about to get your first crash course in combat right about now!" Jamie shouted as she snapped her weapon taut in front of her. She began swinging her right-handed scythe in a circular rotation so fast, it literally formed a perfect, silver disc that appeared to be spinning backwards.

Now I was impressed. She can fight in hand to hand combat, she could classify an unseen fallen quickly, and she could work her weapon like that? Despite her bizarre, semi-sour personality, I guess she was pretty bad-assed.

The underbrush rustled, leaves rushed upwards, and branches snapped signaling their oncoming stampede. Above us, the wind began to pick up speed, kicking up dry leaves, as two large fallen began to dive down towards us from above, like shadowed missiles. Then, they both winked out of view and completely disappeared right in front of our eyes.

Shit!

"Aw hell, not good! They've cloaked themselves!" Jamie exclaimed.

Several medium-sized forms were charging towards us on the ground from all directions; grunting, snorting, and snickering like wild, evil pigs. I didn't freak out this time. An intuition unlike any other I've ever felt since being here began to kick in as we both readied ourselves to fight. I didn't understand Jamie's initial action at first but I did now. I still didn't know what it all meant and if I could trust her at all though.

Glancing at Spencer's inert form on the ground, I felt guilty even though I hadn't been the one who had essentially sucker punched him.

"It might not have been a good idea, knocking him out right about now. What are you gonna tell him when he comes to?"

"He'll get over it" Jamie huffed.

The anticipation of where the hell those fallen were going to emerge and attack from, along with the imps, was definitely way more important —but we didn't have to make a move at all.

In one swift blur, Cam literally swooped down, standing in front of the both of us protectively with his sword in hand, wings splayed out to shield us both, and stopping the two fallen in mid dive as they calculatingly launched themselves at us from the opposite sides.

His heroic instinct, his height, muscular broadness, and the grand span of his majestic, ruined wings, had us both awe-stricken. The intense heat of his power and magic was practically tangible, causing static to crackle and thrum in the air around him.

This was all new to me. I've seen him in battle with that other fallen from the club, but seeing it this close up and feeling it…was a completely different experience.

He stunned the fallen with a spray of long needles formed from light, which forced them to materialize and give away their locations. While they screeched in pain, he quickly took advantage, lighting his black sword and slicing across the line of imps with swift ease. They didn't even know that they had been struck until they began to disintegrate into rank, acrid, steaming smoke. Then, he went for the fallen.

I heard bones breaking, grunting, growling, and the squishy sound of his blade both slicing and tearing into flesh. The cloying smell of putrid blood made me feel nauseous. It literally took him less than five minutes to destroy and kill each and every one of the black, horned imps and the two fallen that hadn't expected him to simply—appear in front of us. The combination of his master sword handling and combat expertise turned me on. A bizarre reaction I know but it couldn't be helped.

I completely understood Jamie's secret fascination with supernatural beings at this very moment.

She was definitely appreciative of his efforts …although given the way she was admiring him as he scouted the perimeter for possibly more fallen, I'd say she was turned on right now by him too. But Cam was mine, just as he claimed that I was his, which meant that yes, I'd rage all over her ass in a heartbeat over him.

"Are you alright?" Cam asked me more than Jamie.

I nodded. Despite our earlier conversation, I was still nervous about Cam appearing before and speaking to me in front of her.

Jamie continued to stare at him with infatuation but there was something else in her eyes.

Yearning and ache.

Snapping out of her trance, she looked at me and then dug into the pocket on the inside of her cloak.

"Here, you're gonna need these." She tossed me a small, dark pouch that I managed to catch and clutch to me in one smooth motion.

What is this? I squeezed it briefly, feeling several small round objects rolling over each other inside of it.

"I meant everything I told you. Go now!" She urged, turning and kneeling down next to Spencer, who had begun to slowly rouse.

Cam had been right. Being an Earthbound Seraphim, in Spencer's case, had put him at a huge vulnerable disadvantage, given that a human warrior could knock him out with one or two hits.

Before I could even speak a word, Cam wasted no time snaking an arm around my waist and holding me firmly against his hard body. He skin was slick and extremely warm, almost hot. The vibration of his magic was still pulsing from him and it made me shiver with desire.

In the next split second, we were airborne. I pulled my blades in quickly, clutching onto him tightly as his legs wrapped around mine to secure me to him. My heart felt as if it were sliding straight down into my stomach. It was like being on a reverse roller coaster. Instead of going down, we were going up at great speed. I kept my eyes shut tightly as we ascended higher and higher into the chilly night sky and above the sparse clouds.

X. CAM`AEL

"I can't believe you did that." Starling said once I landed on the wide, smooth, stone outcropping of rock leading to the front door to my home.

I set her down gently, pulling in my wings and then whispering the brief incantation that would open the entrance.

The five-foot thick slab of rock that served as my door, slowly began to slide open.

"Did what?" I played casual on purpose.

She sighed. "Put yourself at risk like that. I told you, I don't know Jamie despite everything she said. And then Spencer could have seen you too."

"Oh, he wouldn't have seen me. He'd have been down and unconscious before realizing that something or someone hit him. When it comes to your safety, I don't care if the whole damned divine cavalry was out there." I turned around to face her then.

"You know what I mean." She replied but she wasn't looking at me when she spoke. She was looking down into her hands, examining the contents of some small, black pouch. She paused and a mystified expression masked her face.

"What is that?" I asked approaching her.

"Nothing." She said, quickly closing the bag, and inserting it into a hidden pocket in the inside of her cloak.

I smirked as I slowly strode over to her.

"If I really want to see it…I can retrieve it easily." I playfully reminded her.

She placed her hands on her hips. "You mean you can try to."

I smiled. "Is that so?"

Standing in front of her and looking down at her petite stature as she gazed defiantly up at me, I couldn't help but grin.

"There is still one issue that I'd like to get straight with you first…" I then said, purposefully backing her up and forcing her to make a U turn as she slowly began to retreat towards the direction of the open entrance.

She raised a curious brow. "Really? What issue would that be?"

"The issue of trust…" I began.

"Oh, you mean you not trusting me enough to tell me things about you?" She pointed at me and then to herself as she spoke.

"More like the other way around." I corrected her.

She missed the doorway. The stone wall beside it halted her from continuing to retreat from me. I took advantage of that moment.

Her beautiful, pouty lips turned down into a frown and her brows furrowed in confusion. "I think you have that backwards." She replied.

Slowly, she began to rise from the ground. Using just magic, I eased her up the wall and stopped once she was leveled face to face with me. She didn't even react or comment on what I was doing.

I leaned in close, our lips a few centimeters apart.

"No, I think I have it pretty dead on." I whispered.

"You're the one who's keeping things about your past from me."

I eyed her playfully and held up an index finger, "Key word. Past. I'd like to leave it there."

"I'm not asking so I can judge you today."

"Then why do you need to know any of it?"

She narrowed her eyes at me suspiciously. "Why can't you just tell me?"

I couldn't help but smile. She was definitely still the Starling that I fell in love with, without a doubt.

"Besides, you told me that you'd tell me anyway." She insisted.

"I didn't tell you when I would. You're immortal now, so that could mean tomorrow, next week, next month, or five hundred years from now." I grinned.

She gaped at me incredulously.

"Come inside, I need you to do something before we go." I finally said, completely changing the subject as I took a few steps away from her and eased her back down the wall to her feet again.

I headed inside, expecting her to be right behind me but she wasn't. When I turned to head back outside, my eyes widened.

"What are you doing?" I quickly darted over to her.

She was standing at the very edge of the stone platform, facing me—with her back to the nearly 55,000 foot drop down to solid ground...with several protruding cliffs and jagged outcroppings along the way.

I wasn't sure what she had in mind and what she meant, let alone why she was so damned insistent about it, but I had a pretty good idea. Maybe a small part of me didn't fully trust her but I wasn't paying that part any heed. I love her. Of that, I've never been more certain. Surely, she has to know that.

Would she really go this far to prove her trustworthiness to me? She didn't have to go to this extreme.

Her sudden backwards, yet extremely graceful swan-dive over the lip of the ledge had proven me wrong. She immediately began to plummet, back first, down the mountainside. Her black cloak flapped all around the shape of her small frame like crazy bat wings, creating a disturbance in the cloud cover that parted and wisped apart once she quickly disappeared through it.

So, she wanted to play the trust game, huh? I smiled to myself, crossing my arms over my chest while calculating the distance, velocity, and time that it would take for her to just barely come close to hitting the ground. This wasn't a building, this was a mountain—there were no straight lined sides. I pushed out a bit of magick to create a cushion of air and space between her and all the solid, jagged, and deadly obstacles that I knew were part of this mountainside.

In the meantime, my mind wandered to the words that Elohim had revealed to me in the book. It made sense but what was it referring to? It was like a riddle.

'And it will come to pass, before the two worlds divulge, darkness begins to spread its arrogant disease. A weapon will be formed from the life of its master, which shall become the sole source of his absolute destruction.'

I think I had a pretty good idea of its interpretation but I wasn't sure. I suppose that's why I'll have to retrieve the rest of it, which should be an interesting venture.

I wondered why he saw the need to keep this text hidden and who he had implored to write it. Why had he allowed Morning Star to claim a portion of it? And was it a coincidence that Berith had managed to take it from right under his nose and hide it from him, only to place it in my hands? Many things were coincidental lately. I think Edanai had a point when she began to add up all the components surrounding myself and Starling from the beginning.

I immediately sensed the physical change in Starling's now rapidly beating heart.

Panic.

Snapping out of my temporary thoughts, I took a step off the ledge. My wings snapped out and spread wide, and I turned them downward in order to catch the wind. I began to float down slowly at first.

Stray curls had freed themselves from her wildly flailing pony tail, nearly covering her face. I cloaked myself on purpose, diving down and bypassing her by a vertical distance of a few feet. It was apparent that though she was calm, with her arms still splayed out on either side of her, there was a hint of both doubt and a tad bit of anxiety in her heartbeat and expression.

She was as light as a pillow, landing precisely in my arms with a grunt…just several feet from full-on ground impact. I held her cradle style in my arms against my body.

For me, it brought back a memory of when she had been injured by that moronic demon at the hospice. He had injured her ankle and she couldn't walk. I carried her up to her apartment originally with more intent than just being a dutiful cop. It angered me to think about again, so I shifted to the fact that it did lead up to our meeting for the very first time that night too. Even though it was a planned intention on my part, I would treasure and cherish the memory of how and when we met for as long as I existed.

Her heart was racing wildly and her mixture of relief, fear, and slowly mounting anger was incredibly strong…

Shit!

I had no choice but to drop her, literally, like a burning hot coal.

"Ow!" She cried out after landing hard on her ass upon the hard packed earth.

Her body was aglow and white flames began to erupt all over her. She lit up the entire vicinity so intensely, I had to shield my eyes and turn away. Given her current condition, I instantly felt like an asshole for having dropped her the way I did. It was a reflex defensive action. Even though she was superhuman and immortal now, and her body was definitely an extremely strong fortress of protection for our growing child, I still considered her a delicate and fragile human.

This isn't good. She'll draw way too much attention.

The flames around her hands didn't last as long, soon flickering and finally winking out. "I'm sorry," I bit my lip and held a hand out to help her up, " Though I'm sure that was nothing considering what kind of a splat you could have made if I didn't make it on time." I then reminded her.

She grabbed my hand and yanked herself up to her feet gruffly. "Barely! And I know that you waited that long on purpose by the way." She pointed and glared at me. Her anger was slowly subsiding.

I laughed. "Only because it was pointless."

"It wasn't pointless. See? I had complete trust in you the whole time."

"Says the sweat on your face and your erratically beating heart." I commented with a single raised brow.

She looked at me dryly. "Natural human reactions."

"I didn't expect the spontaneous combustion. You really need to gain control of your fire." I told her.

She scowled at me as she dusted off her cloak, form fitting pants, and boots.

"Well, since I'm not a robot or an inanimate object with no emotions, I can't." She replied.

I looked at her curiously. "It's not linked to your emotions…at least it shouldn't be." I told her.

She seemed frustrated. "How would you know that?"

"Because emotions, especially in females, can be wild and out of control. I doubt very seriously that your essence would be of any use if that were its catalyst. More so, I'm referring to the most powerful emotions of all. Love, hate, and fear." I explained to her with a loving smirk.

Though I instantly felt a sudden onrush of hot emotions begin to well up in her, validating what I just said, it was as if she suddenly realized exactly what I was thinking. It was apparent that she opted to bite her tongue instead. I smirked playfully as she eyed me with a slight, defiant pout.

"Well, it's a good thing that I don't hate or fear you then. But I don't like the idea of loving you enough to possibly accidentally hurt or kill you at any given moment either. It's like a cruel twist." Panic masked her eyes with worry and doubt as the flames all over her body finally began to wink out bit by bit.

The visual suddenly made me wonder about our child. Surely it wouldn't be able to sustain itself inside of her whenever she used her fire…if it were solely or even remotely of darkness. Was it even still alive then? Wouldn't she have felt some sort of a physical reaction if that had been the case? That was peculiar and would continue to plague my curiosity until she gave birth—if she managed to give birth. The thought began to sadden and depress me so I pushed it all away for now.

"I know but it's a chance that I'm willing to take. I don't doubt that you'll be able to master it soon."

A sudden shriek split the night air, commanding attention over all the other normal night creatures and sounds. Starling instantly flinched and jumped, turning around to pan the air.

"What was that?" She hissed in a low whisper.

I carefully scanned the darkness of the trees, shadows, and landscape beyond for any scent, movement or signature.

"Yet another reason you should never do something like that again. You'll draw too much attention to yourself if you haven't already," I said reaching for her protectively.

"It's a Psyren. Definitely not females that you'd want to get to know or hang out with. They steal, use, and sell souls and auras." I quickly told her.

Her eyes went wide and sparkled with curiosity as I held her close to me. Her body was taut against mine, slowly kindling arousal and her heart was racing once again. As long as she wasn't feeling fear, I was good.

She glanced up at me and then cocked her ear to listen again. "It sounded like it was right by my ear."

"Never assume that it isn't." I warned her.

Note to self. If her essence is linked to her emotions, never piss her off.

Giving her an affectionate, quick kiss on the lips, I secured my arm around her small waist and we began to ascend once again.

XI: STARLING

Looking down into the small pouch that Jamie had given me, I was speechless. Had she really been telling me the truth? What was her motivation and what did she hope to gain out of me? A confession maybe? She had almost gotten one but instinct told me to remain quiet. So, were these four Divine Hall portal gems in good faith then? I wasn't sure what to think. For all I know, she could be telling the elders everything right now.

However, she did clock Spencer without a second thought. Why would she have risked that though? Maybe it was a sick game of theirs every other night or something. I wondered if she made up that story about Devlin. If it was true, I was curious now myself.

All I know, is that I was glad to be with Cam again…even though I almost set him on fire.

Thinking about it now, I guess it was an insane spur of the moment act. Truth be told, I was wholly afraid, especially when Cam took his sweet time to come after me. The trust thing had been more for me, I think. I wanted to be sure that even though he was a fallen, despite what I knew to be true and what everyone said about his kind, that he was different. Okay, part of it was the thrill too. No doubt his sudden rescue of me and the surge of fear I felt intensified the arousal I had already been feeling in his presence, and being held protectively against his warm, hard body.

Seeing him fighting and engaged in battle up close was both breath-taking and slightly scary for me. Though it appeared effortless on his part, he was vicious and precise, and he held nothing back. Wasn't that what Jamie had described when she was talking about betraying or angering a fallen? Though I knew he was powerful, I had no idea just how strong, deadly, and magical he was—and we were supposed to fight against his kind? It was the more vile, evil, and hardcore ones that I was leery about.

I wondered what Cam wanted me to do first, though I could take a few guesses. I smiled to myself while taking in the décor of Cam's pristine, spotless, cozy, cavern castle, which is what it resembled to me. Even the air was cool, fresh, and clean in here. That surprised me being that it was inside of a mountain and all. It was palatial in size but I suppose it had to be in order to accommodate Cam and his friends comfortably. Cam was a total neat freak. Not that it was a bad thing but that might be where we could have issues.

As I followed close behind him down the wide, oval- shaped corridor to his room, I admired the ripples and contours of muscle gently moving beneath his perfect tanned skin when he moved. He was shirtless, in nothing more than a soft-skinned, sandstone colored pants, and dark brown boots. His 'V' shaped physique was svelte and lithe, and he exuded an incredible, supernatural strength to go with his perfectly chiseled form. His dark hair had begun to grow out a little, curling slightly at the nape of his neck.

Jamie hadn't been kidding about his scent. When I paid closer attention this time, taking in a deep whiff, my senses literally exploded with a delicious aphrodisiac effect, much like when we were first together under the waterfall. It started from the inside of my head, traveling quickly into the tips of my nipples, sliding into my belly, and finally settling in my groin with teasing heat. The tickling sensation came again. How could I be feeling anything like this so soon? I put a hand to my belly just as Cam turned around to face me, standing back to allow me to enter his bed chambers first.

My eyes were immediately drawn to the massive and extremely comfortably bed before anything else. I instantly blushed when I thought back to the intense, unbridled love-making that we had enjoyed not long ago.

The desire and arousal that he was kindling, probably on purpose, was making me shiver with excitement now.

"How are you feeling?" he suddenly asked as his warm hand went to gently rest on my abdomen.

"I feel fine." I assured him.

"You'd tell me if something was wrong or if you were hurting, right?" He raised a single brow as if expecting me to say yes.

I nodded. "Of course I would."

"Good. I have something unique planned." He then grinned mischievously.

"Unique?" I smirked with anticipation.

"As in, it's never been done before." He winked, heading over to his bookshelf and opening an ornate box.

I smiled. "Well, I'm not sure I should be gone too long. They will definitely get suspicious."

"Don't worry, if I decide to take you back at all, you'll only have been gone a few hours at the most." He pulled out something small and compact in his hand.

"If you decide to take me back?"

"That's right." He replied matter-of-factly.

I didn't even know how to respond to that. That may not be such a bad idea considering.

He eyed me. "Would that bother you?"

I thought for a moment as my eyes traveled to the floor, the bed, and then the bathing room off to the right, set in a spacious alcove.

My eyes finally returned meet to his. "No."

He was seemed surprised yet relieved to hear my response though I wasn't sure why. My hesitation had nothing to do with my feelings for him or being pregnant.

I moved over to the bed and sat down on it. The luxuriously soft, thick, fur blanket felt exquisite and warm between my fingertips.

"Has anything else surfaced regarding your memories? I mean, past what I told you and what you already knew?" Cam then asked, joining me on the bed.

He sat down next to me with a cell phone in his hand that immediately caught my attention. He was scrolling through some of the messages and briefly reading them.

"Not really." I replied.

"Do you remember the girl in your photo album? The one with the short, reddish brown hair?"

I shrugged unsurely, trying to remember anything else associated with what Cam told me about her being my best friend. A few images of her came up in my mind but nothing distinct. It frustrated me because she was obviously important to me. She had been in so many of the more recent photos with me.

"What about her?" I peered closer at the phone, "Is that...is that my phone?" I pointed at it and furrowed my brow.

Cam nodded. "I kept it so I could keep you alive as far as your friends know."

I was confused but it didn't take me long to figure out what Cam was trying to tell me and why he had done all of this in the first place.

"How is it still working...here?" I wondered in awe.

He positioned it in between us so that I could see what he was reading and doing, and then he gave me a look that meant, 'Are you really asking me that question?'

"She's been calling and texting often, all of your friends and your places of employment have been. Up until now...I've sort of been stalling and returning the texts—as you. I've even had a female friend emulate your voice when calling her because I didn't want her to worry or think that you were missing and assumed dead, which is the truth, but...well, you know." He tried to explain as if he didn't want me to get upset with him for doing so.

"Emulate my voice?" I was taken aback.

"Yeah, we ah, do that a lot when we want to jack around with humans." He casually explained. Then, his gorgeous face turned into an expression of innocence and chagrin, and with a hand to his chest he clarified, "I don't do it anymore though. I haven't for a really, really long time."

I didn't even know what to say.

Cam handed me the phone. Feeling it in my hands instantly brought on a rush of random memories that I couldn't really make out or piece together but China was in them. A flood of emotions made my chest tighten and my breath caught.

"What's wrong?" Cam asked.

I looked up at him and shook my head, "Nothing." I stared down at the phone again, scrolling through the messages and reading a few. From the looks of it, she was both worried and angry. Angry at me for behaving erratically as if I had lost my mind, or were hiding something and ignoring her. She was telling me that all of my friends were worried about me, wondering why I never talked to them or returned their calls either. She asked if I were coming home for the holidays or what? And what would I do about school since I was so far behind and missing so many days.

It was then that I realized what Cam wanted me to do. It was more for me though, that much I could gather and understand.

"I'm lost. I don't even know what to say. Even if I did tell her that I'd be coming back, how do I explain everything else? Where I've been and stuff? What if I'm not able to stay?"

"You can go anywhere, anytime, whenever you want to and stay for as long as you like. You don't need permission for that, believe me. Anyway, she won't have a clue unless she's chosen, which she isn't, so she won't be able to see your brandings either. However..." Cam trailed off and exhaled slowly.

He looked as if he wanted to say something else but was hesitant.

"What is it?" I asked, straightening my posture and studying his expression.

He paused for a long time and then turned to look down at me. "Don't be surprised to see the young male in your album at the hall soon."

My eyes widened. Even though I barely remembered him too, I was shocked.

"Will he remember me?" I wanted to know.

Cam shook his head. "More than likely not...unless it's by some miracle or gift too."

I felt disappointment.

"It's all up to you though. All this would be pointless if you don't plan to return there, so if you'd rather not, it's understandable."

Did I? Would I?

I could essentially go anywhere I wanted to now but Cam was right. I was glad that he had maintained this connection for me and it seemed as if he'd gone through a lot of trouble to do it too.

All of this had me wondering about the extent of his powers and magic. What all could he do and would he do it? Like, if I wanted several million dollars? What if I wanted to be three inches taller? A mansion on the beach? It was all very tempting but in a way, I really didn't like him using his magic. I wanted things to be real, genuinely felt, known, and experienced not just for me but for him too.

"I tell you what, let's not worry about it right now. Come on." Cam took the phone from me and got up to place it back in the ornate box.

He then quickly crossed the room back to the bed, taking my hand and pulling me to my feet. He led me back outside to the wide, stone slab of jutting rock that cleverly served as an expansive patio or balcony.

"Where are we going?" I asked.

"You'll see." He simply replied. He raised an arm above his head and began to swirl his index finger above his head.

He began to whisper words that I could barely hear let alone make out language wise.

Right before my eyes, the circle he had traced above us began to widen, opening up into an oblong, hazy, purple-tinted tunnel punctuated by many dazzling, glittering things inside.

A portal.

"I've never done this before so if anything happens, just know that I meant well and that I will always love you." Cam looked down at me with a crooked smile.

I grimaced and tried to pull away but he held me firmly to him.

He laughed. "I'm kidding! At the very least a few missing or rearranged limbs won't kill you. You can keep your eyes closed if you want. In fact, that might be best for you anyway. No matter what, do not let go of me, alright?"

My heart began to jackhammer, both excitement and apprehension fighting for dominance.

"Not funny, Cam." I admonished him as I pinched my eyes shut and held my breath.

In a split second, my feet were no longer grounded. The air around us felt like a vacuum, strong with the scent of electricity and ozone. The air pressure changed drastically. It was slightly colder and I felt a pulsing energy pressing against my flesh, making me feel dizzy as if I were—high or drunk.

It probably took no more than a span of a few seconds and Cam's grip on me remained firm. When our feet touched ground once again, I felt my stomach fall back into place and I sucked in a deep, relieving breath since I had been literally holding it the whole time.

There were no distinct sounds but the air smelled hot to me, like burning metal and being inside of a clay oven or microwave oven set on high. Even behind my closed eyelids, everything seemed extremely bright too.

Cam leaned down to whisper to my ear. "You're still in one piece. Open your eyes."

XII: INTERLUDE: MORNING STARS' MEETING ROOM:

His gaze alone was mortifying. It spoke volumes without him having to utter a word. The steady cadence of successive thumping was nerve-wracking. What had they done wrong this time? Who would be punished next? How? And when?

Since Baal and several others had been slain, Morning Star had been in an even more foul temperament than he had been when the girl he had been trying to claim had been killed in the mortal realm. His top soldier was gone and they knew that it only meant that rank and replacement would be put upon a new fallen in their army, maybe.

Those who had been with him the longest, still couldn't read whether or not this meeting would be good news, bad news, or an all-out torture session for the others to behold as a lesson. With Morning Star, there was no telling.

Whatever the case was, he was not happy. That much could be felt in the heavy, oppressive dark energy that weighed upon several of his top arch demon soldiers, his necromancers, and Xyn.

His long silence left fear thick in the air and no one bothered to even speak let alone make a sound out of respect.

Sitting at the head of a long, glossed, onyx table, he appeared quite lax. Leaning back with one arm resting on the arm of his throne chair, Morning Star steadily drummed his fingers on the desk.

"There's been a change in direction." Morning Star finally began after a long bout of silence.

His soldiers all leaned in to pay special close attention.

"And Xyn has been the only one with any common sense to act upon it and report what has been happening right before our eyes. He's managed to single handedly destroy quite a few worthy rebel fallen."

The crow demon remained silent yet rapt at attention, appreciating the recognition and praise from his powerful new master.

"However, he is only one and he has his own tasks to attend, which means that since the murder of Baal, each of you will need to prove yourselves useful to me in order to remain."

"We should destroy one of Cam`ael's top associates too, my lord." Och replied.

Morning Star mechanically turned his head to face Och. His expression appearing bored and stony. "And when he hunts you down and either beheads or eviscerates your cretin ass for doing so, don't look to cower behind me." He flatly replied.

"I only assumed that an eye for an eye was what you sought, your magnificence. It makes sense. Surely you aren't afraid of retaliation from Cam`ael?" Och tried to reason.

Morning Star simply stared at his general calmly, without any sign or hint of annoyance or anger. His powerfully wicked gaze alone was enough to make Och nearly swallow and choke on his own tongue in regret of his words.

Then, in a swift and destructive flash of fire, acrid black and red smoke began to plume in tendrils and curls from Och's chair. He had been reduced to nothing more than a foul, powdery mound of ashes among his burned, and now smoking clothing where he sat.

No one moved, barely breathing as their eyes gaped in fear and shock. Och had been a long-time, high level demon soldier. An expendable one at that apparently.

Morning Star neither moved nor flinched a muscle as his wicked aqua blue eyes panned the rest of the table, "Would anyone else care to take a chance at suggesting something equally senseless and insult me in the process?" he calmly asked.

Everyone eagerly shook their heads almost unanimously,

"No, no my lord!"

"Not at all Master!"

"Good." Morning Star flatly replied as he slowly rose from his chair. He began to pace around the table slow and deliberately, making each one of his top ranking soldiers nervous.

He smiled humorously. "I don't want to have to destroy or punish all of you today. I only planned on a few." He began as his eyes fell upon Sihd.

Sihd stiffened, trembling in his seat beneath his massive armor and quickly shifting eye contact away from Morning Star.

"Sihd." Morning Star spoke, stopping behind him.

Sihd jumped, nearly paralyzed with fear. "Yes, my lord?" he answered dutifully.

"You and your men will be in charge of finding and retrieving both Berith and the book that she thieved from me. If you cannot find the book, I do not want her harmed. That will be my job. If you do uncover the book, and it is damaged or missing parts in any way, think twice before even bothering to return here—is that understood?"

"Indeed, my Lord!" Sihd nodded.

"You're dismissed." Morning Star then said.

Sihd wasted no time rising from his seat and shuffling out quickly.

Morning Star continued his pacing and scanning of the group before him.

"Ganik, I want you and Mephisto to oversee the training, recruiting and preparation of all the dark divines that have already sworn allegiance to me. Gather, influence, and entice as many more as you see fit. That may take a while because I want you to hit every land upon the Earth first, and you may utilize every demon soldier available if needed, so get to it. Do not report until I ask for one."

"Yes, Master!" They both saluted as they rose and quickly left the room without hesitation.

"My gorgeous, dependable Zara. Your task is actually quite easy and should be fun. It will begin at the college that Starling used to attend. There, you will find another chosen. You know what to do— and remember, not a drop of blood spilt. I don't know why this never donned on me before. He was a very close friend of hers while she was mortal. Allow him to come willingly and then bring him to me. I have big plans for him." Morning Star smiled.

"Consider it done, my lord." She smirked with a loyal bow of her head and then she was gone.

Then there were two left. They were his elite soldiers and he had an even greater task for them, for it would be difficult and challenging at best.

"I'm setting the divine one that we've had for quite some time now, free. She's been cooperative for the most part in the last few days and I'm keeping my word. She's going to prove quite useful to me still, so keep an eye on her. You two will also be in charge of bringing me Edanai, even if that means taking out Rahab, which you will have to do, but not until I give the word," Morning Star glanced at Xyn this time.

"I want you to keep an eye out for Cam'ael and Starling. However, use extreme caution in apprehending Starling. She is quite deadly and will offer much resistance as well as putting up a challenging fight. I do not want her harmed in any way. Her essence does not surprise me but it must be contained as soon as possible. Once I have her, Cam'ael will come willingly and I want no one to stop him." Morning Star informed.

Xyn silently gave a perceptible nod of his hood. A few crows flapped about excitedly, cawing as they swarmed into a tornado of black wings and feathers beneath the long, black robe, and he finally disappeared altogether.

Morning Star paused and waited, finally turning to the last one left. His new, single, right-hand soldier. He was the one who had worked in sync with Baal for so long, and now he would have all the duties and responsibilities placed upon his shoulders singly.

"Ammon," Morning Star said, returning to his throne chair at the head of the table but not sitting just yet.

"Yes, Lord?" Ammon sat straight at attention, already confused at why his Lord would not want his life-long rival and arch-nemesis, Cam'ael, stopped before reaching him.

"Ensure that the rifts all over the world, between this realm and the human world are open and ready. Slowly have the voids and shades begin infiltration at even the slightest hints of doubt, hate, and deception, and be ready at the first signs of any large scale catastrophic disaster. Most importantly, do no forget where all of our initial targets lie." Morning Star then said softly.

Ammon nodded and then quirked a brow inquisitively. "Even now? I'm not sure I quite understand, my lord. We currently outnumber all of them, angels and divine warriors combined." He asked, regretting it instantly as his eyes cut to the remaining pile of ash that still smoked where Och had been sitting. He shifted, wishing to take back his reply but to his surprise, Morning Star didn't react the way he had thought he would.

"Always anticipate the unlikely," Morning Star lamented, "We must be ready to move. Call it a hunch." he finally sat back down with a smirk. "I'm leaving you in charge of all of my children and the others. My purpose will be complete once Starling is in my possession. I'll be expecting Cam`ael then." He then said.

Ammon was speechless, gaping at his long-time Master because he now understood what he was preparing for and what it would mean.

"Baal was a fool. I could have intervened to save him but his conceit clouded his judgment. Never underestimate Cam`ael or any of those in his legion, let alone those irksome warriors. It deals a great blow to our army but we will compensate and prevail. Xyn will be able to handle what's left of his dwindling group. Now," Morning Star inhaled as if perusing his own thoughts and fancies. "Let's see, after that meeting I could certainly use some enlightening entertainment of my own to take off the edge. Bring me two female virgins, one male, some soul infused wine with a plate of rare steak and liver, a large screen television with videos of that television show that I really like, and a six of the biggest serpents we have." He grinned diabolically at Ammon.

XIII. CAM`AEL

The look on her face was of utter astonishment. I knew this would definitely be one of the planets that would take her breath away. Though it was completely uninhabited by any living creature, it was nonetheless a most spectacular sight to behold, minus the extreme and mounting heat. The heat waves bending from the gemstone encrusted earth created a mirage of both water and prisms of multi-colored, fractal light.

The entire planet was a giant ball of different grades, weights, and colors of what humans and several other races of beings called, Rhodium, iridium, black opals, palladium, raw diamonds, and many other colored, pure gemstones. Actually, the gems and stones here were far more pure and valuable than the stones of Earth and many other planets. This unnamed planet was one of the hardest to find and get to for many beings, so the value of just a few chips was immeasurable.

Starling gasped in wonder as she took in all the sparkling stalactites, stalagmites, large boulders, and the tips of the vast forest below made up of precious stone columns; all full of shiny, twinkling, bizarre rock formations. Rivers of magma and oil bubbled and churned, branching out like macabre, spidery fingers across the landscape. Even the red and white sand glittered under a mirage of water beneath the light of the three suns facing the north.

Hardly any beings ever ventured here and if they did they didn't stay very long. We wouldn't either. The heat was unlike any other place, past the surface of the actual sun itself. No life could be sustained on this planet whatsoever, regardless of the many pools of boiling water scattered across the unpredictable landscape.

I produced three small pouches, similar to the one she carried her portal gems in.

"This is…incredible." She marveled.

"I know and we don't have much time. The heat will become beyond bearable in a matter of minutes."

She looked up at me quizzically as I handed her the pouches. She took them from me questioningly. "It's already intense. One sun is bad enough." She breathed, fanning her face.

Sweat was already beginning to bead across her forehead and above her upper lip, and a rivulet streamed slowly down her temple. I moved faster. This climate was toxic and way too hot for her. I wouldn't have even brought her here at all but I wanted her to have a chance to see with her own eyes, one of the millions of phenomenal planets that no human has been able to see let alone knows exists.

"I know. There's constant sunlight to the third power here. Your boots will eventually melt into the ground, literally."

"I'm pretty sure my bare feet wouldn't last more than a second after that either. It's like being inside a furnace or fireplace."

"They'd be pulpy burned stumps before you know it."

She scrunched up her face and lifted up each foot, checking out the soles of her black laced up boots. "I believe you. So, what are these for?" She held up the pouches.

I nodded my head for her to follow me.

Scoping a few trunks of diamonds and rhodium, I moved in between them, and created a wide canopy of shade above her using magic.

"Open the first bag and hold it right here." I pointed to a trunk of shiny, green, purplish black metal.

She was still perplexed but she did and I wasted no time slamming my fist into it with all my strength.

The rock shook and cracked as chunks instantly broke away, falling into both the pouch and onto the obsidian streaked ground around her feet.

Her mouth fell, I assumed because she was impressed with what I had done.

"Turn the pouch inside out and use it as a glove to grab those on the ground before they get too hot." I pointed. Then, I sought out a black opal trunk next, and proceeded to do the same thing.

We had managed to gather quite a few different stones and metals before the heat nearly cooked us. We were both drenched in sweat, so it was definitely time to go.

"You just demolished several trunks of pure diamond, dark metal, opal, and solid silver…with your bare fists." Starling pointed at my hands incredulously, looking for some sort of bruising or torn flesh.

I flexed my unscathed hands. "I know. A pickaxe would have

worked better and faster. I'll remember to conjure one up next time since I've managed to impress you already." I winked at her, "Again, hold onto me tightly."

One of my favorite past-times, as well as Edanai's and Rahab's, was dimension or planet hopping. Something no human has ever known or will ever experience…while human anyway. Of course, I'd never take Starling to any of the raunchier cesspools of fleshly pleasures, or any of the dangerous, carnivorous creature infested places. There were many of those out there too. I secured her against me and then we were off to our next destination.

~~~****~~~

Starling took in a deep breath once we landed, tickled by the sudden pop of atmospheric pressure. She immediately began to smile as she opened her eyes.

"Is that barbecue?" She asked with excitement as she eagerly panned the landscape.

"Something like that." I grinned.

She glanced up at me. "Where are we?" She was looking at the entrance of a small hidden city, built below the flat of orange and yellow sand that made up the earth's floor. The street down below teemed with activity and music but was clearly devoid of any voices and laughter.

Starling's brows furrowed. "What are these beings? And why aren't any of them speaking?"

"They're Luminae. Their delicate, nearly see-through skin is why they live underground. They aren't able to withstand ultraviolet rays for very long. The sunlight here remains constant for several years and then it goes dormant for several afterwards, leaving perpetual moonlight. When that happens, they return to their homes above ground to ready crops, livestock and stuff like that before the next phase. Their food supply is actually fed by the power of their moons rather than sunlight, believe it or not."

She was definitely impressed by the extent of my knowledge.

"They can hear but they choose to only speak telepathically, in the same way that we as fallen do—and of course, you and I now."

"You can't speak to them that way?" She inquired.

"No. We don't have any kind of similar wavelength or link. Their language is only known and shared among each other. Gestures and facial expressions are very easily read and interpreted here, so communication with other beings isn't really an issue. Some gestures and symbols are universal no matter where you are or what language you speak."

Starling was fascinated, listening intently to all that I explained to her and at the same time, observing the new beings that were in turn, observing her with keen, welcoming interest.

I continued to give her a quick rundown on them, "These beings have existed for a very, very long time. They've remained undetected by much of the other universe because they keep to themselves. If they had a means of transportation to other worlds, I'm pretty sure that they'd attempt to visit Earth first—like many other beings have been doing for a while now. They are one of the few docile and peace loving races in the entire universe. That's hard to find anywhere these days." I told her.

"So, they won't be hostile being that we're different and crashing in on their city?"

I shook my head no. "They actually welcome visitors of all types." I grabbed her hand and we walked hand in hand down the firm, dirt-carved road that led into the heart of the underground city.

"Do they know what I am? I mean, aside from human?" She then asked.

I nodded. "Yes, and they know what I am too."

"Really? They're all staring but they don't seem afraid of you…of us." She noted.

"I've never given them a reason to be. I keep my wings hidden when I'm come here. They're excited to see them though because they're enchanted by them. The angels sometimes visit here too, so they make the connection but they know that I'm definitely not an angel. Trust me, they aren't staring because of what you or I are."

She glanced down at our interlaced fingers and then back up at me. I know she understood exactly what I meant and she gave my hand a light squeeze in response.

The Luminae's were excited to see us and maybe just a small part of that was actually bewildered confusion, seeing a Divine Warrior and a Fallen holding hands affectionately. The women and children were awed by Starling, not just by her beauty but the powerful essence and aura that she emanated along with her intricate, silver brandings. Or it could have been the fact that I stand at nearly seven feet tall and she's around five feet and barely a couple of inches.

Naturally, she was awestruck by not just their city but the fact that they had three arms; one on each side, and a smaller one on their backs. The extra arm, their oblong shaped heads, their choice of telepathic communication, and their all-white, translucent skin, were the only main differences between human beings and their people.

The melody of a pleasant tune being played on what resembled a large lute, floated through the crowd of pedestrians. A babbling, shallow river flowed through a small canal that split the yellow, dirt packed streets down the middle. Small children were playing alongside the waters' edge, taking turns pushing each other in small boat and smiling with genuine happiness. My thoughts immediately went to our child and I squeezed Starling's hand this time, catching her watching them with adoration too.

The scent of freshly cooking food was drifting out of one of the many open market eateries. Numerous places of business lined the streets with wares from clothing, food, farming tools, jewelry, and toys.

"Hungry?"

"Um, what do they eat here?" She asked.

"It's edible and mostly vegetables. The meat is similar to beef and chicken."

"Similar?" She raised a brow.

I laughed. "I'm pretty discerning about cuisine myself but it's actually really good. They have several native species of animals that they raise for food."

"Species of animals? That doesn't sound very appetizing but you know this place better than I do and I trust you." She gave a smirk.

"Well, first things first. Cleanliness and order is extremely important to me. I'd really like to bathe and change, so I say we hit up a few clothing vendors and see what they have to offer."

She laughed. "Important or an obsession?"

I looked down at her and smirked. "Very important. There are far more valuable things that I choose to place on my personal pedestal of obsession."

A flirtatious fire lit up her sapphire blue eyes.

"As long as I return to the hall in my field wear."

"Speaking of, I failed to tell you just how sexy you are in the entire ensemble."

Her cheeks warmed, turning a soft pink blush at my compliment. "Thanks." She smiled.

We stopped at a market stand, full of an array of prepared foods. The two females were already smiling pleasantly upon our arrival.

I gave a gentle bow and smile and Starling followed suit. The females instantly took to us, now beaming. The younger one of the two offered Starling a native flower, and I retrieved the pouches of jewels that we had collected.

I pointed to an entire basket of freshly baked breads, fruit, and bottles of juice, and then shook out several different chunks of gems and stones into my palm.

Both of their eyes widened, giddy with excitement and surprise and the older of the two females eagerly nodded, trading the whole basket for the handful of the priceless stones I offered her.

"Ah, monetary exchanges." Starling quipped with a smile, and then she inhaled the sweet fragrance of the slender dark purple and blue petals of the flower she held.

"A little is worth a lot out here." I grinned, taking the basket in one hand, and interlacing the fingers of the other with hers as we held hands once again.

XIV: STARLING

I had no words. If Cam was trying to impress me with his fighting abilities, strength, knowledge, and this amazing journey throughout the universe, not to mention his kinship with these friendly alien beings, it was definitely working. My feelings for him were becoming more profound, from the very moment when I first began to remember who he was and how I felt about him before I died.

I was enchanted by these beings and I think it was mutual. Even though they didn't speak words, their spirit and energies were so positive, accepting, and warm, speech wasn't necessary. The gesture of friendship and acceptance was represented through the giving of the beautiful dark purple and blue flower to me. Its scent was light, laced with an exotic sweetness that I've never smelled before, so I had nothing to compare it to and the after effect was really relaxing.

After acquiring a basket of fruits that Cam cleverly bargained for with the stones and gems we collected, we moved on to find somewhere to clean up. We were both allowed access to shower in an underground grotto, beneath a fine misting cavern, which served as a communal shower. Killing two birds with one stone, and given the fact that we were the only ones currently present, we showered…together.

Out of respect, we maintained G rated behavior of light kissing, though we managed to steal a few well-placed, playful, and flirtatious gropes back and forth.

Cam conjured up a change of clothing for himself, and magically dry-cleaned mine while we finished up. I was willing to make a grateful exception for his use of magic in achieving that.

Once we were all cleaned and changed; him now in dark, casual slacks and a loose-fitting button down baby blue dress shirt, which looked exceptionally good on him, and me back in my field wear, we began to stroll through town, hitting up a clothing shop.

I was instantly pulled in by a deep rose colored gown. It could have probably passed for a nightgown or maybe even fancy lingerie, I supposed. Either way, it was an absolutely gorgeous off the shoulder dress of shimmering, flowing, chiffon-like material; all falling in graceful asymmetrical waves that ended at the long trailing hem in the back.

"I already know it will be incredibly stunning on you, so try it on." Cam whispered into my ear.

"It might not fit. It was made for their women, meaning three arm holes instead of two."

"You're as petite as they are. I'd be surprised if it didn't fit perfectly. I can simply get rid of the extra arm hole if you really like it."

"Well, I can't keep it on or with me for that matter." I quickly reminded out loud, more to myself than him. The reasons were obvious.

He sighed and gave me a weary smirk. "If you want it, it's yours. I'll keep it for you, so try the damn dress on already."

I grinned and chewed my lip. I felt like a girl let loose at the mall with a credit card. The whole high of the shopping experience and new clothes was surprisingly something that I still had in me. I did want that dress. I'd be the first of any human girl or guy on Earth to have something made by beings of a whole other planet. What the hell.

It fit like a glove, especially around my breasts and my waist in particular, and one side hung teasingly off my bare shoulder. The material was incredibly light and soft, caressing my body like a whisper of air all around me.

Cam's eyes began to glow with both desire and lust the moment I stepped from behind the screen that separated the make-shift changing area from the main room. I instantly felt it hit me below the waist, spreading warmly down into my legs.

I bit my lip, followed by a soft sigh. *"Not here!"* I communicated to him telepathically.

Cam only smirked devilishly. "It's practically see-through. We'll take it." He wasted no time offering a handful of black opals and diamonds to the shop owner, who graciously accepted the stones for the dress.

As if our date couldn't get any more romantic, our last stop appeared to be...a beach. Well, it was close enough. The colors, like in the spirit realm, were more vibrant and non-conforming, meaning the water was pink yet crystal clear and the sky was a brilliant pastel purple and yellow color.

There was a giant clear sphere or crystal hanging in the sky with several light sources reflected from within its center, casting unique colors across the pearl-like white sand. Was that supposed to be the sun or a source of light or energy? Whatever it was— or this planet was...it was beautiful. Raw and untouched, it was nature in repose as it was supposed to be. Calm, relaxing, and breath-taking.

The beach, or at least this part of the beach, was completely barren of any being or animal, which I found peculiar. A small table, canopied beneath a set of palm leafed trees and accompanied by candlelight, had obviously already been pre-set up before our arrival. Cam completed the entire set-up with the basket of fruit he acquired through trade.

"I don't even know what to say..." I began as I turned to face Cam, who was already naked and prominently— at full salute, just like in the misting grotto. Amorous and an intense libido weren't even the words for him but I wasn't complaining about it.

His flawless body was beyond magnificent. Every appendage and organ was proportionately well-muscled.

"Say you'll stop driving me crazy and start undressing already." Cam quipped.

I smiled, willfully obliging. "Is this an inhabited planet?" I asked, shimmying out of each piece of my field wear after ditching my cloak.

"Only by animals but they're all tame. I'd love you show you around but if I'm going to get you back in a matter of a few hours, I'd rather be doing other things." He grinned.

"I thought we were going to be eating first."

"More like, during."

I flashed a naughty smile, "That's…really kinda kinky."

"Good food stimulates euphoric senses, pair it with arousal, and love-making becomes an incredibly erotic experience."

"Oh. I never thought about it that way." I swallowed, my pulse picking up speed as more of his lust passion warmed over and through me.

"How do you remember where these places and planets are?" I then asked.

I squealed, instantly naked, all of my clothes—vanquished. Cam had abruptly and impatiently stripped me of the last of my remaining cloth barriers using magic. "You talk entirely too much, Starling." He smirked.

Now completely nude, Cam scooped me up into his arms and his mouth nearly devoured mine, definitely to shut me up. His tongue darted into my mouth hungrily and the delicious explosion of being penetrated and explored orally, made me coo and moan deeply into his mouth. The fervor in his kiss, along with everything that I've experienced with him up until now, set both my heart and my body on fire.

Suddenly—I wanted to be the one in control this time, not that I had any idea of what to do or how to do it, but I certainly wanted to try. I kissed him hard both raunchy and fueled by passion, but somehow his eager and probing tongue managed to dominate mine every time.

As if he'd read my intentions, he began to lower himself to theground, his hands on my hips as he began to ease back, ending up flat on his back with me straddled on top of him. I could physically tell by his eager submission that this position alone was equally as wanted and thrilling to him. He conveyed that thought, sliding me forcefully over his hardened shaft and I gasped and quivered at the amount of pleasure derived from a single stroke of skin to skin contact.

He rose up, taking in each of my breasts hungrily, teasing and tasting each nipple expertly. The sensation was erotically explosive, and I didn't want him to stop, almost giving that control back to him.

I pushed him back, forcing him to lay and be still as I began to work my way down, planting soft, suckling kisses along his chiseled jaw and smooth throat. He moaned deeply, his hands stroking, exploring, and massaging my entire body as his hips flexed and writhed teasingly beneath me.

My tongue glazed a hot, wet path down and in between the chiseled planes and curving ripples of hard muscles in his chest and stomach. His skin was soft, hot, and smelled incredibly inviting; like inhaling a potent drug that lowered any inhibitions, while wildly feeding my lust at the same time.

It was as if was no longer in control of my own actions and body. I slid down even further, stopping face to face with his flawless and impressive girth, the source of both his pleasure and mine.

He arched his hips upward with a deep groan of pleasure, his fingers gripping and tangled up in my curls once I encircled my hand around him, my fingertips far from meeting my thumb. His skin near fiery and he was both trembling and throbbing eagerly once I slowly lowered my head with mouth wide open.

XV: CAM`AEL

The sudden eagerness and the amount of lust emanating from Starling's body was a generous surprise that fed my own sexual hunger. Her ardor was much stronger than it had been the first time we made love, which made me a tad nervous, given her out of control hallowed fire.

When she moaned into my mouth, it sent an intense jolt of pleasure straight into my groin, hardening my already pulsing and petrified erection, which ached painfully to be inside of her again.

I wasn't used to this.

I was an Incubus. It was my job to please and both give, as well as take pleasure from, but she was slowly yet fervently taking full control. The heat of her power, the very source of her essence began to warm her skin immediately. I tensed and braced myself, half expecting her to spontaneously ignite once again.

Well, at least I'll die with a big smile on my face if anything, I thought to myself.

Something told me that we wouldn't quite make it to the table, let alone eat anything. The more she kissed me…no—sucked on my mouth and my tongue ravishingly, it was as if she were desperately trying to taste my very soul.

Her enthusiasm both controlled and guided her hands to work hungrily over my back and my arms, raking her nails gently against my scalp, and then clasping my hair between her fingers.

So, she wanted complete control huh? As risky as it might be, I'd give it to her.

Continuing to be kissed deep and wildly by her, I let go of her legs, pulling them around my waist as I eased myself down to the soft sand.

With my hands around her hips, I slid her back slowly, tensing with teeth clenched in pure ecstasy once the wet heat of the softness between her legs glided over my shaft.

I groaned, biting my lip as I rose up to take in a single luscious, soft breast. She cried out, gripping onto my hair as her body trembled. The scent and taste of her skin was addictively delectable and exquisite.

She pulled away, arching her back as a pleasurable half gasp, half wail escaped her throat. I didn't think giving any female this kind of control over me would turn me on as much as it was now, but I know it had to do with the fact that I loved her so much.

The visual of seeing her beautiful body poised over me, marveling at and stroking her breasts, and teasing her hardened nipples, was quickly pushing me closer to the edge of an all- out turbulent and volcanic orgasm.

My eyes began to glow brightly, and if she understood the connection by now, she'd stop teasing me by simply grinding her sex against me.

Where she was going, the further she worked her way down my body, began to make me quiver and lose all of my own control. The moment she grasped me into her small, soft hand, I could already feel the rapid buildup of my climax being coaxed to the surface. And once she took as much of me as she could into her mouth, it was all over with. I would end up drowning her and she would choke if I didn't have her stop now. I planned to return the favor eagerly, right after fulfilling this urgent need first.

I pulled her back up onto me in one fluid motion, unable to wait any longer. Once she was straddled over me again, I reached down to hold myself upright while pressing her hips aggressively down onto me and sliding my tip into her heat.

She tensed, forcing me back down and moving my hand away to take back the control that I almost denied her of in my aching lust.

I obliged obediently, grasping onto her hips as she guided me into her slowly herself.

Tilting my head back, I closed my eyes in extreme rapture as she began to impale herself onto me. She felt soft, hot, slippery…and still incredibly tight.

"Starling." I mumbled through clenched teeth, moaning deep with relief. I wondered if I would be able to slip the essence and power of my lust into her at the same time, the way I normally interacted with women to derive pleasure. Would I be pushing it?

Would I even be able to?

Even though a part of me was already growing inside of her now, and we now shared a telepathic connection as a result, that wouldn't be a good idea especially since her aura was already tainted with my presence as it is.

She was taking her time. Resisting the urge to hold her in place by grabbing her hips and arching my pelvis upwards to sheath myself entirely into her in one complete thrust, was maddening.

I was on the verge of a full-on, hardcore orgasm once she settled fully onto me. It couldn't be helped. It would be the first of several for me anyway, which was common.

As soon as she began to roll and grind her hips, I exploded in a furious release.

Again, instantly the heavens opened up before me behind my eyes. It was a remnant of what I remembered but still I recognized it.

The vision of billions of stars, all forming one uniform body nearly brought tears to my eyes.

I held onto Starling tightly as she shuddered with me, crying out as my orgasm sparked and ignited hers immediately thereafter. I continued to pump her from underneath as her body spasmed, rocked, and quivered in my hands.

It was then, that another vision opened up before me.

This was new.

The image was of a lush, green landscape, and both myself and Starling standing on a gently rolling hill, facing a bountiful glade full of vibrant trees, bushes, and colorful flowers. The field began to spread before me like a painting coming to life. Where was this place and why were we here? Was this a vision of things yet to come? I used to receive visions all of the time as an Angel, but rarely as a Fallen.

The picturesque image began to zoom in like a camera lens coming in for a close up, and my view slowly began to rise and pan around our forms. Once I got closer, I gasped in surprise and pleasant elation. Starling looked the same. She was as beautiful as ever with her full, long curls shining and blowing gently in the breeze. I appeared…different. Different in a distinct way that I couldn't really pinpoint. There was something missing, aside from my wings.

We were each holding an infant, looking down at the sleeping

tiny bundles in our arms with deep adoration.
Babies.
Twins.
Starling was pregnant with twins!

In this precise moment in time, my already intense love for her grew tenfold. Holding her close, skin to skin during the pinnacle of both of our climaxes, immediately began filling me with the very thing that I have been longing to know, understand, have, and feel since my fall from heaven.

Experiencing this sudden bond with Starling, I understood the magnificent power of what love between humans represented and meant. She was going to bear and become the mother of my children. I would crawl on my belly through hot coals, poisoned thorns, or over razor sharp glass from one end of the earth to the other.

I would challenge and fight to defend her from every source and abomination of darkness, including Morning Star himself. I would search each and every galaxy and planet to find her favorite flower, and I would sacrifice my very soul and being a thousand times over in a heartbeat, if it meant that she and my children would live.

Thank you Elohim.

I cherished this…cherished Starling and my children to be, with every ounce, fiber, and molecule of my being. Burying my face into her silken and fragrant curls, I felt the need to weep. Her body trembled against mine, her heart thumped animatedly beneath her breasts as another orgasm pumped more of my seed into her.

The surge of my climax made her stiffen; her thighs clamping tightly around mine as she cried out. I clenched my teeth, tensing and shivering at the tremendous pleasure that went way beyond the connection of our flesh. I will never let her go and I will never hurt her.

Embracing her beautiful face in my hands, my eyes began to glow brightly once again as I leaned in to kiss her obsessively. When we finally gasped for air, breaking from the deep kiss, my fingers slipped gently into her curls and I pulled her face closer to mine. I gazed deeply into the sapphire depths of her eyes. "I love you." I whispered in a low, rasp of breath.

I was amorously compelled to verbalize the words instead of saying them telepathically.

This is what Adam shared with Eve every time he held her in his arms and she looked into his eyes, whenever they made love. It's what every male, human or otherwise felt for the women they were willing to fight and die for. Love was the ultimate power, and power like this could not be broken, infiltrated, or destroyed by any thread of darkness.

XVI: STARLING

Amazing, mind-blowing, and completely satisfying. Those were the only words that came to mind as I lay in the crook of Cam'ael's arm, basking in the afterglow of our love-making.

I noticed that not only had he been extra tender and gentle in letting me have control, but he purposefully chose positions that would make me the most comfortable.

His hand rested on my abdomen, softly massaging in slow circles as we gazed up at the strange, iridescently colorful crystal in the sky. The gentle sound of the waves breaking and churning at the shore was slowly lulling me to sleep, which is all I wanted to do now.

I didn't want to leave let alone be away from him again but I knew he was going to have to take me back soon. When his eyes began to glow brightly, it kind of creeped me out at first but I understood why when he kissed me deeply. It was at that moment when I decided that his intentions, getting me pregnant, and his feelings…had to be genuine. A fallen didn't need to romance a human woman they simply wanted to breed with, not to mention taking the time to be with her like this. I felt guilty for having even thought that about him.

In the momentary silence, I began to think about what Jamie told me, about Fallen loving loyally and deeply and how it becomes the total opposite if they're wronged or betrayed.

Could Cam ever be angry with me enough to try and hurt or even kill me should something ever happen between us? Not that it would but what if?

What would happen if he ever began to hate me for any reason?

I don't know why I was ruining this blissful moment with such negative thoughts.

Suddenly, Cam spoke, "I'm an Incubus. You do know what that is, right?" He whispered softly.

I craned my head to look up at him. He continued to stare up at the enormous crystal, as if in a trance or dream-like state.

When I didn't answer right away, he looked down at me reverently.

I know what an Incubus is but I guess I never really thought about it past the powerful sexual prowess and lust magic that obviously came with it.

Other than incredibly awesome sex? I guess I really didn't know what it really meant.

I pursed my lips and looked away from him when I finally answered, "So what? You're a womanizer? A male fallen whore? You've slept with a lot of women?" I felt myself grow hot with jealousy instantly. I sat up, my back to him as I gazed out onto the rippling pink water. Why was he asking me this now?

After a moment, I felt his hand gently touch my shoulder, urging me back down to lay with him but I shrugged away. I guess he was waiting to see if I'd explode into white flames with my sudden shift in moods. I was actually surprised that I hadn't because my skin and my blood certainly began to warm inside.

I frowned, casting my eyes downward.

He sat up, leaning in close to me. "You wanted to know why I fell." He then said.

I perked up. That made me forget about my brief pouting jealousy. He was going to tell me, finally!

I turned around to face him fully in anticipation.

The hesitation and chagrin brewing in his gorgeous eyes was evident as he glanced down at the pearl infused sand.

"Curiosity." He simply said first.

I remained quiet, expecting him to elaborate.

His eyes returned to mine. I took in and traced every angle, hollow, and contour of his beautiful face, awaiting his confession with undivided attention.

He licked his lips and sighed softly, "My punishment was derived directly from my sin. Lust. When Elohim began the process of creating Eve, we as angels couldn't wait to see what she would look like but we were told we were not allowed to look upon her until after she and Adam had consummated their marriage as husband and wife. She was stunning, with a strong and super bright aura, much like yours." Cam nodded as he examined mine with furrowed brows.

Or what mine used to be, I wanted to comment but I remained silent. I was shocked. Our auras were similar? What did that mean? If Cam knew the answer to that, then he'd tell me —I would think.

Apparently, he did notice the darkness that was smeared into it too. Though he didn't comment about it, I could tell that he was concerned about my not being able to hide it from the others. I imagined that it would only get darker the more I was with him and the further along I became with the pregnancy. I was sure that he was thinking the same thing.

He continued on, "Naturally, many disobeyed out of sheer curiosity. They were cast down to join Morning Star, who had already been cast down for trying to become greater than Elohim in the very beginning.

I was chief Angel of All Powers, given authority, and branded with the sword of resolute and divine justice; as well as the order to take care of any demons and fallen at that time and in the future. At least, that was supposed to have been my duty—had I remained." He paused again, his eyes focused back to the sand.

"Our next command was to never look upon them when they were intimate," he bit his lip and a slight smirk briefly pulled the corner of his mouth upwards when he looked at me.

"Though I never looked or watched…I could hear them. We all could. Eventually, my curiosity got the best of me and I began to wonder what would cause them to want to lie down with each other so often. I saw the way Eve looked at him afterwards and how doting and protective Adam was over her. That connection bound their souls to each other each and every time, and it steadily grew into something beyond powerful. More powerful than any kind of magic that exists. All I know, is that I wanted to feel and understand what made the act of physical intimacy between a man and a woman so special. Like an idiot, I thought I was being crafty by waiting until Adam went off to hunt for food.

I wanted badly to know what that kind of love felt like. Physical love. So, I took his form and approached Eve while she was alone in the garden. I say like an idiot because I didn't even consider that Elohim would know my thoughts and my heart long before I took any action. He let me get far enough before calling me out, condemning, and stripping me of my true-given name and title, and permanently locking me out of the heavens. Forgiveness and apologies aren't options for angels. I was supposed to know better. Despite free will, obedience is expected for the rules that we were given. And being that I was perfect, there was no excuse." Cam swallowed and turned away from me after that last sentence, as if he couldn't even bear for me to look at him then. I could see his jaw tightening.

I didn't really know what to say at first. My lips parted slightly, wanting to say something, anything but nothing came to mind right away. He was waiting for me to respond, already regretting having told me, I'm sure.

"So, your punishment is that you can only know and experience physical pleasure, just like you wanted to with Eve, but you can never actually have or feel love. That's why you're punishment is not just being branded a demon but being an Incubus." I finally whispered.

His gorgeous eyes widened, shimmering with emotional surprise. Apparently, I'd completely stunned him with my understanding. He studied me in amazement, as if seeing me for the first time.

"Not until now." He then said as he reached a hand out and gently brushed my cheek. I smiled.

My next automatic question was itching to be known in the back of my mind but I ignored it. I didn't want to know. It would only reignite my jealousy.

He hadn't mentioned his true God-given name yet but this was enough for me, for now. I rose up on my knees and threw my arms around his neck, pulling myself against him to both hug and embrace him.

"I forgive you and I love you, Cam." I whispered into his ear this time.

I could hear him sigh deeply, as if the tension, embarrassment, and anxiety that he had obviously been feeling while revealing it all to me, had finally began to leave him altogether. My forgiveness of him, even though I wasn't his master or original creator, had meant everything for him to hear. That much I could tell.

His arms tightened around me, hugging me closer to him.

"By the way, we're having twins." He then said.

XVII: CAM`AEL

Starling was silent once she pulled back from our meaningful embrace. Her words, her forgiveness, and her profess of love for me despite my past, touched me in a way that I never believed I could be touched. It meant so much coming from her. What I hadn't expected, was how freeing it was for me to be able to reveal it in its entirety, especially to her—the woman I loved.

Perplexed astonishment immediately contorted her face and her brows knitted together in confusion. You would have thought I'd morphed into another creature right before her eyes.

I smiled.

"Wh—how…" She couldn't even form the words as both of her hands automatically went over her belly. She looked down at her abdomen and I placed my hands over hers. We were both still naked.

"I saw them and I saw us together in a vision not long ago."

She was still at a loss for words.

Her eyes flicked back up to mine. "You saw them?"

"I couldn't see what they looked like or if they were twin girls or boys. They'll have your genes, so I know they're going to be beautiful."

She began to smile, taking in what I had just told her as we both held our hands over her still flat and toned belly.

"You're not so bad looking yourself." she smirked.

I laughed softly.

"So, we were together?" She then whispered.

I nodded unable to contain my own happiness and excitement at the thought the more it began to sink in for the both of us.

"Are you alright with it? I mean, are you happy?" I then asked her.

She gave me a curious look and studied my face. "Why wouldn't I be?" she smiled.

I sighed. She knew why I felt guilty. Her soft hand touched my cheek.

"I'm happy, and I meant exactly what I said, so stop with the guilt, ok?"

I couldn't help but smile at her positivity and acceptance of it all as I leaned down to kiss her lovingly.

~~~****~~~

I had barely gotten her back in time. It was pre-dawn, the sun was just rising—and according to her calculations, the morning bells hadn't tolled yet.

I hadn't heard from her once we parted ways, which was good. I told her to immediately call out to me if there was a problem and I'd find a way to go in and get her.

My first order of business was the texts that Elohim had revealed to me, however, I wanted to get a jump on figuring out how I was going to go about creating this alliance with the Psyrens and Aural Bandits.

First, I would need to take a head count.

Ry, Mac, and Nay had been awfully quiet lately. I didn't want to speculate on the side of negativity with Xyn still around.

"Rahab? Are you and Edanai alright?"

I waited.

"Cam, yes all is well. Edanai has finally found a planet that intrigues her. We've been here ever since."

"Really? So she knew you were following her?"

Rahab chuckled. *"Yes, she knew."*

"Well, as long as you two are safe, that's good. I don't know if she's still pissed off at me but I'll need you two to come back here for a quick head count. I just want to see with my own eyes, how many of us remain."

"Is something wrong? Has something happened?" Rahab's voice turned serious.

"No, not yet anyway. It's just been a while and I want to make sure that everyone is alright. Help me contact any and all who will respond and have them meet at the reservoir now."

"Sure. We'll be there shortly, my friend."

"Great, see you in a bit."

I cut our telepathic connection.

I knew it wouldn't be long before I needed to head to the reservoir myself, so my next plan of action needed to be quick.

Aliks mentioned that I could go about establishing this alliance in any way that I saw fit. I grinned devilishly to myself as I turned my eyes upwards towards the heavens.

This was going to be a ridiculously long shot in the dark but I was going to try it anyway.

"Aliksaeth! I summon thee!" I shouted out loud, turning to face the Eternal Lake.

I watched and listened closely. After a few moments, a sudden flash of lightning lit up the sky and touched down upon the stone in a thunderous crack, spraying a burst of celestial sparks. Aliks' slender form began to materialize and then he floated down to touch the stone surface of the mountain peak several feet from me.

A weary expression was already affixed to his narrow, pale, glittering face.

"Consider this a compliment, Cam`ael. You know that you no longer have the power or the authority to summon Angels, and I didn't know that you knew my full name. However, be thankful that I happened to hear your call, let alone that I even bothered to respond. I don't make it a habit of catering to or associating with demons." He made sure to remind me.

I smirked. "Sure, I'll remember that."

"What is it that you've summoned me for? Questions about your task or your beloved, precious little one?" he raised a single pink brow.

Drakael had been arrogant. Aliks was simply a smart-assed punk to me.

"For your sake, she'd better remain alright." I warned him with every intention of carrying out any threat I would make against him.

He smiled and rocked back on his heels with a hand to his chest. "For my sake? Or what? You'd better be glad that things have turned out the way they have so far. But you and I know that nothing is ever set in stone, don't we? Now state your business or message, I don't have all daybreak."

I felt several nerves twitch when my teeth clenched. It was really hard for me to bite my tongue sometimes and I was getting tired of this charade. He was daring me to kick his ass.

Why couldn't they all be like Sha'rel? I remember dealing with her before when she relayed one of my past requests from Elohim. She was kind and respectful even though it was obvious that she didn't like me.

"I'll make this quick because I do have somewhere I need to be. I just wanted to clarify that you did say that I could use whatever means necessary to forge this alliance, correct?"

He pursed his lips into a thin, tight line, then jammed his hands casually into the faded, loose-fitting jeans that he wore, complete with a green v-neck t-shirt. He was barefoot and his alabaster, shimmering, white feet were unblemished and clean.

I appreciated that.

Where the hell had he been and what was he in the middle of when I summoned him?

"That is correct." He affirmed slowly, already figuring that I was up to something.

"Good. I'm in need of an assistant or a partner to accomplish this request, and there is an additional task that I am needing to complete as well."

He looked at me as if I'd lost my mind and then shrugged, "So pair up with one in your legion. Why are you bothering me with this?" He was annoyed.

I grinned.

His face instantly morphed into a disbelieving frown when he understood my intentions and then he began to laugh jovially.

"You have got to be kidding me! Not only are you bold, you're quite crass. There is no way that I would be caught in the constant company of a fallen, much less an Incubus, unless I was given a direct order to do so. Besides, I've got better things to do, not to mention duties of my own that I..." His words were abruptly cut off. His mouth frozen on the syllable of his next word.

He was still and then, the sweetest expression of appalled disbelief slowly began to rearrange the previous look of disdain and disgust on his face.

My grin widened.

Aliks had just been commanded to assist me.

His lips were pressed tightly once again before he spoke, "Let's get one thing clear, I don't take orders from you. The only thing I am to do is to assist whenever you need me to, got it?" Aliks pointed at me.

I was too busy grinning wickedly to even care let alone agree.

"Though I'm sure that wasn't exactly what you were told, that's fine by me." I nodded, simpering with malice.

His mouth twisted into a grimace as he began to ghost out.

"Whoa, wait a minute!" I held up a hand to stop him.

He slowly began to materialize back to physical form with an agitated and perplexed look about his face.

"What?" He more stated than asked.

"There will be no calling or summoning when I need you, your assistance is required and starts now." I clarified for him.

Aliks narrowed his eyes, apparently about to argue against that stipulation but Elohim was siding with me on this one this time, to my pleasant surprise. I could see his jaw working steadily.

"Fine." He stated flatly.

I was filled with all sorts of possible chastening torture that I could inflict upon him.

~~~****~~~

The reservoir, was a large, water-filled crater that spanned maybe a few hundred feet across in diameter. It formed a long time ago from a fountain of a never-ending, gushing water from an internal, underground spring at the bottom of its center. The fresh water spring was one of many and it was a veritable oasis for many of the local beings and creatures. It was also one of several not far from my own home along this entire ridge of mountains.

When Aliks and I arrived, I was not prepared for what lay before us. The heat of aggression was already mounting at his presence but seeing him with me kept most of those in my legion at temporary bay.

I could have literally taken visual headcount in less than two seconds.

"Ry, this can't be all of us."

"I'm afraid it is. Those that answered are the ones that are still alive or are still on our side."

I couldn't believe what I was seeing and hearing.

Still on our side?

In the beginning, when we first banned together against the other Fallen and Morning Star, our numbers could have covered the entire expanse of the Eternal Waters. Now, it was barely enough to cover the strip of shore surrounding the reservoir itself! It was then that I began to understand exactly why Elohim had wanted me to form an impossible alliance with the Psyrens and Aural Bandits. If he was recommending it, then he was in control of it too, which meant that the alliance with the Divine warriors as a whole, may not be as far-fetched or impossible either.

"This is bad. This is really bad."

"Who are you telling? That demon of crows you mentioned has apparently struck again recently too. Several more have bit it." Ry reported.

"What?! Why didn't anyone say anything?"

"I just heard about it from Vinnah, she barely managed to get away herself. She's here, somewhere."

My heart sank with despair and a feeling of helplessness for a moment.

"What's with the candy faced punk? Why's he here…and with you?" Ry snarled, referring to Aliks.

"We're going to be working together on a new request but I'm thinking that I may need you and Mac with me too."

"I don't work with Angels and I don't believe I'm the only one here who feels that way either." Ry warned.

"Well get used to it. We have no more options, and we're not going to last against Morning Star at this rate, let alone help the warriors if we don't make some drastic exceptions. That was our original plan for creating this legion, wasn't it? Join me up here right now, we need to show some solidarity before I announce a few things."

"Cam'ael, I'm not kidding. I have my limits and I refuse to share *space with him!"*

"Damnit, Ryziel! This isn't a time for hostile prejudices and grudges. This is about survival, for all of us, not just humans!"

I rarely called Ryziel by his full name, so he knew that I was both serious and pissed.

"Rahab, Edanai...I need you both to stand with me and Aliks now."

I called out to the both of them.

Within seconds, they both materialized next to us. Rahab was always the loyal friend, and Edanai, though she gave Aliks a brief side-long glance of annoyance, was an extremely close friend who's never let me down either.

"Nice to see you too." Aliks bowed sarcastically to her with a smirk.

I waited for Ry, feeling my positive mood begin to waver and sink. He was one of my best friends and an incredibly strong and experienced fighter. I couldn't afford his opposition.

"Ry..." I began to call out telepathically.

The buzz and murmur of voices began to rise with the impatience of the rest of those in our legion below.

I sighed and began to speak, my voice carrying loud and clear, "I'll make this brief, because I really don't want to have us all remain congregated in one area for too long, let alone speaking out loud like this for obvious reasons." I began.

"This is a losing revolution, Cam`ael. We will not win against Morning Star and his army. Resisting is proving to be far deadlier than simply going with the flow and making the Earth ours." Someone spoke up.

Suddenly, others were readily agreeing with him.

"If you think that you'll be free to do as you please because you're a fallen, then you're mistaken. You will become subject to Morning Stars' whims just like the humans!" Edanai returned.

"Then so be it. Why should we care this much about the humans when they don't even care about themselves and their own futures?" Someone else asked.

"It's not that they don't care. They are unaware and they are nearly powerless to stop it. They will need our help." Rahab offered.

"That is the job of Elohim, all of the ninth and tenth level Archangels, and the Seraphim soldiers, isn't it?"

I looked at Aliks who affirmed nothing. His expression was difficult to gauge but I was interested in his response to that too.

"And why is he here anyway? What does he care about our situation? They do nothing to stop or help!" A female shouted, referring to Aliks.

"Why do you think he joins us now?" Rahab commented in Aliks defense, which I found noble.

Aliks shifted, apparently surprised by Rahab's words on his behalf, even though that wasn't why Rahab chose to speak in defense of his kin. I could tell that he wanted to say something himself but he was weighing his options in the presence of so many Fallen.

I opened my mouth to add to Rahab's words, only to be cut off abruptly.

"Because we need to work together. We don't have many anymore, all you have to do is just look around. But we do have two things that Morning Star and his massive army will never have." A voice suddenly answered.

I turned to look because the voice literally stunned and filled me with renewed hope.

Though he stood way off to the side, far away from Aliks; Mac, Nay, and Ry had materialized onto the edge of a cliff, adjacent from us. Ry glanced over at me with a cocky smirk and continued to speak, "Resilience and compassion amongst each other." He finished.

The miracle of Ry's change of heart and his words weren't the only things that I took thankful note of, it was the expression that gently came over Aliks's face as he gazed over each one of us after hearing our words. I'd never seen that look upon any angels face before, especially regarding the fallen.

XVIII: STARLING

Twins. I still couldn't believe it. A mixture of several different emotions, thoughts, and scenarios all invaded my mind at once. First and foremost, was that it wouldn't be long before I started to show and I was going to be huge! Should I be seeing a doctor for regular check-ups or something? Like an obstetrician? I wondered. I guess I'll leave all that up to Cam. After all, this wasn't a natural or common thing for a superhuman and a Fallen, was it?

I wanted to make it a point to call and talk to the girl who was my best friend but I wasn't ready to do it just yet. I needed more time to try and reclaim some memory of the level of our friendship. Even though I felt close to her, I still felt like a complete stranger at the same time.

Judging by the sun peering over the horizon in all its brilliant salmon pink, gold, and crystalline blue glory, I'd say we had barely made it back just in time.

Cam stored all the jewelry and clothing that he acquired for me, while we visited the quaint planet of the Luminae, at his place before taking me back to the shore of the Eternal waters. There, I cracked a hall portal gem and quickly ran through after a long, romantic kiss good-bye, or at least until next time.

This time, I allowed no one the time or chance to stare, or wonder about my whereabouts, let alone why I was literally racing back to my room. I also didn't want to allow any of the elemental pets time to start gathering and trailing behind me either.

The breakfast bells began to toll, just as I finished freshening up and dressing.

I made it.

I wasn't hungry, so I had some time to kill before first class…with Spencer. I wondered how everything went down after he came to. Does Jamie really have my back? I was still really confused about her actions, and really unsure about her story regarding Devlin.

I thought about Cam and his vision of our twins. Lifting my shirt I glanced down at my abdomen and smiled to myself, trying to picture what it would soon look like distended. Speaking of, the terror of having to confess still weighed heavily on my mind. How much time was Ilka going to give me anyway? I didn't know but I'd better not assume I'd have another day. How was I going to do it? What would happen then?

I studied my aura in the mirror. To my utter shock and surprise, the dark areas were…gone. It was back to its brilliant white glow, like it was when I first arrived. Now, I was really confused. I had no idea what that meant or why. Nothing had changed, had it? If anything, I had expected it to be even darker but it was quite the opposite.

There was a soft rapping at my door that made me jump slightly. I assumed that everyone was already in the dining hall, so I wondered who it was.

With a hand on the knob, I leaned close to the door first and asked, "Who is it?"

"It's just us, open the door."

It sounded like Lorelei.

"Us?"

"Really, Starling?"

I smiled. That was no doubt, Scarlet. I opened the door and they both stood there with wry expressions.

I took a cursory glance around them for any elemental pets, noting that there were none. Thank goodness.

"Where have you been all night?" Lorelei asked.

"What do you mean?" I played dumb.

"We stopped by to see if you wanted to go to Lorelei's because we planned on having a girls' night thing and you were gone." Scarlet explained.

"Oh, yeah...I went for a walk by the Eternal waters and I guess I must have fallen asleep out there." I hated lying about that to them.

Lorelei's face twisted into a questioning look. "You're weird, Starling. That's kinda risky, I don't recommend making that a habit. Hey, you're aura is back to normal! That's great!" She then beamed as she studied the space around me with a smile.

Relieved, I smiled appreciatively.

Scarlet nodded in agreement, "Yeah, finally. I admit, I was getting worried about you myself. I would have done an exam for you but I'm still under apprenticeship." She smiled.

I forgot that Scarlet was a succor too. Why couldn't I have gone to her to be examined?

"Anyway, you heading to breakfast?" Scarlet then asked.

"In a bit."

"Well, maybe we can do the girls' night tonight, unless you have other plans." Lorelei then suggested.

"Um, no, no plans yet."

"Cool, say tonight? Let's meet behind the training fields, same as last time."

"Yeah, sure." I agreed.

"We're gonna grab some food. Do you want us to wait for you?" Scarlet asked.

"No need to wait, I'm ready. Let's go." I said easing out of my room and closing the door behind me.

I didn't want to eat but I figured that going along for the company to catch up with everyone, especially Durien, was exactly what I needed now that my aura had returned to normal.

"Everything good?" Cam asked.

"Yes. Even my aura has returned to normal."

"Really?"

"Yeah I know, it's bizarre. What do you think it means?"

"I'm not sure. That's really strange but definitely a good thing for you."

"That's for sure."

"I have some things that I've been asked to do, so I may not be around for a bit."

"Some things you've been asked to do?"

"I'll explain what that means later. If you need me though, all

you have to do is speak. It won't take me but a moment to get to you, okay?"

"Okay. Be careful. I love you."

He laughed softly. *"Don't worry. Same thing goes for you. I love you too. I'll see you soon."*

To my pleasant surprise, Durien was already at the table with Anthony and Gabe. He wasn't eating though. It looked like he might have been waiting for me. He smiled big and stood up once I joined them at the table. Lorelei and Scarlet made their way to the food line.

"Morning, guys." I waved first.

"Morning. You look a hundred percent better, aura and all." Anthony replied.

"And minus your trail of elementals too." Gabe joked and they all chuckled.

I flashed a wry smile.

"Trail of elementals?" Durien asked.

Anthony waved a hand, "You had to be here, man."

Durien shrugged and then turned to me with a smirk, "What's up, girl? Glad to see that you made it back." He said, wanting to give me a hug but unsure if I'd allow him to. I initiated the hug first.

"I'm sorry about..." He began to whisper.

"It wasn't your fault at all, so don't worry about it. I'm back and that's all that matters."

"I'm actually curious to what all you saw and had to do to make it back." Gabe then asked.

"Man, I'm sure she's tired of re-telling that story. Just let it go." Durien replied to my surprise.

Once we both sat down, I couldn't help but wonder why Durien didn't ask me that very same question out of curiosity too. I found his reaction and what he said to Gabe in response to his question really odd.

~~~****~~~

I still wasn't used to seeing Spencer in the position of being a teacher, especially given everything that's happened up until today. I wondered how Jamie had soothed over his bruised ego after having knocked him out and what she told him about my whereabouts. I take it she made up something good because from the looks of it, he had no idea where I was or had gone, and if he did then he surely hasn't mentioned it.

Spencer's gorgeous eyes rested on me several times throughout his lecture, as if he had something other than the lecture at hand on his mind.

I hated this.

It felt like school, like…college. The memory was validated with the items that Cam had shown me. A sweatshirt with a college logo was among the various items that he took from my apartment in the mortal realm. I had been a college student and I was sure that I didn't like it then either.

There were three more new risers in here, including myself but I was the still the only one who had already been branded. I wondered what the holdup was on getting theirs done.

"Does anyone know why your memories are erased?" Spencer then asked.

No one made a move to raise a hand just yet and I kept my eyes down, doodling on the blank notepad in front of me.

The first class had been an introduction and tour of the hall. During this class session, we were all given maps of the spirit realm, a guide to the hall, along with conduct rules, and a manuscript that listed all the different types of beings here in this realm; including their descriptions and abilities.

I laughed to myself. I felt like I was reading some sort of players guide to an MMORPG game, like World of Warcraft or something.

A light-skinned girl with gorgeous green eyes and a natural, reddish colored afro, raised her hand.

Spencer pointed to her, "Erika." He addressed.

"Is it so that we aren't recognized by people that knew us?"

Spencer appeared to think about her answer and then nodded. "Close. It's more like the other way around, actually. It's so that we're not distracted by any past baggage, hurts, or knowledge that would deter us from our purpose. That includes your mortal fears of darkness and all of the monsters that are part of it. Good answer though." Spencer flashed a dazzling smile at her.

She nodded. "Has there ever been a case where someone did remember their mortal lives?" She then asked.

Spencer's eyes flicked over to mine for a second, which made me shift slightly in my seat. I averted my eyes back to studying the map of the spirit realm spread out before me.

"Not likely." He answered.

His response made me pause, already feeling his eyes on me but I didn't even bother to look up at him.

That's wrong. It happened for me.

"Once you're trained, any interaction that you have with any dark fallen must be on the basis of defense. That means that you don't attack, especially in the human realm, unless you're being physically threatened or attacked first." Spencer then began.

"Wait, I thought we're supposed to be protecting humans." A guy in the back commented.

Spencer raised a finger and then gestured at all of us in general, "We are, but what we are— what all of you are as warriors and are meant to do, will be crucial in the inevitable aftermath of what's to come. That is our ultimate purpose. We can't afford accidental and premature deaths. However, if a demon is doing something that could cause detection or harm towards humans, then by all means take care of it if you are able to." Spencer backed up to the slate board and began writing something.

When he stepped away, the words.

'Apocalypse = Invasion of Darkness' was written on the board.

"Many of you, though you obviously don't remember, had either constant visions or dreams about what this means when you were mortal," He pointed to the board "Everyone's experience may not have been the same, minus the common thread of being able to see things of this plane or things that normal humans can't see or hear with the naked eye and ear. That's all natural and expected. As a mortal, many aren't even aware of the existence of anything otherworldly, let alone its power.

We were remade in order to forget all that would and could compound our fears once we arrived here, because we can't afford to be or show fear in the presence of darkness, even though we may feel it. They count on and feed off of it. Superhuman and immortal or not, the only thing we have as warriors is unity, each other, and our wits.

That's why physical training and classroom instruction is so important. Though you were chosen, you still have the free will to choose. As you all sit here, you have chosen the path of light. And sadly enough, the reality is that many of your counterparts have already chosen darkness because it was easier and incredibly tempting. We refer to them as dark divines and their numbers grow steadily every day." He paused to connect eyes with me again.

Spencers last two statements left an air of stunned silence to hang in the room. Dark divines. Was that who we were about to fight out there after the whole clubbing disaster? They were humans like us, and they all bore brandings similar to ours but theirs had been black.

"Starling, what do you think about that?" Spencer then asked me on purpose, seeing that I wasn't really paying attention.

All eyes and heads turned to me expectantly.

"About what?"

He smirked. "About still having the free will to choose."

Now I got it. He was asking me on purpose and I was not in the mood for this, especially in front of a class full of new risers.

In my most disinterested expression of annoyance I answered, "It means just that. Choosing is defined by actions, which makes you what you are, not titles."

I got a few whispers of agreement but mostly everyone just looked at me with wide-eyed curiosity.

"That's — quite true. Can you elaborate on what you mean by that though?" Spencer replied, looking at me with suspicious intrigue and silence as if trying to read the thoughts behind my words.

"It's pretty self-explanatory."

He licked his lips and cleared his throat, "So, you're saying that if a demon saves a human from certain death, it changes what he is, making him no longer a demon? Of it a serial killer suddenly donates money to charity, it no longer makes him a serial killer or worthy of being punished for his crimes?" he then asked.

I felt myself flush. Funny that he would make that particular analogy.

I paused and thought about his comparisons for a moment. I think he thought he had me on that reasoning, and—why do I feel like I've lived this moment before?

"No. What I'm saying is that simply calling one a demon or a serial killer, doesn't make them a demon or a serial killer. It's what they do that makes them what they are. If we're all doomed to forever be labeled by stupid decisions, mistakes, or things that may not be in our own direct control or doing, then there's no point in ever rising to be anything more than what we are labeled as. That's it."

Spencer raised a single brow. I was expecting him to come back with something snarky or even more challenging but he didn't.

"Wow, that's deep. I like that." Some girl from the back commented.

"Alright. Yes, that was very interesting. Thank you, Starling. Anyone else want to add or challenge what she's saying?" Spencer then directed to the rest of the class?

Erika looked over at me in awe. "Yeah, I understand. She's saying that just because people may label you as stupid, it doesn't necessarily mean that you are unless all you do is stupid things. Free will means that you can either choose to remain stupid by doing stupid things or change it and choose to do something else that you want to define you. Right?" She directed at me for confirmation.

I nodded and smiled and she smiled back at me.

"How come she's already branded? When will we get ours?" A different guy from earlier pointed at my arms and asked all of a sudden.

"Good question. Very soon, actually. Starling has an interesting story to tell though. One that would behoove all of you to hear. It's a reminder of just how important it is to be cautious, because it can happen to anyone at any time if you're not thoroughly trained. Starling managed to save a fellow warrior and both survived and escaped being taken by a fallen. Care to share your amazing story of bravery with everyone else, Starling?" Spencer encouraged me.

I narrowed my eyes and shifted in my chair again.

The bells began to toll, signaling the end of class instruction for the day. Another save for me.

"I guess we'll pick up on your story tomorrow then," he smiled at me and then turned to the rest of the class, "Remember, go over your codes of conduct and the map. There will be a quiz first thing tomorrow over it, and do not forget to start your journals. Those are important. See you guys tomorrow." Spencer managed to get in as everyone stood and began to file out of the room.

"Starling, hang on a second, I wanted to talk to you." He halted me just as I walked past him.

I groaned internally turning to face him, and then I stiffened.

Shit. Jamie did tell him something.

He waited until everyone was gone and then he moved to close the door.

I tried to maintain a half bored, half innocent expression on purpose.

"If you attempt to molest or kiss me again, I'm screaming." I warned him.

He laughed. "Not the reaction I normally would get but cute. Human world politics don't apply here anyway."

"Fine, I'll just resort to kicking your ass myself then."

He smirked, looking as gorgeous as ever.

"Now that's the Starling that seems more fitting for some reason. I knew you had fire in you. No pun intended." He grinned as he sat on the edge of his desk.

I gave a sarcastic smile. "Why did you want me to stay?"

"I've been wanting to ask you something ever since the inquisition board but you left so fast after being examined, I never got the chance."

Though I felt slightly warm, I had to maintain my pulse and heartbeat. I knew that it was exactly what he was trying to gauge and read in his momentary pause.

"So ask."

"I saw you looking at either end of the table, twice. Who…or what were you looking at specifically?" he then asked.

Huh? Part of me felt instant relief, unless this was the start of another round of invasive questions. Why did he care or want to know?

"Nothing." I said quite simply.

I know he didn't believe that but I didn't care.

He inhaled deeply and then slowly exhaled. He was studying me, looking at my aura and I felt a knot of tension clinch in the pit of my stomach. Or was it the twins?

"Your aura is back to normal, that's good." He then commented.

"Were there any doubts?" I meant to be sarcastic.

He laughed and shrugged. "No, of course not. But in all honesty, I think you're still holding something back."

I looked directly into his eyes then. "Something like what?"

He narrowed his gaze, "I don't know but even more so, I don't understand why you would try to hide it. You should be able to trust everyone here, including me."

"Trust is earned, not automatic." I corrected him.

He bit his lip, "I agree."

I sighed. "Is that all?" I then said.

He finally stood up again.

"Yeah, I'll see you tomorrow and be ready to train. I'm still in charge of helping to acclimate you to using your weapon and your fire." He then said.

I could tell he was both disappointed and annoyed with my curt attitude but I didn't care.

"Are Sean and Diana back yet?" I asked.

He shook his head. "Not yet. There's a really important conference going on at the Eastern hall. It may be a few more days. Why?"

Damn.

"No reason. I can learn to control my own fire on my own though."

He sighed, "You know Starling, I'm actually a little disappointed in you. I mean, I thought you were of a certain mind-set but you're proving to be just the opposite. Your essence and the weapon that chose you is no mistake. You, in particular, stand apart from the majority of the others for a reason. That's a lot of raw power for a new riser both to have and to wield responsibly and I respect that. The question is, do you?"

He looked at me pointedly.

I pursed my lips in annoyance. I couldn't allow myself to be around Spencer that much. I wasn't supposed to be according to Aon and Aliks.

"Maybe you need to have a little faith and let go some of your ego." I replied, turning to make a brisk exit.

I didn't want to allow him the last word. Guilt began to fill the back of my mind soon thereafter.

Spencer was right. He was only doing exactly what he took oaths for as a warrior, even sacrificing his Angelic status to become an Earthbound Seraphim and fight along beside us humans.

It was me who was playing on both sides. It's me who's in love with a fallen...and it's me who's pregnant with the children of a fallen. I didn't know how much longer I could pull this off without giving myself away, even before I started to show. I had hoped that Sean and Diana would be back by now. I felt more comfortable confessing to them and having them pass them message along for me.

I headed straight back to my room, fully aware, and with a heavy heart— prepared to do what I could no longer put off.

XIX: CAM`AEL

It took a bit of persuasion and a whole lot of reminders of what standing idly by and letting Morning Star have both Earth and the humans would ultimately mean. In the end, logic and a sense of independence, pride, and overall repentance; the whole reason we banded together to form this rebel legion against Morning Star in the first place, won out.

My main purpose in calling us all together was to see just how many were left and to warn them all about Xyn. According to Ry, some had recently met him and only one had been able to escape to tell the tale. If I had waited any longer, the next meeting would have simply consisted of myself and my friends alone.

"When are you going to tell the others about Starling and your child?" Edanai's words entered my head, just as the others ghosted away.

"Soon. I won't have a choice."

"Nice. Another bomb." She replied out loud.

I sighed. Yes, another bomb. Edanai didn't know that we were actually having twins.

"Rahab, please stick with Edanai. I've got another request." I made sure to verbalize in front of her.

She sighed and shook her head.

"You don't need me to help?" Rahab asked.

"Not this time. I'd rather you and Edanai remain safe and together."

"As you wish, my Lord." Rahab bowed his head and then he turned to Edanai. I don't know what was said between them telepathically but a slow smile began to spread across Edanai's face.

I pointed at him, about to caution him for starting that again but Edanai pushed my finger aside.

"Accept it. If you could have seen yourself from the point of view of everyone else…you'd realize just how fitting it is right now, so get over it." She then said.

I sighed. I still didn't like it.

When Edanai and Rahab were gone, I turned to Aliks, who still remained focused on the giant pool of water down below.

"You're awfully quiet." I spoke.

He cut his eyes to me. "I've merely been listening and observing. I have nothing to say."

"That doesn't surprise me." I shook my head.

"You said it all quite well, Cam. I'm intrigued. You and the rest of your brethren have impressed me."

I raised a brow. That was an almost compliment I think, especially coming from an Angel.

"No one gives a flying fuck about impressing you." Ry interjected with irritation.

Aliks shook his head derisively as Ry's choice of expletives and attitude.

"Alright, Cam. Where to now?" Mac asked as he sidled up closer to join me but still maintaining a wide berth from Aliks too.

"Care to visit some Psyrens?" I grinned.

Mac's brows shot up and a slow grin pulled each corner of his mouth practically to each of his ears, "Psyrens? Fuck yeah!" His enthusiasm kicking up.

"Aw hell, you didn't say anything about them. Any other being but them. I can't stand them." Ry groaned.

~~~****~~~

To say that I didn't look forward to engaging with the Psyrens myself, would be a flat out lie. Admittedly, they were as gorgeous as the Succubus' and the female fallen who actually took care of their flesh forms, if not more buxom and well-stacked. I personally, have never engaged in sexual contact with any of them though. They were far too treacherous company and quite frankly, their screams and shrieks annoyed the hell out of me.

That brought me back to the whole mind-tripping reason of why Elohim would pick them over all the other beings that existed here to partner up with against Morning Star. They owed me nothing; him…well, I don't know.

"It may be a good idea for you stay out of sight for now." I turned to Aliks, just as we all touched down a few yards from their fiery, dank domain and began to materialize.

We had already been spotted and were being watched.

Something big scuttled off to the left, thrashing through bushes in a grotesque symphony of grunts and squeals. Probably a few of their riding beasts I'm sure.

We readied ourselves for a possible initial attack. The Psyrens and Aural Bandits were deathly afraid of the Fallen. We were powerful and strong, so they were always on the defensive and ready to fight…and die, whenever we got too close.

Shrill screams ripped through the air, making me cringe at not only the sound, but the thought of what lie behind the massive gate made entirely of petrified hell beast bones and their leatherized, armor-plates and scaly skins. The sound of wild laughter, cursing, and tormented cries from all sorts of humans and other-worldly beings that they managed to capture and play with until they became bored, floated up and over the thorny points of the despicable gates.

Aliks pursed his lips with a wry expression, "You don't have to suggest that twice."

"Don't stray too far though." I grinned. He scowled at me as he began to ghost away.

I sighed, repulsed. What could they possibly help us do or accomplish, let alone the humans and divine warriors? On the other hand, Ry and Mac were both stoked and horny.

"What do you want with them anyway?" Mac asked as he moved in to stand next to me. Ry stood on the other side of me.

"I know it's last minute. I'll fill you both in later. As much as I can't even bear the thought of touching or having anything in there touch me, it has to be done."

"Another request?" Ry asked.

"Yes."

"I figured as much."

"Hey, I'm not complaining at all. Psyrens are always up for anything and they don't mind if all you want to do is watch." Mac commented.

"Ready?" I said, turning looking at each of them.

"As ready as I'm gonna get." Ry said, copping his crotch enthusiastically.

"Don't forget, this place is also crawling with bandits too." I reminded him.

"I'm not worried about those brainless, putrid sacks of mismatched body parts." Ry replied.

He was right. Bandits were pretty harmless to us. They were

nothing more than large, goon-like abominations of what would result in the mating of a crater troll and an over-sized Grethlor, the equivalent of a really ugly alligator in the human realm.

We had planned to simply ghost in and observe before making our presence known but to our surprise, the gates slowly began to open right before us, invitingly. A black stone road, leading into a small city spread before us, littered with extremely sexy vixens in all shapes and sizes. Fist sized scorpions and spiders skittered around on armored legs, which clicked loudly as they moved.

Though it was the high point of the afternoon, it was dismal and gray here, like a sheet of dirty cotton, broken up by random flashes of purple lightning every now and then. Numerous posts with glass bulbs dangling from each one, held glowing blue lights. They were actually souls trapped inside the lanterns, to be used as light sources for eternity.

We spotted the bandits and their failed attempts to remain hidden as if setting us up for some ambush. I didn't trust the welcoming gesture but if anything happened, we had the obvious advantages here.

The smell of pungent meat roasting on an open spit floated low, creeping and lingering across the ground like fog. In the mist of smoke, sashayed three incredibly shapely, bodacious silhouettes, all heading towards us.

"No weapons." I whispered to each of them, even though we could distinctly hear the whispers and the clicks of the bandits readying theirs.

The three Psyrens stopped halfway, flanked by one of their vicious pet beasts, resembling a black, mutated lion. The way they exaggerated the sway of their hips was an obvious enticing invitation but one that should be preceded with caution.

We advanced forward slowly to maintain a casual, less threatening presence. Ry and Mac continued to observe and listen, while I kept my sights straight ahead.

The Psyren in the middle struck me as the take charge type for some reason. They all three carried very shapely curves, and were clothed in outfits that pretty much left only the color of their nipples to the imagination. They were smug, only because they believed that they had the attack advantage by having us inconspicuously surrounded.

Really? I couldn't help but find their efforts amusing. We aren't masters of this realm for nothing.

"To what do we owe this unexpected visit?" The one in the middle spoke with a seductive grin. Her completely neon green eyes, devoid of any pupils, were essentially molesting me as she spoke. She had a strange accent and it was nothing that I'd ever heard before. It was like a mix of human language, both Spanish and maybe French.

A large scorpion with an almost humanoid face, came running up and over her shoulder from behind her. Its curled tail and stinger was poised almost erotically as it stroked her cheek with it.

I found that a tad disturbing, personally.

From the corner of my eye, the scarf around the one on her right began to move…no, slither was more like it. Light reflecting off of the shiny, metal scales of the snake that glided around her waist, across her torso, and in between her breasts, finally came to rest around her neck and licked at her skin with its forked tongue.

Damn, the Psyrens were sexy, perverse, and dirty — and obviously not ashamed of it. Strangely enough, they weren't anywhere near being my type but watching…well, that was a different story.

"Vessels to buy or trade, perhaps?" She raised a sultry thin brow, as her eyes went from mine, to Ry's, and then Mac.

The snake charming Psyren, who literally wore an eye-patch for a skirt, and two band aids for a top, was definitely interested in Ry. Ry's interest appeared mutual judging from the smirk on his face.

"No, actually. Curious as to what you do have in stock though." I played the game.

"We show nothing unless you're going to buy or…" The one right was instantly suspicious of us.

The one in the middle brought up her palm swiftly to shut her up. "Wait. I know you…" she smirked as she began to eye rape me again.

"Cam`ael, right?" She grinned big, showcasing glittering rows of shiny, metallic teeth.

That sight of them made me flinch nervously.

"What brings you out this way anyway?" She then asked.

"And you two?" The one on her left asked with a nod of her head.

"Ryziel." Snake Psyren lingered out with a sly grin.

Ry raised his brows and held up a hand, "Please, ladies, no

autographs."

She laughed, an eardrum stinging sound.

"Everyone knows who you guys are. Macai, right?" She then pointed and directed to Mac.

"You're all very notorious around here." The one in the middle commented then.

"And you three are?" I asked to continue with the pleasant small talk. So far, so good.

"What gives? You guys aren't one for small talk. If you've come to steal vessels, it won't be easy this time." The hostile one on her right cut in again.

"Shut up, Saje!" The one in the middle snapped.

The air crackled around Saje, shocking the three of us for a brief moment. She appeared chagrined but she continued to scowl at us and pout silently.

"She's a little on edge, along with all the others around here. Some of your brethren recently tore through and stole what took months to gather." She explained.

"We aren't all of the same company." Mac replied.

"Well, you can understand our apprehension though. I'm Grace." She smiled.

"Grace?" All three of us repeated in unison.

Psyrens had names? They didn't seem so bad off hand but this was just the surface, aside from the wicked looking teeth.

She was affronted, hands on her bodacious hips.

"Yeah. Grace. I happen to like that name. Something wrong with that?"

"You look more like a vamped up Candy, Sasha, or Bambi." Ry smirked.

She smiled sarcastically. "And you look like more of a beefed-up Wednesday Addams, or Marilyn Manson."

Ry grimaced, "Marilyn Manson?! Bitch, I will kick…"

The beast beside the Psyrens instantly leapt forward, growling in warning but all Ry had to do was bare his own fangs and growl back. The ugly attack beast pulled back with a whimper, hiding behind the Psyrens this time.

"Calm down." I stopped him quickly. Really? He was more upset about the Marilyn Manson comparison?

Mac was too busy gaping and drooling over their physical assets to even care or take part in any of the conversation. He seemed mystified by the huge, black scorpion that tittered on Grace's shoulder like a well-trained pet.

"What's with the sunglasses anyway? There's never any sun here." She then chuckled.

Ry raised both brows, "Oh, you wanna see what's up?" He brought a hand up to take the sunglasses off.

I stopped him. This was going to get out of hand quickly. Ry is usually sarcastic and always joking around, I almost forgot about his temper though. He was a loyal friend who would go above and beyond to both defend and seek vengeance on others for you, but once you got on his bad side, you should never turn your back on him. Maybe I should have brought Nay or Rahab instead.

Ry's eyes were extremely hard for any being to look at, especially humans. They had this…freak out effect on others that could literally temporarily blind or drive them insane with fear, which was why he kept the sunglasses on or simply masked them in both realms.

I made an attempt to soothe and start over for all of us. "It's obvious we didn't come with any malicious intent…"

I'd better word this part carefully.

"I've been curious about your stock."

"Same here." Mac affirmed with a grin.

Grace laughed, again, that shrill sound was enough to make me want to rip out her vocal cords with my bare hands.

She held her arms out and turned slowly so that I could get a good look at her ass too. That wasn't what I meant but I sure as hell did take a good, long look. Very nice.

Facing us once again, and with a hand on her hip she said, "Words from fallen don't hold water with me. Now you want to tell me why you all are really here?"

"Simple. I no longer do business with Morning Star."

Grace narrowed her eyes, trying to read and study each one of us for ulterior motives.

"And why is that?"

"Is there somewhere else we can talk?" I asked, scanning the dark alleys and corners were the Bandits stood watching and waiting to attack.

She pursed her full, red lips, looking at the other two, who exchanged some sort of silent communication with her in turn. Then she scanned the area all around us before finally snapping her fingers, "Follow me." She said turning on her heel and sashaying back further into the city.

XX: STARLING

I don't know how long I just sat there, hand poised above the notebook, trying to figure out how to start my journals. I decided that it was something that I needed to do after all. If I happened to get shunned and kicked out of here, at least I've left some version of my explanation behind. Like Sean said, if it wouldn't be for me, maybe someone else would benefit from what I had to say about my experiences and thoughts—or learn what all not to do.

It was hard for me to focus and concentrate though. I was heartbroken and torn. I didn't want to have to choose but I know that I didn't have a choice. There was no way I can have and maintain both loyalties. What if I weren't pregnant? Would I be able to simply give up Cam? Tell him that we couldn't see or be together anymore and hope I didn't have to be put in the position of possibly killing him? I don't know and I would never know. Where it stands right now, there'd be no way that I could ever dream of either hurting or killing Cam, or any of his friends—even if I were ordered to do so.

I bit my lip with a deep sigh. What do I write? Tapping the pencil to the paper, I began to think about Joel. The one that Cam said was also a chosen one. I'd probably never get a chance to see him again. Certainly not here. Would it even matter since he wouldn't know who I was anymore? Maybe some part of his memory would resurface like mine did and whatever our relationship was in the human realm, would continue here on a different level.

What was I going to do? How was I going to do it? Whatever I decided, I had no time to waste. Slowly, I began to write.

~~~****~~~

I was jarred awake by frantic knocking on my door. When had I fallen asleep? My heart raced and I rubbed my eyes, glimpsing down at the notebook. I had written over eleven pages of…I don't know, everything, including a confession.

The knocking came again even more insistent this time.

"Starling!" I heard a muffled voice.

Was that...Lira?

I quickly shut my notebook, the chair falling backwards when I jumped out of it, and rushed to open the door.

When I opened it, Lira was wide-eyed and crying, panting, and nearly breathless.

"Lira? What's wrong?" I was alarmed.

She gasped to catch her breath and stepped back, urging me forward with her hands, "Come, hurry! Jamie told me to come get you!" She blurted out.

"What? Why? Is she hurt?" I began to panic

Lira shook her head and grabbed my hand, pulling me onward to come with her. What was going on?

I let her lead me down the corridor, noting that the halls were nearly empty and everyone else inside was rushing towards the same direction that Lira was pulling me too.

What was happening?

A million thoughts bombarded my mind. What had Jamie done? Was she in trouble? Was it Cam?

Lira led me through the maze of corridors, courtyards, and breezeways throughout the hall, giving up on holding onto my hand when I began to jog at a quick pace. Once outside, I left her behind to quickly join the crowd that began to form on the North lawn.

Guards, elders, and many other warriors all stood crowded at the bordered edge, facing the thick line of trees where the neutral lands began.

"What's going on?" I asked Lira, once she caught up with me. My first thought was, were we being attacked? And if so, by who or what?

The other warriors all stood around at attention as if there was something threatening looming. I couldn't see anything from behind the crowd but then I did begin to pick up on someone softly...sobbing.

"It's Devlin..." Lira whispered.

I stopped and gaped at her.

"Who?"

"She's back." Lira began to cry again.

I tried to get a look, wondering why everyone was crowded around the lawn like this and anything but welcoming of her return.

"Where is she?"

Lira began to cry harder, "They won't...they won't..." her breath was hitching and she couldn't get her words out.

I tried to calm her down. They won't what? Let her back in?

That thought infuriated me. I had to see for myself.

"Where's Jamie?" I then asked Lira.

"She's up there somewhere, I think but I don't see her!" Lira was almost hysterical.

"Okay. Stay here. I'm gonna go find her."

I had to push and force my way through the crowd of warriors, which was annoying and difficult but not nearly as impossible as the wall of warrior guards that lined the very front.

I stooped to peer in between the gaps, scanning the trees beyond for the source of the sobbing.

What I saw made my heart deflate in my chest.

A young, black girl was sitting on the ground with her knees drawn up to her chin. She was rail thin and in nothing but tattered clothing. She looked weak, tired, and now scared as she hugged her thin frame, a lost look in her sallow eyes. Her brandings were still silver, not as shiny as ours but they weren't black, so that was a good sign, wasn't it?

Why weren't they welcoming her back and helping her? She needs help! And then my sorrow turned into incredulous fury. None of the warriors, elders, or guards were making any damned effort to help her.

What the hell?

I forced my way through a small opening, only to have an arm shoot out and block my way.

"Stay back!" The warrior guard gruffly shouted at me.

"She needs help! Why aren't any of you helping her? She's scared!" I screamed at him.

"She's not to be trusted! There's a dark presence in and around her!" he shot back.

"She's one of us!"

"She was. Not anymore. Now stay back!" Another warrior added as he moved in to further block my path.

I couldn't believe this! She was terrified and alone. If that was Devlin, I was pissed that her impossible task of escape only led her back to this welcoming home. She looked emaciated and very weak on top of all that!

"How do you know that?"

"Look, little girl, go back into the hall and let us handle this, okay?" The guard said through clenched teeth. With his shield he nudged me backwards forcefully.

I looked over at Devlin's small form again. She had fallen over to her side, huddled into the fetal position, and her shoulders quivered as she held herself protectively. I didn't know her, and I don't know where she's been or what happened to her but somehow she managed to make it all the way back here, alive. This wasn't right.

Tears began to well up in my eyes and then I launched myself forward and forced my way through with all my strength.

"Hey!" I heard behind me as someone grabbed my arm and several others moved to stop me.

Something ignited in me, charging up my adrenaline. I spun and cocked my arm back; making a firm fist and throwing everything I had straight into the face of the warrior who had my arm. He went stumbling backwards, his shield sliding out of his grip as he skidded along his back a few feet away from me. Shock and anger darkened his face as his lip began to bleed. The force of power behind my strike shocked me.

Had I really punched him that hard? It felt effortless.

"I'm sorry!" I quickly said to him, immediately turning to run out towards Devlin's pathetic, crumpled form.

I ignored the shouts of protest and anger from the other warriors and elders as I slowly began to approach her.

She didn't know me but it didn't matter. We were fellow warriors.

"Devlin?" I called out carefully as I cautiously scanned the forest and trees behind her for any sound or movement.

She began to sob harder.

"Starling! Don't be an idiot, it's an ambush!"

"Get back here!"

I ignored all of them.

Her head slowly began to rise. Clean tear marks streaked her dirty face. Her eyes were swollen from crying and wild from the terrors she was probably trying to block out of her mind, only to be reminded of just how screwed she was when she finally made it back to the hall.

"I'm Starling. I'm a new riser."

She shook her head as more tears fell, and then she turned away from me, almost as if she were shy or too embarrassed to have me see her this way.

"What are you doing, Starling?!" I recognized that voice.

Spencer.

I turned briefly, seeing Spencer with Kaia, Brynn, and Jamie—who stood with a hand cupped over her mouth, crying silently. Lira was still crying hard next to her, and then Lorelei, Scarlet, Crystal, Anthony, and Gabe all stepped from the crowd into view. They looked over at me as if I'd lost my mind but were torn in their own grief, unsure of what to think or do themselves.

"Go get her!" Someone said.

Both Spencer and Jamie ran over to where I knelt about two feet from Devlin.

Jamie and Devlin had been close. That's what Durien told me. If anyone could help her, Jamie could.

"What do you think you're doing? She can't be trusted! Get away from her!" Spencer hissed.

How could he even say that? Right in front of her?

"How do you know? None of you have even bothered to examine her! She's still Devlin, isn't she Jamie?"

Jamie began to cry harder, shaking her head. "I told you Starling…" She was too choked up to finish, looking down at her close friend in conflicted pain.

I wanted to punch Spencer too, and I nearly did when he reached down to hoist me up by the arm as if I were a little child.

Devlin's head rose slowly, her eyes connecting with Jamie's and that's when Jamie lost it. She turned away, putting her face in her hands and crying harder.

I jerked my arm out of his hold. I was beyond pissed now.

Heat was racing through my veins and entire body in a fury, and spreading quickly beneath the surface of my skin. Everyone else simply looked on, shocked, horrified, and scolding. Lorelei, Crystal, and Scarlet were all crying now, and Anthony and Gabe were wide-eyed. The Elders were stoic and eyeing both Devlin and me carefully.

I glanced over all of their faces in disgust. What they were doing, which was nothing for her, was beyond wrong. I thought better of us. This isn't what we as warriors are supposed to represent in the face of a fellow warrior. She had been kidnapped, taken against her will, and then managed to both survive and make it back on her own, what was their deal!?

"I can prove it!" I suddenly blurted, looking at Devlin, and then Spencer and Jamie.

"What are you talking about? This isn't a drill, Starling. This could be disastrous and dangerous. You have no…"

"I'll prove that she still belongs at the hall and that she's still one of us! If I can prove it, will you get them to help her?" I asked him.

He looked at me as if I'd gone insane and pursed his lips, shaking his head. Then he looked at Devlin and I could tell that he was contemplating it but he was too code abiding to take the chance.

"How?"

Jamie turned to face me with a questioning look of hope in her eyes. Every time she looked at Devlin, fresh tears began to stream down her face and she had to look away again.

"You guys need to get back over here now for your own safety!" Someone called out to us.

I turned to look at Devlin again, and a brief image of that girl China, thrashing on the ground in what looked like uncontrollable pain, suddenly made me gasp softly.

I didn't even think, I did what I only knew how do to since I've been here. Sean's words began to echo in my head; 'You can't hurt or destroy your own likeness.'

Light could not harm or destroy light.

If she was still one of us then there was only one way to find out.

Without thinking anymore about it and giving myself time to doubt what I was going to do, I lurched forward and grabbed Devlin into a bear hug, wrapping my arms tightly around her. She felt like a literal bag of bones to me, light and too thin.

Many other voices were shouting at me now, calling me insane, and screaming at me to stop what I was doing but I didn't listen.

I pinched my eyes shut, focusing and seeing nothing but a wall of wildly burning, white fire inside my mind's eye, and then forcing all of my energy, strength, anger, purpose, and sympathy into one enormous detonation of emotion.

A powerful whoosh erupted from me, engulfing the both of us in a conflagration of white flames. Devlin's body went rigid, and she began to scream and buck wildly in my hold. She was incredibly strong, and when I heard an inhuman howling beneath her shrieking screams, I began to panic. Something powerful was trying to escape from her, pressing against my flesh with extreme force as if trying to penetrate and burrow itself into me instead. A stinging sensation began spread along my skin, making me wince as my fire instantly combatted its every attempt.

There had been a dark entity in her after all. She was being used as a vessel to transport it and it was both furious and in severe pain. It tried to fight against me but my fire was too strong for it, consuming and obliterating it swiftly. It screeched in rage as Devlin writhed, her back bent in an almost impossible and painful looking arch, and then she began to tremble as if she were having an exaggerated seizure.

I grit my teeth, forcing more essence and energy into feeding my flames—and then I began to feel…light- headed.

The dark being began to pool out of her ear, no longer fighting and resisting as strongly as it had been initially. It was ugly and vile, twisting and spitting in hostile anger while still trying to attack me. It failed miserably as each part of what was left of its oily black tendrils burned into oblivion. I continued to concentrate on its destruction, refusing to let go of Devlin no matter what.

And then, she stopped moving. Though her breathing was low and raspy, she was still breathing, which was good. Sweat drenched her clothes and her dirty face was slick with tears, sweat, and spittle that dribbled from the corner of her mouth. Her eyes were half closed as she panted softly. Her body felt really light and limp in my arms, it was like holding a bone filled pillow. She was slumped over on her side and I cradled her head consolingly while stroking her dirt-caked, wild and askew hair.

"You're alright now." I whispered to her. I hoped.

Spencer and Jamie looked on in silent, stunned fascination.

I'd done it. I proved to them that she was still one of us. They could help her now.

"She needs a succor!" I called out, scanning the blank faces that looked on questioningly but silent.

The guards looked to the elders for permission but they remained silent and stern, unaffected by what I had just done.

What's wrong with them? She's fine now. Whatever dark thing she had in her was gone.

"I said she needs a succor!" I screamed at them in more of a demanding tone than a pleading one this time.

"She can't be trusted, Starling, regardless of what you think you did. Now come on." Spencer soothed.

"You're just gonna leave her here? Look at her! She needs help!" I shouted angrily at him.

My flames were still going strong, creating a thin, see-through veil between us and them. I began to feel faint as if I were being drained and it confused me. What's wrong with me now? I wondered.

I felt a light, fluttering sensation in my lower belly that made me gasp softly. I had to abruptly stop myself from reflexively bringing a hand to my abdomen in front of so many watchful eyes.

My unborn children were reacting to something. Possibly to what just happened, no doubt, and I hoped that whatever it was didn't affect or impact them negatively. How was I even feeling anything this early? Because this wasn't a normal or natural pregnancy by any means, that's why. Cam was a supernatural being and I was an immortal human. Both of different allegiances. I was of light and he was of dark. But that was just it. To me, he wasn't. In my eyes, he was the very opposite of darkness.

Jamie knelt beside us, and I could tell that she wanted to comfort her long lost friend too but she didn't know how or if she should.

"Return to sanctified land at once! You are all attracting other dark beings. She's brought them with her. They've used her as a decoy!" An elder ordered.

Whether others were coming or not didn't matter to me. I wasn't going to leave Devlin out here like an abandoned animal. I couldn't believe what I was seeing and hearing. Everyone was staring but no one was moving to help.

After a few desolate moments of me being angry and disbelieving, someone finally did.

"Stop, do not go over there!" Someone called out but whoever it was didn't listen.

Scarlet was running towards us and she wasted no time kneeling beside Devlin's near lifeless form. She began to rub her hands and fingertips together while closing her eyes, and then reciting verses that I couldn't understand, softly.

Once she opened her eyes and began to work, tears were glistening on her eyelashes as she proceeded to examine Devlin's skin and eyes.

Scarlet was a succor, and though still under apprenticeship, she was offering to help anyway. I smiled gratefully, gently shifting to ease Devlin down gently onto her back so that Scarlet could go to work on her.

My fire was dying down but I still felt like passing out. It was weird. I tried to stand, only to falter and fall back down on my hands and knees, weak and dizzy. What was wrong with me?

Immediately, I felt a hand at the small of my back and my arm to steady and keep from falling over completely.

"Starling, are you alright? What's wrong?"

I looked up into Lorelei's face, her pretty bright blue eyes were red and wet with tears. Anthony was beside her, offering a hand to me too. Gabe came around to my other side for support, and Lira held my hand.

Crystal took to helping Scarlet by holding Devlin's hand for comfort with her head bowed in prayer.

"I'm...okay. Just a little dizzy, that's all."

"If you all do not return to sanctified land now, I will take your actions of disobedience as a choice. You have been warned. There is no gray, you must choose dark or light. It is clear that she has been past the point of affliction, should you choose to continue to assist her, you are making the choice of dark and in turn, shall all be shunned. Is this your decision?"

What? Was he joking? She was alright now and he was threatening our very destinies and essentially punishing us for helping her?

My god, even the fallen had more sense of loyalty and honor among their kind! During the fight after the club, they had all jumped in to help each other, teaming up to destroy their enemies without hesitation or question. And when Cam's friends thought that I was a threat and that he was in danger, they immediately came to his aid. They had even put their very lives on the line for us as humans and warriors too, with the expectation of nothing else in return except to be despised, hunted, and killed by us.

I was heartbroken, this couldn't be what the warriors represented. Divine backing wouldn't tolerate this level of coldness. I know it can't be what the mantra had been founded upon but the elders seemed unwavering and completely serious.

I exchanged a weary look with everyone else.

"You guys had better go back now while you still can. Thanks." I whispered with a weak smile. My heart was breaking because deep down inside, this had been coming. It was inevitable for me, so I was fine with making my choice now— as sad and devastating as it felt. I was already shunned before having even started.

I appreciated that all of my friends remembered what was more important and risked themselves to do it, but if anyone should be shunned, it should only be me—for more reasons than putting a warrior guard flat on his ass and going against their wishes. I was going to be shunned anyway, so I'd be damned if they were all volunteering to be too for my sake.

"She's right." Spencer added, "Think about the bigger picture and the risks. You helped her, now she's on her own, so let's go while you guys still can."

I didn't even look over at him.

"No way. I'm not going anywhere." Lorelei said defiantly.

Spencer furrowed his brows in confusion.

"Me either." Anthony replied soon thereafter.

No one else moved.

"Jamie." Spencer said, taking a step to head back to the hall grounds and assuming that she'd automatically follow him.

She didn't move.

Instead she walked over to where Scarlet and Crystal remained on either side of Devlin, and knelt down above Devlin, lifting her head gently into her lap and holding her hand.

"You guys don't understand what you're doing. Once you make this decision, there's no coming back." Spencer shook his head.

"Sometimes it isn't a matter of choice but I understand exactly what it means." I whispered.

Spencer was perplexed, studying me with curiosity.

"I'm staying with them too." Lira piped in.

I sighed. Lira didn't have brandings or a weapon. She was too vulnerable out here and way too valuable at the hall.

"No. Lira, you can't. You have to…"

"I'm not staying at the hall without you guys or Devlin now that she's back! I don't care what you say!" her lip quivered as she worked to bite back another burst of tears.

Spencer lingered, staring at all of us incredulous and speechless. Then, he sighed and shook his head, and then turned to jog back to the hall.

"You guys need to go back while you still have the chance. I'm the one that's made this decision."

"Okay, well, we're all making our own decisions now." Lorelei affirmed.

"You should have thought about that before deciding to risk yourself to help yet another fellow warrior." Anthony winked at me with a smile.

I had no idea what to do next. Aon? Where was she when I could use her guidance too?

I didn't want to be responsible for everyone's defection. They were voluntarily accepting shunning on my account. I felt sick inside.

"Kaia, what are you doing?" Spencer suddenly exclaimed.

When I looked over in that direction, I saw Kaia running out towards us.

She paused at his words and then turned around to regard Spencer, sadly shaking her head at him. Then she slowly panned the crowd beyond him. "I'm sorry, Spencer. I've been compelled to join them and I can't explain it. I'm sorry to all of you but in this instance, you are the ones who are wrong." She then said.

That shocked the hell out of me and we all exchanged the same, shocked and questioning glances among each other. I was completely stunned but quickly pulled away from Kaia's unpredictable words and actions—by something else. It was something that made my skin literally shiver and crawl. Apparently, everyone else was hearing it too and they all jumped to immediate alarm and action. Brandings began to glow, readying for battle.

We remained quiet, listening and searching the hidden shadows deep in the forest at the same time. I could hear trees creaking as if moving, and rocks thumping as they hit the ground.

Tree limbs, heavy with leaves, began to crowd over us almost protectively. Then a gust of pungent wind blew through the trees, making the branches tremble. All the small creatures had long since fled into hiding. It was a definite unnatural breeze and we could all distinctly hear a low sighing with words muffled inside of the wind.

"Uh, yeah, might not be a good idea to stay out here. Anyone have a portal gem to their home on them?" Gabe said.

"Hang on, I think I do." Lorelei began to dig into her cloak.

It came again, closer, and this time my blood turned to chill but my body began to grow warm once again, which made me feel even more faint this time. I was completely sapped. I didn't have the energy to bring forth any more fire.

"I have two left." Lorelei offered.

Everyone willed their weapons and were ready. No one on the property of the hall moved but they certainly were watching us with attentively wide eyes.

As if doing nothing wasn't enough, now they were simply going to stand there and watch us possibly get slaughtered?

I was disgusted.

Lorelei cracked a gem...and nothing happened.

"What the hell?" her eyes widened as she turned to look at the row of elders on the hall grounds.

Why hadn't it opened the portal? I wondered in panic. Everyone wondered the same thing.

"I wish I still had the ability to create a portal. I don't anymore." Kaia said sadly.

Had they all been right? Was this an ambush? Nothing emerged or moved but the presence of darkness was beyond palpable and quickly moving in from all sides at once.

"I can't tell exactly what it is, who, or how many." Jamie furrowed her brows.

That wasn't good.

"And they aren't going to help us either." Lorelei frowned with anger at the warriors and guards who were making no moves or effort to offer assistance.

"No, but they sure as hell plan on watching." I affirmed loudly while glaring at them all.

Scarlet and Crystal stood guard over Devlin, who was still barely conscious on the ground. Gabe went to stand in front of all of them with his weapons drawn. His were large, razor sharp, circular blades with the grips in the center. Jamie stood in front of Lira, and Anthony and Kaia both took protective stances in front of me and Lorelei with their weapons primed.

Kaia's weapon was unique. It was a long staff, tipped with a bizarrely shaped, double-sided axe head that curved wickedly in the shape of a crescent moon. It emitted a silvery white glow with tiny inscriptions carved into the blade edge. More than likely it was glorified just like Spencers weapon.

We were all searching the darker parts of the forest further back, awaiting movement or an attack from some direction. Damn! I can smell and feel something but none of us could see anything.

A faint, unearthly, devious voice began to chant, *"Eenie, meenie, minie moe—grab the one with the strongest... Glow!"*

I was jerked off of my feet so hard and so fast, I barely managed a gasp of surprise, let alone had any idea that a flesh-like, ropy, living vine had managed to wrap itself around my ankles. I slammed into the ground, hard and face-first, clumsily trying to either anchor myself to the ground by grabbing onto something, or using both blades to stab into the ground for purchase.

Someone screamed out my name.

XXI: CAM`AEL

A whorehouse was exactly what I was expecting, however what we actually came across, was ingenious. We were all astounded.

"Damn, no need to wonder anymore about how they're able to acquire so many auras and souls." Ry whispered as we gawked at the expensive, well-decorated mansion.

Aside from the spacious foyer and open lounging rooms, there were several grand rooms that were set up with giant, decorative hookah, which served for more than simple smoking sessions. I was certain that there were elements other than tobacco and nicotine in them. I could smell it and it was potent.

The disco room was currently hosting quite a few mortal human guests, all dancing and totally oblivious to the fact that both their souls and their bodies would soon be trapped, sold, and used here forever.

"Interesting. Hang on a sec, I wanna check something. Be right back." Mac mentioned as he ghosted out.

He was probably wondering the same thing that I was thinking just now too.

Class was not something anyone of us associated with Psyrens but this place completely destroyed that pretense altogether. This establishment was immaculate, well-designed, and well-kept.

"See anything you like, just let me know. We'll hook you up." Grace winked over her shoulder. "Except for you, Cam`ael. Here, you're off limits." She made sure to reiterate to her two partners in crime.

I've been around long enough to know what that meant. Please Elohim, don't tell me that I may have to do what I think I have to do in order to gain her trust.

I don't think Starling would appreciate it and I would never do anything to hurt her. Not even this.

Draea continued to watch us suspiciously as Grace led us up a gorgeous, curving staircase that split off into a 'T' at the landing. It was made completely of both smoky glass, and black marble stone, inlaid with pure gold.

Now, either selling souls, vessels, and auras, as well as hooking was extremely good money, or they've earned some incredibly fancy perks from many of those capable of strong magick, like Morning Star.

I don't see how this was going to happen. There was no way I'd ever trust anyone who dealt with him.

Mac ghosted back in and fell into step with us once again. He grinned crookedly. *"I knew it! The other side of this mansion is actually positioned half in the human realm, and it's disguised as a hotel and dance club on that end. Place is crawling with a shit load of hella hot babes; human, Succubus', and Psyrens. It could be anywhere but I'm gonna guess that it's somewhere in the Eastern hemisphere. There's a large variety of women and men with many different accents."* Mac informed us.

Interesting and clever of them. I wouldn't be surprised if more and more beings were doing the same thing. I'm sure it was under Morning Star's advisement. He had ventures, sites, and well-known places set up just like this all over the world. Once any human entered, they were marked as prey and vulnerable. They became open vessels once intoxicated or high, which then allowed them to willingly invite darkness into themselves on a subconscious level.

"Not surprising. Do me a favor, will you two check out the entire mansion? See who's hanging around and if you recognize any from Morning Star's crowd." I relayed to both of them.

"Well, if I must." Mac grinned, rubbing his hands together after spying a group of lingerie clad succubus' and Psyrens waltzing past us at the base of the stairs, purposefully pushing lust magick in our direction—or more like mine.

"You got it, Lord Cam." Ry saluted, mimicking Rahab on purpose with a smirk, and then he turned to head back down the stairs before I could comment.

"Is it alright if they mingle?" I asked Grace who glanced over her shoulder at Mac and Ry's departure.

She appeared stunned that I would even ask.

"Be my guest but I'd prefer for Draea and Saje to escort them. House rules regarding any fallen. And don't be surprised if a few Bandits decide to follow. They're very protective of us." Grace winked at me.

"You mean like a pimp and prostitute?" I replied casually.

She quirked her lips with a slight smirk. "Not quite. More like the other way around."

I wondered what she meant by that.

Ry and Mac were already at the bottom of the stairs, easily disappearing into the crowd with Draea and Saje in tow close behind. If I knew them, they'd end up cloaking and splitting up just to throw confusion.

"Don't do anything to cause trouble, insult, or get them riled up. I'm here to establish trust and create an alliance." I warned Ry.

"Oh, so now it's gone from simple requests to performing miracles?"

"Don't play, Ry."

He laughed, *"Shit, Cam. You take the fun out of every damned thing. Fine, I won't insult but I can't promise that I won't sample a few things. And if Draea keeps following me around, I'm gonna feed that damned snake to her and I don't mean through her mouth."*

I sighed with a chuckle. That was Ry.

Grace led me to her personal boudoir. She had a thing for the Spanish Renaissance décor, from colorful fabrics, to the giltwood and wrought iron framed furniture, all the way down to authentic paintings by El Greco and Juan Van Der Hamen.

She had very good taste in art and design, another surprising discovery. What really stopped me in my tracks was her wall of books, hundreds of books of all sorts.

She reads? I was dumbfounded.

"Care for something to drink or smoke?" She offered as she moved to sit behind a fancy, dark wood desk.

"No thanks." I said, still fascinated by her collection of paintings. I moved closer to the bookshelf, examining the spines of some of the old bound leather.

Tolstoy, Faulkner, The Iliad, obvious first editions of poetry from Greece, Ancient Rome, and Ancient Egypt.

"I've gotten many of those as payments. Most were from the authors and artists themselves. One of my favorites is Shakespeare, actually." She informed me, seeing my intense interest in the books.

"You've…read these?" I had to ask.

"What kind of question is that? Obviously. They aren't for decoration. I see that you have a keen eye for art too. Guess we've both been proven wrong today. I thought all fallen were arrogant warlords who cared for nothing more than fleshly pleasures and conquest." She commented.

I looked at her over my shoulder, "I've assumed the same."

She grinned.

"Alright, let's get down to business then," She lit a long, slender cigarette and sat back in her chair, crossing and propping her shapely legs up on the desk. "What is it that you want because it's evident it isn't about auras or vessels."

I smirked and moved to join her, standing on the other side of the desk. I allowed her time to admire me as if it wasn't obvious.

She licked her upper lip invitingly and raised a brow. "So?"

"This is a smart set-up you have going on here. The humans have no idea and I guess it's no secret who your biggest client is." I began.

"My biggest client or clients? You'd be surprised, actually." She grinned, sensually blowing out a steady stream of intoxicating smoke that took shape of a…cock. She flicked her tongue out, stroking the length of it as it dispersed gently.

I nodded, very impressed.

"You don't have to say anything, Cam`ael. I know why you're here." She eyed me carefully.

"Really?" I smirked.

She laughed soft and low, "I get it. The rivalry between you and Morning Star and what's at stake, along with the earth and everything on it. You don't want him to have it. None of us do. There's been a lot of talk going around though. Many are taking bets on which one of you will rise to power over all when the time comes."

"What's your bet?"

She smirked. "I'm not sure. You are the total opposite of him in many ways but…" She hesitated.

"But what?"

She shook her head, taking another long draw on her cigarette, nearly finishing half of it. She slowly blew out another perverted stream of smoke. Breasts this time.

I take it that she wasn't going to finish that thought for some reason. I watched her body language, admiring her full breasts.

"You still do business with him." I more stated than asked.

"Of course, he pays very well."

"And how long do you think that will last, once he's in power?

He won't need anything from you then. He can do it all on his own. The Earth will be his to rule and rape. What will you do to survive then?"

I wanted to make sure to plant the seed. She was thinking about that.

She had been right though, she knew exactly why I was here, which made me instantly wary. Did Elohim know or see this coming? Yes, more than likely.

"He can do it all on his own now but I won't lie to you, Cam`ael—you do seem pretty cool…on the surface, and no doubt you're very masculine and incredibly sexy. Whatever it is you're looking for, might be easier attained if…"

Here it comes.

"If what?"

"If we start hanging out more."

I raised a single brow. "That's it?"

She snickered and held up a sharp, manicured finger with a determined glimmer in her neon green eyes, "Oh, let me clarify what I mean by, hanging out more. Sex and a relationship. I don't want you to just do me, I want you. You're a powerful fallen with much influence. I find that to be an extra added bonus. If you're trying to make nice with us for whatever reason, then I'm all for it and I can guarantee that it will definitely be well worth your effort too." She smirked, leaning forward to allow her breasts to spill over onto the desk.

I sighed internally. My intuition was rising again. There was no way that this was going to be as simple as it was going so far. Something was amiss here but what?

Either way, Starling would never understand or forgive me for taking Grace up on her offer, pending I could even keep this secret. Maybe I could. It was for the greater good. However, a major part of me already felt guilty for even contemplating it. On top of everything else, if her laughter and shrieks were already painfully irritating and annoying to me, how would she sound in the throes of sex and passion? I cringed internally just thinking about that.

"I'm not interested in an exclusive relationship." I rearranged the truth. I didn't want any of them to know about Starling for the simple fact that she was wanted. More than likely, a very nice reward has been announced and offered by Morning Star for her capture.

She laughed a bit. "Who said anything about exclusive? You're an incubus. Expecting you to be exclusive is like expecting a void to refrain from mimicking a human." She leaned forward on her elbows and flashed a half grin. "I can get sex from anyone and any being at any time. But I want to be with you, right there by and on your side. I can be if you decide to challenge Morning Star and claim this world as your own."

I scoffed. "What makes you think that I want this world?"

She leaned back and eyed me. "Why wouldn't you? It's yours for the taking. Even though Morning Star is well equipped and capable, you're the only one out of the rest of your kin who has the power and ability to destroy him."

I smiled. "Now why would you want me to do that when he's supplying you all of this?" I gestured over the lavish décor.

Her lips pursed into a thin line and twitched. I think I touched a nerve.

"He going to kill you the very first moment that he's allowed." She almost seemed to warn me.

"And the reason that you're trying to tell me something that I don't already know?"

She studied me hard, bewildered by my lackadaisical attitude and nonchalance about it all.

This time I leaned forward and looked her straight in her bizarre eyes. "It isn't the fallen that are going to have to worry about scavenging for food, shelter, and a place to exist. There are thousands upon thousands of distant planets available. Planets that you nor many of the other beings subjected to this realm are able to travel to on their own. The sky arks are commanded to escort and take humans only."

She stared at me nonplussed, and then a flirtatious smirk immediately quirked her mouth. "I'm not an idiot. I know how to play the game, Cam`ael."

"I'll just bet you do."

"So what do you say? You can have me anytime and anywhere you want. I'm yours."

Wait a minute.

She was trying to ensure the safety, protection, and the continuity for her kind —behind me. Maybe I had this whole creating an alliance thing with them backwards or misunderstood. Or… maybe, this was a set-up. I was willing to go with the latter. She inhaled, her breasts rising and jiggling lusciously in the tiny, gem encrusted bustier she wore.

I didn't believe it was possible but Grace was reigniting dark and deviant thoughts in me once again. It was something that I thought I've managed to conquer since being with Starling.

Starling and my children.

I had to think about them. They were the only things that meant everything to me and I didn't want to risk losing them.

It was more than just Grace's body and her offer, it was the fact that I have been completely wrong about the Psyrens for so long, looking around at her taste in décor and literature. Granted, I couldn't stand the obnoxious, deafening screams, and laughter, much less the metal teeth. She was bit too freaky looking for my taste but I couldn't say that I wasn't intrigued. She was indeed voluptuous.

Damn. I could literally feel that corrupted part of me coming to life again, growing steadily and creeping through my veins. The temptation was rising like the pressure building beneath a large volcano. I actually wanted her, physically, and not the way I would normally engage in sexual activity with women.

Wrestling with my own desire and sin, I had to curse myself for even thinking it.

No. I couldn't. I won't.

Starling had my soul and the only one who would have my physical flesh in such an intimate way.

I had to think logically about this though. This seemed conveniently too easy. Something wasn't right about the ease of this conversation either. I didn't trust her, however, wouldn't seeing me hanging with the Psyrens completely confound Morning Star? He absolutely hated me, so surely he would no longer deal with them if he knew I was involved, would he? What did the Psyrens really have to offer in power, magick, or defense? Morning Star wasn't afraid of them and we sure as hell we weren't either. What made having them as allies such a necessity? I wondered.

XXII: STARLING

Something was pulling and dragging me deeper into the forest. Another tentacle like appendage whipped up and swiftly slipped itself around my neck, like a noose. My arms and legs were flailing wildly to find some sort of purchase of resistance. I couldn't get a steady grasp of anything let alone cut through the tentacles and free myself.

Reflexively, I brought my hand up to wedge my fingers in between my throat and the fleshy, rough tentacle, in order to keep from being strangled. I had managed to flip and turn over onto my back.

With one blade wielded, I desperately attempted to once again, bring my free hand up and cut through the tentacle. As soon as I did, another tentacle shot up from out of nowhere and wrapped itself firmly around my wrist, pulling my hand down and away from my neck.

It was scary and dangerous enough to be dragged along the

ground fast and forcefully by some unseen dark thing; but completely another not be able to do a damned thing about it because I was literally rolling, bouncing, and thumping all over the place unsteadily, like a pinball. I was trying to draw forth my fire, only to be met with more physical exhaustion and nothing was happening!

Though the fear of colliding with a large boulder or a large tree trunk passed through my mind, the burn and sting of the ground scraping my exposed skin raw beneath me began to take its toll.

I was now bound by both feet, one wrist, and my throat. I had no choice but to try and slice through the tendril around my neck again. I removed my fingers from the coiling vine around my throat in order to wield my other blade and the tentacle quickly closed the gap once I did.

I began to choke, and before I could bring my second blade up to cut it, yet another tentacle gripped my remaining free wrist. It jerked my arm down to my side forcefully, rendering that blade useless to me now too.

Not again! I refused to be taken again so soon!

My mind screamed.

I could hear the others calling after me, their frantic running footsteps pounding the ground in pursuit. Jagged earth, dry leaves and moss, rocks, and thorny brush, continued to scrape and tear at my clothes and my skin. How far back and where was this diabolical being trying to drag me?

I couldn't get enough air in me to call out to them, so that they'd know which direction I'd been taken. The tendril or tentacle thing began squeezing again, as if it knew that I was about to inhale in order to scream. It was enough to constrict but not enough to completely strangle. Suddenly, the source of the taunting voice grew closer and I was being lifted up off the ground and suspended vertically.

Both my ankles and my wrists were restricted firmly and being pulled taut in opposite directions, which left me spread eagle in mid-air. I was a trapped butterfly in a deadly, thick web—both exposed and vulnerable.

The dim woods masked the four forms into nothing more that dark silhouettes, however, one was obvious even in the minimal light.

There was no mistaking the wings, and I could see where the

tentacles had been coming from now. A dark figure of a woman stood right below me, grinning deviously as the freakishly long, living tentacles of her wild hair continued to hold me captive.

The other two appeared human on the surface to me, aside from the smell, but once their eyes began to glow it was evident that they weren't.

"Sedate her, quickly!" Tentacle head hissed.

I tried to manipulate movement around the strong tendrils secured around my wrists but it was useless. Something sticky, like a mesh netting, began to slide over my forearms, feeling like nasty insects with a million furry legs. I cringed, wanting to scream in revulsion.

Whatever it was, it was keeping me from using my blades.

My only hope was my fire but I couldn't bring it forth at all when I tried a moment ago! I had to try again. Now that I was no longer being ping-ponged along the ground, it might make it a bit easier to focus.

I inhaled deeply, concentrating hard on pulling together every ounce of energy that I had left to salvage. Despite how I felt physically after what I had done for Devlin, I couldn't afford to simply give up and attempt nothing.

My body began to quiver with fatigue in response.

Please, if I didn't have any fire left in me, I was dead.

"Open the portal now!" the fallen shouted to the other two human looking demons. They were both as black as pitch, with this exception of their irises; those were all white, surrounding a small pinpoint of black in the centers. They were the most disturbing and scariest looking beings that I've ever seen on this side so far—aside from the severe medusa woman with the possessed, monstrous, killer hair holding me hostage.

There was no way that I would be able to dodge whatever magic she planned to throw at me, and she was definitely conjuring up something big and bad.

A sickly, yellow ball of light began to form in the middle of her hands. I panicked once she raised her arm, pulled back and then launched it at me. I turned my head as if that would help or make a difference, and at the last minute, a short burst of white flames enveloped me just in time to keep most of the magic from hitting me full on.

The part of the magical, electrified field that did manage to permeate through and hit me, immediately began to take effect. I felt like passing out cold, only one heartbeat away from fainting altogether. A portal shot up a few feet from me and the darkness beyond was lit up sporadically by both red and purple flashes of lightning against a dark, steel gray sky.

I fought hard against giving in and succumbing to the magic while trying to maintain alertness for my own defense. Then I felt myself being lowered to the ground and my head began to droop forward. The urge to go to sleep was undeniably super strong but I managed to quickly catch myself and forcibly snap my head up, thankfully jarred by the impact of the ground.

Though my vision was growing blurry with fatigue, I realized that both of my hands were finally free for the moment. I had to take advantage of that, drowsy or not, or I'd never have the chance again.

My fire had burned off all of the restricting tentacles that were coiled around my wrists and ankles, along with whatever it was that attempted to suppress the movement of my arms and the use of my blades.

My instinct for survival and the fight began to rouse wildly, which made me automatically think of the unborn babies that I had to do everything in my power to protect. I tapped into every grain of remaining energy and strength that I could gather.

The demons began to advance on me quickly. Gripping my blades firmly in my hands, I waited until they were close enough before forcing fire to lick down my arm and into the length of one blade. I swiped forward in a horizontal arc, catching the first demon in the thigh.

At first, he had no clue what just happened, smiling evilly as if what I had done was pointless; until the fire began to grow, expanding, and bursting to consume his entire torso. He began screaming, instantly collapsing as the fire continued to disintegrate him completely where he fell. The smell was horrendous.

"Do it again, quickly! I won't last against her flames! Put her to sleep quickly!" tentacle woman shouted, and then right after— her agonizing scream was cut short. I heard voices, rampant footfalls all around, and I hadn't realized what had happened or who it had done it until I caught sight of all the auras.

The others had finally found me.

A sparking rope was wound tightly around her neck, chest, and waist. It burned into her flesh and she was yanked backwards, the rope pulling through and slicing her into three sections. The pieces began to smoke and melt down into a viscous, dark puddle.

Lorelei was reeling back her scyoto whip, ready to strike again.

Seeing the fate of both of her partners, the other demon began to back away from me but I was already infuriated. I launched myself to my feet, still woozy, and dove at her with blades raised and positioned to both stab and slash.

My flames were gone completely and there was no pulling forth any more. I couldn't even if I wanted to and now a different kind of exhaustion was taking over. I was going to pass out whether I liked it or not.

Seeing that potential weakness in me, the demon reclaimed confidence and watched me closely, waiting for the right moment.

She lunged herself at me, ducking low so that she could go for my legs and waist. I thought she was going to tackle me, so I only managed to slash her once across the chest, quickly bringing my other blade down on her back just as she hoisted me off of my feet while howling in pain, and threw me —straight through the portal of darkness.

I went sailing through, grunting when I landed hard. My head made contact with the ground first and an explosion of stars burst behind my eyelids. My body followed in a crunching slam, skidding, and rolling, which left me momentarily limp and discombobulated all at once.

Damn that hurt! It felt like a few ribs cracked on impact and it was confirmed when I tried to take in a deep breath. I winced and bit my lip to keep from crying out, tasting foul dirt caked to my lips. I spit and gagged, the simple act sending a spike of white hot pain ripping through my body.

I had no choice but to lie still and wait until I healed completely, feeling my bones begin to repair themselves already. The grinding was loud inside my ears and I grit my teeth to stifle the whimper trying to escape my throat.

Looking around, I didn't have to see much to realize where I was. The sky was a dark and depressing gray hue and there was no sign of the sun in sight. The air was humid and fetid, the breeze leaving an oily residue on my skin.

There were many things crawling all over the ground. Oh God…and there were other things too…things that looked like cats, but cats don't have glowing red eyes and they surely don't cackle and snicker.

The portal beyond that I had initially been thrown through, had already closed. Nothing followed me through, thank goodness, but I was beyond screwed and I had no kind of portal gems on me at all. Even if I had hall gems, I would surely be thrown right back out just as easily as I had stepped through it, pending that they would even work. Come to think of it, Lorelei's house gems no longer worked either.

One of the mysterious and potentially deadly creatures began to stalk towards me slowly, scenting me and making the decision whether or not to regard me as prey.

I winced. My bones were still fusing back together but it didn't stop me from backing up and sliding away from it anyway. Keeping my eyes on it, I readied myself to respond to any sudden moves it decided to make. However, that was becoming increasingly difficult for me, being that the effects of the strong magic that had been thrown at me was still working. All I wanted to desperately do right this second, was to close my eyes and sleep.

The closer it got, the more I could see just how big it actually was. It was about the size of a medium-sized tiger —and there were…many of them, all slowly surrounding me.

The strange creature gave a guttural growl and then crouched low, ready to pounce. I quickly pulled myself up to my knees painfully just as it leapt. Swaying slightly, I held my arm up and bent across me protectively with the hilt side pointing towards me. It was a natural defensive action.

When faced with certain death, or painful dismemberment, one was often surprised by the fighting and defensive expertise naturally hidden within.

I jabbed forward, plunging my blade deep into its soft belly and sliced upwards. The beast bellowed as the full, fifteen inches cut through with the ease and power of a laser beam through flesh. Foul, putrid viscera began to spill from its wound and ooze warmly over my hand as it fell onto its side, twitching. I was far too sleepy to be disgusted with both the feel and the smell of it.

And then, they all began to swarm in for the attack at once. All I found myself aware of, besides the angry mob of demonic creatures about to jump me, was the sound of rapidly approaching hoof beats hitting the ground rhythmically. I barely managed to call out, *"Cam...,"* right before I fell forward face down, finally collapsing in helpless exhaustion.

XXIII. CAM`AEL

I needed more time. This was a bit confounding. There were many things that I didn't quite understand or trust. This seemed...way too simple. I wondered how Ry and Mac were faring.

"Ry, Mac. How does it look?"

"I'll get back with you in an hour...or four." Ry replied.

"It looks really, really good, Cam." Mac answered back.

I sighed. *"Be extremely careful and do not get caught up."* I warned them.

That's when I heard a faint voice calling out to me.

"Cam." It was definitely Starling.

I stiffened. *"Starling? What's wrong? What's happening?"* I was instantly on my feet.

Grace stood up and watched me inquisitively.

"What's the matter?" She asked, tensing in response to my abrupt movement.

Starling didn't reply.

"Starling?"

No answer.

"Answer me! Are you hurt?" I was becoming frantic.

Something was definitely wrong. The dark lust that was already swirling in me, immediately shifted into dark anger and it was rising fast at the thought of anything bad happening to her. She was supposed to be at the hall and that sudden whisper of my name, with no further words or response, meant only one thing to me.

"Damnit, Starling, you're about to make me break my promise to you if you don't assure me that you're ok right, now!" I waited for a few more seconds.

Still no reply.

Divine Hall or not—this Fallen was about to go full- fucking-fledged demon.

~~~****~~~

With guns blazing is a popular human cliché, but in my case, it meant darkness waiting to be unleashed.

I wasn't going to go in completely unprepared and clueless though. First, I cloaked myself, and in my spirit form I skirted the perimeter, attempting to find a breach in the protective shield surrounding the hall and the wide acreage of land around it.

My proximity automatically gained the attention of all the guards and other warriors who were out on the training fields, and all over the acres of land beyond, which housed the grazing and riding animals, and most of their gardens.

Darkness formed an electric bolt of lightning that crackled and curled along each of my forearms and fists as I wielded my sword.

"Starling! I'm here, please tell me that you're alright before I do something...very destructive!" I attempted once again.

All remained silent on her end.

With a roar of anger and rage, I stormed swiftly in between bushes, boulders, and above and in between trees, uprooting and tearing through everything like a wild, invisible tornado and ready to cut down anyone who dared to cross my path.

Curiously, warriors, guards, bizarre white creatures, and many of the older men and women were all crowded together on the North lawn, looking out at something about fifty yards away. Whatever it was, it was hidden beneath a canopy of green leaves. There were three female warriors huddled around a young girl lying on the ground, apparently injured in some way.

I automatically thought the worst until I realized that she wasn't Starling. However, the brunette looking in my direction was the same one from the club and from last night. She and a few others, along with the small animals immediately sensed my presence.

The energy building from my magick was pulsing ferociously, awaiting my direction and release. and I know that they could all feel it in the air.

I didn't care.

Remaining cloaked, I purposefully slammed down onto the ground hard and landed in a low crouch. The impact shook the ground with a brief seismic rumble that was surely felt if not heard by everyone, even those on the sanctified land of the hall. The group of unprotected, female warriors behind me were knocked clean off of their feet. I hadn't meant for them to feel the brunt of my attack and rage but it couldn't be helped. Trees shook, some falling completely over, and chunks of rocks tumbled from larger boulders.

I fully released all of the pent up darkness in a single, supersonic, vibrating wave that collided thunderously against their invisible barrier of protection. That enraged me even more. I already knew that I wouldn't be able to get through but it wasn't going to deter me.

The warriors and the guards, braced and readied themselves by drawing and wielding their weapons to both defend and strike back.

"No!" A female screamed from behind me but I ignored her, unleashing another wave of power anyway. I would keep on attacking until the damn shield gave and possibly shattered if that's what it took.

The warriors were stunned, unsure of who or where I was, and searching frantically for a signature. I studied them all, one by one —and then, my eyes locked on his.

The fucking Seraphim cocked his head, focusing on my location and studying my signature with his lightning Bo gripped and ready for attack. He began to whisper, chanting magical defensive verses. Slowly, I began to materialize, grinning at him malignantly to incite his challenge. His expression turned into pensive astonishment, interrupting the flow of his words.

"It's him! That's him! I knew it! He's bound himself to Starling and now he's come for her!" The seraphim exclaimed to the other warriors and elders while pointing at me with his Bo.

Then, he dexterously began to invoke his weak magic with the fingers of one hand while I was gearing up to strike and counter whatever he intended to throw my way. I waited anxiously for him to set one pinky toe outside of the protected, sanctified barrier.

I clenched my teeth as more dark power began to refuel my fury. I was absolutely ready to yank his spine out through his mouth with my bare hands.

The expressions of the elders turned to brief dismay but not disbelief. They didn't say a word to the seraphim in response and they were all quite calm. Interesting, and I now knew why. The girl had spoken the truth about the other fallen after all.

"You shouldn't have come." She then whispered sharply to me.

"Jamie, what's going on?" the Asian girl stood up and asked while wielding her weapon, and then stepping cautiously towards the brunette.

Just then, lightning crashed down, striking the earth in pop of sparks, dirt, and grass. Aliks appeared between both me and the warriors lined up on the hall grounds beyond.

"Stop this!" he hissed at me, but he was glancing over at all of them as well.

"Where is she!?" I growled telepathically to him.

"Revealing yourself was a grave mistake! Do not get yourself destroyed. I was commanded to intervene this time, which means that what you are about to do will result in serious consequences for both sides, so put the weapon away and back down!" Aliks demanded.

"Stay out of this. If you want to continue to stand in between us then be my guest, but let me remind you that I really don't like you very much."

"Do as Elohim has commanded and cease this attack!" He returned out loud in a booming voice that absolutely did not match his slight, physical appearance. His tone took on an authoritative commandment and his eyes began to shimmer brightly.

The glory in his voice, along with the light in his eyes, made me curse and turn away. Though I was furious and I had no intentions of leaving without Starling, I had no choice but to obey.

The brunette girl was stunned, her mouth hung open as she helplessly watched the scene unfold. The look in her eyes seemed to be pleading, wondering why I allowed them to see who I was, and to beg me to back off for my own safety and the lives of the other warriors. But there was something else going on here. Why were they out here like this at all while so many others simply watched them from afar? At least allow me beat the shit out of that Seraphim then.

The Seraphim ceased his efforts in conjuring magick, though he was glaring at me and still caught up in the heat of what would have been a quick fight. He stood in incredulous confusion once Aliks appeared and began to command.

The female warriors behind me joined the brunette, all bewildered. The young, thin, dark-skinned female who had been unconscious initially, slowly began to rouse.

"Where is she?" I asked Aliks in a low, sinister tone. Violence was ebbing in my core, ready to burst forth if he didn't answer me or bring her out here himself right this instant.

"You're going to ruin everything! Now get a grip and calm down." Aliks answered back mentally and firmly.

I was seething beyond the point of continuing on in a mental conversation. *"I don't care about ruining any damned thing, just get her for me!"*

"How are you even aware that anything is wrong at all?" Aliks wondered.

Damn. I was giving everything away in my irrational anger. He was right. I'd better calm down. Who knows what I've already compromised as it is by appearing in front of them. I was sure that they already knew Starling had become soul-tied to me. Her shunning would absolutely be my fault now but I didn't care. I'll take on the full consequences so she won't have to.

"We don't know. She was pulled into the trees by something that was apparently looking for her. The others that were here with us all went after her…," the brunette began to explain with a thumb in the direction of a path that had been roughly disturbed by an imprint on the ground. A trail of some sort.

I immediately thought the worst and a sinking, almost helpless feeling washed over me. Shit! I had no time to waste. There was no telling where she was or who had her. Whatever happened, she had either been rendered silent by a knock-out curse, or she was badly injured. I didn't want to think about that possibility and I was determined to go to any and all measures to find and rescue her. Her aura should make my search a bit easier.

Judging by the looks on the weary faces of the three warriors and a female Seraphim, who were all emerging from the trees without Starling, I felt another rampage building quickly. Please Elohim, don't let her be in Morning Star's hands. I will do anything for you to help me out on this one. She's carrying our children!

The blonde girl had been crying and the other two males looked devastated. The female Seraphim looked at me with resolute surprise. They were all dirty with the scent of fresh, putrid demon blood, still clinging to their clothing.

They stopped short, ready to defend and attack once again and unsure what to make of both my and Aliks' presence.

I turned to Aliks just then, my jaw working and my eyes glowing with fury.

"I don't have time to lose or waste. Tell me where to look for her. Tell me exactly where she is, now!" I breathed deeply. My red anger making me shake in my effort to try and suppress it and remain calm.

I knew that Aliks would be able to pinpoint her location faster than I could, simply because Elohim could see all. He knew and he could tell Aliks.

Aliks glanced at the warriors behind me. "Do not break your oaths," then he turned to regard at the line of guards, warriors, and elders who stood watching pensively in hushed conversations among each other. "You have my word that there is no imminent danger or threat. You stand within the protected hall grounds, so do not retaliate or attack. That is a direct order."

"Yeah, but we're not." I heard the red haired one whisper.

"We aren't in any danger either." Jamie told them all though her eyes remained fixated on me in fascination.

The rest of the small group behind us remained befuddled and shocked by her assurance.

"How do you know that?" The blonde girl asked her though she kept her eyes on me.

The seraphim continued to watch both me and the brunette girl inquisitively, as if trying to figure out a riddle unsuccessfullyThen, like a fool, he stepped out of the protected zone and began to jog over to the group of warriors behind me.

My muscles flexed and twitched, watching him with the eyes of a hunter on its prey.

"Don't you even think it much less do anything." Aliks warned me, already sensing my intent.

The elders were all completely perplexed by Aliks' declaration.

"What's going on?" The male Seraphim asked once he joined the others.

"This doesn't concern you. Return to the hall." Aliks told him.

He appeared affronted.

"You'd better go, Spencer. We're all shunned, remember?" Jamie told him.

They were shunned? All of them? But why? Did that mean that Starling had been too? Did they voluntarily do it...for her? The anger began to simmer down in me just a fraction upon realizing what had just taken place.

His jaw was working when he glanced at the girl on the ground, who was fully awake and sitting up quietly now. Then his eyes connected with mine. I hoped that he could read the: 'I will absolutely fuck you up.' message blazing in my eyes.

The seraphim, Spencer, turned to take one last look at the line of warriors, guards, and elders still standing on the hall grounds in silence.

"You guys are going to need more than one seraphim, no offense Kaia," he smirked at the female seraphim who smiled at him in return.

"I guess I'm willing to accept the price of joining you guys too." He then stated, his eyes then traveled from the female Seraphim, to the brunette girl who ran to and hugged him tightly.

"How do you know about this fallen?" I heard him whisper into her ear.

Aliks sighed deeply. "Is this your choice?" He asked all of the warriors.

They were initially silent, looking at each other for complete affirmation. I was quickly growing agitated again.

"Yes, and we need to rescue Starling. As long as she is shunned, then we are too. We have Devlin back now thanks to her, so we can't let her go out like that." The blonde girl said with conviction, waiting for someone else to oppose.

No one did.

I looked at the dark-skinned girl with curiosity. What did the blonde one mean by that? What had Starling done to help her? Her generosity and sacrifice was admirable but it had gotten her into trouble yet again. She was the one that the dark ones wanted the most out of all of them. That was something she apparently didn't quite understand yet.

The loyalty among her friends in regard to her was touching, and I completely both respected and understood it.

"Alright then, come with me. I am told to assist with a temporary protective sanctuary for you all." Aliks announced, and then he proceeded to head further into the trees, leading the shunned warriors east towards the Eternal waters.

The warriors began to fall into step with Aliks, watching me warily with the exception of the brunette. One of the male warriors hoisted the black girl over his shoulder to carry her. She appeared to be too weak to even stand.

"Aliks..." I growled with insistence again.

"Starling will be fine." he relayed back to me.

XXIV. STARLING

"*Any* day now, sleeping beauty." A soft, soothing voice drifted in from an unknown direction.

I'm still alive? I had expected to be ripped to ribbons and in the lower digestive tract of a demon cat by now, or even imprisoned in the lair of a band of demons.

Who did the voice belong to?

My eyes snapped open and I picked my head up, taking in a deep breath— only to end up gagging. The air was thick, disgusting, and foul. I was hoping to find myself in my room at the hall, or some safe place by some miracle, but no. I was still somewhere in the Darklands, face down on the ground where I had originally keeled over from extreme exhaustion.

Upon seeing the grisly, still smoking, oily, black, dead carcasses of the demonic beasts from last night all around me, I gasped and quickly scrambled to my feet. I immediately began to cough spastically from the acrid stench. I held a hand over my mouth and nose, turning to search for the source of the voice.

Instantly, I squealed and recoiled. "Gross!" I jerked my filthy hand away from my face and tried to desperately wipe it somewhere, anywhere to get the crud off. It was coated with something crusty and black, more disgusting and foul than the air and carcasses around me.

"About time." Someone chuckled, apparently tickled by my situation, which annoyed me even more.

I whirled around with my weapons wielded, only to be shocked and ecstatic.

Aon!

She was decked out in a white jumpsuit and sweet, hot pink Chuck Taylors. Her glittering pink hair was swept to the side as if frozen in an invisible breeze with a ton of gel and hairspray. She was so out of place, sitting atop a large, charred boulder and smirking, with her slim but obviously deadly swords resting over each of her knees.

Had she done all of this? Slaughtered everything within a few yards radius that had been coming for me all by herself? Well, she was an angel. I would think she would have at least picked me up and carried me to safety afterwards though.

I pulled in my blades with a quick look around at the depressing and desolate landscape. There was no life or light here, yet the air of evil hung heavy. I wiped the disgusting taste from my lips with my non-offensively tainted hand, while grimacing. I needed a long soak in a bath or bleach.

"How long was I out?"

"Long enough for me to start feeling like a creeper watching you sleep. All rested up?" She asked.

I was. In fact, I felt really good, way better than normal actually.

I nodded. "Nice shoes." I then complimented.

Her laughter was like the sound of soft chimes. "Starling, you are quite an exceptional yet quirky one by far. I won't even ask how you ended up out here but careless and foolish definitely comes to mind." She scolded.

Careless and foolish? Did she know what happened? Of course she did. Where had she when we needed her though?

"I wouldn't call helping a fellow warrior careless and foolish. No one knew there were dark ones out there waiting. It was an apparent ambush." I replied.

She leapt agilely off the rock and landed gracefully on her feet.

"Helping her by doing what?" Aon fixated her supernatural eyes pointedly on me.

I pursed my lips and shrugged a shoulder, at a loss for an explanation while shaking my head.

"I don't know. I wanted them to see that she was still one of us. That my fire wouldn't kill her."

"Ah, I see. I understand the intent and the logic. So, did it work?" She raised both brows as if she genuinely didn't know the result of my actions.

I sighed, turning away from her and staring down at the black dirt at my feet. "No." I said glumly.

She chuckled. "Precisely. And rescuing a comrade isn't what I'm referring to. Let's get out of here. I can't tell you how many creatures, demons, and fallen that I've had to destroy while you were sleeping. Thankfully, this area is still quite a ways from the really dangerous territories within the Dark lands. I need to make sure that you understand and are aware of a few things first, and then we need to make sure that your man hasn't gone berserk and started a war over you." She then said.

My man?...Cam!? Berserk? Damn. I called out to him before I passed out. I can only imagine what he was thinking, especially since I wasn't able to respond.

Before I could begin to call out and assure him that I was alright, Aon pulled me through a portal of light that nearly blinded me.

~~~~****~~~~

We were literally inside of a clear, white space. A space that appeared domed all around, except for the ground.

There were no visible walls or doors and I couldn't see or hear anything else beyond this place.

"Cam?" I called out anyway while I had the chance.

There was no answer.

Immediate panic began to set in, remembering that Aon had mentioned him potentially starting a war. Had he done something to get himself killed?!

"Cam, please tell me that you're okay. I'm not hurt, and I'm safe now."

Silence.

I really wanted to ask Aon about him, to tell her to take me to him now but I remained quiet about it, going crazy with worry inside of my own mind.

"What is this thing or place?" I asked.

"We are inside of an absolute sphere of light. It's a miniscule place but one of complete protection and privacy. Here, you can see nor hear nothing except for me, and the same goes for anyone else out of this range."

Of course. This bubble must be blocking the mental communication link between us. I desperately hoped that was the explanation.

"Divine warriors are chosen specifically for various reasons. But you must never forget that you, Starling, were given an extremely important purpose and role when you were chosen," Aon began, "That is why you are different from the others and why you are being pursued more so than anyone else. Because of that, you must not allow yourself to be caught or killed so easily. Some things can't be helped but overall, you need to be more cautious about your surroundings and stop being so gullible. You're going to need to pay special and close attention to what I am about to explain to you. More importantly, you need to make sure that you remember all of it, got it?" She was holding up an index finger.

I've been chosen for a specific purpose and role? I'm getting tired of hearing that and not getting any additional reason or explanations past that. I swallowed hard and nodded with apprehension, anxiety, and curiosity all at the same time.

"What's the reason?" I had to know now.

"I don't know. I've only been instructed to make you aware of that much."

I sighed with disappointment. Of course.

"But…I've already accepted being shunned. I'm not a divine warrior anymore, am I?"

Aon shrugged lightly, "I don't know. Are you?" She raised brow.

Was that a trick question?

"I— I want to be. I don't feel different or anything and my brandings are still silver." I observed my arms.

"Well, you did take an oath." Aon reminded me.

Guilt burned my face as I turned away. "I know."

"What do you feel in your heart?"

"The oath still means something. Nothing has changed for me."

"Then there is your answer." Aon smiled.

Okay. So it was that simple, huh? Something has changed though. Being shunned wasn't a good thing. Oh yeah, other than being an open vessel now.

"First things first. You already know that you have the most powerful essence a divine warrior can have, not to mention your weapons," Aon began.

"What do you think fuels your essence, meaning your hallowed fire?" She then asked.

I shrugged a shoulder. "My emotions?"

Aon shook her head.

"Wrong. No wonder you're all over the place with it. Let me try again, what fuels your emotions?" She began to pace around me like a lecturing teacher.

I thought for a moment. "I don't know. My reaction to things and people, I guess."

"Think, Starling. What happened to you after using so much of your essence on your fellow warrior?"

I did think. I felt weak and extremely sleepy.

"I was…really tired."

Aon grinned, "You mean on the verge of passing out?" She sort of corrected me.

"Exactly."

Aon nodded. "And exhaustion comes from the depletion of…" She gestured with her hands, waiting for me to finish the sentence.

I felt stupid.

I sighed, understanding hitting me all at once.

"Energy."

She smiled and pointed at me, "Bingo! You have an essence not a talent. Essences are meant to be used as a very last resort, meaning sparingly when really needed. Granted, it is easier in order to kill many dark ones at once but at what cost? What good does it do if you are unconscious just as you've experienced?"

I pursed my lips and nodded. That made sense.

"Using it wisely, however, in conjunction with your deific blades, is the smartest way to gain mastery over it. Though emotions do require some level of energy, it has nothing to do with your fire and it will take much practice and patience to separate the two." Aon explained.

So, Cam had been right. It doesn't have anything to do with my emotions. I don't know why I doubted that he wouldn't know or understand that.

"Now, turn around." Aon instructed.

I did slowly, surprised to see five tapered candles, all aligned and simply floating in mid-air.

"Now, light them with your fire." Aon ordered.

I glanced at her unsurely. My energy had been replenished, so this was a simple task.

"Okay." I said, approaching the floating candles.

"What are you doing?" Aon asked with a hand on her hip.

I turned to look back at her and frowned in confusion. "Lighting the candles just like you said to do."

"From here." She ordered, pointing down at the space next to her.

My brows furrowed together. "From there?" I pointed.

"Yes."

How in the world was I going to do that? I wondered.

"Well it isn't like you were specific." I mumbled while retreating to the space beside her.

A smiled spread across her youthful, pretty face.

"Okay." I began, facing the candles once again.

"Go for it." She encouraged.

I had no idea how to proceed let alone what to do. The pressure was on and I was both clueless and nervous.

Focusing my energy on bringing forth my fire, without feeling any particular strong emotion, proved almost effortless this time for me, much to my surprise.

However, standing there with flames licking around my hand and fingertips, and trying to figure out how I was going to get it from here to the candle wicks, stumped me completely.

"Very good. It's becoming familiar to you now, I see. Well?"

"I can't. I don't know how." I was frustrated.

"Hmm," Aon studied my fire. "Dilemma." She grinned with her hands behind her back and rocking back and forth on her heels.

I paused, thinking. "The only way I can do it, is if I throw it." I sighed.

Her thin pink brows rose, "Aha! Now there's a solution. Alright, go for it." She said expectantly.

I waved and shook my hand at the candles. Nothing happened.

I tried to think of myself lighting the candles but the flames remained flickering around my hand.

I sighed as tears began forming in the corners of my eyes. "I don't know how."

She studied me with no hint as to what was going through her mind.

"Oh my. From what I'm hearing, it looks like Cam`ael is in trouble. I think he needs you."

I felt an instant swell of panic grip my heart. Tears began to fall and my heart thumped wildly at the thought.

"I'll take you to him…once you light those candles." Aon maintained.

"I can't! I tried to but I can't! If Cam is in trouble, I need to go to him!" I yelled at her.

She was unaffected by my tone, my worry, and my panic over Cam. I wiped the tears from my face and eyes.

Then, her face turned serious. Aon was no longer, witty, playful, and as cheerful as she had been up until now.

"Then light the candles, Starling. This is very important for you to learn how to do."

I bit my lip in anguish and frustration. The fire surrounding my hand began to increase, consuming the energy from my emotions.

How could it not be linked to my emotions? I didn't understand.

I stared at each candle, feeling aggravated.

I zoned in on each individual wick. I had no idea how to do this. In my anger, I pulled my arm back, balling up my fist as if I were about to throw a baseball, and then pitched my arm forward with all my might—and to my surprise, a stream of white fire released itself from my hand, like a long-tailed comet.

The flames engulfed all of the candles, creating a magnificent oracle of fire. After a few moments, once the fire died down, each candle remained flickering with its own single, white, flame.

Aon smiled and slowly clapped her hands. "Very good. But you must remember one thing. Stop making it about your emotions and frustration. It is a weapon and you should be able to bring it forth and throw it at any given moment. This is how you will be able to use it without exhausting your energy. Once your fire has touched darkness, it will continue to spread and destroy anything consisting of darkness in its path."

I wiped the last of my streaming tears. I think I understood now.

I wondered about the babies at this moment then. They were part of Cam. Darkness. How would this affect them? Has it already?

"What about…you know." I gently placed a hand on my abdomen, "Should I be seeing a doctor or a succor…" I asked. I was unsure if Aon was the one that I should be mentioning this to because it wasn't like she didn't know. Who else would I be talking to about it anyway?

She moved forward and gingerly placed her hand on my abdomen. I felt a wash of cleansing energy flash through me at her touch. I tensed. What had she just done?

"Everything is fine. You're superhuman and immortal. Your body can withstand a lot more than a mortal can."

I felt instant relief. "So, I'm…"

"Do you want to know what the sexes are?" Her celestial eyes twinkled.

She knows that they're twins? And she knows their sexes?

I was both excited and curious but hesitant.

"Why is all this happening? I mean, is it supposed to be happening?" I had to ask.

Aon sighed, her lips pressing together. "What is allowed and what is created from that allowance are two different things." She began.

I didn't understand.

"Truthfully, I can't answer that question for you because I don't know. Normally, I can't interfere with the order of events. I'm not a guardian, a messenger, or even an advising angel. I'm a ninth level Seraphim soldier, which means that my job is to battle darkness wherever I see it, nothing more. This is new for me. I have been commanded to both help and watch over you. I appear this way to you because this image is most pleasing and relatable. We don't always appear in human form." She looked at me thoughtfully and smiled,

"You'd be surprised how many mortal people have encountered an angel several times over in their lives at some point without even realizing it. Immortal or not, even as a divine warrior you wouldn't be able to handle the level of glory that is my true form. The same goes for Aliks."

I looked at her in wonder and awe and simply nodded.

"Though Cam`ael has fallen, as a former angel, he knows much of how Elohim works. With that being said, nothing occurs without purpose or reason. All I can tell you is that when the time comes, both you and Cam`ael will know and understand it. But for now, you'll need to know and understand the rules and the universal laws that now apply to you as an immortal human, especially since you have officially become an open vessel. Let's practice this skill a few more times, I'd like you to be more precise in your aim. Afterwards, we can promptly return to the Spirit Realm."

All I could do was stare at Aon, dazzled by her glory. I wasn't even sure what to say or how to respond to all of that.

"Just a second. So, all this has been allowed to happen for a reason though, right?"

"That part is obvious."

I sighed, sort of satisfied with everything she explained to me.

Then I shook my head fervently, "I don't wanna know. The sexes I mean."

"You love the element of surprise? As you wish, I can accept that." Aon smiled with a slight bow of her head.

No, wait! Now it was going to really drive me crazy since I know that she knows. I bit my lip in consternation and then blurted, "Wait, what about Cam? I don't want anyone on either side to get hurt over me! If we wait any longer then…"

She sighed and interjected, "Cam is alright, however, upon your return there are going to be some major issues to work out."

I narrowed my eyes at her tersely, "I thought angels weren't supposed to lie?"

"I didn't lie. He was truly about to face trouble, that is until Aliks intervened." She grinned slyly and winked.

I exhaled, pursing my lips.

"Then what issues are you talking about?" I wanted to know.

"You'll see." Aon simpered.

XXV. CAM`AEL

"You may as well come too, Cam`ael. The cat's out of the bag." Aliks relayed to me with the line of warriors in procession behind him.

I had other things to do. I was about to remind him of those things, as well as the assistance that he had been ordered to provide for me, until something urged me to go along with whatever he had in mind.

These warriors have defected. I wasn't entirely sure of what that would ultimately mean for them unless they chose darkness instead, but they haven't. Not yet anyway.

Though I was still angry, I relented. If Aliks was saying that Starling was fine, I knew that he was telling me the truth. But where was she? What was happening that I still couldn't communicate with her telepathically? There was only one reason that I could think of and it had my curiosity on edge.

I followed them to the northern part of the shore, which ran like a wide swath of curving white sand with shimmering pebbles, flanking the Eternal Lake.

Several small caves lined the rocky ridge that formed drastic angles of carved rock; all jutting out over the water, and complete with waterfalls that cascaded gently over their ledges.

Aliks created a protective dome in a clearing big enough for all of them to fit inside. The invisible barrier was made up of safeguarding symbols, designed to keep all the of the dark ones away and out. I had no choice but to stand along the outskirts and observe.

I could still clearly see and hear them all whispering, just as they could see and hear me.

"Cam, do you still need us? What happened? Where did you go? What happened to hanging with the Psyrens?" Ry reached out.

"It's nothing now. As a matter of fact, I'd like for all of you, with the exception of Atiro, to stand by. I may need you all in a bit but not for battle."

"Alright then. How did it go with Grace?"

"I'm not sure. I may need more time. I don't know how to go about establishing anything remotely trusting with the Psyrens."

"Well, you never know..."

A single brow rose, *"Come again?"*

Ry chuckled. *"I think I'm in love, Cam."*

Ry always had jokes and something sarcastic to say but I know for a fact that he would never joke about that.

"With...who?"

"Man, I can't believe I've wasted all this time hating them."

I grew contemptuous. *"Who?"* I repeated.

"You know, Draea." He said matter-of-factly as if I should have known.

"You're kidding. Snake girl? Whatever happening to shoving it into any and all available orifices?"

Ry laughed. *"The snake should be so lucky. She's been one of the only ones who could withstand looking into my eyes. She thinks they're wicked righteous."*

"Really? You may have just found your soul mate, Ry but I still want you to be extremely careful around her and the rest of them. You know the effect that women, lust, and love on us males."

"Yeah, I know. Anyway, I'll let everyone know, so holla if you need us."

"Alright."

Well, I've seen and heard of far more bizarre things during my existence. Though I would love for Ry to find what I had with Starling, I wished it wasn't with a damned Psyren of all beings. I guess we can't help who we feel attracted to and love. I was a prime example of that.

I listened in on all of the hushed conversations and barely there whispers that were as clear as a bell to my ears. The male warriors worked to gather large logs and various materials to build a fire.

They were all very guarded and wary of me, understandably. The brunette girl, Jamie, was offering no other explanation or information, even to the seraphim when he kept insisting. She had an arm around the mute, dark-skinned girl to console her.

The girl kept her large brown eyes fixated on me. Her eyes were haunted, full of loathing butt she was terrified of me. I recognized that look. Humans that encountered the horrors of what the dark ones perpetrated often looked like that all the time. In her case though, I was sure there was an entirely different reason for the fear and hate in her eyes.

The female Seraphim kept watching me too, as if trying to read my intentions and signature. Good luck with that, I chuckled to myself.

"All of our portal gems are useless marbles now." The blonde girl frowned while crushing something in her hand. The powdery crystal-like substance blew away in the breeze.

"We can't even teleport to our own homes anymore."

"I still can't believe what happened. I mean, I can't believe that they'd cast us out for helping Devlin and Starling like that. They clearly saw that she was no longer afflicted. It makes no sense to me." The Asian girl commented.

"Doesn't matter. We're on our own now, whatever that means." The male with the blonde hair stated as he began to stack rocks in a circular formation to mark the fire pit.

"Lira is the main one I'm concerned about." The dark haired male then said.

"I'll be ok and I'll try not to be a burden." She scowled at him, "Where is Starling? Is she going to be okay?" She then asked Aliks.

"She's safe." Aliks assured.

"That isn't what I meant by that, Lira. And try not to speak out loud too much." The dark haired male said to her with a nod of his head in my direction.

I smirked when the petite girl blushed and turned away from me.

"Why is he standing there? I don't understand. What's going on here? He's clearly a fallen. How long has Starling been messing around with him anyway?" The seraphim pointed at me and asked.

No one bothered to address or answer him.

"I will vouch that he is no threat, meaning that he is not interested in fighting with, possessing, or afflicting anyone." Aliks replied looking sternly at me.

I watched the Seraphim with a dark glimmer in my eyes. Something moved in the trees beyond their protected dome. The aura was one of theirs.

"I can vouch for that too." Jamie finally spoke up.

They all paused their tasks to look at her, including the haunted warrior.

"How do you know?" The blonde male asked.

"I can definitely vouch for him too." A familiar voice said, just before he emerged from the trees.

"Durien!" The petite, dark-haired girl shot up and ran over to him, hugging him firmly.

Durien smiled, taking her in for a brief hug and then nodded at me.

"I would ask what happened and what's going on but I think I already know."

"Does this mean you've also voluntarily accepted shunning?" The dark haired male asked.

"I go where I want to go. I don't live at the hall anymore anyway but technically…yeah, I guess so." Durien glanced my way briefly again.

"But you're a brander." The girl mentioned.

Durien smiled at her, "And you're a scout. From the looks of it, we have fighters, a succor, and some seraphim too. I'd say we're set." He pointed out with positive enthusiasm.

Durien did make an interesting observation.

All of the others contemplated his assessment and then nodded in agreement, with the exception of the seraphim.

Then, he suddenly spoke up again, "You also vouch for him too? He's a fallen and they're not to be trusted, they're manipulative liars, they're…"

"They're not like the other ones." Jamie completed for him to shut him up.

I'm really beginning to like her.

He looked at her as if she'd just slapped him, but then again, he was probably used to it given the way she knocked him out with ease last nightfall. I chuckled to myself thinking back to that scene.

"How can you even say that?" He looked at her with disgust.

Jamie stood with her hands on her hips, and then she glanced at me, "Show them your light power." She directed at me.

This time, everyone, except for Durien looked at her in inquisitive shock and then back at me expectantly.

Muscles flexing, the seraphim looked at me with astonishing anticipation, waiting for me to do it.

"You have light power?" The blonde girl asked softly in surprise.

"How is that possible?" The seraphim demanded to know from Aliks.

"How are many things possible?" Aliks responded simply.

"Hey, someone is missing." Durien commented, looking around the group.

"Missing but safe." Aliks assured.

Durien nodded, glancing at me briefly because he already knew that Starling had been among them.

"Cool, so we've also got one with super deadly weapons and an essence to match." He then smiled at Lira.

"But what are we gonna do now? We can't re-enter the hall and our portal gems don't allow us back into the human realm or to our homes anymore, which sucks because I loved my home and now, none of us have any clothes or anything." The blonde girl said.

Durien thought for a moment and then looked at me briefly before directing his attention back to all of them. "We may have some options but it requires both an open mind and a mutual understanding." He took in a deep breath and cleared his throat.

"I agree with Durien. What happens from here on out is based on many things. Granted, I don't recommend that you make deals with just any being. You all would fare much better in the human realm. At least there, you're protected by universal laws and you are free to go anywhere you'd like — though safety lies in numbers for you at this point. You've all become open vessels, which means that even though you continue to maintain your weapons, essences, and talents, you can also easily become compromised and swayed. You have no other recourse than to seek out assistance but I cannot interfere as an angel."

"What are you saying?" the female seraphim asked Aliks.

Aliks turned to me, "Are you willing to offer your assistance?"

A flat out 'No' was the first thing on the tip of my tongue when I glanced over each of their faces. Half of them were confused as it is already.

"They never stated that they wanted my help." I pointed out.

There was an unsure 'No' in response, and one 'I don't know', but far more 'Yes's', which surprised me. The dark-skinned girl remained silent.

"We don't have a choice. In fact, this collaboration has been a long time coming. It's necessary. In my opinion, we're not gonna win this war against the dark ones without them. I know Cam`ael. Actually, I've been knowing him and his friends for quite a while now. I've been there to see him and his friends quick to jump in and help us fight many times over. They didn't expect and certainly got nothing in return for their help, not even a thanks. Believe it or not, we both share a common enemy. I'm not gonna tell you guys who to trust and who not to trust, that's up to you. But I will say this. He is the reason for Starling making it safely to be rebirthed as a warrior, and he's also the reason that she returned safe and sound after saving Jamie. So you can think what you want but for me, actions speak louder than anything else. I trust him and his circle of friends. They're not like all the others we've come across in the past. We'll need them." Durien explained.

I sincerely appreciated his words. I noted each one of their expressions and the sudden shift in body language and temperatures, regarding his speech. I could tell that it definitely made an impact. Aliks nodded in approval at Durien.

The seraphim grimaced, repulsed at me. "Cam`ael, huh? True God given name?" He inquired suspiciously.

"And what was yours? Oh, that's right. You have no memory of it. Instead you've chosen a flimsy name, which means servile or slave, or in a more fitting human term, a helpless pussy." I grinned wickedly.

Aliks shot me a glare of warning and reproach. *"Stop negating progress, and lose the name calling and dark sarcasm!"*

I could hear the low snickers that were coming from all of the male warriors.

The seraphim's lips tightened into a thin line and he narrowed his eyes, "At least I didn't disobey and fall with dishonor."

"It's never too late." I replied with spite.

The red-haired girl sighed, shaking her head and rolling her eyes, "Really? Males are all alike no matter what being it is, I swear."

The other girls all agreed heartedly.

"I wouldn't make an enemy out of him at this point." Jamie warned him.

"He's already an enemy." The seraphim sneered.

"I'm begging you, allow me to zap him good, just one time." I implored Aliks.

"That would be counter-productive." Aliks replied.

"For who?"

Aliks flashed me a wry gaze.

"I find it disturbing that you both have been colluding with him and his friends all this time." the seraphim then directed at Durien and Jamie.

Durien turned to him with a stern expression. "You call it colluding, I call it creating a strong alliance."

"Cam`ael and those in his circle are the only ones who will be able to create portals for you to move around. It's something to consider but I am merely advising you all. Alliances will be one of your greatest assets as the dark army continues to grow. I say, that if Cam`ael is offering to assist, you'd all be wise to consider it." Aliks added.

"I never offered that. Don't put words in my mouth."

"Work with me here."

I sighed heavily in thought. *"I'll be willing to offer shelter. I'll find them something in the human realm, once Starling has returned safe and sound."*

"I told you that she was fine. She is with Aon, and they will be returning at any moment now. Aon knows what has transpired and she knows where we are now."

I paused again, finally giving in — painfully.

"Portals and a very temporary shelter isn't all that I will offer. You guys have been trained quite thoroughly but it's not good enough, not if you're plan to last against the dark armies. You'll need to learn smarter and more effective counter-attacks, vulnerabilities, and how to dodge magick as well. I as well as my friends would be willing to train you above and beyond what a normal warrior should know. The choice is up to you." I spoke.

I had their attention now and they were definitely thinking about my words, as well as what it would ultimately mean.

"At what price? What do you do get out of it or want in return?" The servant seraphim asked with sarcasm, distrusting of my intentions.

At some point, I'm going to beat the last remaining glorified shit out of him…if there was any left.

"I already have all that I want and I won't make this offer again if you decline it today. Trust goes both ways, and quite frankly, with the exception of Durien, I don't trust any of you either." I told him flatly.

There was a long, silent pause, which allowed all of them time to exchange glances among each other.

Suddenly, Jamie stood up with her hand raised. "I'm in."

The blonde haired girl raised her hand next. "Me too."

Durien's hand was already raised.

"I'm in too." The Asian girl stood up.

Though his hand was halfway up already, the dark haired male leaned in and attempted to whisper quietly to the blonde girl. "You sure it's not because of how he looks?"

She smiled playfully at him. Judging by the scent wafting off of her skin, he assumed absolutely right.

One by one, with the exception of the two seraphim and the dark-skinned girl, they all stood up and joined in the acceptance of my offer.

Jamie turned to look at Spencer in disbelief. "What more do you need? Even the angel vouches for him and he recommends this choice." She hissed.

The seraphim was unmoved, still trying to figure out my motives and hidden agendas.

Then, he shook his head no. "I don't trust him. They are the enemy. You all took oaths, remember?"

"Yeah, but we're all shunned now too, remember?" Jamie replied.

"That shouldn't matter. This is how it starts. The deception and the lies."

"Spencer, give it a rest. If the Angel is on his side, that's all we need to trust." The Asian girl cut him off this time.

"No one is making or begging you stay and accept. I'm sure as hell not. I could care less what you do." I reminded him.

The seraphim's jaw was working now. "What about you, Kaia?" He asked expectantly.

"I made my decision back at the hall already. I'm with them." She said calmly.

"I think you're all making a big mistake." He said in a low whisper that I heard loud and clear.

"As Cam`ael has just pointed out in not so pleasant words, that is your choice, Spencer. They have made theirs. No one is wrong here." Aliks intervened

I narrowed my eyes at him. I may not be able to read minds, but I was definitely picking up something familiar in him that incited the darkest parts of me while completely raising my awareness of his being.

"You already said you were accepting being shunned. What are you gonna do? Where are you gonna go?" Jamie asked. Her eyes turned glassy with fresh tears.

"I don't know. But I refuse to pair up with sworn enemies. You should all be ashamed of yourselves. You're already open vessels, there's no telling what you'll end up subjecting yourselves to." He went on.

Everyone exchanged glances with one another and then turned to Aliks.

"Every choice has its consequence. Do what your spirit tells you to do."

"I've already chosen." Durien replied with confidence.

Jamie wiped her tears, crossing her arms over her middle and turning away from the Seraphim. She returned to sit beside the dark-skinned girl once again.

"So have I." She sniffed, still not looking at him.

"Me too." The female seraphim affirmed.

It was apparent that all of the warriors were maintaining their decisions.

The appeal of what the seraphim was emanating so strongly, wasn't about his clear opposition and distrust of me and my friends, nor the obvious choices of everyone else. I cocked my head, examining him prudently.

And then it hit me. It was similar to the same triggering alarm that went off, seeing it in Drakael in the diner that day with Starling, when she was still mortal.

However, with this seraphim it was different. It was a deadly combination—of pride, doubt, and extreme…jealousy.

XXVI. STARLING

Aon was driving me nuts. I stopped counting how many times she made me practice throwing my fire, but now, I could literally light each wick of up to twenty single candles one by one —with my eyes closed.

I felt drained and tired but not from the use of my fire. I was starving. I had finally learned to completely separate it from my emotions. Now, I could simply bring it forth by sheer will, just like my blades. I even got fancy and began flinging the flames off the tips of each blade to light the candles.

"Alright, you've done remarkably well. I knew you had it in you!" Aon smiled with encouragement.

I didn't even have the mental energy to reply with something smart.

"I'm starving." I whined.

"Me too, actually." She patted her stomach.

I looked at her unbelievingly.

Within an instant, literally, a wave of brighter than bright, supernatural light nearly seared my eyeballs into pools of liquefied jelly, and then...we were standing on the balcony of stone in front of Cam's door to his home.

It wasn't even two seconds before the door rolled opened and Cam was there, looking as hot as ever in a red, loose-fitting shirt and a pair of black lounging pants.

I ran to him and I was lifted off of my feet, and into a firm hug that immediately led to an enthusiastic, deep kiss. He missed me as much as I missed him, and much of the passion in our kiss, was relief that we were both alright.

"You almost made me obliterate everything and everyone at the hall. Are you sure you're alright?"

"Yeah. You promised me, Cam."

"That was hardly part of that promise. I was beyond livid. You're going to have to tell me everything that happened."

"I will, later. I'm really hungry right now."

Aon cleared her throat and announced, "I'll return at daybreak."

We broke from the kiss. I almost forgot she was there. Cam eased me down to the ground and held my hand in his.

"Aliks will be returning too." He told her.

"I know. We've both just been assigned to accompany and assist this—new gathering of alliances. Starling has mastered her essence, something to be celebrated."

Then, she rudely went into that strange language of hers with Cam again.

Cam replied in the same language. The exchange was brief and then she was gone in a silent burst of pretty sparkles that made me 'ooh' and 'ahh'.

"Let me guess, I don't need to know?" I commented.

He laughed. "Precisely. It's not bad, don't worry." He brought my hand up and winked while kissing the top of it.

Cam led me inside, closing the entrance quickly behind us.

Something delicious was cooking and I heard...many voices. Many familiar voices.

I looked at Cam with a questioning glance.

He seemed agitated but acquiescent.

"Spontaneous hosting." He replied as we walked side by side down the, wide, oval-shaped hallway.

I had no idea what that meant, other than it was obvious that there were a lot of people in the dining room and living area.

I gaped, dumbfounded beyond any comprehension of the scene that unfolded in front of me, once we entered the great room that offered a partial view of the kitchen and dining room.

All of Cam's friends…were intermingling —with all of mine.

Durien, Gabe, Anthony, and Jamie were playing a game of pool with several male and female fallen, no surprise there. Lorelei, Scarlet, and Lira were in the living room looking at Cam's massive collection of music with four, gorgeous, female fallen, and Devlin was parked like a zombie in front of a large screen television, watching a movie. From here, I could see and hear both Crystal and Kaia in the kitchen, helping two other female fallen, and a huge, onyx-skinned fallen…to cook?

You would have thought that everyone had been lifetime buddies the way they interacted among one another.

I rubbed my eyes. Was I dreaming, hallucinating or what? I looked up at Cam with dread. "What the…"

Cam leaned down to whisper with a frown, "I know. I told them not to move or mess up anything."

"What's going on?" I asked him in disbelief.

Not that seeing everyone here wasn't a joyful surprise, the shock factor for me was obvious.

"Hey Starling, you're okay! This place is unbelievably gorgeous!" Lorelei called out, waving at me happily.

"And really super clean and organized." Scarlet added with playful emphasis and a thumbs up.

I wanted to giggle because I knew exactly what she meant by the sarcastic compliment.

Lira shuffled quickly over to us and threw her arms around me for a welcoming hug.

"You seem to always make us worry about you."

I was still speechless and paralyzed as I mechanically hugged her back and smiled.

Cam leaned in close to my ear again, "I guess we both have a few things to share. How about I draw you a bath while Rahab is preparing dinner?"

Yeah, I'm gonna need a moment to wrap my brain around this one.

~~~***~~~

After spending quite a while fully submersed in the deep, bowl-shaped tub of steaming water, enhanced with floral scented oils, lit candles placed all around, and bubbles—at my request; I was as calm and relaxed as a light summer breeze over an open field. Cam left me alone while I bathed, but I'm pretty sure it was because he couldn't stand the idea of not being there to police everyone.

I was still shocked but I was definitely happy. Happy because he as a fallen, was willing to take my divine warrior friends in, knowing that we had no place to go now that we were all shunned.

Even if he did volunteer to do it for my sake, especially seeing that he was definitely a private being, I was touched. What fallen does something like this? What fallen would ever consider something like this without something to gain?

He said we can talk when I was done and completely relaxed but before he left, I had him bring me my cell phone. I spent a long while looking through all of the messages. I couldn't check the voicemail because I didn't know the password but I'm sure Cam can fix that.

Since there were no longer any options for me, heading back to pick up where my life left off was becoming more and more appealing. I was feeling a bit more confident in who I was now, and I certainly didn't have much of a choice anymore anyway.

I know that I could always stay here with Cam too, and I wanted to but something was compelling me to return back to the human realm—back to the college that I attended. I don't know why but it may have something to do with protecting all of my friends, especially China. My friend Joel was going to be here in the spirit realm at some point as a warrior, and I would never be able to see or know him again. That part hurt. I wished him well and hoped that he would be able to conform and adjust better than I could.

I was waiting to see if some vision would come to me as I scrolled through all of my pictures. I studied all the text messages, which seemed foreign to me at first, but the longer I read and re-read them, things began to manifest like a distant memory. That part excited me but I was indifferent right now. Then, I ran across a text that really stood out to me. It was from China and it read: *'I keep seeing shadows like u do, especially at night when I'm bout 2 fall asleep. Been happening a lot lately. I feel like they r trying 2 do something 2 me. Steve's been staying here w/me. Very scared, miss u and wish u'd hurry and come home soon. I understand u have 2 do what u need 2 do and I hope everything is ok. Call me plz! Luv u!'*

I stared blankly at it for several seconds. Shadows? How was she seeing them? Cam said she wasn't chosen. It didn't matter, that was the answer for me. The reasoning behind my compulsion to return and to protect all of my friends was revealed. Something was happening in the human realm, that much I could surmise. The date of the text was time stamped on Thursday, November 14th, 2013. That made me curious as to what the current date was in the human realm right now; what date I died; how long I've been gone; how old this text message is; and did it need to be addressed? I didn't see a conversation reply on my part but that didn't mean that Cam didn't have his female friend call her back about it.

I pulled up her name and number in my contacts and tapped on her picture. With my finger poised over the phone icon, I paused. No, I wasn't ready yet. I'd better ask Cam what day it was in the human realm first.

Really, Cam? I thought to myself as I perused the clothing he had been acquiring for me, all hanging inside of a new armoire that hadn't been here before. Where would I wear this? I pulled out a black lace tank top. Though cute, most everything was either sheer and see-through, or really revealing. There were already quite a few maternity shirts and dresses too. Well, if anything he was certainly thinking ahead. Though grateful, and his taste wasn't bad at all, I would much rather pick my own clothes.

"Um, Cam? Any chance I could get something a little more modest and bit less on the nine months pregnant side?" I called out.

"Like what?" His voice came from right above me.

I gasped, tilting my head back and then whirling around to face a mischievously smiling Cam, literally standing right behind and looking down at me. I had expected him to reply telepathically. The fact that I hadn't even detected his presence until he spoke, and how quick and easy he had been able to sneak up on me was not a good thing. My heart raced.

"Damn, you startled me!" I hissed.

"Startled you?"

I cleared my throat, "Yeah, you just caught me off guard, that's all." I lied.

He smiled, not believing that at all. "That's definitely something we'll both have to work on correcting then, starting tomorrow."

"Tomorrow?"

"We're going to be training you guys. Both your friends and mine have agreed and accepted. Now is as good a time as any, much to my apprehension about you in particular because of your condition but you're gonna have to learn sooner or later. For your safety, it will have to be sooner given what almost happened again. Aon filled me in."

I pressed my lips and nodded. "Okay. Do, they know about..." my eyes flicked down to my lower belly. "Your friends, I mean?"

He shook his head. "Not yet."

I wondered why he hadn't told them, then again, mine didn't know either. However, now that we were no longer under the eyes and rules of those at the divine hall, it makes it a lot easier for me to tell…at some point later.

"When should we make the announcement?" I asked.

He inhaled deeply in thought. "I have qualms about too many others knowing, especially since you're not showing yet, but if you want your friends to know now, then we can do it together." He pushed a still slightly damp curl behind my ear and stroked my cheek.

I nodded but I also wondered why he was apprehensive about it. I could take a few guesses, although in a few months we won't have a choice, regardless.

"What day is it? In the human realm?" I then asked.

"You know I don't keep track of time but it won't take but a second to check, just to be sure. And you're curious because?" He wanted me to elaborate.

"I was going through some of the text messages on my phone, that's all."

He nodded. "Oh. Eastern standard, central united States, or pacific mountain time?"

"Wherever it was that I lived last."

"Ok. I'll be right back then." He smiled.

"Thank you…and hey," I stopped him, grabbing onto the front of his shirt, rising up on my tip-toes and pulling him down to me. He leaned down to meet me halfway and I kissed him deep and affectionately.

He was pleasantly surprised and grinning when I pulled away.

He licked his lips, savoring my kiss. "Random but very, very nice."

"You don't know how much all of this means to me. I wished they hadn't chosen to get shunned with me but I guess it's too late for them to turn back now. Anyway, I don't know how to thank you enough."

"You don't need to thank me, at least not until later." He waggled his brows at me.

"Yeah, not with everyone here. I wouldn't feel comfortable." I smiled coyly.

Cam laughed. "You kiss me like that while completely naked and then tell me that you don't feel comfortable making love with everyone here? You don't remember this, but you've just confirmed what I said about you on our first date in the human realm."

I raised a brow. "Oh? And what did you say?"

He smiled. "That you were a tease. I was right."

"Um, after our date last night, you have the nerve to call me a tease?"

He appeared thoughtful while rubbing his chin.

"Excellent reminder. The walls are made of solid stone but if it makes you feel more comfortable, soundproofing them for extra measure is not a problem at all."

I shook my head with a grin. "We'll see."

He playfully reached down and around me, giving one of my cheeks a light squeeze and a quick, playful spank. The temporary sting sparked a shiver of pleasure throughout my pelvis.

"In the meantime, dinner is ready. What do you want to wear?"

My breath caught and I cleared my throat. He knew exactly what reaction his action would generate in me.

"I've always been a t-shirt and jeans kind of girl. Size four, and I wear my shirts in medium. Nothing fancy though."

His eyes traveled the length of my naked body, and then he closed his eyes as if concentrating. When he opened them again, he winked and gave me a quick peck on my lips.

"See you at the dinner table." He whispered, ghosting out instead of leaving through the closed door.

Once he was gone, I spotted the neatly splayed ensemble on his bed. A royal blue, scoop-necked t-shirt and a pair of relaxed fit, low-rise, blue jeans. Cam was pampering and spoiling me rotten.

XXVII. CAM`AEL

I would never admit to it out loud but I was actually enjoying the company, especially the human company. I've always preferred their company over any being of the spirit realm and now, it only reminded me of why. Barriers were being broken and lowered. It was a monumental almost miraculous thing, seeing the interaction between my friends and Starling's, but what really surprised me was when the seraphim decided to stay with them. It wasn't because he trusted us at all, it was because he made a commitment to them when he became earthbound and he was sticking to it, so far. I could definitely respect that but I was watching him closely. Something wasn't fully settled with me about the vibes he was giving off.

I did my best to make sure Starling was occupied and would be for a while during her bath while we all planned for her birthday party. So far, she had no idea. It would be perfect and the fact that her friends were here now, worked out well. Truth be told, it was one of the main reasons that I did make the exception of offering shelter in the first place. It was all for Starling because I knew she would want it this way and that it would make her happy.

Rahab and Edanai were preparing a great feast and a birthday cake and everyone was in on it. My friends offered to escort the girls to requested places so that they could purchase gifts and acquire some articles of clothing, which hadn't taken too long. I had already gotten her gifts from me a while back but there were a few more items that I wanted to try and find too.

"Edanai, I may be a few more minutes, do me a favor and make sure that Starling doesn't head into the dining room until I get back. I want to be there for the surprise part."

Edanai sighed, "*Fine, just hurry back because I think we're all pretty much starving right now.*"

"Thanks."

I invited Atiro and Berith after making a quick check of the city where Starling lived. I could see that it was a week before the Thanksgiving holiday and it was really cold. There were a few other things I wanted to check on and acquire quickly before returning too. I assumed that Starling was making the decision on whether or not to return back to the college she attended, and so I decided to stop by and pay her friend China a visit to announce the news.

She wasn't home. A girl outside of the complex mentioned that she had gone home for the holidays, and that she wouldn't be back until around December the eighteenth. That fact may work in Starlings' favor. The current, U.S human realm date was November the 25th, a Saturday.

I ghosted into the apartment anyway, just to check things out and make sure that all was well and untainted for her return.

There were definitely dark entities that have been playing around here and as to who and why, I had no idea. I placed new feathers strategically throughout the apartment, studying everything in both of their rooms, especially Starlings. Nothing of darkness had been hovering in there, which was a relief. It was apparent that they all knew she had already died.

Beyond the thin curtain and blinds, shadows of several, large and unnatural black crows flapped wildly in an overt showy display meant just for me, outside of the window in her room. It was like an arrogant warning and I already knew who it was. Though I wanted to confront Xyn and battle it out once and for all, I figured that may not be a good idea today. I wanted to be there for Starlings surprise birthday dinner, unscathed and alive.

The table, food, decorations, gifts, cake, and music were already set by the time I returned with Starling's additional present wrapped and in hand. I set it down slightly apart from the others and made my way into the kitchen just to be nosy—because everything did indeed smell delicious.

The seraphim girl and a warrior were both decorating the two tier cake in dark pink, white, and yellow flowers, and making a frosting edging around the base of each tier.

I was thankful that Edanai had managed to stall Starling from entering the kitchen and dining room, being that she was currently still in my bed chamber.

"Is everything ready?" I asked Rahab as I headed back to my

room after a quick inspection for cleanliness.

"Yes, we were all waiting on you. We're all here. Atiro and Berith showed up just a little while ago. I think Edanai managed to stall Starling. She's still in your room."

"Spencer decided to go on and room with me at my place in the human realm." Durien stopped to inform me before I made it to my room.

"You guys do realize that you're no longer protected since you're no longer affiliated with the hall?"

Durien shrugged, "I know. Anyway, he's relying on his own magic if he needs it. I think Jamie and Devlin are gonna be staying with us too but only after we're done training, so we won't be alone if anything happens."

"It could still be dangerous for all of you, and he's an idiot."

Durien laughed and shook his head. "Yeah, I know he can be at times but he's a pretty damned good fighter and friend. He does want to train with you guys though."

I was pensive. That punk had his nerve.

"That doesn't surprise me. And who the hell does he think is going to be taxiing him back and forth between realms for that?"

"I don't know but your friend, Jerilah volunteered pretty quickly though." Durien snickered.

I raised a brow. "Oh, so we're good enough to rely on as methods of transport and training, but he's disgusted and doesn't trust our company?" Another reason why I wanted to serve him up with a righteous ass kicking.

Durien shook his head.

"Man, I appreciate you taking us in at all, let alone even bothering to prepare us like this. If anyone is thankful and grateful for everything…it's definitely me." He then commented.

I nodded. "I just hope that it doesn't back fire in the end." I replied, continuing on to my room to change.

Starling was lying in my bed on her side and facing away from me. She said that she was hungry earlier, so I doubted that she was sleeping and the scent of…oh hell.

She didn't even move to greet me when I entered.

I sighed, crawling onto the bed behind her, and slinking an arm around her waist carefully and lovingly.

She was playing one of the games on it, and she was definitely angry —with me.

"What's wrong? What did I do during the time I wasn't here?" I asked.

She simply shook her head with her lips pressed tightly. It couldn't have been more evident that something was bothering her, and I was grateful that she had learned to separate her fire from her emotions.

"I thought you were hungry." I mentioned, leaning in to kiss her but she shifted away from me and sat up.

"I am." She said flatly, placing her phone on the small table next to my bed, and then proceeded to scoot off the bed and stand, not even looking at me. I reached out and grabbed her hand to stop her. Pregnancy hormones this early? I hoped not. She still had a ways to go.

"Well, you can go when you tell me what's bothering you. Did someone do or say something to you?" I asked.

It seemed like she didn't even want to look at me.

"It doesn't matter. I don't want to talk or think about it, Cam." She brushed off and tried to tug out of my grip.

I wasn't going to let her go. She looked at me, scowling this time.

"Would you please tell me what I did?" I was really confused now.

She exhaled slowly.

"I told you, I'm not really mad. Just thinking." She said, forcing a fake half smile.

I watched her carefully. "About?"

She sighed, turning away from me. "A lot of stuff." She vaguely hinted.

I gauged her carefully, not believing that at all but I let her go.

"Do you love me?" I called out, just as she reached for the door.

That stopped her and she turned to face me.

"Yes, I do. Do you love me?" She raised a brow.

I slid off of my bed and moved over to her. I looked down at her, gazing deeply into the dark, blue depths of her sparkling and trusting, yet searching eyes. "More than my own desire to ever remove myself of my punishment and become an angel again."

If that were even an option for me at all. Either way, it was the honest, sincere truth and I could think of nothing else that would make her believe it enough, apparently.

She seemed surprised, and her face softened into a smile.

"Now, are you going to tell me what's bothering you?" I still wanted to know.

"I told you, Cam. I don't want to bring it up again." She said, and with that she opened the door and left.

I was still unsettled about the whole incident. I wanted to know what made her regard me so coldly when I returned. My mind began to work. There was only one thing I could think of that would make any female turn that quickly. Damn.

I didn't bother to change my clothes at all…at least not the normal way.

As I walked, my clothes quickly morphed into a comfortable silk, blood red-colored, button down shirt, and a pair of black, loose slacks. I followed behind her, though in complete confusion, so that I would be there for the big moment.

As soon as she rounded the living room and headed towards the dining room, everyone jumped up and shouted, 'Surprise!' and 'Happy Birthday!'

She was most definitely surprised.

"A party? What is all of this for?" She was alight with a curious and confused smile on her beautiful face as she gazed over the table, the decorations, her cake, and then all of her presents.

"Well, according to the date on your driver's license, Cam informed us that today is your mortal birthday…based on human realm time." Rahab told her.

Each of her friends took their turns with hugs and brief conversation, and then several of mine moved in to engage her in conversation shortly thereafter—while I looked on from outside of the circle. I was trying to make the connection of just who or what could have led to the source of her sudden change in attitude towards me.

"Birthday? I can't believe you guys did all of this. I…don't even know what to say."

"I can't believe that you're actually twenty." Anthony grinned.

"Me either." Ry commented.

"Yeah, I know." Durien added.

"This is weird, especially since we're immortal now." Starling replied.

"Consider is a party for your rebirth too, then." Lorelei smiled.

"Damn, if that's the case, I've got to be in my late forties then." Durien then said.

"Wanna know how hold I am?" Jerilah smirked.

"Doesn't matter, you don't look a day over twenty in my opinion." Gabe grinned at her.

"Thank, you." Jerilah flirted back.

"The only thing that gains wisdom and age as you all are now, is your sense of knowledge and experiences." Atiro said.

"I agree, and that calls for a toast." Ry urged at the raising of his glass.

Everyone proceeded to raise whatever it was that they were drinking.

"Happy Rebirth, Starling!" he cheered and everyone followed suit, exchanging glass clinks and taking long swigs of their cocktails.

Edanai emerged from the kitchen with a bowl of steaming soup and placed it on the table. "Everything is set. We're all starving and ready to eat. Rahab and the rest of us have been slaving over this meal, so we certainly hope that you like it. You get to sit here, birthday girl." and pointed at the head of the table.

Starling didn't even look at me once…let alone Edanai, at least not in the eye. That was something I picked up on instantly as everyone began to gather around the table and find a seat. I narrowed my gaze at Edanai.

"Did you say something to Starling?" I asked her.

Her amethyst eyes met mine, innocently.

"Something like what?"

"I don't know, that's why I'm asking." I was growing irritated and angry already.

"We were talking. You wanted me to stall her and I did."

"Talking about what?" I felt anger rising in me at Edanai's possible words. Words that may have been intentional.

"Random stuff. She had a lot of questions and I answered them. No biggie, she wanted to know and I wasn't going to lie to her."

I don't think I've ever felt so angry or the urge to either curse Edanai out, or hurt her outright in my entire existence.

It felt as if she had deliberately done this to hurt me or to cause some sort of a fall-out between me and Starling. Why would she do that? Edanai of all people, I've always trusted. Has she really been that jealous and hurt by all of this since finding out that Starling was pregnant with my child?

"What did you say to her, Edanai?!" I was practically yelling at her in my head, and though my face displayed neutral

temperament, my eyes were storming red.

"*Nothing bad or negative. She asked who I was to you and I told her. Now can we not ruin the mood and this birthday dinner for her?*"

I already knew that was not all that Edanai told her. It couldn't have been, not for Starling to be that cold and stand-offish towards me after what happened right before I popped into the human realm very briefly.

"*You already have. Thanks a lot.*" I hissed at her sharply as I turned to head back towards the hallway leading towards the front door, and then ghosted outside.

XXVIII. STARLING

Edanai's words tumbled around in my head like a wild and poisonous bee. I didn't remember her at first, and other than her being absolutely gorgeous, like the other fallen women here, I had no reason to not like her.

She was a really, really close friend of Cam's. She has been for a while and she occasionally stays here…with him.

I didn't think anything bad about it at first, until the whole question of 'what kind of things had Cam done as an incubus before me?' began to rear its ugly head. I hated that I even asked or contemplated wanting to know, especially since I already told myself that it was better that I didn't know.

He was with me now and he loved me just like I loved him. We were about to become parents to two, unique children, soon. It should have been all that I needed to care about and focus on.

But no. I had to ask and she certainly held nothing back whatsoever.

A small part of me did wonder if maybe she was adding in as much detail as she could on purpose, which had me suspicious. Not only did she confirm that she and Cam had been together for a very long time, but that it was a really close and really intimate relationship for a very long time too. Meaning, that they've engaged in all sorts of sexual acts and activities together more times than the earth was old, probably. That knowledge, coupled with the fact that she's been living here with him now, didn't sit very well with the stretches of my imagination.

Then, to add more venom for me to swirl around in my brain, she proceeded to remind me that Cam was an incubus, and the number of women he's been with in his existence as a fallen, could probably span the number of stars in the galaxies. The wild, poisonous bee she had let loose in my brain began to sting and make me crazy with jealousy and anger.

I was beyond angry at both her and him.

Why would she care to say things that would bother me, if she weren't trying to cause issues between me and Cam? And if she was trying to cause issues, maybe she still had feelings for him and she was jealous of me. That part would have been hard to believe, looking at her and looking at me. She was this tall, Amazonian-like, voluptuous yet lean, olive-skinned, ebony-haired goddess; and I was a short, nearly flat-chested human girl with no magic or wings.

I tried not to let those thoughts get in the way of the here and now but it couldn't be helped. The longer I sat with the knowledge, the more resentful and bitter I became. Thoughts and questions began to culminate in my head like, what have I gotten myself into? What future could we both possibly have together, immortal or not, and children or not? How were we going to raise them? What would they become like? Would I have to worry about him getting the urge to go on a screwing spree again? That was the most agonizing of all. How could I possibly be enough for him? But even worse…what if something happened to Cam? He'd be gone forever. I swallowed the emotional lump in my throat and quickly wiped away a tear that had formed and began to fall.

I was making myself ill with both worry, anger, and jealousy until the very thought of even looking at him made me upset. I had brought all that onto myself by asking for the very thing that I should have just left a mystery.

I felt horrible after having reacted to him the way I did, given the fact that he had no clue as to why I was upset when he came back. He's been doing nothing but romancing, protecting, and going above and beyond his own comfort zone to make me happy in various ways and acts; and here I was being angry over things that he did before me, not during…maybe. Then, to make me feel even lower, he had gone through all of this trouble to acknowledge a day that no longer held significance for me now that I was immortal. He had obviously planned a huge party for all of us to enjoy in his home, complete with gifts for me.

I was so confused. I didn't know what I wanted or what to think. Did any of that matter? I didn't want the issue to ruin this party, especially since everything looked so festive, everyone was here and in a good mood despite everything that went down and my second 'almost' abduction, once again.

Though he was gorgeous as hell in the dark red, silk shirt that he magically switched into, which accentuated his flawless tanned skin and dark hair, Cam looked so bewildered and sad just standing there while he watched all of us carrying on.

I saw him glance at Edanai after she pointed out my seat to me, and then I noted a flash of anger flicker in his eyes before he turned to leave.

I instantly hopped up to follow him but when he ghosted out, I stopped.

I don't think I could open the huge, stone doorway by myself, and I think there was some magic spell carved into that served as a lock anyway.

"Where are you going?" I called out to him.

It took him a moment to reply. He was probably shocked that I even asked.

"Giving you some space. I'll be back later, enjoy the party with your friends."

"I want to enjoy it with you. Come back."

"I'll be here when you wake up at daybreak."

"Daybreak? Are you serious?" I was getting angry again but for a different reason this time.

"I've got something I need to do."

Like what? More women? I winced and groaned internally; scolding myself for even making that snarky, and tortuous mental comment to myself.

"Now?"

"It shouldn't take me long. Besides, after the festivities, I want you to rest up. We're going to be training and training hard starting early tomorrow morning, and I'm going to have to figure out how to get around your condition."

"I'm not made of glass. I'll be alright."

"Still. I love you, Starling."

I sighed. *"I love you too, Cam. Be safe. I want you here when I wake up first thing."*

"Don't worry, I will be."

~~~****~~~

The food was amazing and the company even more so. Who would have ever thought that partying with fallen would be this fun and interesting? We all had a blast, dancing, playing, talking, being amazed and charmed by the male fallen and their cool magic.

The weird girl Berith, who was obviously not human though she appeared to be on the surface, seemed friendly enough but something about the way she kept looking at me was starting to get on my nerves. We all finally got in some girl time, and that included enjoying the company of the other female fallen as well. The glamour magic…wickedly awesome.

Spencer being here was a complete shock, especially hearing that he had accepted shunning along with us too. He really didn't say much to me, and he spent the majority of the time brooding up until all of Cam's friends got ready to leave. They took everyone, including Lira back to Duriens place in the human realm, where they were all going to stay for right now. Lorelei was irked that she couldn't remember the exact location of her house, other than it was secluded in the French countryside.

In the morning, Cam's friends would bring them back and we'd all meet up for the first day of arduous, yet valuable training here in the Spirit Realm. That would be the plan for however long it took.

I was told by Rahab, that by placing a feather of their own in and around the house, it would act as a marker or signature to ward off other potential fallen to think twice before entering or attacking. That made me feel better because I was really worried about Lira. I knew everyone would be extra watchful of her, and Jamie and Spencer would keep her protected. That, I was sure of as well as Devlin's safety now that she was back.

Speaking of Devlin, she hadn't said a word much less displayed any emotion the entire time that she was here. She barely even ate anything. I didn't expect a thank you from her, it was a given, so I understood her state of mind after all of that. Did she even remember that part? I wondered.

I couldn't even begin to imagine what she's been through and endured, what she's seen, or what she must be thinking being around all of these fallen, who might be reminding her of the one that she had become close to too. Maybe after a while, she'd come around.

"Have you noticed anything about her that kind of seems…familiar?" I heard whispering coming from the somewhere.

There were only three fallen left; Rahab, Edanai, Atiro, and then that weird inhuman girl who introduced herself as Berith.

The voices were female but where were they coming from? There was no one in the kitchen or the living room.

"Familiar? Like what? I'm sure she didn't appreciate you staring at her all night like that either."

"I wasn't staring. I was studying."

"Whatever you want to call it, it was creepy. She was way too nice to tell you off and I was about to do it for her."

"There's something about her that I can't quite place other than she's definitely dangerous and looks are always deceiving, you know."

"Tell me about it. Anyway, the party is over. You can leave now."

"Where has Cam`ael been?"

"He's mad at me."

"Mad? Over what?"

"Bye, Berith." The other voice was imperative.

I heard a heavy sigh, mumbling, and then it was quiet.

I waited for Berith to appear from wherever the voices were coming from but she didn't. Instead, Atiro simply vanished and then I heard someone in the kitchen.

Damn, being around so many supernatural beings was unsettling. I wasn't too crazy about the whispers, the vanishing, the appearing, and the magic but I supposed I'd better get used to it.

Out of automatic consideration, I began to help with the clean-up. Now that it was quiet, I began to ponder things once again.

"No need to do all of that. I'll take care of it." I heard Edanai say from behind me, just as I began to clear away a few plates.

I set them back down slowly and watched her.

Rahab was busy inspecting everything for damage, rearrangement, and messes.

"In case you haven't figured it out by now, filth and disorder turns Cam`ael into a raving, demonic lunatic. He's very anal about it." She then smiled at me.

I returned a weak smile, not really knowing what to say to her at this point.

"I know." I replied.

She laughed and then paused.

There was a gap of silence that hung in the air, and then she pulled out a chair, sitting down.

"I hope that I didn't give you the wrong impression about him. I didn't mean to make it sound as if he was untrustworthy or deceptive, so I apologize for that,"

I tilted my head, wondering why she was backtracking now all of a sudden, and then I slowly sat down across from her.

She held her palm forward with the other crossed over her middle, "I'm not saying that it isn't true, just that I shouldn't have told you any of it." She clarified.

Then she sighed and rested her forearms on the table, staring down at her long, painted fingernails, "If anything, you're very fortunate to have him bind himself to you the way he has. He's absolutely crazy about and very deeply in love with you."

I only nodded with a half-smile, thinking about him.

She went on, "There was no mistake that you two ended up together. A relationship between a fallen and a warrior is not something that happens. He took an insane risk but he made a very good choice."

Her compliment made me raise both brows in surprise.

She finally made eye contact with me again, studying me. "You bring out a softer, more at peace side of him that means a lot for me to see. So I guess I can say it now. I'm jealous of you."

"Jealous of me?"

She nodded, averting her jewel-like eyes from me.

"You've given him the very thing that he's been searching for and wanting badly since falling. Something that no woman has ever be able to give him, not even me."

I studied her beautiful, oval shaped face in fascination. What could a being as gorgeous as she was, who could have any male, mortal or immortal that she wanted, and magical abilities and powers, be so sad about?

She hesitated and then her gaze rested on nothing in particular.

"Some of us will never have the very thing we fell in the first place over but Cam`ael does with you, and that gives us all hope for something better, and possible redemption." She finished, her eyes finding mine when she said that.

Reading my facial expression, she went on, "A part of him grows in you right now."

"How did you know about that?" I whispered.

I thought Cam hadn't told any of his friends yet?

"He didn't reveal it to me. Believe it or not, Cam`ael is a horrible liar. Very cunning and a great bull-shitter, but a horrible liar. I guess maybe I've just known him too long. Anyway, the bottom line is that fallen in general, especially Incubus', are very sexually potent. Your becoming pregnant was inevitable from the very first time…and that's all I'll say about that. Though he will never admit to it, he's a very caring being with a big heart, and I'm honored to have him as my very close and best friend. But I do have one thing that I feel I should warn you about."

I stiffened in alarm, my heart beginning to thump wildly.

"What?"

She leaned in closer to me before speaking again, "Fallen do not handle devastation very well. If you ever broke things off and decided that you wanted nothing to do with him anymore…he'd fight you to the death."

I felt the blood rush from my face. I was nonplussed. I suddenly understood what Jamie meant and what she told me. Fight to the death? I couldn't even picture it let alone fathom it. I closed my eyes and shook my head, swallowing hard.

I glanced over at Rahab from the corner of my eye. He continued to busy himself with cleaning and dusting but I could tell with the slight cock of his head, that he had been listening to our conversation too.

"I would never…are you telling me what I think you're telling me? That he'd hate me enough to…"

Edanai pursed her lips and shook her head, "Not your death. His."

I stared at her blankly with my mouth open.

She was apparently letting that sink in, seeing the fearful expression frozen on my face.

She leaned back, hesitating for a moment.

"We were angels once. We feel great sorrow, intense pain, and love far deeper than any human can ever imagine. That part of ourselves is still true, even as fallen. Those that wanted to not feel anything at all anymore, chose darkness and Morning Star. Your relationship, Cam`ael's feelings, and the bond that you've both created between each other, especially now that you are about to become the mother of his child, are all very passionate things, so I hope you're prepared.

We can't kill ourselves, that's part of the terms of our

punishment. As fallen, we have way too much pride and power to simply stand by and allow ourselves to be killed by others of our kind either. You have the power to destroy him both physically and emotionally. He knows and accepts that." She leaned closer to me again, her eyes sparkling as they bore into mine.

She held a finger up to make her point, "Do not tell him we had this conversation, ever. And if you ever hurt him on any level...I will come after you myself. And don't worry, I don't mean killing you. Every child needs its mother."

Several thoughts ran through my mind in that instance, especially the longer that I stared into her gorgeous, light purple eyes— and then it hit me.

I do remember her, or more so...something about her.

I narrowed my gaze and this time I leaned forward with a smirk, "I haven't forgotten about the whole spider incident."

She was surprised at first and then she laughed.

Returning to Cam's room, I sighed, still seeing no sign of him having returned yet but there was another small, gift-wrapped package sitting in the middle of the bed for me. I melted, he had already gotten me several nice, expensive gifts ranging from clothes to electronics, so it made me wonder what this small one could be.

Just as I sat on the bed and reached for it, my cell phone began to ring on the table next to the bed where I had left it.

I glanced over at it, frozen and blinking for several seconds before quickly crawling over to and picking it up. China's profile picture as an icon, along with her cell phone number were displayed on the screen. I swallowed, hesitating for a few more seconds. Then, with a nervous and shaking finger, I tapped on the answer button and held the phone to my ear.

Pausing to find my voice, I waited for her to speak first.

"Oh my freaking God, Star. What the hell? What is wrong with you? Why have you been seriously tripping? You've never done anything like this. You don't call or text back, and you told me that you'd be back by Thanksgiving!" She rattled off.

I did? Crap.

I probably shouldn't have answered. Though the very sound of her voice invoked a flash of random images and memories of her, I had no idea what to say.

"Um...I know and I still plan on it..."

There was silence. "Are you doing drugs? Did you sustain a massive head injury resulting in a coma? Star, I am really worried about you now. This isn't funny."

"No...I..."

"Thanksgiving was two days ago and if you tell me that you won't be home by Christmas, I will fly out there with my parents, Steve, Toya, Jenna, Vanessa, and the fucking FBI to get you and bring you back home. Everyone is worried about you. You've got a ton of mail, several from the University marked time-sensitive, that are probably what I think they are, and I haven't seen or heard from Joel for a while now either — not since he started dating some weird chic. Is everything really okay? You wouldn't be into some sort of weird cult or something, would you? Has Cam been out there to see you? You said he planned on it, which makes me feel a little better about your absence and safety. He did stop by once to tell me that you were okay but no one has seen him around here since then. Is he still out there with you? I mean, cop or not, how well do you know him? You allowed him to come out there to see and support you but not me?"

Damn.

My God, I was seriously getting chewed out. I had no memory of China and her ability to fuss and say so much in one breath. This wasn't going well. I shouldn't have answered.

In my panic, I had to think of something because I did plan to return soon.

Playing off of her words, I finally responded, "China..." My mouth hung open, my words suspended in my throat as my heart hammered wildly. I said the only thing that quickly came to mind and it had nothing to do with her barrage of questions.

I sighed. "I know, I'm sorry about everything. Nothing is wrong though. Cam has been here too—and I'm...pregnant."

It went completely silent on her end.

XXIX. CAM`AEL

I felt betrayed by Edanai. As much as we all had to battle against the stigma, the hate, and being marked forever as demons; she managed to send me right back to that place with words alone. It was even worse this time because she had replanted that image in Starling's mind.

I was both pissed and devastated, wondering if Starling would ever be able to look at me the same again.

Though I didn't want to leave the party, I felt that it would be best before the anger sloughing off of me began to fester negatively in the air and ruin everyone's mood.

At first, I planned to simply just fly off somewhere to vent off my anger but then I remembered the mysterious text. This would probably be more of a perfect time than any to retrieve the rest but I needed my assistant for translation purposes.

I almost stopped and returned back inside, shocked when Starling's voice entered my head, especially when she said that she wanted me to stay. Did that mean she was okay with the information that Edanai had generously dumped on her? Did she still want me?

I wanted to go back as soon as I heard her voice but I needed to release the dark anger first. I don't know if I'd ever forgive Edanai for causing this painful rift of doubt between myself and the only human being that has ever held my wicked yet fragile heart in her hands. She may as well have killed me herself because it was practically what she's done.

It was cold on this small, miniscule, dusty gray planet, which was barren of any life form. I don't think it was because the atmosphere was lethal but because it was small, nearly insignificant, and derived purely of glorified stone and light. The ground emitted a soft, pale glow and there was no sky to divide it from the heavens. That told me all that I needed to know about its origins and history. The original text had been buried here by an angel. Possibly an angel who had eventually fallen, and only managed to salvage part of it to take with him, eventually ending up in the hands of Morning Star.

I didn't have enough light in me to withstand contact with the ground, so I was left to hover at about a foot or so above with wings out.

"Why didn't you just have me do this when I was with you earlier? And what are we doing anyway?" Aliks grumbled, looking up at me.

I had him meet me and then we both tunneled in from a portal. I would have lost my feet entirely had I not quickly reacted upon realizing that the earth was created of light. It was way different from the sanctified lands of the divine hall.

"I didn't plan on doing this just yet. I was attempting the whole Psyren kumbaya thing, remember? You don't know anything about part of a text that's entitled, End to End All, the Genesis of Divine Warriors, do you? It's written in the very first language of Angels." I looked at him questioningly.

A single, pink brow rose with interest, "There were many texts written in that language. Where is it?"

"I only have a portion of it and I didn't bring it with me. It was given to me by one of Morning Star's former lovers. He had it. I'm pretty sure you're about to get a briefing on it now if you haven't already. Elohim disclosed the location of the rest of it to me but I can't read it much less retrieve it, obviously, so I wasn't sure what he was thinking. That's where you'll come in and prove to be useful." I nodded at him.

Aliks inhaled. His lips tightened as his gaze went to the heavens above in silence.

I waited.

Then he trained his eyes back on me. "You'll need to cut yourself and allow your blood to flow and fall upon the ground."

"What?" I was taken aback.

"What part did you not hear?"

"What good will my blood do? I can't even stand on the ground." I argued.

"I didn't say you had to stand on the ground. In case you haven't noticed, there are no landmarks or X's on the ground to mark the actual location of the text. You were given the location of this book. Elohim entrusted you with it for a reason and I was told to help you for that same reason. I am simply relaying a direct command if you want to find it. Now, cut yourself and let's get this done." Aliks was serious.

I didn't understand what my cursed blood would do except to completely disintegrate upon impact. Why couldn't Elohim just tell me all of this directly? Apparently, I needed Aliks or any other angel to help me accomplish this anyway. I imagined that was why he commanded him to assist me but he couldn't have known that I would request it though.

What am I saying? Of course he did.

That was Elohim.

Reluctantly, I conjured my trusty but deadly blade. I hadn't used this one in a while. It was the very one that I had used many times before to cut myself with for the guilt of having partied in Morning Star's domain.

"How much blood?" I asked.

"Let it flow until it stops on its own."

I dug the tip of the blade in deep, flinching slightly and biting my bottom lip as I pressed down and sliced a, long, deep cut into my forearm and then across the veins in my wrists. Dark, crimson blood immediately began to spurt and gush, splattering the landscape in a soft, pattering rhythm.

The earth hissed, steamed, and crackled like crazy, just like I had predicted. Black smoke began to rise, and the smell of electricity, like wires burning, began to waft upwards. It was hard to see anything beyond the smoke at first but as it cleared…something strange began to emerge.

Aliks began to rise with his wings out and beating silently, slowly. We both stared down at the ground in amazement and awe.

My blood began to run swiftly in several different directions, spreading far and wide, creating angles and lines of blackened fissures carved into the ground in its wake.

Our eyes followed the dark, snaking trails as they branched out, forming a pattern that actually began to resemble shapes. When my skin completely healed over and the last drop of my blood fell, I ascended higher as Aliks flew further towards the north end to inspect the complete phenomenon.

I had no words, I was completely astonished.

"Cam`ael, come look at this. Rise up higher so you can see it better." Aliks called out to me as he began to ascend a few more feet.

I did and then flew over to join him. What I saw left me both stunned and mute.

The design that had been carved by my blood created uniform steps of a stairway. It was wide on the outer edges, tapering the closer it got to a solid black circle in the center. It reminded me of the landscape art, communication codes, and greetings that many of the sky arks would playfully leave behind in wide open fields in the human realm.

Aliks looked at me. "There's your safe path. You've actually created it yourself. I'm guessing you need to start digging in the center of the circle."

"You think?" I mumbled sarcastically.

I slowly descended, keeping my wings out and folded against me, just in case it wasn't completely safe for me.

I tensed once I touched the ground.

Nothing happened.

How would I have known to do this if Aliks hadn't told me to?

I hated having to work with others like this, especially an angel. It wasn't my style.

"How is everything going with the warriors?" He was making small talk now.

"Not as bad as I thought it would be but that doesn't mean I like a house full of humans—and warriors at that either. Starling is the obvious exception to my rule though."

Aliks grinned. "It's a new and uncomfortable experience for all. It's only when we put aside our hate, fears, and differences for the greater good that peace and harmony can be achieved."

I looked at him wryly. "Who are you talking to? Good luck trying to spread that ideology among beings with free will."

Aliks chuckled.

It was an age old conversation among the angels. One that I remembered having many times very well.

"I would say that should apply to your side as well but even I don't associate with the majority of the fallen." I added.

"Precisely. However, having accompanied you earlier today when you met with those in your circle, I was left with many things to ponder."

I eyed him in surprise but didn't respond.

I stepped carefully along the one dimensional stair steps that led to a blackened circle of dirt. Aliks met me on the other side of it, landing softly to observe in fascination.

I kneeled and held a hand over the center of the roughly three feet in diameter circle.

If my blood did all of this, then my magic should suffice. The dirt began to swirl, resembling a whirlpool, and then it began to collapse in the center as a sinkhole would. The way it moved and responded to my magic, reminded me of iron filaments reacting to a magnetic force from above.

Apparently, my blood had blackened the ground beneath the surface from what I could see so far. After about a foot or so down, a gold box began to appear beneath the crumbling dirt. I quickly reached in and picked it up carefully, brushing the rest of the tainted dirt away. It was bound in a different grade of yellow-gold from the one Berith gave me.

"Interesting." Aliks breathed.

I stood up, handling and examining it closely.

"I'll probably need to put the rest with it though, so it will make sense to you." I told him.

"Let me get a look anyway. I can probably read a few parts of it now to get an idea." Aliks held his hand out for it.

I gave it to him and watched as he studied it carefully. Then, he finally opened the cover and eyed the pages in awe.

He was silent for a long time, which began to get on my nerves. His facial expression never changed but then…his eyes widened.

"What? What is it?" I impatiently demanded to know.

After carefully flipping through the pages one after the other, he finally closed the book and a look of utter confusion and bewilderment masked his face.

I didn't like that combination at all.

"What is it, Aliks?" I was shouting at him now.

"I don't know. I'm not sure yet. I'll have to consult with a few arch angels about this first before I can validate its meaning and get the permission to disclose it to you, and I'll definitely need the rest of it."

"Disclose it to me? Elohim gave me the instructions on where to find it! Don't play games with me Aliks! Just tell me what you read! I'm keeping the book with me." I told him, taking it from him forcefully.

He didn't resist.

"Fine, keep and put it with the rest and continue to keep it secured. I'll get back with you soon."

"Give me a hint at least! I know it has something to do with a weapon. I figured out that much on my own."

"It does but it's not what you think. You have my word, Cam`ael. I'll get back to you with its full interpretation and when I do…be prepared to accept it. That's all I will say for now." He said.

What? What the hell does that mean? He ghosted away before I could scream and curse him out for leaving me hanging with such an ominous statement like that.

Damned angels!

~~~****~~~

I slaughtered a few chasm trolls, two feral, poison-barbed felines, and even kicked a few pesky imp asses before finally returning back to my home and Starling.

I had to. It was either that or something sexually deviant to get rid of the darkness about to boil over in me. Paying Grace another visit had been a fleeting thought but a very minor one at that. I was sure that she was probably still anticipating or awaiting my return and I hadn't decided when that would be.

I cloaked myself and slipped into my bed chamber silently as not to disturb her. The fireplace was crackling softly, casting warm, amber light against her sleeping form in my bed.

Everyone except for Edanai and Rahab, were gone.

Thank goodness.

I'd inspect the place later but my friends knew me best, so I knew that they made sure to both clean and arrange everything back the way I liked to keep my place.

"Where is everyone?" I asked Rahab.

"The others returned them to the home of Durien. We placed feathers around his house for a little protection. They'll bring them back in the morning for training."

"Great. Thank you for all you have done my friend."

"Anytime."

I didn't feel like speaking to Edanai right now at all.

I carefully placed the book with the other portion together in the hiding space behind my bookshelf, and then proceeded to bathe before retiring to rest next to Starling. I noticed the present that I had left for her was still unwrapped on the tableside. I wondered why she hadn't opened it yet. Was she still upset with me?

I heard her shift and move just as I finished drying myself off. Naked, I stepped from the alcove of my bathing room, surprised to see her fully awake.

"I thought you were asleep."

"No. I was waiting for you. I almost dozed off until I felt your presence." Her voice was a whisper.

She was becoming keen to recognizing my signature.

"Is it safe to assume that I'm no longer as they say, in the dog house?"

She laughed and then sighed softly. "You never were."

I could tell that wasn't entirely true but I wasn't going to push it. I was relieved.

If my eyes served me correctly, she was naked underneath the covers and that thought automatically aroused me. She smirked when her eyes flicked down the length of my body.

"So where did you go?" She wanted to know.

I shook my head slowly walking to the end of the bed.

"I had to retrieve something that was revealed to me by Elohim."

She beamed at me incredulously.

"Are you serious? From God himself? You talk to God?"

I shook my head and moved to the bed. "Not directly anymore. It's part of my condemnation. But every now and then, he places requests or tasks on me and since I still give him my allegiance, I do them."

She nodded slowly. "To get back into heaven?"

"No. That option doesn't and will never exist."

I eased into the softness of my bed with a sigh of relief. I didn't want to talk about this subject with Starling, simply because it made me look neurotic and pathetic.

She looked at me curiously but with admiration, finally understanding that I really didn't want to get too in depth with this conversation.

"You didn't open your gift?" I asked to quickly change the subject.

"I know. I was waiting for you since you missed me opening the others. Thank you, for everything and the presents but you don't have to buy me expensive things, Cam."

I slowly moved in beside her. She shifted to sit up a little more, bringing the blanket up with her to cover her breasts, as if hiding something.

I playfully eyed her curiously, and then leaned down to plant soft, nibbling kisses along her bare shoulder. Aside from the naturally enticing scent of her skin, something else smelled sweet and sugary, like vanilla.

"I know. But it means something to me to be able to give you everything that your heart desires." I whispered close to her ear.

She looked up at me, her gentle hand went to my cheek.

"All I desire is you. In fact, I saved you some cake too." She then smiled slyly.

Even though cake was the last thing on my mind, I glanced over at all of the tables in my room, seeing no sign of any cake.

"Where is it?"

She lifted the covers slightly, her eyes flicking downwards with a sensual and flirtatious twinkle.

I grinned, seeing that she had strategically placed a bit of frosting on each of her nipples, and several dots in a small trail down her lower belly…leading straight to one of my most favorite spots of all on her body.

Taking hold of the covers and pulling them away completely, I positioned myself over her.

"I see. Guess I won't be needing a fork then."

I leaned down with a long, slow flick of my tongue over the sweet, creamy frosting, and applying enough pressure to graze firmly over her hardened nipple.

Grasping onto my hair, she gasped loudly, moaning as she arched upwards and began to writhe beneath me in response.

"Oh damn, here we go again. I'm out of here." Edanai's voice carried into my room.

"Wait for me." Rahab grumbled next.

I laughed to myself. No need to worry about soundproofing the walls after all.

XXX: STARLING

I was very well rested, pumped, and ready to begin training bright and early this morning. Though it saddened me, it was a relief not hearing the divine hall bells tolling at the break of dawn. Cam managed to completely take care of most of the negative images that had been created in my head by Edanai's sharing of his past habits.

Continuing to spoil me, he even served me breakfast in bed. He held out the small present in front of me, just as I finished dressing in the brand new training wear that he had had a female fallen friend of his design and conjure for me. I loved them. They were light, comfortable, easy to move in, and form fitting. All of my tops were reinforced with an extra protective chain mail layer inserted between the material that covered my torso and abdominal areas.

Cam was going to be a major distraction for me. He was absolutely gorgeous and sexy in his own battle wear. He was practically shirtless, in nothing but a pair of black, soft leather pants, black boots, a black and chrome chest covering that extended into shoulder plates over his muscularly broad shoulders.

"I guess we got way too distracted last night. Why don't you open this one now?" There was a glimmer and glow in his eyes when he smiled.

I couldn't help but smile and blush, taking the small box from him and tearing at the tiny bow and wrapping. I opened the small lid to the gold colored box inside, already breathless at the black velvet ring box inside.

I looked up at him, speechless.

He took the box from me and opened it, revealing a diamond encrusted, white gold, or whatever material he had probably managed to gather from that microwave oven planet, cuff ring.

It was beyond unique. I studied the design closely, realizing that it sort of mimicked a portion of the pattern of my brandings on one side—and his on the other.

Tears began to form in my eyes.

He took my left hand, lifting my ring finger up and gently sliding the cool, gorgeous, breath-taking metal onto my finger where it fit perfectly.

"I guess as immortals, we'll have to devise our own method of commitment—that is if you're willing to accept this as that token." Cam then said.

He wiped away the single tear that managed to escape my eye.

My heart was fluttering.

"Are you asking me to marry you?"

"Humans call it marriage but I guess it's kind of the same meaning. For me...or for us, it's more of a bonding of souls and it goes way deeper than flesh. I'm asking for yours and I want for you to accept mine exclusively."

More tears fell slowly. I sniffed and he wiped them away for me.

I didn't know what to say, not that I was going to tell him no. Was he asking me for my soul? What exactly did that entail? There was no hesitation. I was already carrying his children but I needed some time to think and be sure about this part.

"That idea scares you, doesn't it?" he suddenly said, lowering his lids and looking down at me.

I didn't deny or admit to that, averting my eyes from his for just a second.

"I understand." He then said softly, kissing the top of my head.

I looked up at him, suddenly realizing what my hesitation must seem like.

"I'm not saying no. I just want to understand what exactly it means when you say, the willing giving of souls."

He smiled slightly. "I'm not Morning Star if that makes you feel better about the significance. I love you very much, Starling. My soul...or what's left of it is in your hands."

I felt guilt for having second thoughts about his intent.

"You have more soul in one feather than some of the humans that call themselves elders have in their entire bodies. I love you too." I whispered.

Cam brushed my chin with his finger, a slight smile playing at his the corner of his mouth.

It was silent as I admired the gorgeous, skillfully-crafted ring. Cam suddenly lifted me up gently, kissing me slow and deep, which sent fireworks straight into my groin once again. I was actually surprised that I could walk at all this morning let alone instantly feel arousal so soon after.

When he pulled away, he leaned in close to my ear.

"My first, true Elohim given name is…Ao`thiel."

My eyes went round. The revelation of finally hearing his true-given name echoed inside my ears over and over again, and the sound of it was beautiful. Once he set me back down on my feet, I was overcome with amazement and emotion at the meaning behind his finally revealing his true name to me.

He brushed a stray curl from across my forehead before speaking again, "Elohim gives us several names each, so that no man can ever learn or gain knowledge of our true, first-given names. Knowledge of a true name can give human beings complete power and control over the being attached to it. Universal law prohibits angels as well as the fallen from revealing, writing, or saying the true first name of another out loud in the presence of humans unless given permission to by that being. Some humans have been given the information through Morning Star but only for the fallen who follow him. They want to be used by humans in order to create chaos, dominance, and destruction in the human realm.

I was a tenth level archangel, which means that I was one of the very first angels created in the heavens. Not only did I hold and have access to a great amount of power, I was also responsible for the thwarting of opposition, which later became known as demons, and the policing of all other powers among all of the lower level angels. I was the eyes and the controller of divine light." He went on to tell me.

I felt my legs give out from underneath me but he swiftly caught and supported me, holding me against him. I wondered if that was why he still possessed light and why he has so much more heart and character, which separates him and his friends from all of the other fallen out there.

I couldn't understand why I reacted the way I did, other than I no longer saw him as just a fallen that I was in love with anymore. He was so much more than that —he's always been so much more than that even to all of his friends. The thought of being bound to a being of his caliber, fallen or not and carrying his children on top of that, was absolutely mind-blowing for me to even begin to comprehend.

"Are you alright?" has asked casually, as if he'd know this was going to be my reaction.

I nodded, still speechless as I reverently stared into his gorgeous, perfect face; seeing beyond the dark, purple blue, green, and gold rimmed color of his eyes, eyes that tended to give me chills every now and then when they began to glow.

"So now—you have absolute and complete control over me…not that you don't already." He said softly and winked.

~~~****~~~

The spot that Cam picked for us to train, was an island with a large open field, just beyond a large body of water that he called, the Infinite lakes. That was because unlike the healing properties of light that the Eternal waters were made up of, it wouldn't be lethal to his friends.

It was a gorgeous field, surrounded by lush, fruity smelling trees, like a tropical oasis.

I was already on cloud nine with our little soul binding commitment, which I agreed to make with Cam before we arrived. It was scary but not for the reasons that were obvious. I have no idea what the future holds, but either way—it will involve becoming parents soon. That alone was enough to get me to accept.

I was happy to see everyone out here already, including Aon. There were an even number of Cam's friends, one for each one of us, and a few others that I assumed wanted to sit and watch or something.

Everyone was here; Devlin, Durien, Spencer, even Lira. She was sitting with Aon underneath a small gazebo that had been set up, complete with snacks, water and other items like…bandages and first aid salves? I wondered exactly what they were for considering that we heal quickly.

Okay, now I was getting both nervous and antsy.

Lorelei ran over to meet up with me just as we landed.

"I'm going to do a quick head count and figure out a game plan before we get started." Cam whispered to me and then he was off across the field.

"Hey, kick ass outfit, I love that. Damn, having a supernatural boyfriend has many advantages. How does it feel to be twenty now?" She joked with a grin.

"Ask me when I should be sixty or even a hundred and we'll see."

We both laughed.

"That was a hell of a party last night. I never thought I'd ever say this, but I really enjoyed partying with them. It never once dawned on me that they were actually fallen— except for the magic." Lorelei giggled, "Oh and I figured out where my place was after all with the help of Jerilah, so us girls are rooming there. Jerilah and this other fallen named Vinnah stayed with us last night for protection, which was really cool of them to do. Wish you had come with us at least just to hang out. Are you going to be staying with Cam?" Lorelei then asked.

"For a while, yeah." I nodded.

It was quiet for a moment then Lorelei spoke low, "I wonder what's happening at the hall right now. I'm sure Sean and Diana have already gotten word. If anything, I hope they understand."

I didn't know what to say to that but guilt made my face burn.

"Me too." I said softly.

"Is he the same one that everyone knew you were with before you died? I mean, how did you two get together so fast that you would trust him like this? Did you remember him?"

I hesitated answering her question but then I thought about it. I looked her directly in the eyes, "He remembered me, actually. Some things were meant to be I guess."

She nodded. Jamie, Crystal, Scarlet and Lira were heading towards us.

I frowned when I glanced across the field to see Spencer, sitting off to the left of everyone else, alone.

"I guess Spencer doesn't share the same sentiment."

Jamie followed my gaze and glanced over at him with her brows knitted together. "He's still in hardcore divine warrior creed mode. But I'm sure that he'll come around after a while when he sees how much of a necessity this is. He's here and he defected with the rest of us, so that counts for something."

"How is Devlin?" I then asked her.

"Same."

"She's still not speaking?"

She shook her head no. "She's still bruised, I think. If you guys know what I mean."

Lorelei nodded sympathetically.

I sighed. "Maybe I should talk to her."

"I don't know...but there is one thing that she did want to know, if you could ask him. Cam, I mean."

That got my attention. I looked at her carefully. Even Lorelei leaned in closer.

"Ask him what?"

Jamie inhaled and turned to glance back at Devlin, who was watching all of us expectantly.

"She wanted to know…if he could somehow, find him. The one I told you about that night? And if he could bring him back…for her."

I had no idea how to respond or what to even say to that.

XXXI: CAM`AEL

Quite frankly, I would have loved nothing more than to take this opportunity to pound the seraphim into the ground. Why was he even here? That attitude was going to get him hurt, badly. He was already irritating to me just looking at him, sitting there melancholy and pensive. No one asked him to come and no one was certainly making him stay. I didn't have time for him.

I had many other things on my mind, one of which was the anticipation of what Aliks would tell me about the text. If it weren't for Starling pledging to become soul bound to me, I wouldn't be in such a productive, positive, and patient mood right now.

"I've secured and shielded the island all around and I will do it each time that you all come to train. Take as much time as you all will need without being seen or possibly distracted." Aon's voice filtered into my head.

"I was just about to ask being that this was the only logical area that offered some seclusion and space. I don't know how to go about this with Starling."

Aon chuckled, "Do not underestimate her ability even in her current condition. Starling will be absolutely fine. In fact, her spirit and compassion, her essence, her weapons, and her will, all make her one of the most fierce and aggressive warriors that I've seen in a very long time. Never underestimate the power, strength, and courage of a mother protecting her young. Ever seen a mother bear, wolverine, lioness, or even a mother impling go head to head with any beast twice her size who are threatening her babies?"

I've actually seen all four before, I mused.

"Good point."

I looked over at Starling briefly thereafter, trying to picture that level of ferocity in her. Strangely, I actually could.

Those of my friends who volunteered, aside from my closer friends who I knew wouldn't let me down, all showed up on time. I'm sure a part of that anticipation was the chance to both attack and fight against the warriors, even if it were just on a training level basis. I wasn't sure how I wanted to go about this, so I wanted to meet with my friends first to get it all figured out.

Everyone began to crowd in around me...very enthused to get started. I even noted a few who were here for more spectatorship than anything else, which was fine with me.

"How shall we proceed, oh fearless leader?" Ry quipped with a grin.

"First and foremost, I don't want this to be some sort of a class or military style drilling. The best way to learn is by doing but there are a few things that I want to ask of them and to make sure that they understand first."

"No special treatment for your woman though, right?" Mac commented.

Edanai stood in the background, arms folded across her chest as if trying to read me. She knew that I was still angry with her though, so she remained silent for now.

"No, of course not."

"Yeah, well I hope she has control of that fire of hers, otherwise...I'm out." Nay said, holding his hands up to clarify.

Nay's tattoos were superb and original but they were really distracting.

"Correction, if she doesn't then we may all be out and I don't mean ghosting out either." Ry joked and a few others laughed, though uneasily.

"She's already learned to master control over it. I was told by Aon, so no need to worry about that either but that does give me an idea. I think this may flow better if we find out what each one can do first, meaning their essences, strengths, and weaknesses. Then we can go from there but we should pair up. One of us with each one of them so that each demonstration can be practiced afterwards. How does that sound?" I looked at everyone for confirmation.

"Sure."

"Fine."

"Cool. In that case, I think you should be the one to pair up with your woman." Nay grinned.

I shot him a disparaging glance.

"Sounds good to me too, as long as they know that we aren't going to hold back. Are we?" Rahab asked unsurely.

"No. Hold nothing back but be very careful. We're helping not fighting them and we don't want any permanent or long lasting injuries, which goes for magick attacks as well."

"Agreed." Mac replied. Osiel, Sinma, and Jerilah all nodded affirmation.

I turned around to face the warriors who were scattered about, some conversing and others warming up.

"I need you all to gather over here with us so that we can go over a few guidelines before we start." I called out and beckoned all of them over. The others began to spread out and form a line-up behind me, standing with their wings out but folded behind them.

The warriors gathered around, forming a semi-circle in front of us with me in the middle. I didn't even look at the seraphim.

"I have something to ask you when we're done. It's about Devlin, the one Jamie was telling me about that night, who also befriended a fallen." Starling's voice entered my train of thought.

I glanced at her. *"I can already guess what that something is. The problem is that even if I knew his true given name, I don't have the power to un-banish him."*

"Oh."

"But...I know who does, so I'll look into it for you."
She smiled.

Now that I had their attentions, it was time to get down to business.

"First of all, I want to say that the timeframe we may have... and quite frankly, the time and patience of some others," I glanced over my shoulder at Ry and Nay, "Is not a guarantee. But I did say that we would help to prepare you guys and that's exactly what we intend to do on our end. You either want to learn or you don't, none of us will force or wait on anyone to make up their minds." I pierced the seraphim with a hard glare. He remained stoic.

Then, I paused and chuckled a bit, my friends sharing the same sentiment of humor because they knew it was going to come up eventually. I began to pace up and down the line of warriors to make eye contact as I spoke, feeling like a general talking to his army before battle.

"I have to address this first, only because I've seen you guys try time and time again but to no avail and certainly not in vain, so don't take this the wrong way," I looked each and every one of them directly in the eyes before I stated concisely that, "You will never outrun a fallen. Ever. The only choice and option that you have is to make yourself as difficult as possible to be caught— but let me warn you all that we are just as adamant about capturing you as you are about getting away. Ultimately, if we want you…we will catch you, and of course you all already know that females are at much more of a higher risk, so we're really going to be working with you seven in that area." I gave a nod to Starling and the eight females, including the female seraphim, Kaia.

I was already making some shift uncomfortably but it had to be said in order to give them something to think about.

It was truth.

"And why is that?" the seraphim was skeptical of my words.

I looked over at him and grinned.

"We don't just cloak, we teleport through portal pockets of both space and air. Why do you think we appear to be moving so fast and stealthily? I guess that's something you must have forgotten along with everything else. Damned shame."

His face reddened.

"Allow me to demonstrate." Mac flexed the muscles in his biceps and rolled his head as if stretching in preparation, just for show sake. He took flight in less than a split second thereafter.

Mac was nothing more than a dark streak, moving unbelievable fast, literally as if he were blinking in and out of sight. One minute he had been standing behind me with everyone else, and the next literal second…Lira squealed.

She was airborne with him as he glided upwards, making a wide arc and then slowly swooping low as to not freak her out or anything.

"Damn!" Anthony remarked.

"I didn't think ya'll were that freaking fast!" Durien exclaimed, shaking his head incredulously as Mac set a giggling but wide-eyed Lira, gently back down on her feet.

"Well, you obviously haven't seen Starling outrun one of you guys then." Jamie quipped with a confident grin but I could tell that it was more to get me off of the seraphim's back.

I glanced at Starling with a twinkle in my eye.

"I've heard. Care to demonstrate? Any volunteers?" I asked any of the others behind me.

"Uh, yeah. That machine was nowhere near that fast. I really don't think I could…"

"I know you can." The seraphim said assuredly to Starling and she was surprised.

"So do I." Kaia, piped in with an encouraging smile and a glimmer in her eyes.

I had to admit, I believed that she probably could too, but I was even more impressed with the support from all of her friends and from both seraphim.

"I'll volunteer for this one." Nay said cockily and stepped forward.

Everyone else began to cheer Starling on. She seemed uneasy until I nodded and winked my own encouragement at her.

I looked around for a possible course, then pointed towards a distant stand of foliage and trees, "Run to those two trees there, then back around and past the gazebo, ending up right back here. This isn't really a race. I want to know exactly what your speed is. If Nay manages to catch you, it will prove my point. This will be something that you will all end up being put to the challenge of by using the techniques that we'll show you."

Starling readied herself. Ry and the others were hyped and ready to see this, as was I. They were more set to mock Nay if Starling did indeed outrun him. If he didn't catch her, he'd never hear the end of it, I mused to myself.

"Ready?" I began.

She nodded, getting into position. The adrenaline building in her body was incredibly strong, I could literally feel it thrumming simply standing next to her.

She was focused and determined and she may just prove us all wrong.

"Come on, Starling, you can do it!" Durien clapped and the other rallied around his words.

"Ten second head start?" Nay asked her.

Starling shook her head and smiled confidently, "If you think you need it."

"Ohhh! Damn! Ouch!" Ry exclaimed as he and the rest of us, along with Starling's friends, all broke out in instigating laughter.

Nay pursed his lips and nodded with a grin, appreciating her humor, "Alright. No mercy, girl. Don't say I didn't offer." He began to ascend slowly, wings beating and ready.

"Go!" I shouted.

To my utter surprise, Starling was off like a literal shot, leaving nothing but the trailing blur of her light brown and ash blonde, curly pony tail whipping and flying wildly behind her.

Nay left a hard rush of wind behind in his wake that kicked up a whirlwind of dust and grass.

I could not believe my own eyes—and that was saying a lot. I didn't think that she could impress me any more than she has already. When Starling came flying back towards the group, though Nay was right on her heels, cheers and shouts of joy erupted all around us once Starling stopped. She was barely breathless.

"Holy shit, no way!" Ry exclaimed, incredulous as he gaped at Starling through his shades.

"I'm speechless. That's unheard of. If I didn't just see it, I wouldn't believe it." Jerilah said.

"I want a rematch." Nay said, slamming into the ground and already enduring the ridicule by everyone, especially those who came to just watch it all.

It was apparent that they were all intrigued with a newfound respect for Starling.

She had beaten him. She actually outran one of us. I saw her in a whole new light. She was not only going to be deadly, she was going to be damned near invincible.

"Very well done. You never cease to shock the hell out of me." I told her.

She smiled, pushing a curl from her face.

"Let me give it a run." Mac stepped forward and said.

"Later, we'll all get a chance," I grinned at Starling and she looked at me wryly.

"That was a very impressive demonstration. You guys were right but I never had a doubt that Starling was fast. Now that we know what we're working with, I have one last thing to address before we get started," My eyes went to the petite girl, Lira. She blushed.

"Why the hell do they not teach your scouts to fight with weapons?"

No one really had an answer, glancing at each other, especially the seraphim.

"Honestly, do they actually expect them to stay forever behind the walls of the hall? Scouts are the most favored of all the fallen because of what they can do. They go for high prices and since they're rare, she's going to be in the worst kind of danger…always."

"I can make her a weapon." Durien offered, looking at the tiny girl who stared back at me, incredulous that I was even saying it.

She pointed to herself. "Me? Fight? And I get my own weapon too? Awesome!" She bounced with a big smile, thrilled at prospect.

"One of you might want to teach her how to fight in hand to hand combat as well. That's always good to know."

"Fighting you guys would be impossible." Starling mentioned.

"After seeing what you just did, nothing is impossible," I told her.

"But I will offer you all this one guarded secret, even though I know that some of us won't be happy about it," I was already getting warning looks from the others, and throat clearing with covert grunts of protest from the rest.

I didn't want to reveal anything sacred either but this was a very crucial part of giving these warriors full advantage over all of the other warriors, so I continued on anyway, "Fallen, cannot fly, create portals, or cloak if their wing or wings have been badly injured. If you ever end up coming against one of us, that had better be the first thing that you try to take out or maim. We're the most vulnerable after taking wing damage and waiting to heal."

More disbelieving groans of disapproval came from behind me.

The warriors were both intrigued and appreciative of that top secret tip, remaining very attentive. At the same time, it was evident that another layer of trust had just been added to our collaboration. That had been part of my intent.

"Be assured that it won't be easy though. We know better than any other being, exactly what makes us vulnerable. That being said, you will all still more than likely get your asses handed back to you, of course, but at least it gives you more of a fighting chance when it comes to hand to hand combat. So now, would you all wield your weapons for us to see?" I then asked next.

"Man, you almost fucked up there. Too much information may backfire." Mac spoke first.

"Don't give too much, Cam. Not yet anyway. I don't trust that seraphim, Spencer." Ry warned.

"I don't either but I know what I'm doing. This is pointless if we're not helping to elevate their skills and knowledge of the fallen. I'm keeping tabs on every aspect about him, don't worry."

"I hope you didn't just murder all of us." Nay commented next.

I glanced at each one of them wryly, and then we all too a moment to observe each of the different types of weapons that we were going to be working with. As I went down the line, I pointed to the blonde girl first.

"Yours may be a problem but we can try and work around it. Durien, I'm not sure about yours. First, let me ask this. Have any of you ever tried to throw your weapons?"

"What do you mean?" Durien asked.

"Does the word throw have more than one meaning?"

Durien looked at me wryly.

"Has anyone ever thrown their weapons by letting them go?" I humored him with a smirk.

"We can't. It's attached and a part of us." Jamie replied.

I furrowed my brow. "That's not what I asked. I'm taking your answers to be no, none of you have even tried. Starling, yours will be perfect to demonstrate. Throw one of your blades over there." I pointed to the same copse of tropical trees in the far distance.

She looked at me unsurely as she stepped forward and raised her arm to throw it.

"Just let it go as you would a baseball." I encouraged her.

"Okay." She said, and with a slight grunt, she sent her blade sailing swiftly end over end towards the trees where we all clearly heard it embed itself in a trunk with a thump.

A few gasps of surprise immediately sounded from behind her, even she was stunned.

"Very nice." I complimented her aim, and it was more than just being partial.

"This is lesson number one. You want to know how to avoid most magic attacks, this will be the way to do it. Always keep your arms and your hand over your face protectively because that's where we tend to throw it first. A curse and magick spell are two different things and neither one can be cast simultaneously. Your biggest advantage, is to never remain in groups because even we can't get everyone at once. Fallen are more vulnerable while casting magic but you'd better move superfast because timing is everything. Now, pull your blades in." I then told her.

Her looked at me inquisitively and then she glanced over at her friends.

"Um…"

"Just trust me." I winked.

"This is another advantage if you happen to be hit by any magick. Magick, is meant to restrain both you and the use of your weapon. Throwing it away from you, keeps that weapon from being affected and..."

Starling's blade returned to her smoothly, like a well-directed boomerang, tethered to her palm by an invisible string. It was a blur as it whipped past us all but she caught it by the hilt expertly with a surprised look on her face.

Her skill was impressive. I can only imagine how lethal she'll become after training and practice.

"It will always return to you. When thrown, it temporarily becomes separate from you, which means that it will not be subject to whatever spell your body has been afflicted by. So when you pull them back in, they become projectiles bearing your light, which will destroy or break any dark magick spell. Consider that technique to be a highly effective alternate line of defense."

Each one of them were very pleasantly surprised but the seraphim still remained somewhat cynical.

"How did you know that we could do that?" He then asked.

"Yeah, we were never told that was an option." Lorelei added. Several others agreed with nods.

I sighed, popping my neck with slow annoyance at his game.

"We have brandings in common..." I began, wielding my short, diamond edged blade and flinging it at him, all in one obscuring motion.

It whistled as it sailed through the air at high speed but he managed to dodge it just in time, crouching low and nearly falling back on his ass with a stunned expression that quickly turned into a scowl. He twirled his iridescently glowing, lightning-shaped bo and held it out defensively in front of him.

Clumsy but nice dodge.

My blade swiftly returned to me and I clasped the thick hilt with ease.

"Whoa, wicked sweet!" Gabe exclaimed enthusiastically. The rest of them all made similar comments in awe. Devlin's face remained passive but intrigued by me, my words, and my demonstration.

"Our weapons were both cleaved and forged in the same manner. That's why. Any more questions?" I regarded the seraphim with a raised a brow.

XXXII: STARLING

I had to admit, I was highly impressed with myself and even more confident in all of my abilities after beating Nay. After that, the first few days of training with the fallen were extremely hard. No one escaped without some sort of injury or injuries, either physical or by magic. It was all very difficult but in the end, it was all very valuable and highly necessary.

It was suggested by Cam, that working in and as a group could overpower any fallen or a few at one time. We also learned, that fallen could only do one thing at a time, either fight in combat or throw magic—even in flight, but not both. We should always be ready to react and take advantage of the few precious seconds that we would have to attack or even escape.

Since a few of my natural talents included super running speed, flexibility, and acrobatics, Cam used me for most of the demonstrations. However, when it came time to pair up to practice, none of the other fallen wanted to be my partner, even though I had proven and shown them all that I had complete control over my fire now. Cam was stuck with me — and I may have accidentally burned him one or twice but they were very minor.

I had to continually check on the dates after several more training sessions because Cam said that for every one day cycle here, it was two in the human realm. That meant that it was getting close to Christmas time in the human realm and I told China that I would be back by then.

She had fainted on the phone when I told her that I was pregnant, so I just hung up. When she came to, she called right back and immediately wanted to know everything. I told her I'd save that for when I returned and she was giddy that she was going to be an aunt. It gave both of us something to look forward too on my return. I hoped.

As for Joel, I was still indifferent about him but given the fact that she said he was acting different because of this new girl he was dating, I wasn't sure what to think. I believed her though, about the darkness that she felt was trying to mess with her now. I somehow felt responsible for that, so I had to go back, soon.

On our final day of training, we decided to not just celebrate a newly found alliance with fallen, but becoming closer as a group of warriors and friends as well. It was one last major dinner together before finally returning to the human realm where we would all room together for safety purposes.

Cam had been a superior teacher and trainer. He even went the extra mile in scouting out a place big enough for all of us in an inconspicuous part of town where I went to school.

I didn't want everyone to feel as if they had to stay wherever I went; they had their own lives to lead even as warriors but they agreed that we should all stick together. The beginning of the horrors to come haven't even begun, so if we don't maintain solidarity now, then we weren't going to survive.

No one wanted to return to lives that they didn't even remember for the most part anyway.

We all wanted to show appreciation to the fallen, so the majority of us, well the girls anyway, helped Rahab to cook up a huge gourmet dinner for everyone.

Spencer declined to join us, heading back to Durien's by himself, which I found rude and ungrateful. He got the training and now he wanted nothing to do with the fallen. Jerk.

Devlin began to open up just a bit but she spoke very few words. Of course, Cam offered to host the dinner at his place—and the size four jeans that I was used to wearing...were starting to feel a little snug.

"Any word on who would be able to reach Devlin's fallen friend?" I asked Cam once we all sat at the table.

She hadn't said anymore about it but I hadn't forgotten.

"I'll have to wait until I see Aliks. He's supposed to be getting back to me soon anyway about something else. Have I told you yet, what an ass-kicking, deadly on so many levels, including by virtue of your beauty, of a warrior you are?" Cam replied, pulling out my chair for me as I sat.

I giggled out loud. *"You haven't really told me that verbally but you've certainly shown me just about each and every night after training."*

He groaned with desire, low enough so that only I could hear, and then kissed me on the side of my neck in front of everyone.

It was all good because after each training session, and even through all of the injuries, I always found myself incredibly turned on just like that first day on the training field at the hall.

"Well, even though I'm afraid of you it won't stop me from showing you again tonight too. I live dangerously."

I smiled, blushing. *"I know."*

There were other fallen here too, the ones that had started out simply watching the training, and then ended up helping out and becoming more acquainted with us. Cam left the doorway to his home open and they all sat out on the stone balcony, drinking and laughing while engaged in conversations with Jamie, Gabe, Anthony, and Durien until it was time to eat.

I admit, it couldn't get any better than this. Everyone was getting along and there was delicious food to go along with the hip hop music playing in the background.

Lira loved to dance. She was showing off some of her hip-hop dance moves and entertaining the female fallen who watched her with fascination.

"The food is ready but I would like to propose a toast first before we all sit down to eat." Rahab suddenly announced while tapping a spoon to his wineglass.

It was kind of comical seeing his massive taloned fingers curled around the delicate stem. Though he was scary looking, he was actually one of my favorites. He was well-spoken, polite, and considerate — kind of like a giant teddy bear. Ry on the other hand, well, I've never seen his eyes but he was cool and funny. Atiro didn't speak much so I wasn't sure what to make of him. Mac and Nay were smart alecks but really nice once you stripped all the sarcasm away. Of course, Nay was still determined and ready to chase me again anytime, anywhere. Edanai, I wasn't sure what to make of her just yet either but Cam told me that her specialties and gifts lie in healing, nurturing, and masking.

Everyone stopped their conversations, and the fallen who had been outside came filtering in to crowd around the table with their drinks already in hand.

Rahab waited patiently for everyone to raise their glasses before speaking again.

"Just for show, you shouldn't drink." Edanai whispered to me as she handed me a red wine-filled glass.

"To new alliances and hopefully long-lasting friendships." He began.

"And to probably the only warriors who stood fast against hard-assed training and did very well." Mac tilted his glass.

"To exciting and new arrivals both big and small." Edanai smiled with a tip of her wineglass.

I narrowed my eyes at her and I could see Cam cut his eyes at her immediately too. Then, his head snapped to Ry a curious and agitated glare.

Ry immediately jumped up from the table.

"It's Draea, don't attack them! She's my woman!" He proclaimed as he swiftly made his way outside, "Hold your thoughts, I'll be right back." He quickly said over his shoulder.

"What the hell are they doing here?" Cam looked pissed as he stood up and followed him.

Okay, what was going on?

"Who the hell is Draea?" Edanai inquired, getting up from the table too.

I couldn't help but be nosy, so I hurried out after all three of them. Peering out of the door, I eased out from behind Edanai to get a better view only because I was amazed at what I saw. It was something straight out of a fairy tale book…or a nightmare tale more like it.

There were two incredibly sexy, barely clothed, centerfold girls, sitting astride a really long, scaly, sharp-fanged thing that resembled a snake with a lion's head…and wings.

One of them hopped off and ran into Ry's arms and they kissed like two long lost lovers in a romance movie. I couldn't help but smile.

"Cam'ael, we come in peace and alone, I promise. I wanted to make sure that you were alright. May I approach?" The girl still sitting on the strange beast called out. There were two weird looking, ugly, hulks of something mounted on two more creatures on either side of her in the distance, watching,

I glanced up at Cam with a hand on my hip. He looked at down at me out of the corner of his eye, surprised to see me standing here and I could tell that he was really annoyed.

"Go back inside now." He hissed at me, quickly moving in front of me and somehow keeping me from moving around him to see anything else.

"Why? What's going on? Who is that she-thing?"

"What are you both doing here? How did you even know where…" Cam began to ask her until Ry and that freaky girl stopped sucking face.

The girl looked at Cam. "I brought her here. I don't know if you know but I was the one who brought Berith here that day. We're old friends and I owed her a favor. Grace was worried about you, so I showed her the way." Draea explained.

Grace? Jealousy began to rear its ugly head again.

I tried to peer around Cam but he wouldn't let me past him. He held his arms out behind him to keep me from moving, like guard rails. Though I should have been able to move, I couldn't. I couldn't even duck beneath him. He was holding me in place with magic. Tip-toeing to see above him was out of the question, he towered over me by almost two feet at least.

"I don't want either of them to see you, now go back inside."

"Why not?" My thoughts instantly went to the worst, like when Edanai gave me the run-down of his past.

"They work for Morning Star."

"So what?"

He wasn't budging.

"Fine. I'm going but don't close the door." I pouted with attitude but it didn't faze him.

I tried to force myself to move and take a step, only to end up tripping and stumbling sideways, once his magic hold on me had dissipated. Cam's hand shot out in a stealth blur, catching me before I hit the ground and intent on keeping me hidden, but he failed. At that point, I was able to get another look at this girl and she could fully see me now.

"Shit." Cam groaned.

The creature thing floated closer and I could see her a little better. Her crazy, neon green eyes immediately zoned in me with curiosity at first, and then she simply stared at me in astonishment. Her eyes then returned to Cam, and then back to me once again.

"You should really go inside now, Starling." Edanai urged quietly.

Cam was really annoyed and ticked. It was evident on his beautiful face. His jaw tensed, really working.

I already knew what she was thinking. What I wanted to know was, who the hell she was to him?

"What's this? You bought a pet from Morning Star? No…wait…"

"Oh wow!" She then grinned, displaying eye-shocking, gleaming metallic teeth. "A divine warrior?! For breeding purposes too? How did you manage to snag one of her caliber, and for how much? Her aura is spell-bindingly bright." She was ecstatic now.

When Cam ignored her questions, the girl continued on, "Before you blow me out of the sky, I'm here because you left my room so fast and without a word, I wasn't sure what to think. I assume all is alright since it looks like you're having a party. I'm hurt that I didn't get an invite. We didn't finish our conversation either." Grace then smiled flirtatiously.

"What?" I snapped with an attitude over all of her comments and assumptions—but more so, her last few sentences in particular.

"Wait inside, Starling. Please." Cam patiently told me again. He let me go and I took my time backing away from him towards the doorway. I knew he could use magic to hurry me along if he wanted to but he didn't, probably because there was no longer any point. He was obviously taken aback by my aggressive insistence.

"Who is she...or what is she?" I demanded to know first.

"You let your pet talk to you that way and roam around freely?"

"She's not my pet! You didn't have to come out here." He stated firmly to her.

"Not your pet? And not for breeding purposes, eh? Then what is she to you? And why is she with child?" The girl persisted with a surreptitious grin slowly spreading across her face.

She knows? How can she tell that I'm pregnant? My hand automatically went to my belly.

All of Cam's friends, including the ones from inside who had just joined us, slowly turned to look at me as if I were some bizarre thing. You could have heard a bubble pop in that precise moment.

"Okay, I'm going inside now...and feel free to close the door too." I finally gave in to Cam.

I could be stubborn, I know.

XXXIII: CA'MAEL

I didn't think it was possible for me to be as pissed, annoyed, and any more near ballistic than I already was right now. First, at Draea for having the gall to bring both herself and Grace here; at Ry for acting like it was no big deal, knowing how I am about my space; at Edanai for telling Starling all of my past business; and then at Starling, for being so damned stubborn. Now, she's been seen by Grace and even worse...Grace knows that she's pregnant. That meant that Morning Star would soon know too. I could only portend doom and very bad things from this point on.

Starling took a step towards the door, only to stop short. The doorway was crowded with both her friends and the rest of mine.

This just kept getting better and better. Not the way I wanted everyone to find out but it was out of my hands now. If I really wanted to be an ass, I'd throw a huge gush of wind filled with light at Grace, Draea, and the two goons in the distance but I lost my window of opportunity several moments ago.

"Did she just say what we think she said?" Durien asked Starling.

She bit her lip, casting her eyes down to the ground and slowly nodded.

"Whoa." One of her friends breathed softly.

The rest were quiet, probably in shock.

"Is everything okay, Cam?" Rahab asked.

"Not really, Rahab but no threats." I informed him warily.

"I suppose I'm going to be an uncle now?" he then asked for verification.

I wanted to chuckle. In the midst of the moment, leave it to Rahab to remain positive and supportive, not that I didn't think he wouldn't have been no matter what the circumstances.

"It looks that way, my friend."

"Congratulations, Cam."

Rahab, a long time close friend, both knew and understood what Starling having my children meant to me.

"Thank you, Rahab."

Now, I had no choice but to hurry and get Starling and all of her warrior friends the hell out of my place and back in to the human realm, where they'd all fare better and safer for the time being.

All of my friends, except for Edanai were staring at me. Well, it was going to come out eventually. I wanted nothing more than to ghost away right now.

"Pregnant with your child, how very interesting." Grace reiterated, looking me over curiously and then at Starling again.

I already didn't trust her, even more so, the way she phrased that.

If I told her to leave, it could jeopardize any alliance but I didn't care about that at this point.

"Is Starling really pregnant?" Ry asked me privately for verification. His question held more of a disbelieving tone. Draea was still draped all over him like a wet towel.

"Yes."

"Not that it surprises me at all but how was that even possible? And how long were you going to wait before telling us? Damn, you had her doing all that hardcore training too? She can't be too far along, she's not showing yet."

"Now is not the time to talk about all that but yes, I was going to tell everyone eventually. Aon and Aliks already know, they said she would be fine and —well…she sure as hell did everything and very well, too."

"True. So, the angels know and they're cool with that?"

"Yeah."

Ry was silent at first and then he began to laugh hysterically in his head.

I glanced at him in question.

"Nay got owned by a human female—and a pregnant one at that. Sweet!"

I pursed my lips. Ry shook his head with a huge grin on his face.

"I'll meet you at your place to talk later at nightfall." I finally told Grace.

I had to make sure that the threat of her reporting this to Morning Star was nullified somehow.

I could feel the heat of Starling's unhappy glare on my face right then.

In the next instant, I literally felt something in the air—change. To us fallen and supernatural beings, the anomaly was evident. Even Kaia, the female seraphim emerged from my home with a serious look on her face as she scanned the horizon.

Draea and Grace also reacted, we just didn't know what we were looking at or expecting other than it being something…negative.

"What's going on? What's everyone looking at?" Starling asked, moving in next to me.

I automatically put my arm around her and pulled her to me protectively, scanning the skies in the far distance suspiciously.

"I'm not sure yet." I whispered.

"You felt that too, huh?" Mac said, appearing on my other side as he gazed over the horizon.

"Do me a favor, take them all inside and tell everyone to get ready for transport into the human realm. We need to get them out of here, now. I have a bad feeling about this." I told him.

"About what? I'm not going anywhere without you." Starling panicked.

"Starling, this isn't up for debate and your stubbornness won't work this time. I'll be fine, your safety is my main concern."

Even Grace and her Bandit cronies began to inch closer towards my home, turning around to face the unknown force that was pressing heavily in the atmosphere, growing stronger by the minute.

The only thing I could think of, the only thing that I was sure that we could all think of…was Morning Star.

What the hell was he doing and why now?

I turned to face the rest of the warriors, gently pushing Starling in the direction of the doorway.

"All of you, get inside now. I'm going to seal the door closed."

"No!" Starling screamed, holding onto me tighter.

I started to just pick her up and carry her inside myself, when an extremely loud and powerful explosion rocked both the air and the ground in a sonic boom that reverberated against the mountains, hurting even *my* ears.

Starling jumped, gripping onto me tighter and gasping in horror with a hand clamped over her mouth to keep from screaming aloud. Her eyes went wide, immediately filling with tears.

Several of the warriors verbally exclaimed their shock out loud, and the girls all screamed in horror, falling to their knees in tears. Even the female seraphim began to cry. An enormous, fiery ball billowed up like a rising, flaming sun in the far distance.

I was struck speechless, feeling helpless and paralyzed with revulsion. I did feel a sense of guilt for being relieved that Starling hadn't been there at the time. It didn't take much to guess what had just happened. It was just impossible for me to even begin to comprehend.

The Divine Hall had just been completely—obliterated.

XXXIV: STARLING

Paralyzed in horror, I couldn't help but cry. I felt sick, my knees about ready to give out on me but Cam supported me to keep me from collapsing. I wasn't really sure what had happened until I heard both Lorelei and Scarlet scream, and then saw them both fall to their knees in horrified despair.

I still couldn't believe it let alone understand how that happened. Then confusion began to intercept my grief. Even the fallen were silent and frozen as we all stared out into the far distance at what was once the grand Divine Hall.

"How did that just happen?" I asked Cam.

He hugged me tighter against him and then glanced down at me. I never thought I'd see uncertainty in his eyes but I was seeing it now and it worried me.

"I don't know."

Suddenly, both Aon and Aliks appeared and they didn't seem at all alarmed. I supposed it was because they already knew.

"I'll see you tonight then." Grace said quickly in reaction to their arrival.

Ry and Draea kissed their good-byes and she was back on the beast with Grace in a flash. Then, they all took off swiftly towards the Northern horizon.

Cam turned to address his friends, "Could you all take the warriors to the location I set aside for them now?"

"How was that allowed let alone able to happen?" Anthony looked at both Aon and Aliks for an answer.

"Nothing is ever allowed to happen. For every action, there is an opposite reaction." Aon said.

"So a bunch of innocent warriors, animals, and people were killed for no reason?" Lorelei's voice was quivering.

"What it because we all defected?" Scarlet sniffed, confused.

Both Aon and Aliks remained passive and stoic but Aliks shook his head no. I was angry at them right now too.

"Why didn't you two warn them? Or better yet, stopped it? What kind of an action and reaction caused that?" I spat with a gesture towards the inferno in the distance.

Aon looked at me and Cam matter-of-factly and calmly replied, "Why do you think?"

I froze, my anger halted as I crossed my arms over my middle. My voice quickly toned down to an innocent whisper. "What? But I thought that…"

Cam cut in and spoke to Aon, "There are enough eyes and ears out here and I don't mean everyone here." Then he turned to me urgently, "Starling, go inside. Ry is taking you out of here."

So this was all mine and Cam's fault? I felt like fainting. Guilt burned my face and threatened to make me throw up. Was everyone going to blame and hate me now too? I didn't even want to meet their eyes.

Lira was the most hysterical.

"I-I- need to see what h-h-happened." She could barely speak.

"No, it's way too dangerous for you." Edanai told her.

Lira got up, almost stumbling as she ran back inside.

Cam's friends began to usher everyone else inside.

Durien was standing stock still like a statue, simply staring in silence.

The only one who wasn't crying at all, and I was even surprised that she was out here, was Devlin.

She seemed unaffected by the scene and I couldn't blame her on the surface but there were many innocent people over there.

"The hall has many underground tunnels, tunnels that span a great distance and converge into one main hall in the central hemisphere…" Kaia began to say softly.

"There's no way they could have been prepared or saw that coming. There wouldn't have been any time for anyone to have seen that coming." Durien replied.

"But they do have a ton of portal gems. They could have easily used them before it happened." Gabe offered.

"The only problem with that possibility is that they had no idea it was going to happen." Anthony replied.

It was upsettingly silent for the next few moments.

"Wait! Spencer. We need to check on Spencer too!" Jamie suddenly said before they were all ushered inside.

Once inside, Scarlet was screaming Lira's name. I ran into the living room to see Lira, lying on her back as if she were in a peaceful sleep on the couch. Her arms were gently resting over her stomach and she wasn't moving. We all knew what she had done and both Scarlet and Crystal were in tears again.

"Can one of you find her and tell her to come back!" Lorelei asked any of the Fallen.

"How do you usually wake her up when she does this?"

"We can't. Her spirit is already gone. Unless it returns, she's like a corpse save for the fact that she's still breathing."

"Then her physical body will be fine here. It will have to remain here for her return anyway, right?" Edanai pointed out.

Scarlet nodded.

"I need to get to Spencer before we leave!" Jamie said again frantically to Rahab.

"I'll go with you guys just in case." Durien offered her.

"I will too." Kaia stepped up.

"If he's there and won't come with us, then what?" Durien asked Jamie.

"Then I'll stay with him and try to convince him." Jamie replied.

"I don't know." Rahab shook his head.

"Please!" Jamie begged him.

I could only look on at the plight of everyone in both shame and sadness.

"If Spencer is in the human realm, isn't he safer than all of us right now? I mean, he's not gonna be in the same place, but the human realm is where we're going now too, isn't it?" I pointed out.

"It's just a feeling I have, Starling. He's by himself right and he's going to be devastated when he finds out what just happened. He's a part of this group too and I want to make sure that he's with us. There's no limit to anything anymore after that brazen act." Jamie countered.

She was right.

"What do you think this all means? Do you think this is it? This is the start of it all, isn't it?" Lorelei asked anyone who would answer.

"No, not necessarily." Nay replied.

"But it was shocking and really odd." Mac said.

This was all my fault. They would all be looking at me next. I was the one responsible for the death of so many. Why had God and the Angels allowed so many warriors, elders, and elementals to die like that? We needed all the help we could get!

The table in the dining room was still full of the savory dishes we cooked, all untouched. I turned to head back to Cam's room to sulk and grieve in private. I had no words of support or anything right now, and I didn't want to look anyone in the eye. A hand stopped me firmly.

"Starling, start grabbing your clothes. We're getting all of you out of this realm, now." It was Ry.

I shook my head. "I'm staying with Cam."

"Touching—but no, he's not gonna be on my ass for leaving you here."

"He won't."

I gasped and squealed in surprise when he leaned down, reached under my arms, and hoisted me up with fluid ease so that I was eye level with him. I could only look at my reflection in the sunglasses that masked his mysterious eyes. It was amazing to me how he managed to keep them on during all of the training drills too.

"Apparently, you don't understand how we fallen interact with one another. He wants you safe in your condition. Normally, I wouldn't give a shit but Cam is my friend and he'd do it for me, now get your things and let's go. If anything, you'll be back in your own familiar territory anyway."

"I'll deal with him then."

"Damn, you're more stubborn than I am. Edanai!" Ry called over his shoulder.

"Put me down, please." I stated.

"What?" Edanai answered him.

"Need a little assistance here. Starling isn't quite working with me or getting any of this. Can you get her stuff later?"

"Later? Hey, put me down, Ry! I said I'm not going!" I began to writhe and squirm in his grip.

"Aw hell, hurry before she lights my ass up!" he called again said.

I wouldn't have done that to him but it didn't matter. Before I could even make a move to do anything at all, I lost total and complete consciousness.

XXXV: CAM`AEL

"*Are* you telling me what I think you're telling me?" I asked Aon acidly.

"That depends, what do you think I'm telling you?" She replied.

"Enough with the cryptic! You know exactly what I'm asking! And you, you owe me a decoded text!" I said to Aliks.

We had all three popped out into another dimension to quickly converse with each other. There were things I didn't want my friends, the warriors, and whatever dark beings that were lurking out there to hear and to know. I knew my friends would quickly get the warriors out of there and continue to protect and watch over them in the human realm, especially Starling.

"Starling has been pregnant, Cam`ael, do you really believe that was the cause?" Aon reasoned.

"They why did you make her believe that?"

"I didn't make her believe anything."

"Why did you guys allow that to happen? And don't give me that cause and effect shit! This is exactly why the darkness is winning and you all just stand by and watch!"

I was fuming now.

"Cam`ael, you need to calm down. I'm not finished decoding or gaining permission to reveal yet. I only came on the spur of the moment because Aon asked me to meet her at your place." Aliks said.

"Have you no faith Cam`ael? After all you've been given, you still act as if you know nothing." Aon said.

I glared at her, not in the mood for any bullshit or placating.

"If anyone did it, it was you." She then said.

I narrowed my eyes at her.

"Now you're blaming me?!"

"Somehow, their protective force field was weakened considerably enough that it left them vulnerable. You know, when you threw that fit over Starling not long ago?" Aliks reminded me.

How the hell had I managed to weaken an indestructible field of light?

"So you are saying that I'm responsible for all of their deaths? Is that it?" I was both sorrowful and angry at the same time.

"No." Aon shook her head and she was serious.
"Then what the hell are you two saying?"
"There were no deaths, Cam'ael."
I was perplexed. We all saw it.
"How is that possible?"
"Again, ye of little faith." She then grinned.
There was a momentary silence, one that they allowed for my own benefit as I began to think.
"They got out in time, animals and all—didn't they?" I finally figured out.
Aon clapped patronizingly, "By George, he's a genius."
Aliks grinned slightly.
"Why? How did they know?"
"The plan was already in place. They were given a foretelling message. A meeting was called for and held at the Northern Hall over several day breaks ago. The move was decided then. A simultaneous portal gem breaking, if you will." Aon smiled.
Why did I feel relief? I could care less. I supposed it was because Starling and her friends would no longer be devastated and traumatized, once they were told.
"What was the message?"
"Now that part, is none of your business. Divine warrior confidentiality." Aon tsked with a wagging finger.
I rolled my eyes and sighed heavily. I was still anxious and getting really impatient about knowing what the texts were talking about, too. It was cruel not to explain this to the hysterical warriors when they both arrived at my place, but I already assumed that they were leaving that part up to me.
"Soon." I pointed to Aliks as a reminder, and then I created a portal and ghosted through, back home.

~~~****~~~

When I made it to the abandoned warehouse that sat in a field by a small lake in the country, everyone was in the midst of getting their things together and setting up in whichever room that they chose.
Everything inside was made brand new, right down to the paint over the insulated steel walls. I set up the utilities, all new appliances, furniture, and even cable television. There were a total

of seven bedrooms, three bathrooms, a large kitchen and dining room, and an equally large living room. I even threw in a few extras, like a state of the art gaming system, sound system, and a hot tub. The rest was up to them.

No one really spoke and a few people were missing. The only ones here were Lorelei, Gabe, Anthony, Ry, Nay, and Atiro.

"Where's Berith?" I asked Atiro.

"She's safe on a tropical planet with a few others. I thought it would be best for her in light of everything that's just transpired."

I nodded, "Good thinking."

I then turned to the three warriors that remained. "Where are Jamie, Durien, Kaia, and Lira?"

"Jamie, Durien, and Kaia all went with Rahab, Jerilah, and Sinma to check on Spencer, and Lira is at your place with Crystal, Scarlet, and Edanai— unconscious. She went to see what happened at the hall." Lorelei explained, melancholy. Her eyes were red.

Great.

"Well, there's something I need to tell everyone but I'll wait until they all return so I won't have to repeat it." I told her.

"I hope its good news." Gabe said.

"And Starling is unconscious in that room up there but she's alright." Anthony pointed.

"Unconscious?" I was up the metal spiral staircase in a flash.

"I had to do it, man. She was fighting me to stay with you." Ry informed me, "And I've already scoped the place out. It's clear. I placed a few feathers around and Vinnah placed some protective spells around the windows and doors, and about a mile radius all around. If anything, it might be a really good disguise. Not many would think that warriors were here, if you know what I mean." Ry went on to explain as he headed back down the stairs in the opposite direction.

He glanced over his shoulder while throwing a quick peace sign, "I'll be at Draea's if you need me."

"Thanks." I nodded.

I quietly peered into the room, seeing Starling sleeping peacefully on the bed. I would have woke her up but I wanted her to rest.

She needed it.

Being pregnant, and pregnant with twins wasn't easy yet she exuded both energy and strength beyond my expectations and even that of her friends. The ring I gave her shimmered softly on her finger. Her hand rested on her stomach and it winked with the slow rise and fall of her rhythmic breathing. It was a symbol of my undying love and loyalty to her. She was already professing hers to me by virtue of carrying and having my children.

Someone was approaching. I backed out of the doorway and glanced down the short hallway at the landing of the metal, spiral steps.

Devlin stopped, eyeing me carefully. She was apprehensive, taking timid steps. I didn't even notice her when I got here. She stopped, still several feet from me once we made eye contact.

It seemed like she wanted to speak to me but she was afraid. Then she softly cleared her throat.

"Is…Is she really pregnant?" She asked me in thin, hoarse voice and her eyes shifted to the room where Starling slept.

That wasn't the question that I was prepared for her to ask me but there was no point in lying about it.

I sighed and nodded.

"How was that possible?"

I didn't know that I wanted to answer that question, aside from the birds and the bees talk. Then I realized exactly why she was asking it. This was the girl that Starling helped. She had endured and suffered in Morning Star's capture and I was pretty sure I knew why he let her go. Morning Star never lets his captives and servants go, at least not sane; all in one piece; or alive for that matter, so it made me a little wary of her.

Leaning with her back to the wall behind her, she laughed quietly to herself as if thinking of a private joke, and then slid down to sit, pulling her legs up and hugging her knees. We were probably about four or five feet from each other. I leaned against the opposite wall on my shoulder and crossed my arms.

She inhaled, taking in a deep breath as if she were about to speak and then she paused. We could hear the other four bustling about downstairs and engaged in low conversations about what just happened.

For the most part, it was pretty quiet.

I needed to tell them the truth, soon. I wondered what was taking so long to check on that damned seraphim.

"Who took Jamie, Durien, and Kaia to get the seraphim?" I called out to everyone at once.

"We did. Me, Jerilah, and Sinma are here. The seraphim is gone *and I suspect foul play but you know they didn't kill him. There are lots of lingering dark signatures left behind here. No trace of a struggle but there's not a body either, which makes me very suspicious."* Rahab reported back.

No trace of a struggle? That was odd unless he was also broadsided and overpowered, which was very likely. Earthbound seraphim were the third in line for most valuable in the Spirit Realm because they were very rare. I know for a fact that whoever took him didn't kill him, and they don't plan on it either.

They want him for the light he has and for reproductive purposes. I couldn't see him choosing darkness, which is exactly what they're hoping.

Damn. I groaned. More bad news.

"You must already know what we're thinking. Jamie is hysterical. She thinks he might have just gone somewhere and she wants to wait for him to possibly come back but I don't think that's gonna happen. This place is miles from any town and he has no access to portals. The others are scouting the area with the other warriors right now."

Great. I hate to say that I already knew what could have happened. Dark armies didn't believe in ransom and surely wouldn't have picked him for it either if they were trying to get to me and maybe Starling. This was unfortunate but he was just too damned hard-headed.

"Be safe and bring her back anyway. It's got Morning Star written all over it, though I can't figure out how they were able to track and find him so quickly. I knew they were watching and I don't think it was a coincidence on the heels of what just happened at the hall either. I'm pretty sure that the two occurrences are linked. Hurry and return here with the warriors. I'll send an image and an address of the location."

Devlin began to speak again, having no idea that I was in my own mental communication.

"I can't blame them for not trusting me but they didn't deserve that sucker attack. He set me up to be a mite, hoping that they'd accept me back in and I'd be his eyes and ears." It seemed like she didn't want to face me at first, keeping her eyes fixated on the blank wall across from her.

"I know what he did but I had nowhere else to go. I tried to…I wanted to just…" She shook her head and sniffed, her eyes closing briefly to stop her tears.

Sadly, I knew what she was going to say and what she had tried to do. I remained quiet, lending her the ear that she needed.

"He wanted me to try and lure Starling to him. I didn't know who she was at the time but when she did what she did…I understood exactly why then. She's gonna have to be really, really careful here too. She has no idea how many he has out to get her for him."

"I do and that's all that matters. He won't so much as see her let alone get his hands on her while I'm around."

She nodded slowly and then paused again.

"He's been trying for the longest time. As long as he had me, he's been trying but he can't do it, not even with all the magic and servants that do that stuff. He still can't. None of them can. Evil and hate-filled aren't even strong enough words to describe him." She then laughed softly to herself, scratching her chin on her knee in thought.

"All of that power yet the one thing he can't do is what he wants more than anything."

"He can impregnate humans. We all can. All of his children are expendable. The dark divines chose darkness, there's no light left in them anymore so they're of no use to him except to fight."

Her brows furrowed. "I know but how? Light and dark can't exist in the same body."

She made a good point and it was true.

"I have both."

Awe brightened her eyes and then she was perplexed.

"I guess that's why she's pregnant now." She glanced at the open door where Starling slept.

"I don't know if you planned it or not…but I do know that if it wasn't born of love, it wouldn't have happened. At least, that's what I believe. You'd better make sure to keep her protected. If he finds out, he will go above and beyond to kidnap her and your child." She whispered ominously.

I was nonchalant.

"He's evil, bold, annoying, insane, and powerful but he's not stupid, and by that I mean he would never try and attack me directly or anything I hold dear."

She chuckled. "No shit. I get why he's scared of you now. He really hates you, which means you guys must be doing something good." She smiled crookedly.

I nodded, flattered.

There was another long pause and I thought about her words. I wanted to know and hear everything that she had to say, only because she hadn't spoken for so long since rejoining the other warriors.

"What's the name of the fallen that befriended you?" I asked her.

A light seemed to turn on in her eyes all of a sudden and she appeared both hopeful yet sad at the same time.

"Xavien. You—you can call him back?"

"I can't make any guarantees. I'll see what I can do."

Her shoulders slumped a bit but she nodded.

Why did that name seem…familiar?

XXXVI: STARLING

My eyes slowly fluttered open. The room was a bit chilly but a thick comforter had been pulled up to my chin.

Where was I?

I sat up quickly and looked around the unfamiliar, dim room. It was cozy, and set-up with the smell of brand new furniture but it wasn't anything or anywhere I'd been before. Am I in the human realm now?

Voices carried from below, sounding familiar and then Cam stepped into the room with a tray of— bless him, a nice juicy burger, fries, a coke, and a shake!

The smell alone made me salivate for the fattening meal, and though I felt ornery, I began to grin gratefully.

He was obviously alright but then the sadness of what had just happened suddenly slammed back into my gut and I wasn't as hungry anymore.

He waited for me to sit up before setting the tray across my lap.

"I figured you'd be starving. You woke up sooner than I thought."

I pursed my lips.

"That was low down of Ry and Edanai."

"You didn't give them much of a choice."

Cam kissed me softly on the lips right before I shoved a hot, salty, delicious French fry in my mouth.

"Is everyone here? And where is here? It's cold."

He shook his head. "Still waiting on a few others. We're back in the city where you went to school. It's out in the country and it's the middle of winter."

He paused.

"I've just turned the heat up a bit." He then said.

Anxiety slammed into me with a mixture of nostalgia at simply being back in the human world and what was to come, once I came face to face with China again.

"Is Lira back yet?" I had to ask, feeling my gut twist and my chest burning already, threatening to bring the fry back up.

"I don't really know what she did or what she was trying to do but I'm gonna guess that it shouldn't take this long. That's what your friends said"

I sighed, depressed at the bad thoughts that suddenly filtered into my mind.

Cam wasn't finished yet, that much I could read on his face. He sighed before continuing, "And Jamie isn't doing so well."

I tensed. "Why?"

Cam sat down on the bed beside me.

"The seraphim, Spencer, was apparently kidnapped at some point after he was last with us."

I nearly spit out a spray of chewed up potato, coughing with a hand over my mouth as I sat up straighter in the bed and nearly toppling the tray that Cam held steady. He handed me the coke but I didn't want it.

I leapt out of bed, stumbled out of the doorway into a strange, dark hallway, and raced towards the source of light and voices in the direction of what looked like stairs.

I was at the bottom of the spiral staircase in a flash, my eyes searching for faces, seeing only Durien, Anthony, and Gabe sitting in the kitchen, eating.

"Where is everyone?" I asked.

"In their rooms. No one has much of an appetite right now, especially Jamie." Gabe said.

"Poor Kaia looks physically sick. I think that as an earthbound seraphim, she and Spencer are kindred-linked. She was the most devastated and she's been in a deep state of meditation ever since we made the discovery." Durien explained.

Cam was behind me already, "I'd let them all rest. Everyone has had a really big shock and this news doesn't help." He soothed with his hands gently massaging my shoulders.

I whirled around to face him in panic. "What about Lira?"

Cam went silent. I wondered if he were going into another mental conversation.

Then, his eyes darkened, almost making my skin crawl and I took a step away from him. I'd never seen him do that before. It temporarily reminded me of what he truly was for a split second.

"Cam, what's wrong?"

The darkness lifted when he looked down at me, and without an explanation he quickly said, "Stay put. No one leaves. I'll be right back."

"Hey...wait!" I reached for him but he ghosted away and was gone in an instant.

"Cam, tell me what's wrong, please!"

"I will as soon as I know."

"Be careful."

I sighed, feeling drained already even though I had just woken from a deep sleep.

I was afraid, wondering what had happened and praying that it wouldn't be more bad news.

"What's the deal with Spencer? What happened?" I asked, joining the guys at the table.

Durien shook his head and shrugged, though he was definitely upset. "I don't know and I don't get it. Nothing looked out of place. I don't understand who or what managed to get him so easily either. There wasn't a body or any blood. Spencer would never let himself go out like that, not without a good fight and magic. He was a damned good fighter."

"But he didn't have any way of calling any of us for help either. If several or more powerful demons got to him, he didn't stand a chance no matter what he was throwing at them." Anthony added.

I sighed in despair, thinking of the short amount of time that I got to know Spencer, and our last meaningful conversation. He was a playboy and a flirt, he was also Jamie's man, I think. Though he was rigid and by the book...we really needed him. I agreed with Durien in that he was a very good fighter. He was knowledgeable and he had access to some defensive magic.

It was quiet. Too quiet and I didn't like it.

A door creaked open softly and both Devlin and Lorelei emerged, weary.

"You're up." Lorelei tried to smile despite the circumstances.

She looked around the room, "Where did they go?"

We all figured that she was referring to our new, fallen allies and friends.

"They'll be back. We're still waiting on Lira, Crystal, and Scarlet. Lira hasn't returned to her body yet." Gabe answered.

Lorelei looked pained again as she pulled out a chair and sat down beside Anthony, eyeing the bags of fast food in the middle of the table with disinterest.

Devlin hopped up onto the counter next to the stove. She seemed different to me now. More alive, normal, and engaging in conversations.

"It took forever to get Jamie to calm down. She finally cried herself to sleep and Kaia has basically zoned out too." She said.

I felt bad for her but I didn't know what to do. None of us did.

"I still can't believe that you're pregnant." Lorelei flicked her eyes up to meet mine. I could see that her thoughts went beyond that simple statement and realization; like what was it like sleeping with a fallen and one of Cam's size, too.

I wasn't sure how to take her expression and statement.

Should I feel guilt or embarrassment?

"I can." Devlin stated.

We all turned to look at her. Her expression was actually bright and almost playful.

"How far along are you?"

I shrugged.

"Pretty early I imagine. You're not showing at all." Durien pointed out.

"Do you feel sick or anything?" Lorelei then asked.

"No."

"What are you going to do when you get bigger?" Anthony asked.

"Probably not much of anything." I tried to joke.

I didn't like being the center of so many questions but I couldn't blame them for having them.

Procreation, let alone love between a fallen and a warrior, was absolutely forbidden. I didn't have to be one for very long to know and understand that much.

"What about prenatal care? I mean, how did you find out anyway?" Lorelei inquired next.

I shifted in my chair. "I was told and it was confirmed by Ilka first, then Cam, and then Aon. Essentially, I was the last to know."

They all gaped.

"No shit! Ilka knew?" Durien replied.

I nodded.

"Yep, they all know now then." Gabe nodded in assurance.

"Damn. It's so weird. I mean, you didn't know that you could get pregnant?" Lorelei then asked as if I should have known better.

I sighed. "You're making me feel like an afterschool special now.

I did know but I didn't know, meaning that it never crossed my mind since we're immortal now."

Lorelei thought about that as if the possibility didn't dawn on her either, and then she turned her head, once Anthony moved in behind her and touched her shoulders gently.

I suddenly understood why she was asking. Had she and Anthony been trying to have a child? Why would they want to bring a child into this world now with all that we had to face as warriors anyway? The worst was yet to come. Then again, look at me.

Anthony remained quiet, simply listening with his hands massaging her shoulders.

"How do you feel about it?" Durien then asked.

I thought for a moment and then shrugged a shoulder.

"It was definitely a shock but I'm cool with it now. It's not like there's any other choice for me."

"And because she loves him as much as he obviously loves her. He'd die for her. That much I do know. That's how the fallen are. I for one can't wait to see this baby. It's gonna be special. It has to be, that's the only reason it was allowed." Devlin sort of answered him for me.

We all looked over at her in surprise. She was serious about that statement and it meant a lot for me to have a fellow warrior understand and back me up in that regard.

I would have told them it was going to be twins but I really didn't want to get that conversation started right now.

"Hey, is that a ring?" Lorelei took notice of the ring Cam gave me.

I didn't wear it during training because I didn't want to get it messed up, and I really hadn't worn it since Cam first gave it to me. It wasn't that I didn't love it, it was to avoid an explanation to the others about it—like right now.

Lorelei leaned forward and pulled my hand to her, and then everyone began to crowd around to gawk at it. It twinkled and sparkled beneath the low kitchen light hanging over the table.

"Damn, are all of those real diamonds?" Gabe asked.

I nodded.

"No guess as to who gave you that." Devlin grinned.

They all looked at me, awaiting confirmation.

"So does that mean you two are like engaged or something then?" Anthony asked.

"Something like that."

"It's gorgeous. It looks like...the design of your brandings on this side." Lorelei pointed with a smile.

"Wow, that's cool." Devlin commented.

I pulled my hand away from the center of attention. "We need some soothing music or something." I suddenly stood up, wanting to break the silence and change the subject. I began searching for the remote to the stereo.

"Your car is parked outside. I want you to head first thing in the morning to the University and go on as if nothing has happened. Alright?" Cam's voice filtered into my head.

My heart began to pound with anxiety, feeling as if something was wrong— and then my mind went to that weird chic on that ugly beast, Grace.

Didn't he say he was going to meet her at her place later?

I mumbled to myself.

"Starling? You're spacing out. Are you okay?"

I turned to look behind me. Everyone was staring at me as if I'd lost my mind, standing here with the remote poised but not turning on the television.

"Oh, yeah." I nodded and clicked it on. "Here, someone want to pick a movie or something?" I set the remote down and Devlin came over to retrieve it, looking at me strangely.

"I'm not really in the mood or hungry. I think I'm gonna take a bath and just go to sleep." Lorelei said quietly as she rose from the table.

"What is there to do here in Indianapolis anyway?" Anthony asked.

"Like she'd remember." Durien said.

"Oh, yeah. Sorry." He sheepishly grinned.

"Google it." Gabe got up and went to retrieve the laptop sitting on the kitchen counter and powering it on, "I'm hoping we have some sort of internet connection." he commented.

I sat down on the comfy, single recliner and pretended to watch the television while Devlin scrolled through the channels.

"Where are you? When are you coming back?"

"I'm in the spirit realm. There's an issue but I'm taking care of it. Jerilah, Rahab, and Vinnah should be showing up at any minute with Crystal and Scarlet. Your friend, Lira is still unconscious but her body is safe. I don't want you to worry about anything right

now. Go on as if life is normal and if you need any references when you meet your friend China again, let me know but be sure to arrive with the luggage that I already put in your trunk. They're mainly for show but they do have some of the items, shoes, and clothing that I've gotten for you already in them. Get yourself some winter clothing. I've left enough money for all of you on the bedside table in your room to get what you need...including cars."

My brows went up. Was it that easy for Cam to provide a crap load of real money at any given time? Whenever we needed it? Apparently, yes.

"My room? Do you think I should stay here as opposed to my apartment with China?"

"Now that you've told her you're pregnant, I don't think she'll get too suspicious if you've decided to stay with me and we're eloping. It's your room here. For the most part I want you with me at my place."

Eloping? Well, we were already spiritually bonded. The equivalent of marriage for supernatural beings with the exception of me being human.

"She fainted with the pregnancy news so I don't know how she'll take that. She already thinks that I fell and hit my head. What if she wants to visit? She's gonna want to know who everyone else is."

"We'll cross that bridge when we get to it. For now, resume as normally as possible until I return."

I sighed. *"Cam, I don't have a good feeling about this. What about Spencer? How long will you be gone?"*

"I can make a million guesses but I have no idea where to start. I'll have to confer with Aliks on that. We'll try and find him though. The others will be around you all to make sure that you stay safe. And...this is straight from Aon and Aliks, let the others know that no one died at the Hall. Apparently, they've known that something was going to happen. Animals and all have journeyed to another Hall long before this happened. I don't know how long I'll be but it shouldn't be too long."

A huge, internal sigh of relief took away the tension in my entire body and all of the sadness weighing heavily on my psyche.

"How long have you known that and why did you look like something was wrong before you left?"

He paused. I know he probably didn't want to tell me.

"Edanai went to look for your friend, Lira. She's missing now

and she's not answering me at all."

Oh no. I felt sick again.

"Cam, you don't think that..."

"I don't know. Just promise me that you won't be stubborn and remember the original promise that you made to me too. I'll be back soon, you know I can't stay away from you that long anyway. I love you."

Why did I feel my heart breaking already? I was feeling the despair that Cam was probably feeling, given that realization. I didn't particularly like Edanai but I certainly hoped that she was okay.

"I love you, too."

XXXVII: CAM`AEL

Another vision began to play behind my eyes. It was of Starling, lying on her back, her belly huge and round. She was alone in a lush, green field filled with white, bell-shaped flowers…in the full-blown throes —of labor. Sweat glistened on her forehead and temples, her beautiful face was contorted in pain and determination. I wanted…no, I needed to go to her but I couldn't. That part alarmed me and I was infuriated at my inability to do anything to help and be with her.

Why couldn't I move?!

In the distance, the dismal horizon began to shift and morph as if alive and it was menacing. Blood-red, fiery clouds began to coalesce, billowing and rushing in from afar at great speed. Darkness began to slither across the green grass, killing and tainting it with its oily, thick presence from across the field. Morning Star's mocking, triumphantly resonating laughter began to rumble, coming from everywhere at once. I began to curse, feeling helpless as I watched it creep even closer to Starling once she began to push with a scream.

The vision suddenly snapped closed like a thick, black curtain, shutting the scene away from my eyes completely.

I found myself gritting my teeth, wanting to howl in agony at my uselessness.

My eyes flew open as I came to and inhaled a deep breath only to grunt and nearly choke. I couldn't see initially, feeling the weight of a lot of leaves, dirt, and grass packed over my body. More dirt, grass, and leaves invaded my mouth when I took another breath only to gag and spit angrily. A steady, pounding pain still lingered in the back of my skull.

I couldn't remember exactly what had happened shortly after talking to Starling telepathically.

What the hell had happened? I remembered flying towards the destroyed, smoking remnants of the hall because I caught a glimpse of Edanai's signature, then sheer physical pain erupted all over my flesh, and all went black.

I quickly sat up taking immediate note of my surroundings. It was obvious that I had been purposefully buried beneath all this brush.

Leaves and grass crunched nearby. The moon and the illumination from the rubble of what was left of the hall allowed some light, even though I could see perfectly in the dark. There was another fallen here and I was on my feet in a flash, ready to wield my sword and pull forth light.

It was Edanai and she was alright.

My breathing was still ragged as I tried to shake off the last images of that disturbing vision.

I could never leave Starling alone, which meant that I'd better hurry back to her as soon as I can. I'm sure that Morning Star was already up to devastation number three, and I knew that it wouldn't be long before he found out that Starling was pregnant. Then again, I wouldn't be surprised if he already knew. He knew when we were together, and he knew that her becoming pregnant was a very likely probability. In fact, I'm sure that he was both banking on and anticipating it.

"Sorry. If I hadn't been zapped and knocked unconscious myself too, I could've warned you, although I would think that your light would've offered you some sort of a buffer. Guess not." She smiled.

"What the hell was that?" I groaned, rubbing the soreness in the back of my neck.

"Apparently, there's a strong, protective, sanctified force field still surrounding the remains of what's left. I just came to myself about five minutes ago. Luckily the forest guardians managed to conceal our vulnerable bodies, hence the mouth and face full of leaves, dirt, twigs, and berries." She grinned.

I was appreciative and I scanned the trees, boulders, and bushes with acknowledgment and a nod of thanks. They rustled softly in response.

Well, that made sense. It explained why Edanai couldn't answer me earlier either.

Edanai still had a few stray leaves in her long, dark hair and her bangs wisped gently across her forehead in the slight night breeze. She was wearing a cream colored halter style breastplate, and dark brown, leather shorts with thigh high boots. Her smooth, olive toned skin shimmered with a thin layer of sweat, enhancing her long, muscular legs and the gentle ridges of muscle in her flat torso and abdomen.

"Oh, and the girl isn't even here. If she's not back in her body by now, it may be safe to assume that she might have been captured and taken."

"Shit." I sighed, vigorously running my fingers through my hair to comb through and shake out the debris.

Edanai studied me as I did so for a while in silence. My guess is that she was trying determine if I was still angry with her for all that she told Starling earlier. I was but there were much bigger things to worry about right now, like the vision I just had.

"Would you mind checking to make sure first? I'd like you to either remain at my place or join the others where they are in the human realm for now, to also help protect them until I get there. Bring Lira with you if she's back."

"Sure." She replied half-heartedly.

I shook my head looking over the massive destruction beyond. She turned to look too.

"I still don't get it. But for some reason, I have a feeling that they know more about Morning Star's plans than we do. They were warned though, that much was told to me by Aon and Aliks."

"Warned by who? And why now?"

"That is all we are privy to know." I replied with sarcasm.

She looked as if she wanted to say something else but she didn't. She turned around to stare off into the distance of about a few hundred yards.

The shell of what was once a great hall, one of several that has been around for many, many millennia, still sat smoking and burning in a mass of nothing but charred stone and blackened, burnt wood. Nothing prominent remained despite the protective field, which had purposefully been left behind.

"You be careful. I hope we do find her. I'll be in touch." Edanai said as her wings snapped out and then she began to ascend, cloaking herself as she did.

Then, I was alone. I sighed. My first personal thought was that Lira was as good as gone but then I thought of another avenue that I could take.

Aliks was certainly taking his sweet time with the deciphering of the text and it didn't make sense to me. It should not take this long, let alone for permission to disclose it but maybe it was because I was a fallen, I supposed. Elohim had shown me where the rest was, and even led me directly to it, allowing me access to dig it up. I had a right to know...I'm supposed to know. My patience was wearing thin.

I needed assistance once again.

He seemed to be expecting me to summon him this time, which made me wonder if he had finally completed his task.

No. He hadn't.

"I need to know if Lira is still free, and if she is then why hasn't she returned to her body yet?"

"How would I know that?"

I looked at him wryly.

"She has her own free will. Her spirit isn't being monitored. Her talent is her own to use wisely." He shrugged.

I shook my head in exasperation.

"Can you at least tell me if she's in trouble?'

"How long has it been since she's been out of her body?"

"A very long time. She was coming here to see what happened and as you can see, she's not here now."

"There's no telling then." He lamented.

"You're absolutely useless, you know that?" I barked with irritation.

He sighed with boredom at my insulting tone, "Is this what you summoned me for?"

Then, a thought hit me.

"No. I need your truth meter. I've got a particular Psyren to interrogate and I'll need you there to tell me if she's lying or not."

"You don't need me for that. What would she be lying about anyway?"

"Everything. I also need to ask you something...a request of my own, if you will."

He gauged me, waiting for me to get on with it.

I paused, finding it strangely hard for me to even say the words let alone think of the possibility.

"I want to make sure that if anything ever happens to me, that Starling and my children will be protected from Morning Star."

Aliks was surprised and he stared at me blankly for a moment before speaking.

"Why do you think that something would happen to you?"

"Just allow me the peace of mind and guarantee, please."

I was dead serious.

That word alone raised both of his brows.

"I can't interfere…"

I sighed heavily and turned away from him to stave off my rising frustration and temper, while resisting the urge to lash out at him.

"But…I can watch over them as both Aon and I have already been instructed. You know that we are not allowed to impede upon the divine path of any being." He added.

"Fine. I understand that and that's all I ask. Now let's go." I said through clenched teeth.

~~~****~~~

Apparently, not having expected both an angel and a fallen to arrive and arrive…together, the City of Psyrens was left nearly deserted, yet glowering eyes watched from dark alleys and homes with intense curiosity. Even the aural bandits scattered and cowered in fear and confusion.

Even if Grace didn't have Lira, she may be able to negotiate her back from whoever did—pending that it wasn't Morning Star.

But then again, Lira was a scout. That possibility was slim to none. No one would give her up or make the trade. She was way too valuable in that regard.

"She's not here, Cam." Edanai reported to me.

I sighed dejectedly.

"Ok, thanks. You stay safe and keep in touch in the meantime."

"I always do. The same goes for you too. You'd better stay alive…for all of us."

Now why did she have to put that kind of pressure on me now? I laughed emptily to myself.

We continued to walk with caution, observing everything and every being as we made our way to the large, luxurious mansion, sitting right in the middle at the very end of a long road that was flanked by homes, bars, and shops.

"Starling, are you okay?" I then asked.

"Damn you, Cam! Where have you been? I've been calling out to you forever!"

"Sorry. Is everything okay?"

"Yeah, it's fine. I was checking on you. Any word? What happened to you?"

"Carelessness." Was all that I was going to tell her and admit.

"Is that supposed to make me feel better?"

I chuckled. *"You worry way too much, Starling but coming from you, it means a lot. How's the reunion?"* I said to redirect her annoyance.

"She's not here yet. I hope it goes well though."

"It will. I'll try not to be long. And please don't give Rahab and Ry a hard time. You know what I mean."

I heard her sigh softly. *"Fine. I love you."*

I laughed. *"I'll be back soon. I love you too."*

"You'd better."

XXXVIII: STARLING

Despite the good news that Cam gave about the Hall and then delivering it to the others, who were also relieved and ecstatic, I was still worried. We were all worried sick.

Spencer was still missing and Lira was still unconscious. It shouldn't have taken her this long to return to her body. Deep down, I wanted to stay positive but I was already grieving inside. Even shopping didn't' help us girls when we went to the local mall to stock up on winter clothes.

Her absence from her body and her missing soul was painstakingly hard to take because we all had to face the possible truth that she could truly be gone forever, especially with numerous dark beings stalking every corner of the spirit realm. Why did she have to go have a look at anything? There was nothing to see or report. We all knew who was responsible for it. The whole thing had me wondering though, is their current location where Sean and Diana were all this time? Did they know this was going to happen when I had met with them for orientation? I wondered.

Well, at least they were all safe. I wanted to be mad at Lira but she was too much like me in that regard. I could understand now why Cam and his friends, as well as mine, all had to be stern with me.

The others did their car shopping without me since I already had one, apparently. A black Honda Civic was sitting out on the snow covered lawn, just like Cam said it would be. The first thing I had done was to go through it for any key items of interest that could possibly both fill me in on the blank pieces of my mortal life or trigger more memories.

The next thing we did was to acquire and exchange cell phone and cell numbers, so that we could all keep in touch with each other. Cam's friends could find us in a heartbeat, especially knowing where we were now. They had their own built in cellphone like communication and of course, no one knew that both Cam and I were also connected.

I was a bit nervous at first. People didn't seem to notice that we were different. Though our arms were covered, our hands were still marked with brandings. Thank goodness it was winter now but we couldn't wear gloves forever. However, I already knew that unless one was chosen or of the spirit realm, they wouldn't be able to see them anyway.

I then thought of Joel. When and if I saw him, how would I explain them? How would I even talk to him? Cam didn't mention anything about a history with him even though he was obviously a close friend of mine. I was afraid of the reunion, more so being clueless and seeming weird.

The only other worry I had was giving ourselves away. I mean, young adults paying cash for brand new cars, clothes, and cellphones? I prayed that we wouldn't be mistaken for an organized criminal gang or something.

I wondered how I ever managed to drive through the falling snow before. Had I done it before? I must have. There wasn't a lot of traffic on the road until I got closer to the city. I was fine with the slow moving traffic because it stalled me, giving me time to think. Apprehension gripped my insides. None of the sights were familiar…however, many normal things now looked strange to me.

I passed many pretty twinkling holiday lights, decorated trees, cars, storefronts, and a lot of festive holiday cheer spread all over the place. Every sound was clarified and every living thing had an aura. I was more aware of everything, which meant that I could instantly tell if they were friend or foe too.

It was all incredibly fascinating, being able to see and switch back and forth beyond the veil of reality and into parts of the spirit realm that could be seen in hidden places. I don't know if that was a good or bad thing but it made me wonder if I'd end up having to confront a dark being at any given moment. If I could see them, they were most definitely seeing me, so it was a possibility.

"Not wise to be by yourself." I heard from the backseat.

I gasped, jerking the steering wheel to the right and almost wrecking. I slammed on the brakes, slightly skidding and fishtailing towards the guardrail.

Someone honked angrily.

I pulled alongside the guardrail into the shoulder and stopped.

Looking in the rearview mirror, Aon was sitting in the backseat.

"You scared the crap out of me. I can't drive in snow as it is! I assume that there's going to be a lot of people around that

University, so I'll be alright." I hissed and then scowled.

She smiled innocently. "Driving in snow? There's nothing to it. Besides, I was referring to you leaving your friends vulnerable too. Your power is far deadlier, effective, and long reaching. Without you, they stand the most danger."

"That's why most of Cam's friends are with them now."

Aon raised a brow. "I see. Do you even know where you're going?"

"Yes...at least with the help of the GPS app on my cell phone and the address on my drivers' license." I said glancing over at my phone, which was inserted into a hands free holder that suctioned to my windshield.

She nodded.

"Reuniting with your friend? Did you bother to call her ahead of time to tell her that you'd be coming?"

"Should I have?"

"She's still at the home of her family, approximately four hours away. Many of the students are away for the holiday season."

"Good. That will give me some time to get settled and try to remember some things before she gets back. I'll tell her that I'm back a little later on then."

"Just remember, play it cool and be careful. You're protected by universal laws in a sense but that doesn't mean anything. They will take the attack and destruction of the hall as full reign and permission."

"I know. Have you heard from Cam?"

She shook her head. "Cam has been around a long, long time and he's very powerful, not just physically. He knows what he's doing...most of the time, and he'll be alright, especially now that you've given him a reason to fight and exist."

Her unexpected sentiment surprised me and I was touched.

"I still worry about him."

"I know. You're female and you're pregnant." She smirked. "You may want to familiarize yourself with the Universal laws soon. After all, you are subject to the rules too. No display of weapons, essences, or physical abilities in front of mortal eyes."

"And if I'm attacked first?"

"That is why you should not venture alone."

"What does that matter? So darkness can attack us but we can't defend?"

"I didn't say that."
"Then what should I do?"
"Run."
I pursed my lips and looked back at her wryly.
"Not my style."
"Then make it your style. You're already being watched and hunted, and quite frankly, I don't want to have to knock your man out or worse for throwing another tantrum over you if anything were to happen. In this world, I can't readily assist as I can in the spirit realm."
"I'll be alright. The others are here and so are Cam's friends."
"They too, are bound by laws."
"Well, if the darkness can break them then we should be able to too. The field has to be leveled somewhere."
"Starling, Starling, Starling…"Aon sounded chastising but there was a deviant sparkle in her celestial eyes.
"What?"
"No wonder you and Cam`ael are so drawn together, like charged ions of opposite polarities. I suppose that is why they call it…chemistry." She chuckled melodically.
And then, she was gone.

~~~****~~~

Pulling into the parking lot of the three-story, all gray brick building with the circular placard mounted high beneath the eaves that read: **Wayford Hall Luxury Apartments**, I already began to feel anxious. So far, nothing really rang a bell but I did feel as if I were home. That was a good sign, right?

Ry tapped on the passenger side window, startling me. I should be able to detect other supernatural beings better than this. I sighed, pressing the 'window down' button.

Though I could tell it was probably more for show, he was bundled up in a black leather jacket, thick long sleeved thermal shirt, dark jeans, and sunglasses. Speckles of falling snow contrasted against his long, ebony mo-hawk that draped down the length of his back.

"Me, Rahab, and Mac are gonna be in the area while you're here but we'll be cloaked. I'm pretty sure you can feel some trace of lingering dark activity here, so be aware of your surroundings.

Don't hesitate to do what you do best and light each and every fucker coming at you up. I mean that, I don't care what Aon or Aliks said. Got it?" He pointed a finger at me.

He heard her?

I smiled. "Okay."

Disobeying an angel? At the mercy of taking the advice from a fallen who knew what he was talking about...I still didn't know if I could do that knowingly and willingly.

Ry gave me a thumbs up before he turned and headed in the opposite direction of my car.

"Hey Ry!" I called out.

He turned and looked at me over his shoulder.

"Be careful!"

Ry shook his head and chuckled with the tips of his fangs showing. "Yes ma'am." He humored me anyway with a salute, continuing onward towards an empty courtyard, packed with random mounds of snow.

Once alone, I hesitated again, looking around to take note of everything just like Ry had mentioned.

What about seeing snowfall blanketing everything in white beneath a silver, gray sky, makes everything seem so...calm and peaceful? It was just a ruse and I was getting cold, so it was time to go on and get this over with now.

Hoping to regain the memories of an apartment that barely registered with me, and trying to play off my slight confusion at the same time was difficult. Once inside, after perusing the first floor and realizing that none of the apartment numbers matched the one on my license, I figured that I was gonna have to wander each floor without looking too much like a weirdo. It would have been worse to ask the people who have known me, 'Hey, I know I've been here for almost a year, but...what apartment do I live in again?'

With the two pieces of expensive luggage that Cam left for me in my trunk, I trudged up the stair well to the second floor. Bingo! The numbers were getting close to mine as I made my way down the corridor.

Luckily, I hadn't run across anyone familiar when I first entered the building, at least...they didn't seem to care that I had returned. The building actually seemed a little deserted. I chalked that up to the fact that more than likely many of them, China included, were all out of town and visiting family and friends for the holidays. This was definitely in my favor.

It took me about ten minutes to figure out which key on my key ring would open the apartment door. Why the hell did I have so many keys anyway? What did they go to?

When I finally got the door open, the scent of sweet honeysuckle candles, long since burned out, lingered in the air. It instantly hit me with a sense of belonging and a memory suddenly flashed behind my eyes. I remember sitting at that kitchen counter, writing something. China had been doing something to my back and I associated some sort of discomfort and pain with whatever she was doing in that memory.

Then, I remembered sitting on that couch, watching movies and doing homework.

The apartment wasn't that fancy but it was a nicely decorated and spacious. An immediate brooding, negative energy caught my awareness and that immediately put me on edge. Could it be the darkness that China said was trying to mess with her? I left the suitcases by the door and closed it behind me.

I poked around in the kitchen and the nearly empty refrigerator, glancing at some of the notes and photos that were held by magnets on the freezer. Some were of me and China, others were of her and some stocky built guy with light brown, spiky hair, and some were of me and Joel. He was really handsome, too. My fingers lingered on the photo, waiting on some kind of a memory of interacting with him but none came.

I sighed and wandered into the living room, looking at all of the décor and sitting down on the couch for a moment, just staring at the blank fifty inch flat screen television.

Nice.

China had already put up a small tree with a few lights, and shiny red garland, surrounded by small Christmas figurines, and stockings along the sofa table next to the tree.

There were several presents left under the tree. Curiously I walked over and looked at each one. Three were to me from China, two were from both Jenna and Vanessa, one was from Toya—and then there was a small one with a red envelope that was from Joel. I felt tears well up at the thought. She anticipated my return, all of my friends did and that meant a lot for me to see. I picked up the envelope from Joel, turning it over in my hands and debating on whether or not to open it. Should I call him too? Hesitating, I just kept and carried it with me as I continued to inspect my former home.

I took in all of the distinct scents while listening closely to every sound. Someone was playing music in an apartment nearby. Another was having a get together. I was amazed at how clearly I could pick it all up. Spying the room closest to where I stood near the tree, I entered it first.

It was neat and clean and the bed was made perfectly but I could already tell that it wasn't mine. There were a few photos of that guy and China all along the dresser— and disturbingly, the negative energy was the strongest in here. I carefully panned every corner, checking the closet, and even underneath the bed for anything but there was nothing here now.

I paused before taking a deep breath and venturing across the living room to the other room with the closed door, my room. I stopped and eyed the coffee table for some reason. I found myself staring at it for a few moments, expecting an instant barrage of memories to come flooding through…but nothing happened.

Strange.

I finally stood at my bedroom door and slowly opened it. It was dim and warm, being that the blinds were half closed and it was gray and snowing outside. I flipped on the light and proceeded to step cautiously inside.

I took my time gazing at everything from my dresser, to my bed and comforter, to the television, curtains, and all of the pictures and posters adorning my walls. There were University of Indianapolis at Bloomington collegiate memorabilia scattered about, from lanyards, sweatpants, shirts, and a few cream and crimson colored pennants with the word, 'Hoosiers' in red lettering on it.

It was quiet in here with the exception of the steady humming of the heating system in the background. I began to hear a few voices drifting in from several directions, which made me feel a small sense of relief. I turned the television on, wanting to catch up on the events of the world today, and find out exactly what day and time it was right now. I set the card from Joel on my dresser, finding the remote next to a jewelry box, and clicked on the television.

The sound was comforting. I flipped through a few channels until I found a local station. Then I spied my closet and immediately began to raid it, going through all of my clothes, photos, backpack, and shoes...most of which I planned to pack inside the suitcases and take with me.

My cell phone began to chime and I pulled it out of my coat pocket.

It was China.

Perfect timing.

Well, so much for waiting before telling her that I was back, might as well get it over with now. Besides, it would take her a few hours to drive back even if she did decide to come home right now, which I highly doubted that she would leave the rest of her family right before Christmas just for me— best friend or not.

"Hey." I answered first.

"What up girlfriend or shall I say mom to be. How are you?"

I smiled. "Great, how about you?"

"Eh, family drama...same as every year. They were all wondering why you didn't come with me this year though, and I had to explain to them that you're having an extreme case of random psychosis but you needed to connect with family you've never met. So, it's two days before Christmas and I thought I'd call for a status update — although if you haven't caught a flight yet...you're not gonna make it and I'm am going to be severely upset if that's the case."

"Well, I don't want you to be upset so...I'm giving you part of my Christmas present now."

She giggled. "Oh really? And what is it? An e-gift card?"

I laughed. "No. I'm home. Merry Christmas."

I heard her gasp and she paused.

"You'd better not be messing with me about that, Star! Are you serious?" her voice went up an octave with excitement.

"I would not lie to you about that. I'm standing in my room right now as we speak."

China squealed long and loud. I had to hold my cell phone away from my ear for the duration.

"I'm there! I can cut the four hour drive by half so you'd better not disappear on me again!" She warned.

"I won't. Don't speed and rush though, it's snowing right now." I certainly hoped I'd be able to keep my word.

"Please, I could care less about the snow, you know that I'm used to it. This is going to be the best Christmas yet! I will see you in a few hours!"

"Okay. I'll see you when you get here." I clicked off.

Now, to go through everything, including watching the news so that this would not turn into a disaster after all.

XXXIX: CA'MAEL

Grace was lounging in one of the parlor rooms, smoking on a hookah pipe. A human slave was on all fours, serving as a table with a bowl of fruit on his back next to her. A gag was strapped across his mouth and there was a blank, submissive far away stare in his eyes. A few books, with one lying face down and open as if she'd taken a break from reading it, littered the table in front of her.

That large scorpion was perched on the back rest portion of the chaise lounging chair, next to her head. It appeared to be nibbling on a slice of apple. I was pretty sure that there was a male human soul inside of that scorpion she had made her close pet.

She didn't seemed surprised to see me but she was almost fearful when she saw Aliks. She immediately sat up straight and her eyes bulged.

"Relax, we're not here for anything more but your help." I assured her.

She looked confused. "My help? I thought you were looking for something else. I was waiting for you." She told me but kept her eyes on Aliks.

I didn't doubt that she probably was waiting for me. She was wearing a veil thin slinky skirt fringed with gold beads that hung low on her slim waist, and a top that looked like two scarves crisscrossed over each of her voluptuous, tanned breasts just to cover the nipples.

Under normal circumstances, I'd have been all over and in that…the way I normally do it, not physically, but I wasn't feeling any of it. The current situation and my love for Starling suppressed all of my dark lust and sinful desires. What I had and felt was derived from the purest form of love, and it was because of Starling and reserved only for her.

"He's not here to judge, spy, or condemn. He's assisting me." I added to explain Aliks' presence.

She looked confounded probably because Aliks was with me at all let alone assisting me with anything.

"I don't understand. What do you need my help with then?" She asked, waving away someone that we didn't notice outright, though we did feel their signatures camouflaged in the darkened corners.

Two bandits grunted as they lumbered and shuffled out of the parlor, making extremely wide and cautionary berths around us to get out, and quickly closed the door behind them.

"Well, I don't know what Angels eat but I have some fresh fruit." Grace waved a hand over her human table.

Her green eyes glowed softly, she was absolutely fascinated with Aliks from what I was picking up from her but definitely nervous. Maybe it was from the memory of having been an angel too. Psyrens were formerly of the lower Demisiph or seraph classes of servile angels.

They all used to be guardian angels.

No wonder they were so smitten with the fallen yet they feared us at the same time. That was something I'd forgotten myself until just now. So to her, Aliks, even as dainty as he appeared to me, was an absolute stud.

They had been damned for having begun consorting with dark beings. When she waved her hand and the bandits immediately obeyed, it had me thinking. Though I knew it was obvious how the Psyrens, being sexy females, could hold power over the male goons, they in turn seemed readily obedient and protective of them…like children.

I'll be damned.

Elohim was having us partner up with all the races of former angels for this war with Morning Star and those in his legion. No wonder the Psyrens didn't like nor care for the Succubus'. They were former lower level angels too but that didn't mean they couldn't choose the side of good and light either. We all could. The option and choice was never taken away from us despite being condemned and fallen. So, would an alliance with the Succubus' be the next request? That could get very ugly.

His plan was beyond clever and sneaky, and something that would never happen on its own if left up to us individually. The possibility and option to even try never dawned on me once.

The tricky part though, would be to get everyone to cooperate and work together but if Elohim didn't think it was possible, possible for everyone to remember what they used to be…then he wouldn't have made the request.

"No thank you." Aliks politely declined.

"Then please, have a seat and make yourselves at home." She then pointed to the two plush chairs right behind us.

"I'll make this quick and short because we're actually in a hurry." I began.

Grace cocked her head and looked at me, awaiting what I wanted from her. She played innocent very well.

"There's a warrior scout that's gone missing. Her spirit was supposedly last seen at the site of the hall shortly after the explosion."

She cut me off and folded her arms across her chest looking offended, "You think I or someone here claimed her?"

"I don't know, that's why I'm asking."

Her eyes shifted from me to Aliks and then she harrumphed and sat back down.

"Say that we did have her, what is she worth?" She then asked smugly.

"Don't put a price on her, Grace. This is very important. We can't afford to be at odds with each other. This is about survival of the end, for all of us." I told her in all seriousness.

She appeared thoughtful to my plea.

"I don't have her nor have I seen her. I can ask around but none of us have gone on any runs since the explosion. It's very risqué right now. Many of Morning Star's army is roaming around and I wouldn't doubt that he probably does have her. If that's the case, I'm sorry. You're more than likely not going to get her back at all, ever."

I sighed and looked over at Aliks. He nodded slightly.

Grace was telling the truth.

"Have you thought about my offer and what we talked about earlier?" She then asked me.

"I can't do it." I flatly replied.

She studied me with surprise and then disappointment.

"Then I don't know what you're needing or expecting from me. I can't retrieve the girl."

"You can make a trade."

"Of what? Who?" She looked at me incredulously.

I had to think of something. This wouldn't be as important to me if the girl wasn't a warrior. Before further possibly humiliating myself, Aliks had to go.

He had served his purpose for me.

"The next time I see you, you had better have a fully, deciphered text for me. That seraphim is still missing, so if you know where he might be, let me know. And thanks." I told him.

"You're welcome. I'll keep an eye out but there are no guarantees. I surmise that I should be close to finishing and gaining permission once we've all met about it...pending you quit summoning me for every little thing." He replied sharply before swiftly ghosting out in a beam of bright light that quickly winked out after his departure.

"You keep interesting company. I had no idea that was allowed." Grace then commented, turning on the seductive charm now that we were alone.

"You'd be surprised what things are allowed once you stop associating with Morning Star."

She appeared to be thinking about that statement and then she slowly sashayed towards me, her hips swaying enticingly as she began to assess me from head to toe with a flick of her tongue over her lips.

"I don't *associate* with him. We do business. It's nothing more than money and survival."

I looked down at her, "And I told you, it is…for now."

She ran a finger down my chest and smirked, "Now, with you on the other hand…"

I tensed and exhaled slowly at her touch on my bare chest.

She stepped back and unclipped the back of her top, letting it fall gently and cascade around her waist.

Her nipples looked painted on, dusted in light pink glitter. Interesting.

"I'm not asking for anything you can't do or aren't known for," She smiled with a devious flash in her neon green eyes.

"I'd be more willing to help…" She said leaning in and brushing her lips against my chest. Her tongue flicked out softly, instantly stimulating a hint of arousal but not enough for me to want to react.

"Don't." I gently pushed her away from me.

Ego bruised, she was definitely hurt. Looking deeply into my eyes, she bit her lip as if trying to keep herself from either saying something ugly…or maybe even shedding a tear. Accepting the fact that she had just been turned down by a fallen, an Incubus, she stepped away from me with a slight smirk.

"Wow. I get it now. The human warrior girl who's pregnant with your child. You love her too." She stated more so than asked.

I didn't say anything, not that it wasn't true but she took my silence as an affirmation.

She laughed softly. "You're right, Cam`ael. I've seen and heard of many strange things but seeing you walking side by side with an angel in peace, and your love for a human…warrior who carries your child…leaves me utterly speechless. I don't understand any of it. Why? Why now?" She was truly befuddled.

I think I got her suspicious inquiry. She was right though. These things were never known because it was assumed that it was not supposed to be. That we were all forever doomed to live one way and be one thing, just because of one mistake. I know because it was exactly my mindset until I was granted permission to actually meet and be with Starling, even though she was a chosen.

"What does it matter? I don't know if you remember but this is how we used to exist. We are what we create, be it of light or darkness and the darkness is only dark when it is used for that purpose. You know that."

I was adamant that I was getting through to her, she was definitely thinking about my words.

She pulled her top back up, adjusting the sheer strips back over her breasts and then moved to sit back down, silent at first.

"What do you want from us? We have no power or influence." She then said.

"Alone, you and your kin may have not have as much."

If this what Elohim wanted for me to do in order to gain the Psyrens as an ally, then I believe that I finally understood.

There was a long pregnant pause before Grace finally met my eyes and spoke, "I think I know who may have this warrior scout."

I raised a brow.

She then rose, "Give me a moment to prepare myself for possible battle and gather a few bandits to ride with us."

A sudden, thunderous cacophony of high pitched screeching and cawing came from every side of the mansion.

Shouts, cries and screams could be heard throughout the house and from outside.

Then, there was massive cawing. Crows.

I could only think of one demon associated with those birds. I wielded my sword and Grace looked at me with alarm and confusion.

"Stay put. This one is dangerous." I told her.

"Something's attacking my city! I'm not going to sit idly by!" She said, bursting through the doors of the parlor, and dashing through the chaos that began to ensue throughout the mansion, and swiftly up to her room.

By the time she suited up, it could be too late. Though I was apprehensive about taking on Xyn myself, I knew that I was the only one who could do it right now. Why was he here? Did he follow me? What the hell did he want with the Psyrens?

I began to pull light forth, forming it into a sphere as I ghosted out and onto the roof of the mansion to get a better look.

It was like a mad tornado of black, screaming birds swarming over, dive-bombing city dwellers, and taking them down in large groups. Several Psyren warrior women had already mounted their war Chimeras, and the lion heads were roaring, blowing streams of fire from their mouths.

They all began to converge on the many crows that made up Xyn. They were screeching and cawing madly as they were being roasted alive in mid-air. The smell of chicken meat and dank, burnt feathers began to permeate the air in a vaporous haze of red and black smoke.

I thought that might have been enough but it only enraged him. All of the crows began to glow, red with fury and moving in together to form a massive homing missile that arced beneath one Chimera. The group of crows literally lanced through its plated underbelly like a razor tipped torpedo with ease. The war beast growled and howled in pain as its belly was torn open and eviscerated. It spun wildly, slamming down to the ground with a loud thud, which finished it off completely.

"Xyn!" I called for his attention to break him from them.

I wasn't sure he had heard me, until the birds began to swarm in together to form a funnel, twisting down into a single, robed form that began to levitate until it was level with me, finally.

It was apprehensive, eyeing the sphere of light in my hand. I couldn't afford to miss. He'd just disperse and dodge my light attack anyway.

I wasn't going to go down without giving it all I had. I had way too much to live for.

Though I didn't want to risk any of them, I needed at least three of my best fighters for a distraction to help me out but they were helping to protect Starling.

Damn.

I finally decided on Osiel, Nay, and Sinma.

XL: STARLING

Nothing much of interest on the news with the exception of an increasing number of crimes all over the world. There was an influx of many natural disasters in one place after the other, like massive Tsunamis', large scale magnitude earthquakes in many places that had never experienced any before. Landslides, deadly tornadoes, and major snowstorms were being reported all around the world in places that typically never experienced those disasters, too. I wondered if it were all a sign of what was to come, and why everything was so off kilter. The darkness and its army had to be behind it all.

The thought of what the Earth would become, and what would happen to the billions of humans on it, made me shiver despite being a warrior and having access to the power and weapons that cleaved themselves to me. How could we as a small number of warriors, stand in between humans and all the deadly powers of the darkness? I lay on my bed in front of the television with the Christmas card that Joel left for me back in my hands.

I began to open it, smiling once I pulled out the card that featured sun-tanning snowman, one that was actually made from sand instead of snow, wearing swimming trunks with a strip of sunscreen on his carrot nose. He was tanning on a small island with a bright sun in the sky, and lying beneath a palm tree decorated to look like a Christmas tree above him. The caption read: 'Merry Christmas, Mon!' in Jamaican speak and the theme featured Jamaica's native colors of green, black, and yellow.

It automatically warmed my heart. I opened it to a coupon paper-clipped inside, good for a free bento box from Zen to Five Sushi and Karaoke Bar. There was a lengthy note on the inside flap that read.

'*Hey Starling, I hate that I'm gonna be missing you for Christmas too but I do hope this card and gift finds you in time. I can't say that I understand what you're going through and why you had to leave like that, but I wish that you'd at least talk to me. I don't know if you ever got any of my phone messages or texts, I'm sure that you did. I've missed you badly. I never meant to make you mad by insulting the guy you're feeling. It's just that something about him bothered me, call it a vibe. I guess that's one of the things we've always had in common. Either way, I'll say it again then. I love you. I've been in love with you since the day that we met. It's been hard because I don't know if I'd ruin our friendship had I told you before but when you told me you wanted me to be your first, and then you were going out with ol' cop or whatever he is...I didn't know what to think. It actually hurt me, but I only want to see you happy. Be careful around him. I have my reasons. China told me what she thinks might have been bothering you but you know you could have talked to me. You know that I've seen things before too, the shadows and dark things that you used to tell me about. I told you that before. If you can talk to anyone about it, please know that you can always talk to me. I'll be thinking of you and hope to see you when you get back. Take care and don't forget to use the coupon soon, you know my aunt don't like to give away any free food! Enjoy your gifts, (you're gonna have to see me in person to get your birthday gift) Happy late Birthday and Merry Christmas! Love you always~ Joel.'*

Tears were flowing out my eyes by the end of the note. Though I had no particular memories of him, his words alone gave me a pretty good idea of what he probably meant to me. I already knew he was chosen too, so that verifies that. How did I never know, or did I? I wondered if he were still in town right now? Where did he live anyway? I was sure that his address was somewhere around here or maybe on my phone. Should I just go ahead and call him then? I'd hate that I might never get to speak to him, especially when his time came. Where would he go now that the Hall was destroyed?

I heard a shuffle outside of the apartment door and I wouldn't have thought anything about it until I heard the doorknob rattle.

China? Had it been a few hours already since she told me she was on her way?

I immediately sat up, bringing my legs over and getting up out of my bed.

Listening, I waited for the key to be inserted into the lock—but nothing happened.

My senses began to click and adrenaline began to filter into my veins.

I stepped softly, slowly, and cautiously outside of my room, taking in every object, shadow, noise, and scent, both in and outside of the apartment.

Automatically, my eyes went to the locked deadbolt and doorknob, waiting for something—anything to happen.

I could literally feel a negative energy begin to expand and my first reflex action was to wield my blades, but what if it wasn't anything sinister or of darkness? I wasn't supposed to be exposing them in the human realm.

Waiting for a few beats for any other sound, movement, or turn of the knob, I carefully and stealthily made my way to the door, leaning against it and listening once again.

It was silent. No voices, no music, nothing.

I then peered out of the peep hole, not sure of what I was expecting to see. There was nothing out of the ordinary.

I swallowed and debated opening the door to make double sure.

The negative energy was faint but still present. Ignoring it wouldn't make it go away. Someone or something had jiggled the doorknob from the outside. A robber maybe? I could handle a potential thief but a potential human thief wouldn't emit such a distinct signature and scent of…something a tad familiar.

My heart began to hammer wildly and my brandings began to glow softly. Even pulling down my long sleeves further wouldn't fully cover my hands.

I waited a moment longer. This door would be useless against any dark force anyway, so it was pointless to think that not opening it would render me safe.

I'd better be prepared to draw my blades and my fire anyway, just like Ry told me to do.

Speaking of, I wondered if they were still somewhere nearby. Maybe it had been Ry or Rahab.

No. They wouldn't have done that without showing up in the flesh to check on me and make sure that all was alright.

I inhaled and exhaled slowly before reaching for the lock, slowly turning both deadbolts, and then closing my hand over the knob to turn and pull the door slowly open.

I peered out of the narrow crack a tiny bit first before slowly opening the door wider and bracing myself for any possible swift attack to come.

I was surprised to find the hallway both quiet and empty...except for the small, gold foil wrapped gift with a pretty, metallic red bow. That definitely hadn't been there before.

Instant suspicion roused my instincts about its origins and purpose. I leaned out slowly, glancing down each end of the wide hallway while keeping one arm hidden from view inside of the apartment...a single blade was fully extended in my grip.

The door to the stairwell opened at the end of the hallway where I had come up earlier, and out stepped a really tall police officer...I tensed but quickly sighed in relief once I realized who it was.

Cam! Damn, why didn't he just tell me he was coming or better yet why didn't he just materialize or ghost into the apartment?

"I should have known it was you." I shook my head.

He was smiling as he approached me. I reached down to pick up the gift.

The tag simply said: 'To Starling'

"This is early. I haven't gotten you anything yet." I said gesturing with the small present and meeting him halfway for a hug and kiss.

He looked breathtakingly hot in the black police uniform. I was about to ask why he was wearing it at all but I remembered seeing him in it in one of my random memory flashes. It was a disguise obviously, and a damned sexy one at that.

"Merry Christmas." He said, lifting me up and into his arms and hugging me firmly. He kissed my neck and a rush of instant arousal began to tingle in my groin.

"You smell good. Is she back yet?" He whispered into my hair.

"Not yet but soon I imagine."

He kissed me hard—and he was definitely happy to see me.

Though I was touched, I found it odd that he seemed so frisky in spite of everything currently happening.

I was breathless when we broke from the kiss and he was already backing us up into the apartment, closing the door behind him, with me still in his arms.

"Wait, so...did you find Lira or Spencer?"

"Not yet."

I felt guilty for making love just knowing that they were both still missing and possibly in trouble.

I was about to say something else but he kissed me again with extreme passion and hunger.

There was something different about his kiss. All of the romance, love, and tenderness —was gone.

I pulled back and jerked away from him just as he backed me up to my bed where he let me down and began to undo his weapons belt.

Cam would never take me like this, not that I didn't find it appealing but...something wasn't right.

Come to think of it...he smelled a little off too, not like the fresh spring rain and earthy cinnamon that he normally emanated.

"Not here. She'll be here at any moment now." I told him.

"I doubt it. When you want something done, you have to do it yourself. Know what I mean?"

What? No, I had no idea what he meant. What the hell was he talking about?

All of my senses were suddenly on high alert.

"Cam, what's wrong with you? What are you talking about?"
I called out to him first.

There was no telepathic response from him at all.

"Cam?"

This was all wrong. Something was wrong with him.

And then it hit me. This was definitely not Cam.

If it wasn't Cam, then who was this? Why didn't Cam answer me at all?

I eyed the open door of my bedroom out of my periphery.

Reacting with resistance, and violently at that, was going to cause an instant...really bad and really violent reaction in return.

I needed a split second distraction. Running down an open field was one thing, but running through an apartment complex and stairwells might be a bit of a challenge although not impossible.

If I ignited my fire, it could get messy and loud and I'd end up breaking whatever universal law that stated we had to be sitting ducks and wimps in the face of danger.

I had to play dumb, as if I wasn't even aware of the revelation.

"Wait." I said scooting backwards on the bed and standing as I began to pull my shirt up.

He watched me with a lustful grin, his eyes beginning to glow...but not like Cam's. His were a greenish tint and that was all the confirmation I needed.

In a flash, I swiftly wielded my blade and whipped it downward in a slashing motion.

To my shock, I was grabbed by an unseen force and flung across the room, slamming hard into the wall with a loud, vibrating thud that shook the entire length of the wall and door.

I slammed onto the floor hard, surprising myself that although it had been shocking, it didn't really hurt or disorient me as it probably would have if I weren't superhuman. I swiftly rolled onto my back and crab-walked backwards, taking advantage of the gap between us by turning to kip up onto my feet and make a break for the door.

When I opened it, I froze. I was faced with a solid brick wall. I pressed my hands flat against it and pushed, trying to see if it were real or just an illusion. It was definitely real.

"I don't plan on hurting you, so stop all the damned fancy escape attempts and moves. You're only going to piss me off even more." I heard behind me.

I whirled around, pressing myself flat against the wall for protection and to allow time to calculate my next move.

I had no choice but to either fight him with weapons or simply use my fire.

"I guess I underestimated that you'd be easily fooled...but I almost had you going." He pointed at me and flashed a dazzling smile.

It blew my mind because it was Cam's face and body, and nearly identical at that, but it was no longer his voice.

"Damn, you certainly know your man. I'm envious." He added.

The energy that began to fill the room was incredibly strong and powerful. It was beginning to make me feel dizzy.

"Do you think I'd really risk the chance of losing the child that Cam`ael promised me?"

What?!

With both blades out now, I was ready to strike.

Right before my eyes, he began to morph. His body changing slightly though he was still tall and very muscular.

His hair lengthened, now hanging past his shoulders in light waves and light brown in color. He had the prettiest, crystalline, aqua blue eyes that I'd ever seen. They sparkled like pure gemstones under sunlight but they were tainted by his eerie, catlike pupils.

He was wearing a dark blue, expensive three piece business suit, and he was incredibly beautiful...almost mesmerizingly so, but the dark energy vibrating and emanating from him was very strong and sickening to me.

I should be terrified, and I was to an extent but not because I couldn't fight him if I had to, I just wasn't fully prepared...at least not on my own. I had to turn away so that my eyes wouldn't be influenced over who this was...Morning Star.

"Don't look so surprised, sweetheart," he laughed. "I mean really? Do I really offend? I don't think I'm all that bad looking. Now come on, put those things away before I have to hurt or knock you out. I promise that you won't be able to hurt or defeat me no matter what you do but I'll certainly let you try. I'll even allow you to think that you're winning for a while, too." He smiled casually as he sat down comfortably in the armchair, swiveling it around so that he was facing me.

He knew he had me and he seemed very lax about anything that I might do.

"Let me let you in on a little something before I claim what's mine, Starling—love the name by the way," he winked as he shifted in the chair and crossed a leg over the other, ankle resting over his opposite knee.

His tone was scathing. "You see, your boyfriend Cam'ael, promised me something a little while back, sort of a deal if you will." He steepled his index fingers together and then pointed to my abdomen with them.

"Both you and that child... are mine." He then said with a serious and sinister glimmer that flashed in both of his eyes.

Almost instantly, an extremely powerful force pinned me firmly against the random brick wall behind me, and then closed in like secure vices around my shoulders, each wrist, my ankles, and my waist.

My legs nearly gave out. Not necessarily from fear but from what he was telling me. He didn't know that we were having twins, which definitely proves that he was lying. If Cam had done this, which I did not believe, then he would have told him that we were having twins.

"Bullshit. You can't claim anything from a dead body and I'll die before letting you touch me or my child!" I spat out angrily. Even though I couldn't move my hands or arms, my flames began to lick down each blade, burning brightly—ready to be thrown.

He beamed, entranced. "Hallowed fire. Very nice and very fitting for you. I love my women both beautiful and deadly that way. Be careful what you wish for though…and before you even consider using your fire…" He snapped his fingers with a sarcastic smirk plastered to his gorgeous face. A body instantly fell through a portal that had opened and expanded right above him.

I flinched and gasped when it landed on the ground with a heavy thud in a crumpled heap.

It wasn't hard for me to figure out who it was from the long, sleek black hair and the firm, amazon-like, slender body.

Edanai!

But was it really her? What was wrong with her? Was she…dead?

"Don't worry, she wouldn't be of much value to me dead." He said as if he'd read my mind.

Her body began to slowly rise, being levitated by magic until she hovered limply just slightly above his lap, and then her body came to rest gently in it as if she were an invalid that he was lovingly rocking to sleep.

He began to stroke her hair, gently brushing it from her pretty face, which remained still in a peaceful repose.

Launching a ball of fire at him it would burn her too and he knew that. Damn him!

"You see, you humans place way too much value, attachment, and feelings on things, other people, and beings. For the side of light, that is and will be your biggest downfall. It certainly will be for Cam`ael. Now I don't doubt that Cam`ael would ever leave you alone for this long, especially when he has no idea that I have Edanai too—yet…so, we'll just wait a little longer. He's probably occupied with something else right now anyway. He can't resist beautiful women and virgins, you know. It's probably one of the reasons why he wanted you so badly, and you gave yourself to him foolishly." He tormented, using his words to stab doubt and hurt into my heart about Cam. Shut up! My mind screamed. I can't allow myself to listen to his false words. He knew exactly what he was doing, awaiting my reaction or reply with a confident half smile.

He shrugged nonchalantly, stroking Edanai's hair as if she were a pet in his lap, "Don't look so surprised or hurt. He's a fallen, it's what we do best. You should never trust one, dear. We're all of the same mindset. We're all liars no matter what you were told or what you want to believe, and that will never change…not even with love. In the meantime, let's get a little more acquainted, seeing as you're not going to doing anything stupid that involves using fire, and we're all going to be one big happy family very soon." He smiled satisfactorily.

I felt like throwing up. Though I know he was full of shit, a tiny part of me...began to believe it. How had he known that I was a virgin? I hated that part and I wished he would just stop talking! I couldn't let him see that his words were affecting me at all. I quickly sucked up the tears that almost fell and tried to focus on something else.

This was a set up. He was setting Cam up for something and both Edanai and I were bait—bait that he was certainly going to keep.

"Just take me. Leave her here and leave everyone else alone. I'll go with you willingly." I pleaded.

He raised a brow as if considering my offer. "You're willingly giving yourself to me?" He asked carefully.

"I said I'd go with you willingly, not that I was giving myself to you willingly." I clarified through clenched teeth.

"Oh. Well that's too bad. Say, isn't your friend...what's her name, China? Isn't she on her way to see you right now? Snow can sometimes prove treacherous to maneuver a vehicle in safely. Did you know that most accidents happen within three to five miles of the home?" he pointed at me as if he were actually asking me the question, and about to embark on some sort of speech about public safety.

I paled and felt myself grow cold and numb inside, only because he had the power to do something easily at any given moment. He was merciless and cruel.

"Please, this has nothing to do with her! Leave her alone! She has a family and a future!" I was both scared and angry at the same time.

He laughed softly at my desperation and useless pleading.

"That all depends on you. How much do both of their lives mean to you? You know, accidents happen all of the time and I promise you that I have nothing to do with any of them...well, most of them at least."

He smiled dangerously.

"What do you want me to do?" I said helplessly. I had no options at this point. He could easily kill China in a split second and I'd never see or talk to her again.

"I want you to willingly give yourself to me. Your soul and physical vessel."

I pressed my lips together as tears began to well into my eyes again. My heart was breaking slowly with despair, defiance, anger, and absolute torture all chipping away at it. I couldn't allow him to see me hurting and weak. He was evidently enjoying this, sucking it all up. He wanted to torture me emotionally and it was working, only because I knew he'd follow through and make good on his threats.

If this was what I had to do to save China and Edanai— then I'd do it. It may be easier to kill him when he least expects it, and to do that, I'd have to be close to him when he's the most vulnerable.

He awaited my answer, apparently already knowing that I wasn't going to agree and say yes that easily or readily if at all.

He huffed with a diabolical grin, "Doesn't matter anyway, I'll have all three of you soon. She's more of a consolation prize in the mix." He shook his head and nodded at Edanai. He then began to slowly trace a line across Edanai's cheek that began to ooze dark blood. She didn't move or react but it looked painful. I jerked in automatic reflex, pinned like a butterfly to a board while in attack mode and left to stare in horror, helpless.

"Stop that!" I screamed at him uselessly.

My God, how much more lame could I be? I was actually sitting here telling Satan to stop being cruel and evil? I tried to force my weight and strength against the invisible restraints against my wrists, ankles, and waist once again but I still couldn't move. The pressure was way too strong and unyielding.

He laughed, low and taunting at my pointless efforts.

Cam wouldn't know or think to come unless Ry or Rahab showed up at any moment now and summoned him. I couldn't call out to him. I wasn't going to lure him to this trap. For some reason, Morning Star wanted him to come, but why? Cam would go ballistic and destroy him on sight, especially seeing that he had Edanai too.

Was that what he wanted him to do?

—Wait...the fallen could communicate telepathically among one another. Did one of those fallen include Morning Star?

"Cam, whatever you do...don't listen to Morning Star. It's a trap!" I attempted to relay to Cam, just in case.

Morning Star suddenly pierced me with a confident glint in his eyes, and a grin that made him look both deadly and gorgeous at the same time.

A burst of strange light broke through from somewhere, and then a large, dark blur forcefully rushed out of thin air right above my head. I didn't even see what it was until the explosion of glass, wood, and steel burst outward, and the apartment fell away like jagged shards of glass from a window pane. The armchair that Morning Star had been sitting in, had been totally obliterated.

The magical restraints holding me in place were suddenly released, and I was propelled forward inside the wake that created a suction of powerful wind from whatever it was that darted out and attacked Morning Star. I was pulled into the tunnel of wind, through the destroyed wall that was part of my apartment, into the spirit realm plane, and then deposited on a long, stone bridge. I dove and rolled agilely, coming to a low crouch with one knee up and the other down, as if I were about to spring forward.

I frantically searched for both Edanai and whatever it was that shot out like a raging bullet from the portal that had been above me, which was now closed. Edanai's body lie on the stony ground several feet behind me now, instead of on my living room floor.

Morning Star, and whoever it was that had attacked him faster than the speed of light itself, were nowhere to be seen. My jaw dropped when I looked at the spirit realm landscape that replaced my apartment.

It was bleak and lightning flashed treacherously across a red and purple painted sky. We were both on a strip of dark stone, a bridge with a long drop on each side. Down below were two huge, deep, cavernous pits in the ground that resembled giant maws. Hundreds of sharp rocks jutted inward from the sides, which formed what looked like sharp pointed teeth, and there were literally hundreds of thousands of human skeletons and skulls lying at the very bottom.

I ran over to Edanai, placing a hand on her chest to see if she was breathing. She was and then she suddenly began to rouse. I supposed that when Morning Star was attacked, whatever magic or spell he had over her was instantly released too, but she was still groggy and out of it.

"Edanai, you have to get out of here. Now!" I shook her.

Her eyes snapped up to mine, trying to focus on my face as she rubbed the top of her head. Then she shook her head no and tried to stand, only to falter and sit back down.

What was wrong with her?

"I'm not going anywhere. Do you see all of this?" She pointed. Her eyes were round with uncertainty.

"Yeah and they're all after me, so get out of here! You're hurt and I can't protect you without possibly or accidentally killing you!" I pleaded with her, tears welling up in my eyes.

"No. No way! Whatever you have to do... you'd better do it and do it big! It's you they all want, and I promised myself and Cam that I would keep them away from you even if it costs my own existence, so don't you dare worry about me! You have a baby to protect, and besides, Morning Star injured both of my wings badly, I can't fly or cloak for a while until they heal." She shouted harsh and fervently while pointing at me.

The normal Edanai was coming back. She appeared to be gaining more lucidity and she was quickly on her feet, broken wings splayed. I gasped in horror. They had been nearly torn to shreds, and blood ran in between each feather. I wished I could help her but I had no idea of what to do.

"Don't worry, I'll be fine. They're healing already, though slowly." She mentioned seeing the expression on my face.

I shook my head no, firmly pursing my lips to keep myself from bawling. We didn't have time to stand here debating and I wasn't budging.

Large shadows and dark flying things continued to rise all around us. The air turned foul, beginning to steam, and the haunting cries of torture and anguish could be heard from way down below. It tore at both my heart and my ears painfully. I knew where this place was.

In the far distance somewhere, I could distinctly hear Morning Star's chiding, booming voice. Then, he was laughing mockingly and victoriously beneath the loud battle that could distinctly be heard.

Whoever his opponent was, sounded both furious and vengeful; unleashing a stormy wrath of rage and power that you could literally feel and see in the air.

Suddenly, we were surrounded by several more fallen. I wasn't sure who or what they were amid the melee and chaos, but when I saw them begin to attack the rising dark things that had begun surrounding both Edanai and myself, I instantly knew who they were then.

The earth began to rumble and shake. Edanai had fully regained her composure and was now standing, ready to both fight and attack, even though she couldn't fly. She threw some sort of spell that created a black, web like netting that both wrapped around a group of huge, mutated vulture- looking creatures. They began to shriek and howl in frustration. She was right, they were all after me. With my blades out and ready to throw fire, I immediately ran over to her when she collapsed once again, down on one knee after having done that.

Rahab swooped in low and swift, coming to her aid.

"Rahab, get her out of here!" I told him.

"Not without you too." He growled.

Something humongous, rank, and beastly began to rise from one of the pits below. It reminded me of some sort of a zombie, mega pterodactyl creature…a hairy one at that, with razor sharp teeth along its curved beak. At the end of each leathery black wing were capable hands. It's shadow closed in over us and all I could initially do was stare at it with my mouth open.

Rahab flew up at it with both his claws and his sword out, ready to strike. He was swift but not swift enough as the creature batted him away as if he were a tiny fly.

I screamed.

Edanai screamed out. "Rahab!"

Then, determination and anger overpowered my frozen fear. There was too much going on, all of the others were occupied, and somewhere beyond all of this, Cam was fighting a potentially deadly battle with the ultimate evil of all time!

I spun to gain momentum and flung a single blade directly at the creature.

My blade was a streak of light and I assumed that on impact, the creature would be injured enough for the others to finish him off.

Lord knows it needed a really big breath mint.

My smirk of determination and confidence was shattered when the creature actually caught my blade in its hand with ease.

What?

It actually sounded as if it were…laughing.

"Starling…go…" Edanai was crying. She was actually —crying.

I'd never seen or known a fallen to cry.

Go where?

I had to fight back my own tears. With resolute determination, I turned my attention back to the creature and narrowed my eyes.

Holding my hand out to catch my blade once I pulled them in, I smirked. The beast had no idea what it was truly holding. I had never tried this before, even in training, but now was a good a time as any. I forced fire into both of my blades.

The mutant pterodactyl…began to screech at an unreal, eardrum-shattering decibel. My flames began to consume its flesh, rapidly working its way up this arms, his wings, and quickly over his entire body.

Rahab was flying back towards the creature, charging with weapons held up and ready to strike.

"Rahab, no!" Edanai screamed as she immediately forced herself to take flight, only to tumble back to the ground as the creature began to reach for her, attempting to take her with it in its dying descent back into the pits below.

I paled.

"No!" I screamed.

Something rushed me, pushing me over the bridge just as I caught the blade I had thrown at the disgusting, now dying, flying demon.

I was plummeting down, heat was almost like fire against my skin but it wasn't my fire. It was a stinging, vile fire and sweat began to drench my clothes.

I grunted, slamming into something else, hard. Another being. Another fallen caught me, and I prayed that it was one of Cam's friends.

I turned and craned my head up to look.

"Please, do not accidentally kill me!"

I wanted to cry and laugh at the same time. It was Ry!

"Wait, Rahab…Edanai!" I couldn't get my words out.

"I'm getting you the hell out of here now!" He said, and then a portal began to open up in front of us.

"No! Cam is still here!" I screamed at the top of my lungs defiantly.

He wasn't listening to me at all.

What I heard next, as we neared the portal, echoed all across the skies and made my blood chill.

"You're so predictable Cam`ael, but alas—you have stricken the first injury… and you know what that means…"

I'd never seen or felt this level of his power coming from him before. Though I wasn't there to witness this current battle, I could tell that this was way different. It was epic and beyond dangerous.

It was with Morning Star. The true dark prince of hate, destruction, and evil.

My adrenaline began to surge like crazy. My body and mind automatically going into protective mode as I fought against Ry uselessly.

"Hey! Chill! I don't want to have to drop you, Starling, but I sure as hell will if you burst into flames on me." He warned me.

We had just entered the portal, when Morning Star's voice came again, this time mimicking Michael Buffer's voice exactly, "LET'S GET READY TO RUMBLE!"

In the next moment...the ground began to tremble even more violently and it was really loud. Giant tears began to rip all across the red and purple sky of the spirit realm that hovered over the dark lands, parting to reveal a periwinkle blue sky with fluffy white clouds that belonged to the human realm beyond.

There was no need to enter the portal anymore. It had actually began to disappear right before our eyes.

"Ah shit!" Ry whispered.

I didn't have to ask him what was happening to understand what was taking place all of a sudden.

This was it. This is what it took to bring it about, and now—there was no stopping it.

Cam had apparently just broken a major universal law…

END

COMING IN THE FALL OF 2014
THE FINAL INSTALLMENT AND
CONCLUSION OF THE
DIVINITY SAGA

*DIVINITY: REALM OF
ANNIHILATION:
BOOK FOUR*

Personal note from the author: If you've enjoyed the Divinity Saga so far, please be so kind as to leave a review for others. Your effort and time is greatly appreciated by me! Thank you!

ABOUT THE AUTHOR

The Divinity Saga came about from a recurring dream. From the start, the character of Starling came to fruition. At first, Divinity the Gathering was meant to be just one book but she couldn't see how both Starling and Cam`ael's story would be complete in just one. She doesn't have any impressive accolades, collaborations, or a long list of awards to mention as far as her writing history goes, though she's been writing for many, many years. She's thrilled to know that people are reading the worlds she has created in her mind and even more so, really loving what they are reading. This is the first time that she has decided to finally try her hand at publishing something.

Though she dabbles in many genres, she tends to gravitate more towards urban and dark fantasy and the paranormal. In her spare time, books replace television and she loves reading horror. She loves trying new things, and since she loves to cook and bake, much of that creative energy ends up on the dinner table whether it be a meal or dessert. Susan resides in the Lonestar state with her two children and two well-fed cats.

In addition to writing, she does work a nine to five job in Law Enforcement in order to supplement both her writing and reading habits. She is very approachable and does respond to and engage with her fans from all over; from twitter, facebook, linkedin, and through Goodreads. Feel free to drop her a comment or just say hello anytime! She maintains a blog page, and a Facebook page dedicated to the saga as well. She loves to watch martial arts movies with her teenaged son, and volunteers often to be the guinea pig for her aspiring Esthetician adult daughter!

Please visit your favorite online retailers to discover other books by Susan Reid:

Divinity: The Gathering Book One
Divinity: Transcendence Book Two
Divinity: Immolation: Book Three
Divinity: Realm of Annihilation: Book Four (To be released in the Fall of 2014)
The Divinity Saga Prequel: Divinity: Anathema: Book Five (Release date TBA)
Companion Novel: Fall to Flesh: Diary of Cam`ael (Title not yet confirmed. Release date TBA)
H.U.M.A.N.S (The first book in a brand new series coming in Summer of 2014)

Connect with Author Susan Reid

Follow on twitter @BabyNewt38
Linkedin: Susan Reid
Visit on Facebook at:
 http://www.facebook.com/DivinityTheGatheringBookOne
http://divinitysagabooks.wordpress.com/
Goodreads

Made in the USA
Charleston, SC
05 June 2014